CLINICAL

ISBN: 145647510X
ISBN-13: 9781456475109
Library of Congress Control Number:
2010919322

To my brother Stephen for a hell of an idea and to Haley for putting up with me through everything.

Clinical Lycanthropy

By
Tim Garrity

I

The jets rumbled overhead, the ground quaking beneath them. Hurtling headlong towards their target, the two F-16 fighter planes ripped through the air, the desert sun glinting off their dull gray surfaces and rattling the teeth of those on the ground as they screamed past with their single engines thrusting at full. Within seconds they had released their deadly cargo, climbing steadily as two black dots fell silently towards the surface. There was a flash of light followed by a pair of thunderous explosions, their combined concussive force shaking the onlookers more violently than the engine noise before. Soon the jets had disappeared, nothing more than small specks in a cloudless azure sky, leaving the destruction they had wrought in their wake.

Specialist Mark Enos hunkered down, clutching his rifle close as a cloud of sand wafted past, covering his position entirely. Soon the sediment-created fog settled, revealing a small grouping of American soldiers, each one covered with a fine coating of silt and dust. Enos shook his head, casting a small beach's worth of sand from his helmet, still keeping his mouth and nose covered with a thick green scarf. The shooting had stopped, but he knew better than most that it didn't mean much.

"Think Hajji's gone?" Private First Class Steve Frey asked Enos.

Enos slowly shook his head no, choosing to stay silent and keep his face covered. One of his closest friends, Frey could annoy Enos from time to time with his incessant, often asinine questions. Enos watched as members of the small army team began to stir, individually dusting themselves off.

A large, gruff looking individual stood up, his M-4 rifle clutched by his waist. A thin coating of sweat clung to his chocolate-colored skin and dripped beneath the collar of his tan and brown uniform. His arched eyebrows, clenched jaw, and cruel looking mouth betrayed his unpleasant disposition. "All right, move out," Staff Sergeant Glen Kelly barked.

In response the squad of ten soldiers rose up and scaled a small ridge of sand. "Fire team one flank left, Fire team two with me," Kelly commanded. Obligingly Enos fell in behind Kelly as they all broke into a slow trot, their weapons raised and pointed forwards. Enos trudged on through the desert heat, kicking up small puffs of sand with his combat boots. He could hear Frey breathing heavily just behind him as they advanced towards a smoldering ruin of a house.

It was slung low, appearing as more of an earthen mound than a small hut. A mud and stone fence, crumbling in places due to the bomb blast, lined the perimeter of the property, and an acrid column of black and gray smoke billowed skyward. A horrible smell hit Enos has they approached, a mixture of charred beef and burnt hair. He knew what it was and shuddered at the source, burning human flesh. Arriving at the base of the stone wall, Kelly hunkered down, five soldiers lining directly behind him. Across the way Enos watched as another grouping of four soldiers fell into a similar position.

Not speaking, Kelly made a series of hand movements towards the soldier facing him. The soldier nodded, and on a silent count of three Kelly and the soldier rose to their feet and stormed through an opening in the wall, followed swiftly by the rest of the squad. The soldiers fanned out, training their weapons on different points and scanning the perimeter. Nothing moved.

Enos winced as he viewed a few unlucky souls who had been lying in the open as the jets had passed, their bodies smoldering and their simple cotton clothes singed in various places. Enos noted the number of dead goats who also littered the courtyard. Nearly every corpse clutched a

Kalashnikov rifle in their blackened hands. *At least they weren't civilians,* Enos comforted himself. Kelly moved forward, his rifle trained upon the ruined opening of the house. The interior appeared to be pitch black, and smoke emanated from the roof. Enos joined Kelly, and together they entered the interior of the house. It was even worse than outside.

The roof had collapsed, pinning the house's occupants beneath the rubble. Those faces still recognizable in the debris lay with their eyes open, their teeth clenched in a horrible death mask of anguish and anger. The coarse hair of their black beards still burned, filling the air with a most unpleasant odor. Advancing further Kelly inspected one of the more intact corpses intently before lowering his rifle and turning towards Enos. "I think we're clear."

Enos nodded, uncovering his mouth, "I think so too."

Kelly and Enos emerged from the small hut, their weapons pointed towards the ground. In response the team of soldiers lowered the guards, their postures becoming more relaxed. "Ramirez," Kelly growled, "get your ass on the radio; tell him we're clear."

Breathing a sigh of relief, Enos approached Frey, who stood just inside the perimeter wall. Now that the danger had passed he felt the heaviness in his tired legs as the adrenaline drained from his body. The heat was overwhelming here in the desert, and the heavy combat gear he wore seemed to retain his body heat. Frey looked even worse for wear; the sweat poured forth from his forehead, and his expression was one of discomfort. "I told you they got them," Frey offered as Enos approached.

"Shut up," Enos grumbled, "motherfuckers usually find a way to survive the strikes."

"Not this time," Frey said, smiling.

Enos smiled back and opened his mouth to speak, "Smar—"

"Aaaarrrgghhh!"

The blood-curdling scream made the hairs on the back of Enos' neck stand on end. Wheeling around, he struggled to comprehend just what he was seeing. A seemingly dead militant, his legs missing and his waist a tattered, red mess, clutched at Enos' squad mate Tom Reilly's leg. Reilly screamed as the legless man bit into his calf, dragging the torso across the desert floor as he struggled to get away.

"Holy shit!" Frey exclaimed as the two watched the bizarre struggle.

Reilly gritted his teeth and began to fire into the man's center mass, the bullets hitting the flesh with a sickening thud; yet the militant refused to let go, keeping his mouth clamped onto the soldier's leg. Soon there was another scream followed by the rat-a-tat of another rifle. Enos turned to see another soldier being attacked by the walking dead. Enos began to hyperventilate as he watched the still-smoldering corpses begin to stir, their faces morphing into the visages of horrible, fanged demons. They rose and set upon the soldiers, tearing into their flesh with long, dagger-like talons and sharpened canines. Enos began to sweat profusely, frozen in place by fear and confusion, watching as the soldiers fired shot after shot to no avail, their bullets passing harmlessly through the zombie-like attackers.

Enos watched as Kelly moved against the wall of the house, firing short bursts into a group of approaching militants. He bared his teeth and growled like a madman as shot after shot did little to slow the coming onslaught. "You want some, motherfuckers? Huh, you want some?" He hissed as he fired. A yellow-green hand emerged from the nearby doorway and clawed at the Staff Sergeant's face, causing him to drop his rifle. He screamed as he clutched at the open wound on his cheek, drawing his sidearm and turning to face the new attacker, only to be pounced upon by the old ones. Enos watched in horror as the Sergeant was torn to pieces, the militants greedily feasting upon his red, wet flesh.

Frey called out, and Enos turned, only to see one of the zombies sink its teeth into Frey's neck. Frey looked into Enos' eyes with a pained and frightened look. The blood trickled forth from Frey's throat, staining the top of his uniform and seeping over his green flak jacket. The zombie flicked its head back, tearing a small piece of meat from Frey's neck, and Enos was hit with the warm spray of arterial blood. The militant dropped Frey's now lifeless body and hissed at Enos, the piece of flesh still hinged in its jaws.

Enos felt his heart thundering in his chest, and as he scanned the yard, he realized, much to his horror, that he was the only member of his squad left. The zombie militants surrounded him, hissing in anger. Their lifeless yellow eyes affixed on him, and each bared bloodstained fangs and claws. Enos raised his rifle and depressed the trigger, hearing only a clicking sound rather than the roar of gunshots. His gun had jammed. Dropping the rifle, Enos grabbed his sidearm, aiming at the nearest zombie and firing, only to hear a click again. Pressing the trigger again and again, Enos whimpered as he realized his sidearm too was jammed.

The seething militants closed in, several crawling towards him, as they were just torsos. Withdrawing his KA-BAR knife from his holster, he swiped at the nearest zombie, inflicting a large, bloodless wound. Flailing wildly, Enos screamed in pain as the attackers seized him and dug into his flesh, tearing chunks of meat from his body. Slipping deeper into the attacking crowd, Enos watched helplessly as one of the attackers displayed its fangs demonstratively before plunging them deep into his throat, ending it all . . .

Enos awoke violently, sitting up in his bed. Hyperventilating, his body was covered in sweat, which seeped through his white, cotton sheets. Still frightened, he scanned the dark room for any sign of attacking zombies, only to find a small collection of action figures, model airplanes, and dirty clothes. *Just another dream*, he assured himself.

His breathing became deeper, returning to a normal pace. Casting the white sheet aside, he flipped his legs over the tiny bed and sat with his face in his hands. His head hurt, his body ached, and he had not had a good night sleep in ages. Rubbing his fingers through his hair, he took a deep breath and looked at the desk which sat astride his bed.

Kelly, Frey, and him, smiling faces all, stared back at him, their arms draped over each other's shoulders and a pristine desert landscape stretching for miles behind them. He hadn't spoken to either of them since he had returned from Iraq; he wouldn't really know what to say. Things hadn't been the same since he had come home. He felt out of place, overly stressed. He sped up when driving under overpasses, constantly expected the sidewalk to detonate as he walked upon it, and then there were the dreams. They were terrible, nonsensical things that prevented him from resting properly and caused him to dread closing his eyes at night.

Rising up on wobbly knees, Enos stumbled past the bed and towards the bedroom door. The hinges creaked, and an old heavy metal poster upon the wall fluttered loudly as he pried the door open. Exiting the room, he slowly began to walk down the narrow hallway. The hardwood floor was excruciatingly cold, and he quickly picked up the soles of his feet as if he were walking upon hot sand at the beach. With each footstep there was a corresponding groan from the aging red oak floorboards.

Feeling along the wall, he located a light switch and flicked it on before entering the bathroom. The lavatory was a cramped, overly perfumed place. The walls were a powder blue, though the wallpaper was yellowing and peeling in places from years of neglect. The porcelain sink and toilet were also light blue in color, a thin lining of black mildew coating the cracks and crevices of both. The shower was a dingy off white, the curtain a clear vinyl.

Enos stumbled towards the sink and turned the water on. A rushing, cold torrent poured forth from the spigot. Leaning closer, he splashed his face, enjoying the cold shock of the frigid liquid. He rubbed it through his hair and splashed even more upon his face before bracing himself against the sink and taking several deep breaths. The water formed small rivulets that ran through his short, dirty blond hair and through the creases on his troubled forehead before reaching his nose and dropping back into the porcelain basin. Turning off the faucet, he stood there for several moments listening to the plinking sound the water made as it hit the small pool at the bottom of the sink.

"Mark?" A raspy voice called out, "Mark, are you all right?"

"Yeah, Ma, I'm fine," Enos called out, turning his head towards the doorway before adding, "Go back to bed."

"Was it another dream?" his mother asked, her voice slightly muffled, as her room was down the hall.

Frowning, Enos answered, "No, Ma, I just had to go to the bathroom. Go back to bed."

"Are you sure you're okay?" she asked again.

Aggravated by the repetitive nature of her questioning, Enos bit his lip, fighting the urge to scream. He knew she was simply trying to be helpful, that it wasn't her intention to annoy him. Swallowing his rage, he calmed himself before replying, "Yeah, Mom, I'm okay."

"All right then, good night; see you in the morning," she called out.

Enos turned away from the door and looked into the mirror. His skin was a pale white; his eyes were sunken and lined with light purple bags. His cheekbones seemed ready to poke through his skin, and overall he just had a skeletal look about him. *It is tough to eat lately as well.* Sleep was the first priority, he decided.

Pulling a handle on the mirror's frame, he revealed the medicine cabinet concealed behind it. Scanning the myriad of multi-colored boxes and orange pill containers he located just what he was looking for. Removing a small foil-lined container, he popped out a small blue pill and threw it in his mouth. Fighting a case of dry mouth, he choked the sleeping pill down and closed the mirror.

Staring at his reflection once again, he looked deep into his bloodshot, blue eyes. They looked weary, yet restless at the same time, reflecting exactly how he felt. At least the pills would help with his sleeping problem, for tonight anyways. Taking a deep breath, he stared into the mirror. "I'll be okay." He then stepped away from the sink, shutting off the light and walking back towards his bedroom.

There was the clinking of silverware on plates, the occasional scrape of a knife upon a ceramic surface. Now and then one of them would slurp from a drink or clear their throat, but none of them spoke. Enos sat at the dinner table in uncomfortable silence with his mother, Virginia, and his older brother, Stephen.

Not bothering to look up, he focused his attention on the food in front of him a hearty dinner of fast food fried chicken, mashed potatoes, and mixed vegetables. His mother had never been much of a cook, but this was ridiculous. It seemed a little disrespectful to invite his brother over to celebrate Mark's return home from Iraq and serve takeout, but then again that had always been her way. Slowly, he shoveled another bite of the greasy chicken into his mouth, chewing slowly and praying that someone would break the silence.

There was little Enos could do to spark conversation. Most of the stories he possessed and loved to tell were crude, full of sexual innuendo and toilet humor, befitting of a locker room, not the dinner table. Unable to think of anything to say, Enos remained silent and continued to eat. Eyes still affixed to his plate, Enos could sense that his mother had set down her fork and was preparing to speak. *Thank God.*

"How are the kids, Steve?" She asked.

Enos looked up and watched as his brother swallowed his last bite of food and cleared a lock of black hair from his face before answering. "They're good, Mom, getting big. Real handfuls."

Virginia smiled, her plump cheeks rising up and squinting her eyes. "That's good, real good. And how's Marie?"

"She's good as well, Mom," Stephen answered. "I just figured this was more of an immediate family thing. You know just me, you, and Mark."

His mother interlocked her chubby digits and rested her chin upon her hands, a frown upon her face. "You could've brought them. I bought plenty of food, and you know I always love to see my grandchildren."

Enos looked at his brother, awaiting a response to his mother's subtle scolding, and found a look of discomfort upon Stephen's face. Sensing that his brother was searching for the right words, Enos moved in to play defense. "Yeah, speaking of the food, Mom, I'd just like to say thanks. You really pulled out all the stops and slaved hard over a hot phone to make this meal special."

His mother's face crinkled in mock disgust as Stephen let out a guffaw in reply to Mark's remark. She turned towards her youngest son. "Oh, always so good to have you both home at the same time. Welcome home, smart ass."

Mark raised his glass of soda towards her in salute before sipping from it. Stephen chuckled silently before looking at his younger brother. "So Mom tells me you're working."

"Yeah," Mark nodded, "Mr. Lamperti from across the street got me a job over at the All-Mart working in the warehouse."

"That Mr. Lamperti is such a nice man," Virginia said. "You should really thank him for getting you that job, Mark," she added, wagging a finger at Mark, her perm shifting on her head as she did so.

"All-Mart?" Stephen asked, pretending to be impressed.

"Yes, I know it's not like your nice job with the state, but it's something for the time being," Mark responded.

Stephen smiled wryly while taking another bite; Mark smiled as well, ignoring the small dig at his new choice of employment. Mark looked at his brother as he hadn't seen him since leaving for Iraq. Slightly taller than Mark, he was roughly the same body shape, yet Stephen lacked the sinewy muscularity of his brother. Mark kept his straw-colored hair in a spiky crew cut, whereas Stephen kept his black hair relatively long for a man, parting it in the middle and letting it flow around his face.

Mark noted that even their wardrobes were dramatically different. Mark looked as if he had plucked his clothes out of a dirty laundry bin, wearing a faded, gray army t-shirt and a tattered pair of blue jeans. Stephen, on the other hand, was clad in a button down white shirt with light red stripes running vertically along the surface. He also wore a pair of black slacks and looked rather professional. Yet despite the difference in appearances, Mark was comforted by the fact that they were remarkably similar in personality. Or at least they had been before he left for the army.

"In all seriousness though, you two," their mother sounded, "it is great to have you guys under the same roof again." She then zoned out, casting a sorrowful look at the table. "I just wish your father could be here."

"Jesus, Mom," Stephen sneered, "this is supposed to be a happy occasion."

"Yeah come on, Mom, don't be a downer," Mark chimed in.

Virginia ran her hands over her face before raising them defensively. "Okay, okay. You're right; it is supposed to be a happy time."

They all became silent once again, returning to their plates and not looking up, the clinking and scraping of silverware once again the only thing filling the air.

* * *

Enos settled into the rocking chair located on the porch of the small, ranch style home. Gently swaying back and forth, he noted the weathered condition of his childhood home. The red paint flaked in places; chips scattered upon the dark, rotting wood of the porch; and there was the heavy smell of mildew that surrounded the domicile. Lost in his own thoughts, he did not hear the screech of the screen door as it opened and was not aware of another's presence until he felt a cold, wet sensation upon his shoulder. Not bothering to look up, he accepted the beer from his brother and cradled it upon his lap.

"I'm sorry I couldn't make it when you got off the plane," Stephen said, moving in front of Mark and leaning against the off-white railing of the porch.

"Not a problem, man," Mark responded flippantly as he cracked open his beer and took a sip.

"Well, good to have you home, Bro," Stephen said, extending his can in a toast.

Mark made eye contact and with a nod touched his beverage to his brother's. "Thanks, good to be home . . . I guess."

Stephen frowned before taking another swig. Swallowing he spoke. "You guess?"

"Yeah," Mark shrugged, "just getting used to being back stateside."

"Mom did tell me you were having a little problem adjusting," Stephen confessed.

Mark sighed. "Did she?"

"Yeah," Stephen nodded, "she's just worried about you, man. She says you're having problems getting to sleep at night; that you're having nightmares."

Mark grimaced; he didn't appreciate his mother sharing the intimate details of his life with people, even his older brother. "I can deal with the nightmares, man; they gave me pills for those. Bad dreams aren't the problem."

"Then what is?" Stephen asked, his brow furrowed in concern.

"Just life I guess." Mark shrugged.

What do you mean?"

"I mean this isn't really what I expected it to be like growing up. I certainly never aspired to working at the fucking All-Mart at twenty-three," Mark lamented. "I guess I just wanted more."

"Why didn't you stay in the army?" Stephen questioned.

"I couldn't have done that, Steve." Mark shook his head. "That part of my life is over."

Stephen sipped from his beer. "I think you're just getting overwhelmed, Bro, it's not like

All-Mart is a career move. It's just something for you to do until you get on your feet and decide what you want to do in life."

"Ah, see, that's the problem, man. I don't know what I want to do in life. Everything's just so complicated," Mark complained. Taking another swig of his beer, Mark pondered what to say next.

"Do you remember when Nana and Papa would take us to Wompatuck every Labor Day?" Mark asked, referring to an annual camping trip their mother's parents would take them on every Labor Day weekend to a local state park.

"Yeah," Stephen nodded before adding, "Christ those trips were so awful. Why do you ask?"

Mark smiled. "Yeah they were really boring, but I bring them up because I'd trade where I'm at right now for a million of those weekends. As boring and long as they were, we really had no concerns, not a care in the fucking world. Nana cooked all our food; we fished, rode bikes. I really don't know why we complained so much."

"Well, there was that one time I got poison ivy on my crotch from pissing in the woods," Stephen cracked.

"Yeah that sucked," Mark smiled, "but seriously there were no bills to pay, nothing really expected of you, no 'getting on your feet,' and for me, no fucking nightmares." Mark shook his head before saying, "I'd give anything to live like that again." Still shaking his head he downed some more of his beer while rocking back and forth in his chair.

"Mark," Stephen sighed, "I really think you just need to relax, man. Things will turn out all right. Besides, I think you're forgetting how cold it was in those tents, the way Nana farted in her sleep, and the bugs you would find in your sleeping bag."

Mark smiled, "I suppose you're right."

"Just take it one day at a time man, and you'll be okay." Stephen nodded before extending his arm towards Mark once again. "Again, man, it's good to have you home."

Mark knocked cans for a second time with his brother, responding, "It's good to be home."

Mark watched forlornly, a weak smile upon his face, as the headlights of Stephen's car retreated from the driveway, the aging transmission emitting a high-pitched whir. Waving his hand from the porch, he waited until the crimson brake lights had faded from view, and he was engulfed in darkness once again. An unspeakable sadness overcame him; he felt as if he was now the last man on Earth. Backing up, he collapsed in his rocking chair, choosing to sit in the shadows rather than retreat indoors.

He enjoyed his brother's company, immensely so. It had taken thousands of miles and the heat of a guerilla war to impress upon him just how much he needed his older sibling. With a sigh, he fingered the lid of his beer can and leaned his head back, his feet only touching the floor intermittently. There was a lump in his throat and for a moment he thought he might cry, only to swallow it back down and resume normal breathing.

He had been happy once, a long time ago. People were always remarking on what a sparkplug and a joy to be around he had been as a small child. That had all changed of course when his father, Ron, had passed away. The sudden, crushing realization that Daddy was not getting out of bed had destroyed him, extinguishing the flame of his childhood exuberance in an instant. He couldn't remember much: his mother's sorrowful wailing, the horror of his father's open casket, and the endless rows of tombstones as Ron was interred. The memory still stung all these years later, and he thought he might burst into tears as he sat there. *Why the fuck did she have to bring that up?* He cursed his mother.

It was after his father's death, he had decided long ago, that he truly turned to Stephen as his best friend. Bonded together through the shared emotion of the moment and the fact that their mother had withdrawn, becoming emotionally unavailable for years, meant that they developed a closeness only brothers could experience. Stephen seemed to recover from Ron's death much more rapidly than Mark ever could. Perhaps it was the difference in age; Mark was never really able to pinpoint a single factor.

Mark, however, withdrew completely and drifted into a decidedly dreary adolescence. Not big enough to be a bully and not small enough to be a victim, he had settled into his role as the quiet, brooding child in the corner of the classroom. Over time he adjusted and acquired the ability to act like a normal human being, smiling at the right moment and even laughing on occasion, but the emotional wounds had never fully healed. Pretending to be human throughout his teenage years, he thought of himself as something more, deeper than his classmates, something other than human.

He lacked true emotions and had never even attempted to form anything other than a shallow bond with other students. He had no friends, just schoolyard acquaintances. No girlfriend, just a series of females he had fumbled around in the backseat of his car, never anything deep. Which is why he needed Stephen; his brother was the only one he had ever felt close to after his father's death. Stephen was his only true friend.

He had joined the army shortly after high school in the years following the September Eleventh attacks, not out of any deep seeded sense of patriotism or rage, but simply because it was something to do. There was never any question of college; the money really wasn't there, and he wasn't even sure of what he wanted to do. The army seemed simplistic, regimented, and thus perfect for a man like him. He was well aware of the certainty of combat following his initial training, but for someone as cold and hardened as he was, he shrugged it off. He was a robot, an automaton, truly the perfect soldier.

This illusion was shattered on the battlefield of Iraq. As the bombs exploded and the bullets flew, Mark felt fear for the first time in years. Viewing the dead bodies of men he had known and the crumpled forms of innocent civilians, he felt a profound sadness in his heart. The smell of burning cordite, singed flesh, and even the coppery scent of blood brought a rush of emotions to the forefront. Then there was the enemy. The few times Mark had actually been forced to discharge his weapon, a torrent of terrible thoughts cascaded through his mind. Had his round hit its mark? The very thought of his bullet tearing through skin, splintering bone, and lodging itself in the grey matter of a man's brain or the meaty redness of his heart tore at Mark's insides. He felt a profound sense of guilt, the indescribable weight of having ended a man's life, even an evil man, taking its toll on the younger Enos.

Faced with constant reminders of his own mortality, Mark was bombarded by long dormant feelings and thoughts. For the first time in forever, he wanted to live, wanted to continue being a human being. It was like coming up for air after being submerged for several minutes, like being reborn. Mark could even feel himself gasping at times. The totality of it all was too much too take. His brain overloaded from sensory input, and thus he cracked, his thin veil of sanity shattering there in the desert.

He could remember sobbing at first, but this was replaced by a sternly clenched jaw. He found it difficult to sleep, and this only contributed to his failing mental state. He was irritable, paranoid, and generally unapproachable. He could remember clocking an Iraqi merchant for no discernable reason, his own paranoia dictating that this man was a threat. Mark cringed at the memory of his rifle butt making contact with the softness of the man's cheek and shattering the jaw bones below. It was at that very moment that his commanding officer, Kelley, sent him to be evaluated.

Battle fatigue, that's what he had been diagnosed with initially. During the Second World War they had described it innocently enough as "shellshock," and it wasn't until after Vietnam that they came up with a professional sounding diagnosis, Post Traumatic Stress Disorder. Ordinarily, men were sent home for such things, honorably discharged and sent out amongst the living, the civilian population, trying to pick up the pieces of their shattered lives. However, Iraq was no ordinary time. The professional US army was overstretched, forced to do more with less, and thus they could not afford to lose any able-bodied individual. Mark was therefore told he was battle fatigued and sent to a recreational facility at a nearby base for a few days of "R and R" and subjected to a heavy diet of pills. It was here that he learned the healing power of drugs.

They allowed you to escape within your own mind, giving the feeling of ecstasy even in the most untenable or horrifying of conditions. They made him placid, "normal," and he needed more. At first the soothing drugs the army doctors had administered had been adequate, allowing him to interact with fellow humans and calming his nerves, but he knew they wouldn't do the trick for long.

His hunch was confirmed upon rejoining his unit, as the stress of limited combat and the enemy's guerilla tactics began to take their toll, and so he committed himself to searching for everything he could get his hands on. Acquiring a nice little stash, he experimented with all types of chemicals, seeking the perfect cocktail to put his mind at ease. He never found it of course, but the drugs had allowed him to reassume the appearance of normality and to finish out his tour of duty. He was even regarded as an above-average soldier by those above him, but he knew there were whispers amongst the ranks of his fragile hold on sanity.

Returning stateside, he was subjected to an array of army psychiatrists and psychologists: the Government's attempts at assuring he was safe for life outside of the military, that they were not releasing some wild animal upon the general populace. He answered all their questions, all the while continuing to pursue the drugs which now made him tick. He was more than pleased with the bounty he could procure in America; the marketplace dwarfed that which he had found in the Middle East.

It would be months before they sent him home, an honorable discharge in his hand. His mind had been ravaged by war, and his savings drained by his endless pursuit of narcotics; he arrived home a broken man at only the age of twenty-three. The meeting with his mother at the airport had been cordial yet strained; the two had never formed that close bond which existed between many mothers and sons. He had arrived home destitute, financially and emotionally, taking up residence in his old bedroom racked by the new horrors that plagued his mind.

The nightmares had only intensified since he had come home, and he couldn't tell if it was due to the heavy doses of drugs he was ingesting or the lack of army shrinks ready to analyze him at a moment's notice. He felt lost and useless, suicidal even, and it had only been tonight, when he had enjoyed the company of his lone brother, that he had first felt at ease, happy even. Stephen humanized him, reminded him that there was hope for him. Mark realized now more than ever that he truly needed his brother, his one emotional contact point in the entire world, and that is why he had felt so sad as he watched him back out of the driveway and leave. Sure, he would be back again, and it wasn't as if he lived that far away, but Mark felt as though he needed him there in perpetuity, a constant companion. Stephen was the only one, he was sure of it, he could ever open up to and explain everything that had plagued him for months, detail the horrors he had witnessed.

Now, sitting alone in the dark, rocking back and forth, Mark felt more isolated than he had since coming home. He was fearful too, unwilling to return indoors as he knew the terrors which awaited him the minute he closed his eyes. The nightmares that refused to leave him alone were waiting for him in his bedroom, secure in their fortress behind his eyes. He felt like a small child, unwilling to go to bed for fear of the bogeyman hiding in his closet. Cursing himself, he looked skyward. *Tonight's going to be a bad one.* He could feel it.

IV

There was a flash of light, followed by a tremendous explosion that sent the tan Humvee somersaulting across the road. Already baking in the hot desert sun, it began to burn slowly, the flames licking the surface of the entire vehicle. As a column of black smoke rose from the damaged vehicle, a crowd of stunned onlookers moved forth and gathered round. Every one of them clad in what could only be described as decorative frocks, they started to chatter and scream at one another excitedly, several of them retrieving their cell phones.

Bleeding from his face and still strapped into his seat, Mark came to, his vision fogged and his head aching beneath his helmet. He began to cough as he inhaled the fuel vapors and the smoke. The familiar smell of burning meat reached him, a scent akin to a pig roast, and he knew he was surrounded by burning bodies.

Looking to the driver's seat, Mark noticed that the driver had lost consciousness, slumped against the roof of the vehicle. Facing away from him, Mark could only view the soldier's backside, but he could tell the soldier was a burly man, and he spied thinning, white hair peeking out from underneath his helmet. Removing the man's helmet, Mark turned the soldier's head. He looked into the face of his father, Ron Enos. Fully dressed in army uniform, his eyes were closed. Blood splattered across his flak jacket, and Mark knew instantly he was gone once again. A tinge of sadness tugged at his heart as Enos realized that he had just lost his father for the second time in his life. Ron Enos had been a bear of a man, full of life and perpetually happy until his heart stopped beating one night as he slept, the victim of a massive heart attack. His eyes watering, a lump in the back of his throat, Mark forgot the fact that he was in mortal peril for a moment and stared at his beloved father, sobbing softly.

Still crying, he looked out the windshield and saw that the world had turned upside down, the blue sky now resting upon the car floor. It dawned on him that the car had rolled. A powerful concussion had flung the nearly three-ton vehicle clear across the street.

The stench of gasoline began to overtake the smell of burning meat, and Mark began to panic, forgetting his dead father as he realized the fuel tanks had ruptured. In a burning vehicle, it was only a matter of time before the resulting explosion finished the job the improvised bomb had started. He began to hyperventilate, aware of his perilous position, when something else literally screamed for his attention, drawing him to look to the backseat of the Humvee.

Another soldier was screaming at the top of his lungs, apparently also coming to the conclusion that they were about to die. As Mark looked back, he was mortified to see that the soldier was none other than his brother, Stephen. Pinned against the roof by his own equipment, Stephen struggled to free himself as the flames lapped at his skin, searing the flesh of his cheeks and causing the skin to bubble.

"Stephen!" Mark called.

"Mark, fucking save me!" Stephen yelled, "Fucking save me!"

Undoing his seat restraint Mark fell to the roof of the Humvee, and he fought to right himself. He turned and reached for his brother's hand, determined to pull him from the wreck. Stephen continued to yell, stretching out his hand as the flames flew under his helmet and singed his hair, the resulting smell making Mark want to vomit. As their fingers touched, Mark realized it was too late; there was no way he would rescue them both. Time seemed to stand still for a moment as the gasoline met the orange flames, and the fireball overtook them both, incinerating them in an unholy fire.

Mark awoke with a jolt, the sweat dripping from his forehead and his chest heaving uncontrollably. It had seemed so real, as if he and his brother had just been burned alive. Clasping a hand to his face, he slicked back his hair as he began to calm himself. This was becoming ridiculous, a nightly ritual for him. The dreams seemed like they would never end.

He couldn't understand why he suffered from such night terrors, while others in his unit had been able to function normally. He felt weak and inadequate, as if he lacked internal fortitude. While he had seen combat in Iraq, had heard the bullets fired in anger whizz by his head in brutal firefights, his unit had actually remained relatively unscathed. While there had been few men lost, there had been no mass casualties like those depicted in numerous war movies. Rather it was the unpredictability of the guerilla war the enemy waged which had frayed Mark's sanity and shattered his nerves. Just the thought that your next step could be your last, that some faceless enemy had placed an improvised explosive device in a sidewalk or a market cart and was determined to blow you to kingdom come as you passed by. It had rattled his nerves, deprived him of countless hours of sleep, and had affected him severely. He had never believed he would make it home alive. He always truly believed he would succumb to an insurgent attack, become just another statistic related in the back of the daily paper.

His thoughts now turned to his long-deceased father. *Why the fuck did Mom have to bring him up?* It had taken years for him to get over the sudden death of his father, so much time before he could function normally. It wasn't fair to Mark that his mother had thrust the memory of Ron Enos to the forefront of his mind, and it certainly wasn't fair to him that the thought had penetrated his nightmares. *As if I don't have enough shit to deal with.*

Flipping off his covers, he moved towards his dresser. He needed heavy shit, something that would really calm him down and take the edge off. While the army doctors had prescribed Alprazalom, a powerful anti-anxiety drug, to deal with what they termed his "severe post traumatic stress disorder," Mark had acquired even more potent substances to help him cope. Opening the top drawer, he sifted through the underwear and socks he used to conceal the drugs, unearthing his secret stash.

An impressive collection of drugs, he had accumulated it over a period of months while he was in the army. It was amazing the amount of pills, powders, and other substances one could acquire on the average army base. Everywhere you went, someone seemed willing to sell or barter a variety of supplements and drugs. Mark now had a vast selection of uppers, downers, and anti-depressants, and he searched for just the right pill to do the trick. Moving aside foil wrappers and orange pill containers, he smiled as he selected a potent little drug, Diazepam or Valium, and popped a number of pills in his mouth.

Swallowing, he closed the drawer and marched back to bed, slipping under the covers. As he felt the drugs take effect, he found himself smiling in ecstasy as he fell asleep, a trail of spittle running from his mouth as he began to snore.

V

Mark Enos thought that after two tours of duty in Iraq over a span of four years he knew what hell was like. Enduring combat in the sweltering heat of an Iraqi summer, experiencing the smells and sounds of war had surely steeled him for any extreme that life could throw at him, prepared him for any hardship. Or so he had thought.

As the inoffensive, mind-numbing music droned on in the background and the glare from the fluorescent lights blinded him, Mark now knew what hell was truly like. Hell was the late shift at the local All-Mart. Instead of the imposing fatigues of a battle-hardened soldier, he now wore an unflattering, loose-fitting blue vest over his street clothes. A white nametag announced his name to the world and annoyingly clacked against a yellow smiley face button affixed to his work vest.

Wheeling a large plastic-wrapped pallet of electronics behind him, he shuffled aimlessly through the rows of flat-screen televisions, home furnishings, and children's toys. Only two hours into his first shift, he found that his body was on autopilot. A response, he decided, to the fact that his mind had shut itself down out of the sheer boredom which overwhelmed it.

Enos was like an automaton, mindlessly walking through the world to the point where he barely avoided colliding with an elderly woman emerging from an aisle. Snapping into focus, he stopped short, wincing in pain as the heavy pallet continued on moving, driven by inertia and pinching the skin upon his ankles. The woman glared at him in a manner befitting a boarding school nun before harrumphing in disapproval and continuing on to the next aisle.

Mark shook his head and peeled the back of his feet from the pallet, waiting for the pain to subside. *How much longer do I have to be here?* Dragging the pallet a few aisles down he arrived in front of an empty shelf and removed a small razor blade from his vest pocket. After making a few incisions in the plastic wrap he peeled the cellophane from the uneven stack of boxes and began to slowly place them upon the white, aluminum shelf.

He felt tired; he was still not sleeping well despite the pills. Even the act of lifting a small, plastic toaster in a box and placing it on the ledge required some sort of Herculean effort on his part.

His body felt weak and listless, kept running only by downing a considerable amount of coffee and the ingestion of a few diet pills he had purchased at a local convenience store. Filling the shelf in front of him, he was convinced he had least burned some time, that he was a little closer to going home. Glancing at his cell phone, he felt his shoulders slump as he realized only five minutes had passed.

"You're not allowed to have those during your shift," a gravelly voice whispered.

Enos looked up and cringed at the owner of the voice. Carol, one of his new coworkers, stood leaning against a pallet of her own. Somewhere in her mid fifties, Carol was hideous, possessing a body that was both languid and wiry. Her back hunched, her brown hair was unkempt, and a pair of thick glasses perched atop her Romanesque, pointed nose.

Fighting the urge to hurl an insult at her, Enos nodded at her instead. "Sorry, won't happen again."

"Just don't want to see you get in trouble," Carol said, winking at him in a provocative manner.

Enos almost vomited in response.

"Have you taken your break yet?" Carol asked.

"No, not yet."

Carol smiled, revealing a mouthful of discolored teeth badly in need of orthodontic assistance. "Well come on then, I haven't either."

Mark searched for any reason to refuse the woman, looking around the aisle in desperation.

His eyes settled upon the pallet behind him. "I'd like to, but I have to finish stocking all this stuff."

Carol waved her hand dismissively. "Oh don't worry about that. It'll be there when you're finished. They don't care if you leave them in the aisles as long as the customer's can get by them."

Mark realized that he was defeated, that all avenues of escape had been cut off. With his head bowed, he shambled towards Carol, who was waving him towards her. Placing her weathered and liver-spotted hand upon him, she crowed, "Going to break is the best part of the day."

* * *

The employee break room was dimly lit, as the fluorescent light bulbs embedded in the paneled ceiling were dying. Cold, multicolored linoleum covered the floor, and the walls were painted a dull gray, broken only by a series of motivational posters and a wooden notification board. They sat at a round table, just next to the break room's refrigerator and microwave.

Enos watched in disgust as Carol excitedly shoveled gobs of blueberry yogurt into her mouth. Much of the thick, viscous material was expelled from her mouth, meandering through the large gaps in her teeth and dribbling down her chin before landing upon the table. Making matters worse, she made a sickening slurping noise as she ate and continually spoke with her mouth full.

"Not eating?" Carol questioned, expelling a spattering of yogurt towards Enos.

"Not hungry," Enos muttered.

"So this your first shift?"

"Uh huh," Enos nodded, pretending to be looking around the room, looking at anything but Carol.

"I remember my first shift like it was yesterday," Carol laughed before sucking in more yogurt.

"How long have you worked here, Carol?" Enos asked, intrigued to hear her answer.

"Oh God," Carol paused, swallowing as she thought, "Come December I'll have been here fourteen years."

Enos felt his blood run cold. *Dear God*, he pondered, *I couldn't imagine being here for fourteen more minutes, let alone fourteen years.*

"By the way, bucko," Carol scolded, "you've got to pick it up from November to December if you plan on sticking around. One and a half pallets in two hours isn't going to cut it with all the Christmas shoppers that come through here, let me tell you." She sampled another spoonful of yogurt before adding, "Although they might keep you around just 'cause you're so cute." She winked again and turned back to her yogurt.

Revolting, Enos thought before nodding at her. "Noted." There had to be a way out of this. Scanning the room, he noticed a door painted in a similar manner to the break room walls and emblazoned with the white figures which denoted that it was a restroom. That was where he needed to go. "Excuse me for a minute, I just need to use the bathroom," he said.

"Oh, by all means," Carol responded, waving her spindly fingers dismissively.

Enos scurried towards the bathroom and quickly closed the door behind him, locking it just in case Carol decided to surprise him. Moving towards the sink, he turned it on, hoping the sound of rushing water would drown out the sound of Carol eating. It failed to do so. *This is terrible.* There was no way he could make it through this entire shift and still maintain his sanity, especially if Carol was going to be his constant companion throughout the night.

He needed chemical assistance, something that would make the duration of his night at least bearable. Luckily, he had come prepared. Removing a small mint tin from his pants pocket, he opened up and removed a tiny white pill, which he promptly placed in his mouth. Containing the powerful painkiller Oxycodone, the pill took effect in less than a minute. Enos felt his muscles relax and a wave of orgasmic bliss overtake him. Rather than being overwhelmed by boredom or disgust for Carol, he simply felt happy. Now all he would have to do was ride the drug-induced wave of ecstasy and his shift would be over in no time. He could then just drive home, collapse in bed, and forget all about Carol and this awful place.

He suddenly became aware of a buzzing in his vest pocket. Reaching in, he retrieved his cell phone. Raising the receiver to his ear, he pressed a button and heard the voicemail he had just received begin to play. *"Hello, Mark, it's Mom,"* a tinny voice sounded. *"I hope you're enjoying the new job. I told Mr. Lamperti that you were so thankful that you would love to take Toby out tonight. He said he'd leave the gate open for you and that Toby will be waiting for you when you get out of work. I'm going to bed; I'll see you in the morning. Love ya, Goodnight."*

Mark hung up the phone. *Shit,* he thought to himself. He couldn't take Toby out tonight, not in the condition he was going to be in by the time he got home. Why in the hell would his mother make such a promise to the old man? Besides, it wasn't as if Toby and he had ever gotten along. This night just kept getting worse. Still bemoaning his mother's decision, he heard a knock at the door.

"Yeah?" Mark asked, turning off the faucet.

"Just wanted to let you know to finish up in there, wipe yourself or whatever you have to," Carol's muffled voice reverberated. "We only get a fifteen-minute break."

VI

The moon sat pregnant and suspended overhead. Surrounded by an ethereal yellow hallow, it appeared preternaturally close to the earth, allowing even the naked eye to observe the craters which dotted its pockmarked and cragged face. Enos and Toby strolled along the darkened suburban street, silhouetted in the moonlight.

Occasionally Toby would saunter just a little too far ahead for Mark's liking, and he would be forced to tug upon the leash in his hand to rein the mutt in. Toby was Mr. Lamperti's Irish setter. The neighborhood, led by Mark's mother, had chipped in years back to purchase the dog for the elderly Lamperti shortly after his wife had passed away, feeling that the elderly man needed a companion. Mark always assumed his mother had been so dogged about purchasing the pooch as payback for the support the Lamperti's had provided when Mark's father had died unexpectedly.

While Mark had no quarrel with Mr. Lamperti, he and Toby had never quite gotten along. Even when Mark was a teenager and Toby just a puppy, there were problems. Toby would snap at Mark's hand when he went to pet him, and later, as Toby matured, the dog would growl and bark at the young man as he walked by. It was not until shortly before Mark was to leave for the army that their relationship had devolved into an uneasy truce between man and beast. Mark refused to go near the animal, and Toby had ceased to bark incessantly as he walked by.

This made their present situation all the more curious to Mark. Enos had expected the dog to raise a tremendous racket as he approached, and he was prepared for the dog to shy away in protest when he sought to hitch the leash to his collar. However, he found Toby to be quite placid, readily approaching Mark and acquiescing to the application of his leash. *Maybe he's getting too old to fight with me*, Mark thought, *or maybe he's just forgotten who I am.*

Whatever the reason for the dog's change in disposition and approach to him, Enos was not about to look a gift horse in the mouth. In his drug-addled state, he was exhausted and too weakened physically to fight with the canine. As the dog trotted along at a stately and respectable pace, Enos struggled to keep up, often scuffing his toes upon the pavement and finding himself dragged along by Toby. With a yawn, he tugged on Toby's rein, signaling that the dog needed to slow down.

Slowly they made their way down Talbot Road, walking away from the house lamps and streetlights which illuminated much of the street. As they became ensconced in the shadows, Mark craned his neck and determined that they were roughly a hundred feet from the nearest home. *More than enough distance.* Tugging hard on Toby's leash, Enos brought the procession to a grinding halt. The dog whimpered in displeasure and walked in a large circle before placing his rump upon the asphalt.

"Good boy," Mark muttered while reaching into his coat pocket and producing a joint. Placing the marijuana cigarette between his lips, he retrieved a lighter from his pants pocket and cupped his hands around the end of the joint before igniting the lighter. The golden light of the flame flickered momentarily between his fingers before disappearing, replaced by the dull orange glow of the joint. Enos took a long drag off the crudely rolled cigarette, holding the smoke in his lungs for a few moments before exhaling a long column of gray, acrid smoke.

As the fumes left his mouth, he erupted into a violent coughing fit, his eyes watering as he did so. Closing his mouth he stifled the coughing, feeling his diaphragm muscles convulse, which in turn caused a brief bout of hiccups. As the coughing subsided, Mark looked down at Toby. The dog had perked up, his head tilted and his ears raised as he stared at Mark in curiosity.

"You want some?" Mark croaked, holding the joint towards Toby. The dog let out what could only be interpreted as a groan and placed his head upon his forearms, looking tired and bored. Mark laughed, eliciting another round of coughing, which prompted him to take another drag of his joint.

Toby's ears pricked up, and the dog raised his head as if sniffing the air. Suddenly agitated the dog stood on all fours and unleashed a threatening growl.

"Would you relax," Mark said as he blew more smoke into the air. "We'll move in a minute."

Toby refused to stop growling and the dog arched his back.

"Cut the shit," Mark said angrily. Looking down at the dog, he realized Toby was not growling at him, but rather staring intently at the grove of trees just ahead of them. Mark strained to see through the darkness and his watery eyes, but couldn't make out anything in the undergrowth. *Probably just a raccoon*, Mark determined.

Toby began to bark menacingly in the direction of the bushes, lips peeled back to reveal yellowing teeth. The dog continued to yap and snarl, becoming more and more animated by the minute. He started towards the woods, only to be pulled back by his leash. Still barking, Toby continued to pull against his leash, rising up on two feet momentarily before succumbing to Enos's refusal to relinquish control.

"Calm the fuck down," Enos growled. "There's nothing there." No sooner had he said this than he heard the sharp snap of a breaking twig. There was something in the woods, and it apparently was not frightened off by Toby's barking. The dog ceased to yip and returned to a series of low, guttural growls. Enos fumbled around in his pocket for his lighter and held it forward, his arm extended towards the forest.

Flicking it on, he waved the flame back and forth, hoping to see just what had upset Toby. His heart thundered in his chest, his adrenaline surging from the fear of the great unknown. It was unnerving knowing that something or someone was spying on them from the cover of the forest. Making another sweep of his hand, his blood went cold as the flame allowed him to catch sight of something. Two yellow-green dots stared back at him, the flame flickering upon their shiny surface in the unmistakable reflection of a nocturnal animal's eye shine. Mark felt his blood run cold and the hairs on the back of his neck stand on end. Though he couldn't accurately ascertain the animal's size, he simply knew that it was big.

"Holy shi—," Mark began to exclaim just as the unseen beast burst forth from the underbrush. Dropping the lighter, Mark extended his hands in an instinctive defensive posture only to have the attacking animal latch on to his right hand. As it pulled him to the ground, Mark marveled at the animal's power. Just as it clamped its fangs down, his survival instincts took over. His face was filled with the sight of black fur, and he screamed as the animal jerked its head back and forth, tearing flesh and ripping tendons.

Mark released Toby's leash and began to pound away at the beast, feeling his blows land harmlessly upon the animal's muscular body. He could hear the beast snarling along with Toby barking excitedly, and could feel himself being dragged along the asphalt by his attacker. He had to escape the animal's clutches; he desperately needed to free himself. There was only one way out this, a comical thought which crept into the back of his mind at this peculiar moment in time. Feeling along the underside of the animal, he located the attacker's scrotum and clutched it in his hand, squeezing as hard as he could. The beast released his hand, howling in pain. Yanking both hands to his chest and curling up in a ball, Mark watched as the animal stumbled forward shaking its head.

It was only then that he got a clearer look at the beast. It was canine in appearance, but was exceptionally large and heavily muscled. Still shaking its head, Mark only caught glimpses of the animal's snout and its yellow eyes. He only viewed its spectacularly long fangs for a moment before, still snarling, it bounded across the street and into the forest.

Mark felt himself go limp, his strength fading fast. As he lay upon the ground, chest heaving from exertion, he viewed Toby taking off down the street. The dog had fled out of fear, taking off at a full gallop with his leash in tow. Woozy and unable to see clearly, Mark continued to watch until the dog disappeared in the darkness. Coughing, Mark lay prostrate, unable to move. Staring up at the sky, he viewed the moon, gazing at the heavens for only a moment before succumbing to exhaustion and closing his eyes.

VII

The police cruiser rolled up slowly, the glare from a myriad of red flashing lights gleaming upon its shiny, white exterior. As the tires ground to a halt, the driver's side door opened, allowing Sergeant Eric Kaplan to exit the vehicle. Heavily muscled and broad shouldered, Kaplan ran a hand through his flat, auburn-colored hair before slamming the door shut and walking towards the crowd ahead.

His black boots grated upon the asphalt and he began to weave through the crowd of onlookers who had gathered upon the throughway, each one of them jostling for position trying to catch a glimpse of what was going on. "Excuse me," Kaplan muttered as he shouldered past one middle-aged woman.

"Move aside please," he ordered another woman. Patiently he continued to make way through the group, each individual moving aside deferentially as they realized it was a police officer pushing them aside. Suddenly a worn and weathered hand grabbed hold of Kaplan's cerulean uniform top.

"My dog," an elderly man wheezed, peering at Kaplan through a pair of horn-rimmed glasses. "Officer, I can't find my dog."

The man appeared to be on death's doorstep, his skin loosely hanging upon his small frame and a smattering of brown liver spots decorating his face. Long strands of thin, white hair were brushed back upon the man's balding head, and a bushy mustache along with the aforementioned glasses sat upon his countenance. Kaplan gently removed the man's hand from his chest, "Okay, Mister,"

"Lamperti," the man gasped, "Bill Lamperti. I can't find my dog Toby."

"Okay, sir," Kaplan soothed, still moving forward, "we'll get right on that. Just let me attend to this matter."

Kaplan released the man's hand pointing towards the collection of fire trucks and ambulances which waited ahead. Lamperti moved his mouth, yet made no sound, choosing to remain silent, looking forlorn and dejected as Kaplan moved on. The remaining members of the crowd parted, and Kaplan emerged next to the rear end of a red fire truck.

"What's going on?" A fireman asked rhetorically as Kaplan approached.

"You tell me," Kaplan cracked. He did not recognize the fireman, but then again, they all looked and sounded the same to him. Clad in the thick yellow-black patterned fire jacket and pants common to all firefighters, this rendered the man undistinguishable from his peers.

"Some type of animal attack," the fireman responded, motioning for Kaplan to follow him.

"What type of animal?" Kaplan asked as they walked through the maze of rescue vehicles.

"Don't know," the fireman shrugged, "the guy couldn't really say what it was. Animal control's out searching the woods for it now, though."

"Okay," Kaplan nodded, "how bad is the victim?"

"Didn't look too bad when we first got here; it looks like just a few bites on his hand. His mother found him lying passed out in the street. I'd say he's just shaken up."

"Do we need all this for a few bites on a hand?" Kaplan asked in disbelief, motioning towards all the vehicles surrounding them.

"Hey, what can I tell you man?" The fireman laughed. "It's a slow night."

Kaplan continued walking forward shaking his head. Just ahead there was an ambulance, the rear doors opened outwards and the harsh, white light of its interior pouring forth. A stout woman stood with a hand to her mouth and a look of concern upon her face. Even from a distance Kaplan could detect the red, swollenness of her eyes and knew that she had recently been crying. Two medical technicians milled about a young man who sat with his legs dangling out the rear of the ambulance, his hand outstretched and his body wrapped in a brown, itchy looking blanket.

The young man's eyes were glossed over and buttressed by thick, purple bags. Hunched over and slack jawed, he just had a world weary and tired air about him. He didn't even look up as Kaplan approached the group.

"Hello, guys," Kaplan greeted, announcing his presence to the gathering.

"What's up?" One of the technicians nodded at Kaplan as he bandaged up the young man's hand.

Kaplan ignored the technician and moved towards the young man. "I'm Officer Eric Kaplan. And you are?"

The young man blinked for what seemed like the first time and looked up at Kaplan. "Mark."

"I'm Mark's mother," the woman to the left of the ambulance stated, "Virginia Enos." She extended her hand in greeting towards Kaplan.

Shaking her hand, Kaplan turned back towards Mark. "Okay so, Mark, can you fill me in on what happened tonight?"

"I was attacked," Mark answered drowsily.

"Okay," Kaplan nodded, his tone dangerously close to being considered condescending, "can you tell me what attacked you?"

"Not really." Mark shook his head. "I didn't get a real clear view of it."

"Just try for me," Kaplan urged.

"It was big," Mark answered, "and black, I can remember that. It looked kind of like a dog, but it wasn't really. I guess I'd say it looked like a wolf."

"A wolf?" Kaplan asked, releasing Virginia's hand and bringing a fist to his chin.

"Yeah, if I had to pick an animal, that'd be it." Mark nodded. "But like I said, I didn't get a good look at it, and it was a lot bigger than I thought a wolf would be."

"And it just rushed you?"

"Pretty much," Mark replied. "I was walking the neighbor's dog, and the thing just came out of nowhere and attacked me."

"Mr. Lamperti's dog, Toby?" Kaplan questioned.

"Yeah, you know him?"

"We actually just met," Kaplan mused. "So how'd you get away from this thing?"

Mark smiled. "Actually I kind of grabbed it by the balls, and it just let go of my hand."

"Jesus," Kaplan replied, smiling and shaking his head, "and what'd it do, just run away?"

"Yeah," Mark answered, "it let go and just ran off into the woods."

"And Toby?"

"Before I passed out, I saw Toby running down the street."

"All right." Kaplan nodded before turning his attention to the medical technicians. "How's the hand look?"

A female technician scribbling upon a chart paused and answered, "We're taking him to South Shore Hospital now for a few cautionary X-rays and so a doctor can look at his hand. We're also going to give him a rabies shot before he can go home."

"Awesome," Kaplan boomed facetiously while tapping Mark upon the shoulder. "Hear that, Mark? You've got some good times in front of you."

"Thanks," Mark responded sarcastically.

Kaplan gave Mark's shoulder a squeeze. "Just get some rest, Mark. We'll be in touch." Before moving off, Kaplan nodded towards Virginia. "Ma'am."

Walking away from the ambulance Kaplan scanned the scene, locating another officer just near the tree line to his right.

A thin, lithe individual, Kaplan recognized him instantly. "McGuire," he called.

The officer looked in Kaplan's direction and nodded in recognition. Kaplan approached quickly and leaned forward towards McGuire. "You got anything?"

"Yeah," McGuire answered, peering over Kaplan's shoulder to make sure he was out of earshot of the ambulance. "When we got here, we found a nice looking roach next to where the kid said he was attacked."

Kaplan crossed his arms and looked back at the ambulance. "He said he was just walking the dog when the thing rushed him."

"Amongst other things," McGuire laughed, "I figure he was walking the dog, paused to light his joint, and the thing ambushed him."

"Sounds reasonable," Kaplan said. "What do you think it was?"

"I don't know," McGuire shrugged, "probably just another dog. Animal control's out searching for it."

"I've heard," Kaplan replied. "Well I'm heading back. Just wanted to check it out for myself. Keep me up to date if anything happens. You've got my cell, right?"

"Yeah," McGuire answered, "what do you want me to do about the weed?"

Kaplan peered back at Enos, thinking for a moment before turning back towards McGuire. "Fuck it. The kid's been through enough tonight."

Kaplan turned and began to walk back towards the crowd. The same elderly gentleman who had accosted him before stood at the front of the crowd a lost and lonely look about him. His wide, sad eyes stared forth through his thick glasses and he periodically stood on his tip toes so as to see just what was happening. Kaplan stopped and looked back at McGuire. "And tell somebody to find Mr. Lamperti's dog too."

McGuire looked at the escaping Kaplan's backside with his arms spread wide. "Who the hell is Mr. Lamperti?"

VIII

Enos awoke with a yawn, his eyes flying open. His face was squished against the mattress, and he had to pry himself off of the bed as a thin coating of dried drool acted like an adhesive upon the sheets. His mouth was dry, tongue like sandpaper, and he had to shake his head vigorously to wake himself up. Still groggy, he rolled out of the bed and stumbled towards the door.

Emerging into the hallway, he felt along the wall, only to find his sense of touch dulled by the bandages which encased his hand. Pausing for a moment, Enos withdrew his hand from the wall and inspected it. His hand was clubbed, with only the thumb retaining its original shape. The white gauze was stained a light brown in areas where the blood had attempted to seep through. *Jesus, that really happened last night.* Mark snorted.

As he continued down the hallway, he was forced to blink furiously as the sunlight which poured through the windows blinded him. His eyes ached as if they had not been forced to deal with any source of light in ages. His head throbbed, and it suddenly occurred to Mark that he felt as if he were dealing with a tremendous hangover. *I must be really dehydrated.*

Mark entered the kitchen, the smell of bacon and burnt toast pervading his nostrils. There was also the slight hint of stale coffee in the air. The prodigious rump of his mother sat swaying back and forth in front of the sink, the sound of clinking plates and running water indicating she was washing dishes. Humming to herself, her perm jostled upon her head, and she turned towards him. "Well, good morning!" she exclaimed, turning off the faucet as she did so.

"Morning," he replied, rubbing his free hand upon his eyes.

"How's the hand?"

"Um," Mark answered, pausing for a moment to reinspect his hand. It only now occurred to him that he was not in extreme pain. There was only a mild soreness in his hand, similar to the ache after a bout of heavy weight lifting, but nothing debilitating. As he gingerly flexed his wounded appendage he sensed a slight burning, itching sensation emanating from the injury, but again it was nothing excruciating. "Um, it actually feels all right," he answered finally.

"Rested are we?" Virginia asked in an annoyingly sing-song tone.

"Yeah, actually I am," he responded. It occurred to him now that he had slept through the night without waking and without the assistance of a sleep aid. Perhaps it was due to shock or his previously drug-addled state, but he had experienced his first disturbance free night in ages. In fact, he felt extremely rested and rejuvenated. For the first time in a long time he felt decidedly normal.

"Well, you should be with how long you slept," Virginia said.

"Why? What time is it?"

"It's ten thirty in the morning," she answered.

Mark furrowed his brow, "That's not that late. We didn't get back from the hospital until two."

A concerned look spread across Virginia's face, "Mark, honey, its ten thirty in the morning, Wednesday. You've been asleep for a day and a half."

Her last statement took Mark back. "You let me sleep for over thirty hours, Ma?"

"Well, I was afraid at first when you didn't wake up, but I figured you hadn't had a good night's sleep in so long, so I just let you go."

"I had to work yesterday," he groaned.

She raised her hands in a defensive manner and shook her head. "I took care of that. I called in for you, and they said take as much time as you need."

Mark steadied himself against a nearby chair. "Jesus, Mom, you called in for me? They're going to think I'm some fucking invalid here."

"No, no, no," she said dismissively. "I explained everything, and they totally understood. Here, honey, sit down. Are you hungry?"

Mark slumped into the chair he was leaning against and just nodded his head. Placing his elbow upon the table, he rested his aching head upon his hand as his mother set a plate in front of him. Mark looked down and inspected the plate. Watery looking yellow eggs stared back at him along with blackened strips of bacon and charred wheat toast. Under normal conditions, Mark would have refused the plate, but his mouth began to water, and his belly gurgled and churned. God, he was hungry. Grabbing a fork, he attacked the horrid looking meal in front of him.

Shoveling bites of slippery eggs into his gullet and snapping off chunks of bacon with his teeth, he would hardly finish chewing before taking another bite. His mother had retreated to the refrigerator to fetch a glass of orange juice and upon turning she gasped, "Mark, honey, slow down. You'll just give yourself a stomach ache."

Ignoring her, Mark continued to lap up his breakfast. Not bothering to look up, he grabbed the glass of juice she offered and downed the entire cup before thrusting the glass back to her. Virginia set the glass down and sat across from him, watching as he hungrily gnawed away at the hardened slices of bread she had prepared for him. His cheeks bulged with food waiting to enter his throat, and she watched intently as he continued to shove more into his mouth.

"Mark, slow down," she said sternly.

With lips barely containing the food backed up in his mouth, he set down his fork and swallowed hard, a loud, wet, sloshing sound coming from his throat. Swallowing again, he looked at his mother. "Sorry."

"That's fine," she soothed. "It's good to see you hungry. I just didn't want to see you choke."

Returning to his plate, Mark was now more conscientious with how he ate, slowly bringing small bites up to his mouth. Finishing the last few bites, he pushed the plate away and leaned back in the chair.

"All done?" his mother asked.

Mark simply nodded in return.

Looking out the window, Virginia sighed, "They still haven't found Toby."

"No?" Mark asked.

"No," his mother answered, shaking her head. "That poor, poor man."

"I'm sure he'll be fine," Mark said, waving her off.

"He was out there all last night calling Toby's name," Virginia continued, ignoring her son's flippancy.

"The thing that bit me probably ate Toby," Mark cracked.

Virginia playfully slapped Mark. "Oh, don't say that. That'd kill Mr. Lamperti, and you know it."

"Yeah, that or the impending stroke," Mark snorted.

"Well, since you're so concerned about our neighbor, you'll be happy to know that I've told him that you feel so bad that you'd be more than willing to help find his dog," Virginia smiled.

"Oh, what the hell, Ma?" Mark moaned. "Why'd you tell him that?"

"Well, you're the one that lost him, Mark," she answered.

"It's not like I let the thing run away. I was attacked," he retorted.

"Oh, come on, you'd be lifting the old man's spirits."

"What about my spirits?" he grumbled.

"We'll deal with those later, but right now you have to go jump in the shower," she said as she stood up from her chair, clearing Mark's dish from the table.

"Why's that?" Mark asked.

"Because I told Mr. Lamperti you'd be over right after breakfast," she answered with a broad smile; turning away from the table and leaving Mark slouched in his chair.

IX

They walked in awkward silence, nary a word spoken between them. Occasionally one of them would snap his fingers and let loose with a weak whistle, usually followed by a mumbled, "Here boy." Walking down the road, Mark held his head down, only half-heartedly searching for Mr. Lamperti's lost canine. *Goddamn it, Mom, how the hell did I let you talk me into this?* It struck him that in all his years knowing Mr. Lamperti, he had never been alone with the old man, usually only encountering him on the street or at a local barbeque. It was a strained atmosphere; they simply had no common ground with which to spark conversation. *This is agonizing.* Swatting at a nearby tall weed, he looked up and shuddered as they passed the spot where he had been attacked.

It was his first time walking by the area since the incident, and the memories were still fresh in his mind. It was simply a wooded area, overgrown with underbrush, yet he viewed as the perfect spot from which a predator could ambush its unsuspecting prey. Closing his eyes, he visualized the animal lunging forth from the forest and sinking it's fangs into his flesh. Involuntarily, he shivered and shook his head to clear the image from his mind. *You've got to forget about it, man. It was an isolated incident.*

As if reading the young man's thoughts, Bill Lamperti nodded towards the area. "You know it just hit me; they never told me exactly what it was that got ya."

Mark met Lamperti's gaze and responded with a shrug of his shoulders. "You know, I really don't know what it was either. I think it was a wolf from the looks of it."

"Hell of a thing to happen," Lamperti said, shaking his head. "Toby fight it off?"

"He started barking at the thing when we stopped," Mark answered, "but nah, he didn't fight it."

"That's a shame, figured him a braver dog than that," Lamperti said disappointedly. Walking a few more feet, Lamperti's eyebrows rose, "why'd you guys stop?"

Shit. Mark winced. It had been a careless slip; he hadn't meant to mention that they had been stationary when they were attacked. He couldn't tell the truth; he sincerely doubted that the old man would understand or appreciate the fact that he had paused to light a joint. "Oh, um, you know, we stopped because Toby started barking, and I wanted to know why."

"Oh," Lamperti nodded, "makes sense, suppose I would have done the same thing. Doubt I'd have taken the thing too well though, being how old I am." Chuckling lightly, Lamperti gestured towards Mark wounded appendage. "How is the hand anyways?"

"Oh this?" Mark asked, holding up the red-spotted bandage which hid his hand. "It's actually a lot better than it looks."

"Ha, well I'm sure your mother will be happy to hear that, hell of a lady."

"Yeah," Mark responded. "She's um, she's something."

"How you handling being back stateside?"

"I'm doing okay," Mark lied, noting that the old man seemed to make conversation easily once he got started, whereas he himself still found their interaction awkward and forced.

"Besides a wolf attack," Lamperti smiled.

"Well yeah," Mark replied, forcing a smile.

"Scary over there?" Lamperti pressed.

Though the question made him uncomfortable, Mark felt obligated to answer in a casual manner. "It wasn't fun."

"I was in the service myself years ago," Lamperti offered.

"Really?" Mark asked, perking up, "which war?"

"Oh Jesus," Lamperti laughed, "no war, never did see combat. I spent most of my time in the army on bases in Korea."

"Oh," Mark replied, lowering his head again as he realized there was no connection being made between the two of them.

Lamperti kept speaking though, as if walking in silence with the young man unnerved him. "So Toby ran away after the thing came at you?"

"Yeah," Mark nodded, "last thing I saw before passing out was him running away, just down the road."

"Was the wolf after him?" Lamperti asked, his face a mask of concern.

"I don't know," Mark answered, shaking his head. "I don't think so." As they neared the end of the road, Mark sighed and looked towards the old man. The worried look the old man wore when asking about his dog told Mark all he needed to know about the importance of Toby in Lamperti's life; clearly the dog was all this old man had left. *Must be sad, living for an animal.* "Look, Mr. Lamperti I just want to apologize for losing your dog."

"No, no," Lamperti wheezed, emphatically waving Mark off, "wasn't your fault, could've happened to anybody."

Reaching the end of the road, Lamperti stared off into the distance, coming to a complete stop. Looking dejected and resigned to spending yet another day alone, he slumped his shoulders. "Well, I guess that's enough for today."

"Are you sure?" Mark asked, "I mean we can go grab my mom's car and take a spin around town."

"Nah," Lamperti croaked, "I spent all day yesterday searching for him. He's a good dog; he'll find his way home, probably still a little scared that's all." Turning around he began to shuffle back the way they had come. "If you're hungry, I've got a few sandwiches at the house."

"That's alrigh—," Mark cut himself off, realizing that he wouldn't mind feasting once again. This was odd as he had never been one for gluttony, yet despite having eaten breakfast no more than an hour before, he found himself salivating at the thought of eating again. He had a feeling of intense hunger. *Probably just from sleeping all day yesterday,* he assured himself. That had to be it, just his calorie-starved body yearning for more sustenance. "Um, yeah, all right, I could eat."

"Well come on then," Lamperti smiled, "I could use the company."

* * *

Mark sat at Lamperti's kitchen table, ignoring the strange smells of the house as he greedily tore into his roast beef sandwich. It was the good kind, the type carved from an actual roast rather than some type of processed mystery loaf. Ragged strips of red meat dangled from his roll as he took more and more of it into his mouth. Lamperti, who had hardly touched his own sandwich, watched Mark in amazement. "Calm down, son, no one's coming to take that from you."

In a repeat performance of his breakfast antics, Mark slowly set down his nearly finished sandwich and swallowed hard. "Sorry," he mumbled.

"It's quite all right, good to see you've got an appetite," Lamperti said. "Used to have one myself when I was your age, but that like a lot of things goes with age."

"I've heard," Mark nodded, finding his attention drawn back to the meat on his plate. The crimson meat in all its slimy glory beckoned him with its salty flavor; it drove him wild. Yet he restrained himself, knowing that he was embarrassing himself in front of the old man. Eating like a wild animal in front of his mother was one thing, but his elderly neighbor was quite another. He was ravenous, however, the allure of the beef threatening his sanity. *What the hell is wrong with you, man?*

He had never acted like this, and yet here he was for the second time in the span of an hour trying to tear apart a meal as if it were his last. Was it the drugs he had been taking? Perhaps they acted like an appetite suppressant, and now his body, starved of them for over twenty-four hours, was expressing its desire to feed and feed well. Whatever it was, he wasn't a huge fan of it. Reaching the limits of his willpower, Mark snuck a stray strip of beef from his plate into his mouth.

"Don't not eat on my account," Lamperti said, laughing. "I just didn't want you to get sick here in my kitchen."

"Ha," Mark offered, not finding anything particularly funny. Picking up the remnants of his sandwich, he resumed his feast, albeit at a slower pace.

Noticing that Mark's eyes had wandered towards his own sandwich, Lamperti shoved his plate forward. "Have at it, son. I'm not that hungry."

Wanting to refuse the old man's offer, he felt powerless to resist, relenting to his unceasing hunger. Finishing his own sandwich, he snatched up Lamperti's. "Thank you," he said, his voice muffled by the contents of his mouth.

"My pleasure," Lamperti smiled.

I really hope this isn't permanent, Mark lamented. *I'll be four hundred fucking pounds if I keep eating like this.*

X

The two of them ran through the parking lot, revealing themselves intermittently in the glow of several interspaced streetlights. The hulking man-beast and his four-legged companion, they weaved in between the various cars, never taking their eyes off the lit store front up ahead. Mark could sense that his gait was different, and the closer he came to the All-Mart entrance, the closer he got to the ground. Soon he too was lumbering forward as a quadruped, yet somehow he managed to keep pace with the beast to his right.

There were other changes, things he couldn't quite see, but knew they had happened. In the light of yet another streetlamp, he caught a glimpse of himself in the aluminum siding of a nearby vehicle. He was grotesque, his face contorted and no longer resembling a man's but rather that of a predatory animal. Large fangs sprouted forth from his mouth, and his nose had been replaced with what could only be called an animal's snout, short angular and canine in appearance. Hair had sprouted everywhere, and as he looked down, he could see that his fingers had elongated, each digit tapering into a spear-like claw. He could feel his clothes ripping, and he knew that he was stronger, more muscular than he had ever been.

He could feel the changes coming on, and he relished the transformation, each bounding stride bringing him closer to his inner beast. Looking to his right, he knew now what he was traveling with. The black sheen of the fur, the rippling muscles, Mark had seen them both before. It was the unidentified animal that had attacked him and Toby that fateful night, and though he recognized this and was knowledgeable of the animal's fierce nature, he did not recoil in fear. He could sense there was no danger; he realized they were as one, two kindred spirits hurtling headlong for the same destination.

They burst through the sliding door of the All-Mart and encountered their first victim, a stocky, older gentleman who Mark remembered as being named David. Ignoring their ghastly appearance and threatening posture, David smiled and waved towards them. "Hello and good evening, welcome to All-Mart." They ignored his good-natured salutation and set upon him, each of them tearing into the soft belly which sat behind his blue vest. David screamed and fell to the ground, where

Mark's animal companion finished him off with a vicious bite to the throat, snapping his neck and nearly decapitating him. Not content with their fallen prey, the two beasts headed off into the store seeking new quarry.

There were the excited screams of employees and customers as they viewed the attacking animals and began to view the results of their rampage. Mark and the animal broke off from one another, each dispatching a number of victims. The beast leapt upon a fleeing cashier, tearing her apart just outside of the bathrooms and splattering blood upon the white-painted walls of the store.

Mark moved for a young man taking off into the maze of the men's department. The young man hurled t-shirts and jeans at his attacker, but to no avail as Mark was upon him within seconds. Mark took great glee as his claws stabbed deep into the man's flesh and reveled in the sensation of tearing out the man's throat with his fangs. The blood was warm and metallic in flavor as it washed over his tongue, but to Mark it may as well have been beef gravy; it tasted so good. Not satisfied, he returned to the front of the store, pairing up with the beast to terrorize the remaining customers.

They fell by the score, their blood smacking upon the linoleum floors and washing over the smiling faces staring out from celebrity magazines. A cardboard cutout of a racecar driver endorsing a brand of batteries was stained red, the driver's gleaming white teeth now a dark crimson.

The screams of the dying victims rose and fell, usually accompanied by the snarls of the attackers along with the wet slap of gore upon the storefront's surfaces. In a brief moment of lucidity, just as he swiped his claws across the gut of an old woman, Mark noted that the soft music of the store's intercom system continued to drone on throughout the massacre.

Soon they were finished, the floors awash in body parts and viscera, a romantic country tune playing in the background. Mark stood up, his chest heaving from exertion. Turning to his partner, they met each other's gaze before emitting a pair of mournful howls, their heads pointed towards the ceiling. It was a celebratory gesture, acknowledging each other in a job well done. Howling a few more times for good measure, they moved to feast upon the spoils of their murderous venture. There was the snapping of bones and the ripping of flesh as they began to enjoy the smorgasbord which lay before them. Tearing into a particularly fine cut of a victim's thigh, Mark stopped, his pointed ears pricking up.

Swallowing, he lifted his head, sampling the air. His nostrils flared and he let loose with a growl as something had disturbed him. Dropping the thigh muscle, he ambled into the store's interior passing through the aisles and shelves of various departments in search of his prey. He could smell it; he knew it was here. Getting low to the ground, he came around the corner of the electronics aisle and spied what he was after.

Carol stood shivering against a bank of television screens, all showing cheery scenes from an animated film. Holding her price gun forward, she warned him off, "Don't you come any closer to me, Mark, you hear?" Her back against the televisions, she saw fit to add, "Even if you are cute." Baring her gross teeth, she winked and smiled at the approaching man-beast.

Mark flew into a rage, bounding towards the hideous woman. Slashing at her upper torso Mark heard her speak one last time as he bit into her neck. "I don't get paid enough for this shit."

His eyes fluttered open, a wry smile upon his face. Inspecting himself thoroughly, he assured himself that he was not a beast, the furry appendages of his murderous rampage replaced with his usual pink flesh. His hands were not clawed weapons either, the only abnormality about them being his still-bandaged hand. With a yawn he sat up, still chuckling to himself about his bizarre dream.

Could that be categorized as a nightmare? No, he reasoned, *that was too much fun.* The dream, though morbid and disgusting, had been exhilarating, no doubt a manifestation of his hatred for All-Mart and his lingering fear from the animal attack. He had especially enjoyed dispatching Carol at the end, though he acknowledged it was macabre to derive any enjoyment out of such a thought.

He did find it rather strange, however, that the animal that had attacked him had become his ally in the dream. The beast still stoked fearful images in his mind, and he found the thought that the animal was still free, roaming about the woods, a terrifying one. Yet in the dream, the animal had been his pack mate, a partner in crime. That was odd to him, and he didn't know from which part of his subconscious such a concept had originated. Either way, it had been an entertaining dream.

Looking towards the clock upon his nightstand, he noted that it was only six in the morning. The sun was up, and the birds were chirping outside his window, but he saw no real reason to rise from his bed. Resting his head back upon the pillows, he pulled the covers tight and drifted back to sleep, the smile refusing to leave his face.

XI

The phone buzzed upon Kaplan's desk, causing him to frown. Swallowing, he placed the turkey sandwich down on the newspaper he was reading and picked up the receiver. "Sergeant Kaplan," he chimed.

"Hey, Officer Kaplan, how's it going?" A gruff voice called.

"I'm good," Kaplan answered, a little confused. "Sorry, who's this?"

"Oh, jeez, sorry," the voice apologized, "this is Rob Lambert from animal control."

"Okay, Rob, How can I help you?" Kaplan asked.

"I think I found your dog," Lambert boomed.

"I'm sorry?" Kaplan questioned, his eyebrows still raised in confusion.

"Your dog, Toby," Lambert answered.

"Oh, right," Kaplan said, smacking his head with an open palm. Smiling, he leaned back in his chair. "So how is he?"

"Um," Lambert replied, the change in his tone indicating that something was amiss, "I think you better come down here and see for yourself."

* * *

Kaplan steered the cruiser down Summer Street, the blue waters of Walton Cove and Hingham Harbor off to his right and the green, brackish water of Broad Cove to his left. The stretch of road was a picturesque piece of real estate, underscoring the fact that Hingham was a stereotypical New England town, the type of town which people who had never been to the region pictured in their heads. Just off to the left as he continued to speed down the road sat The Lobster Pound, a fish shack which specialized in fried seafood. The smell of hydrogenated oil and cooking shellfish permeated Kaplan's car and wafted past his nostrils.

Nosing the car down Otis Street, Kaplan sped by number of small, residential units, each one whizzing past in a blur of blue and gray. Gripping the steering column, Kaplan edged the car around a curb and gently depressed the brake as the sight of a white van filled his windshield. Pulling up behind the van, Kaplan caught his first glimpse of Rob Lambert.

A stocky man with ill-fitting clothes, Kaplan judged him to be somewhere in his mid fifties. He wore a navy blue ball cap and dark tinted glasses, which sat upon his nose and just above his thick, bristly, salt-and-pepper-colored beard. Lambert was leaning against the van, and he smiled as Kaplan pulled up, waving his hand as if they were old friends.

Kaplan cut the engine and exited the vehicle, extending his hand in greeting as he approached Lambert. "How are you? You must be Rob."

Lambert peeled himself off of the van and accepted Kaplan's hand, squeezing it tight and shaking it vigorously. "That's right. Glad to meet you, Officer Kaplan."

"Call me Eric," Kaplan smiled, struggling to wrest his hand from Lambert's grip as he did so.

With his hand still throbbing, Kaplan nodded towards the van emblazoned with the words MASSACHUSETTS ANIMAL CONTROL upon its side. "Is Toby in there?" There were several cabinet style doors adorning the side of the van and Kaplan could hear the muffled barking of dogs emanating from inside.

Lambert's smiled faded, "Nope." He then nodded towards an embankment beside them. "No, I'm afraid your mutt's down there."

Kaplan stared down at the embankment, his view obscured by a mess of red and brown foliage. The occasional evergreen furthered prevented him from seeing just what Lambert was pointing at. "Well, how do we do this? What do we lure him out with a treat or something?" Kaplan asked.

Lambert laughed, "Uh, I think it's a little more complicated than that."

Kaplan smiled nervously. "I'm afraid I don't follow."

"Follow me," Lambert beckoned, moving towards the hill.

Is this guy serious? Kaplan frowned before falling in behind Lambert and timidly starting down the hill.

"Watch yourself here, it's pretty tricky footing wise," Lambert cautioned, bracing himself as they more or less slid down the embankment. As the two men reached the bottom, Kaplan swatted away the branches which scratched at his face, listening as Lambert droned on, "We're pretty lucky we found him at all down here."

"Yeah, how did you find him down here?" Kaplan asked, annoying slapping away leaves.

"I saw a whole mess of blackbirds take off from here while I was searching for him, and we all know what that means," Lambert harrumphed.

"Yeah," Kaplan replied, having no clue what the man was babbling about. *What the hell do blackbirds signify?*

Placing a hand upon a bush, Lambert turned towards Kaplan. "So I shimmied down here and found him." With that Lambert peeled back the branches and revealed a most grisly sight.

A medium-sized, brown dog laid on its side, neck arched backward in the throes of death and its pink tongue dangling out. The underbelly of the canine had been torn to shreds, and its entrails littered the ground before it, blanketed by ragged bits of brick-red flesh. The pelt was matted in places, freckled with dried blood, and the entirety of the dog's body appeared deflated, as if it were a teddy bear that had been torn open and the stuffing pulled out.

"Oh, Jesus Christ," Kaplan winced, pulling away from the macabre display.

"Yeah, it's pretty bad," Lambert remarked. "Look, you can even see where the birds pecked at his eyes."

"I don't need to see that," Kaplan hissed. "Are you sure it's Toby?"

"Yeah," Lambert responded, "tags match up."

"What happened to him?" Kaplan asked, still shaking his head.

"Well, if I had to guess, I'd say something got after him. Had itself a real nice meal."

"What do you think that something was?" Kaplan demanded.

"I don't know," Lambert shrugged, "probably another dog or maybe a coyote."

"What about a wolf?" Kaplan asked.

"No, no," Lambert answered shaking his head. "Not possible, there are no wolves in Massachusetts." Lambert continued to shake his head. "Why do you ask?"

"Because the kid who was with this dog said he thought it was a wolf that attacked him."

"You're boy most likely saw a coyote then; people often mistake big ones for wolves. We've got coyotes all over the South Shore," Lambert offered. Thinking for a minute Lambert added. "Come to the think of it, me and the missus, we love to watch those nature shows on TV, and I remember watching one that said coyotes and wolves sometimes attack people with dogs; drives them nuts apparently, like they see the dog as a competitor or something. Yeah, you're boy probably was attacked by a coyote."

"He said it was big, real big and black. Does that sound like a coyote?" Kaplan asked, legitimately seeking Lambert's opinion. "I mean, how big do these things get?"

"Not too, too big," Lambert answered. "I mean they're usually about two feet tall and probably 'bout three feet long. It's real rare for them to attack a human, but if it really wanted Toby here, it'd go for it no question."

"Yeah, but he said it was big and that it originally came for him," Kaplan countered.

Lambert frowned, running his hand through his beard as he thought. "I'd say it was another dog then, especially if he said it was black. Coyotes are usually gray in color I believe. He's probably mistaken about it coming for him though, it was definitely after Toby; thing tore him to shreds."

"Okay," Kaplan nodded, satisfied with Lambert's answers. "Thanks for your help, Rob." He thought about shaking Lambert's hand once again, but remembered the painful experience that was their first greeting. Instead Kaplan waved sheepishly and turned to amble up the embankment.

"Um, wait what do you want me to do with the dog?" Lambert called after him.

Kaplan paused and looked back at the pitiful form on the ground behind them. "I don't know. Burn it, get rid of it somehow."

"You don't want to give the tags to the owner?" Lambert asked, seemingly dismayed by Kaplan's response.

"Something tells me the owner's better off believing his dog simply ran away rather than knowing it was something's lunch. Like I said, cremate it." Kaplan then turned and began to gingerly claw his way up the embankment towards his car.

XII

Mark awoke, not with a jolt, but gently and relaxed. Blinking his eyes a few times, he was disoriented, as it was dark in the room. Yawning, the familiar images of his bedroom became clear. He frowned as he noticed his gauze wrapped hand. There was light spotting as some blood continued to trickle through his stitches, and it was still sore as he flexed his fingers.

Had he been dreaming? He couldn't remember, but why else would he have awoken in the middle of the night? It had been a number of days since his last nightmare, but he had anticipated they would resume soon enough. Mark couldn't remember a time when they weren't his constant bedtime companion. Confused, he attempted to recall just what he had been imagining during his slumber, to remember just what had hurtled him back into consciousness.

In a flash, there was a tickle in his midsection, and he began to squirm in discomfort. As it dawned on him what was happening, he flung the covers off and ran into the hall. Running clumsily he flung himself into the bathroom, shimmied off his boxers, and lifted the toilet seat before unleashing a powerful stream of urine. As the pouring water echoed off the walls of the bathroom, Mark began to laugh, struggling to maintain his aim. He had been that close to wetting his bed in his early twenties; it would have been hell explaining that to his mother.

Finishing up, he flushed before pulling up his underwear and exiting the bathroom. As he walked down the hall, he continued to chuckle to himself, his knees wobbling as he did so. Covering his mouth, he stumbled back into his bedroom and collapsed on the bed. Checking his sheets he sighed in relief as he realized there had been no mishap, no sprinkling of piss on his sheets. As he curled up, he squeezed his eyes shut and attempted to go back to sleep.

He flipped over, trying to find a more comfortable position. Tossing and turning, he finally slapped at his pillow in frustration, realizing that sleep would not come as easily as he would have liked. Sitting up in bed, he swung his legs over the side and walked to his dresser. *This always works.*

Sliding open the door he began to search for the right medication, the correct pill which would deliver him to dreamland the quickest. As he threw aside one foil wrapper full of non-descript white pills he paused. He didn't need this; it was absurd that he relied so heavily on these chemicals for relief. It dawned on Mark that the pills, liquids, and powders he possessed in this drawer were a crutch, something he had leaned upon to simply get by. *I don't want to live this way.*

Pulling out the underwear and socks that he used to conceal the drugs, he threw them on the floor before turning back to the drawer. Like a man possessed he began to collect every wrapper, every orange pill container, and every plastic bag that sat in the drawer, finally holding the bundle of substances in his arms. Cradling the drugs he exited the room and returned to the bathroom. Dumping his bounty in the sink he flicked on the lights and began to open the individual containers, dumping their contents in the toilet.

Flush after flush, he watched as a rainbow of pills and powders swirled around the bowl before disappearing down the drain. There was something infinitely satisfying about watching the drugs go away, the pills becoming caught up in the whirlpool before disappearing into the pipes. He felt liberated, like he was taking his life back. Free from the shackles of controlled substances, he had regained his independence and would seek to start anew. But he wasn't done just yet. There were still more drugs to be eliminated.

Opening the medicine cabinet, he began to empty it as well, disposing of the medicines his mother knew he had been prescribed. Emptying the anti-depressant containers before disposing of them in the trash he searched for something else, finally finding the opiates he had been given for his bite. *Do I keep these to deal with the pain?*

Looking down at his hand, Mark reflected that he wasn't actually in a great deal of pain. Though he still struggled with the occasional ache, and the itching along with the burning had yet to subside, Mark decided there was no appreciable need for the pills. Shrugging his shoulders, he popped open the top and they too went into the hopper.

Satisfied with his course of action, Mark collected the empty containers before walking back to his room. Throwing the empties back into his sock drawer, he returned his underwear back to its original position, covering the now depleted containers. He couldn't throw the vessels away in the trash and risk his mother finding them. She would want to sit down and have a long chat, something he had no desire for. Closing the drawer he smiled. *I'll get rid of them some other time. Right now, I'm fucking going back to bed.* Jumping back on his mattress he slowly drifted off to sleep.

XIII

Enos continued to run steadily, gracefully placing one foot in front of another. His breath came not in ragged, short gasps but rather deep, calm inhalations. Buoyed by a source of newfound energy, he had taken up running in the weeks after the attack. He had not so much as jogged ten feet since leaving the army, but he found no difficulty in tackling mile after mile just days after being set upon by the unknown predatory animal.

Following his little mishap, he had taken to exercising vigorously, unearthing an old set of rusty weights in the garage and lifting them religiously. Where he had once felt weak and listless, he now felt reinvigorated and alive. His muscles felt taut and toned, his heartbeat slow and rhythmic. Simply put, he felt amazing, as if he had a new lease on life.

The chemical induced highs were now replaced by the endorphin release of vigorous, sustained physical activity. It was no longer how many pills he could stack together, but how much weight he could stack on the barbell during his next workout. He felt driven and purposeful, becoming more and more surprised with his rapidly increasing strength.

Life had progressed steadily and pleasurably since the attack. Working had allowed him to accumulate a small amount of money in his bank account, cash he would surely put to use in moving out of his mother's house. Mr. Lamperti had released him from his charge of looking for Toby after just a day of searching, although the poor old fool continued to hope the mutt would come home, continually calling for the dog from his yard every night. He had also managed to control his intense hunger pangs, returning to a normal, healthy eating schedule. Best of all, Mark had been sleeping well ever since that fateful day, and he hadn't so much as touched an aspirin tablet in a month. Besides the bandages which still encased his hand, things were going just fine for Mark Enos.

The wound itself did not bother Mark at all. In fact, the only hindrance to his quality of life had proved to be the gauze and tape which were wrapped around his left hand. The slight burning and itching sensation, which had been nothing more than a nuisance following the injury, had disappeared within days, and there had been little to no pain with which to speak of since. Mark had retained the full range of motion in his hand and the skin appeared to be healing quickly, yet his mother insisted on keeping the wound wrapped until a doctor had given the all clear. *Hopefully*, Mark reflected, *that should happen today*. He had his one-month check-up later on that afternoon.

Coming around a bend in the road, he passed the small patch of foliage from which the beast had set upon him. Amazingly, he felt no attachment to the area, no traumatic fear of the spot. There was no shiver up his spine, no hair standing on end as he jogged past. Perhaps after seeing combat in Iraq, he was too jaded to be fazed by such events, he reasoned. Ambling forward, he could now see his house just ahead.

A beat-up looking, green station wagon was parked in the driveway, and Mark smiled because he knew it meant his brother had stopped by for a surprise visit. Sure enough, Stephen exited the domicile just as Mark slogged into the driveway. Coming to a stop, Mark bent over at the waist, bracing himself upon his knees and panting heavily.

"Working out?" Stephen asked as he approached, offering Mark a glass of water.

"Yeah," Mark answered, accepting the glass. "Thanks," he gasped, taking a pull from the cup.

"Mom was just telling me about your new fitness regimen. Says you're a real Richard Simmons," Stephen joked, leaning against the station wagon.

"Shut up, asshole. Just getting back into shape," Mark said. "What are you doing here anyways?"

"I got off work early and brought Alicia by to see Mom," Stephen answered. Alicia was his oldest daughter, and Mark's niece, having just recently turned five years old.

"Oh, where's she now?" Mark asked.

"In the house," Stephen said, motioning with a nod towards the house, "showing Mom her new cat."

"You got a fucking cat?" Mark asked incredulously before taking another sip of water.

"Yeah," Stephen laughed, "some lady at work is moving and had to give it away. So, I figured what the hell."

"What's the wife think of that?"

"She doesn't know yet," Stephen replied, smiling sheepishly. "Do you need a ride later on? Mom told me you have that doctor's appointment today."

"Nah, I'm going to just take Mom's car," Mark answered before adding, "Thanks for the offer, though."

They turned as the screen door clanged against the house, watching as a small brunette toddled out clutching a furry white cat in her arms. The little girl wore a broad smile, her two front teeth missing and her pigtails swayed back and forth as she waddled forward and ambled down the steps. "Hi, Uncle Mark," she exclaimed in her high-pitched voice, "Look what Daddy got me!"

"I heard," Mark answered, his voice raised an octave and his tone noticeably gentler. "What did you name it?" He asked as he walked towards her hunched over so as to be at her level.

"Sasha," she answered.

"Is it even a girl?" Mark asked, looking back at his brother.

"I have no clue," Stephen shrugged.

"Say hi to Mark, Sasha," Alicia cooed, pointing the seemingly copasetic feline towards Mark.

"Hi Sasha," Mark chirped, moving to pet the animal.

Immediately the cat drew back, arching its back as it did so. With a hiss, it bared its tiny fangs and swatted a paw in the direction of Mark's hand. Confused, Mark stood there staring blankly at the animal. This seemed to agitate the cat further as just Enos' mere presence was causing it to act erratically. The cat pounced backwards, attempting to leap over Alicia's shoulder in an attempt to get away from Mark.

Alicia squealed as the cat's claws dug into the flesh of her shoulder, and it clawed at her face as it sought to make its escape. The little girl flapped her arms, causing the cat to hit the asphalt with a thud before skittering away to the perceived safety of the station wagon's undercarriage. She began to cry hysterically as small drops of blood seeped through the thin slits on her face. "Daddy! Daddy!" she cried.

"Jesus Christ!" Stephen yelled, swooping his daughter up into his arms. "Oh, baby," he soothed as the girl continued to cry, her eyes squeezed shut. "It's okay, it's okay."

Through it all, Mark stood dumbfounded, unsure of what had just happened. He could hear the cat's continued growls and hisses from underneath the car, knowing full well that they were addressed towards him.

"Stupid fucking cat," Stephen grumbled, looking angrily towards where the feline had fled. Still jostling his crying child Stephen pulled open the screen door. "Mom, I need some hydrogen Peroxide!"

Standing in the driveway Mark could hear the muffled screaming of his mother and Alicia's sobbing. Shaking his head he noticed that the cat had poked its furry head out from its hiding spot. As man and beast made eye contact, the cat closed its eyes while letting loose with another threatening hiss. Staring at the agitated animal for a moment, Mark began to walk gingerly towards the house, still confused by the animal's reaction.

XIV

Enos sat with his feet dangling over the medical bench. The bench's vinyl and paper covering clung to his bare backside, and he felt a slight chill, since only a thin hospital gown covered him. The smell of caustic, heavy duty cleaning chemicals hung in the air, and the sterile, white walls of the hospital room stung his eyes. While he knew it had only been a matter of minutes, he felt as if he had been waiting in the room for hours on end.

His mother had subdued Alicia quickly, plying her from her crying fit with the promise of ice cream. They had cleaned her superficial wounds in seconds, and Stephen had vanished with the child before Mark had even exited the shower. Mark hadn't bothered inquiring about the fate of the petulant Sasha; he simply assumed his brother would return the cat to its original owner. Still, the cat's reaction was startling, and Mark got the sense that the pet had been rather placid until he arrived on scene. He wondered why that had been the case.

His thoughts were interrupted by the door of the room opening slowly. A tall man waltzed in looking at a chart and not bothering to glance up at Mark. He looked like a stereotypical doctor, wearing wire-framed glasses and a long white lab coat. A stethoscope hung around his neck, the harsh fluorescent lighting glinting off his bald head. Taking a final look at his chart, he spoke, "Hello, Mister . . . " Embarrassed, he glanced back down at his records, "Enos. How are you doing today?"

"I'm good," Mark nodded.

"Good, good," the doctor said. "I'm Doctor Andrews, and we're here to check on your injury, correct?"

"Yeah," Mark affirmed.

"And you're going to receive another dose of the rabies vaccine, it says here," Andrews said, his tone matter of fact, holding up the chart in his hand. "Did they give you the immunoglobulin yet?"

Mark shrugged. "If that's the crap they shot me up with the day of, then yeah."

Andrews smiled while taking a seat on a rolling stool. "Was the shot painful?"

"Didn't feel good," Mark answered.

"Then yeah, that was the immunoglobulin," Andrews laughed. Rubbing a hand over his bald head, Andrews retrieved the stethoscope from around his neck and wheeled towards Enos, "All right, so let's just get the basics here first."

"Okay," Mark answered.

"Feeling okay overall?" Andrews asked.

"Yeah, actually I've been feeling great."

"That's good," Andrews remarked, scribbling notes down on the chart. Standing for a moment he positioned himself in front of Enos and placed the stethoscope prongs in his ear. Mark gasped as the cold, metal disc of the instrument was placed against the bare skin of his back. "Deep breath," Andrews instructed.

Doing as he was told Mark inhaled deeply.

"Hold it," Andrews ordered. Several seconds elapsed before Andrews spoke, "and breathe out."

Mark, just having acclimated himself to the cold steel upon his back, winced as Andrews moved the disc to his chest; not allowing the young man to recover from the shock before instructing, "And same thing here."

Ignoring the cold Mark breathed deeply, repeating the same sequence he had when the disc was on his back. "Okay, excellent," Andrews remarked, placing the stethoscope back around his neck. Returning to his stool he scribbled some more notes on his chart. Placing the pen down, he crossed his legs and met Enos's gaze. "Okay, so you were attacked by a dog?"

"I think it was a wolf," Enos replied.

"A wolf?" Andrews asked, his brow furrowing in disbelief.

"Yeah, I didn't get a good look at thing, but I'm pretty sure it wasn't a dog."

"Are there even wolves in Massachusetts?" Andrews questioned.

"I . . . I don't know," Enos shrugged.

"Well, that's beside the point," Andrews said, waving his hand. "Let's just see the wound itself."

Enos held out his hand and Andrews wheeled forward. Gently and with great care he began to undo the gauze and tape which encased Enos' left hand. Enos could feel the gauze lightly scrape and tickle his skin, but otherwise felt nothing out of the ordinary as Andrews undid the bandages. Andrews removed the last of the gauze, disposing of it in a small plastic bin to his right, ensconced with orange labels warning it was medical waste. Wheeling back towards Enos he stopped short. "Holy shit," he gasped.

Confused, Enos looked down at his hand, not knowing what the doctor was referring to. "Something wrong?" Enos asked worriedly.

"What?" Andrews questioned, looking up at Enos before shaking his head. "No, no there's nothing wrong, sorry. It's just it doesn't look like there's anything wrong with your hand."

Enos inspected his left hand. Besides a slight pinkish hue to the skin around where the animal had grabbed him, he noted that the doctor was right; it didn't appear as if anything was wrong with his hand. There was no oozing, puss-filled wound or hideous scab to speak of. The skin was smooth and supple looking. For the first time, Mark noted that there wasn't even the faint hint of a scar where the wolf-like beast had bitten him.

Andrews looked over his charts again, thumbing through the pages upon it, "You were attacked a month ago?"

"Yeah," Mark responded.

Flabbergasted, Andrews placed the chart back upon his lap. "It says here your hand was in pretty bad shape when they brought you in."

"I don't know what to tell you." Mark shrugged, still holding out his hand. "It didn't look great for the first week."

"Can you move it?" Andrews interrogated. "For example, can you make a fist?"

Mark flexed his fingers slowly in response before balling up his hand in a fist. The doctor sat there, mouth agape, looking at his young patient in shock. "You shouldn't be able to do that, "Andrews stuttered. "It says you severed tendons, that you'd probably need surgery to regain the full use of your hand."

Enos placed his hand back at his side. "I don't know what to tell ya, Doc. I feel fine."

"I can see that," Andrews said, shaking his head slowly. "What was it that attacked you again, a wolf?"

"Yeah, I think," Mark answered.

"Jesus," Andrews remarked, retrieving his pen and scribbling upon his chart. Done writing, he raised his eyebrows and waved his hand, indicating that he had no idea with how to proceed. "Well, I guess I'll have a nurse come in and give you that next rabies shot, and then after that . . . " His voice trailed off as the doctor seemed lost in his thoughts. Collecting himself, he shook his head. "I guess let's just have you come back in two weeks, and we'll see how you're doing then."

"Okay." Mark nodded as the doctor rose slowly from his stool and move to exit the hospital room.

Stopping at the door, Andrews looked back. "A wolf?"

"I guess." Mark shrugged. *What the hell does this guy want me to say?*

Andrews opened the door and exited the room, still shaking his head in disbelief. Mark watched the doctor trudge down the hall grumbling to himself as the door slowly closed shut.

XV

Mark proceeded slowly, moving along with the meandering rush hour traffic. Rapping his fingers upon the steering wheel, he had long since tuned out the warbling of the car radio, preoccupied with his own thoughts. It had been a bizarre day, with the cat attacking his niece and a doctor who seemed genuinely perplexed by Mark's condition. *Just what is going on exactly?* Mark shook his head. *It's all a coincidence. The cat was probably unstable to begin with, and I've always been a quick healer*, he assured himself.

There was, however, a nagging question that lingered in his mind. Just what had attacked him? Having seen coyotes before, he was absolutely certain that the beast that had lashed out at him that night was anything but. He was also sure that it had not been a large dog. Then again, it had all happened so quickly, and he had been under the influence. *You can't be sure what you saw,* he scolded. Still pondering the identity of the aggressive animal, he happened to glimpse a familiar signpost out of the corner of his eye.

A weathered, bent metallic sign stood lonely upon the road's shoulder. Its brown coloring threatened to blend in with the early autumn foliage, and the only thing that alerted passing motorists of its presence was its white, reflective lettering. "WOMPATUCK STATE PARK – NEXT RIGHT" it announced. Passing by at a snail's pace, Mark remembered speaking of the location with his brother shortly after arriving home. Recalling fond memories of summers past, Mark sat upright in his chair as something hit him.

Ahead, the trees lining the road gave way, and the tall, white spire of a church rose skyward. The church parking lot sat empty, as if the building had long since been abandoned, and a small stretch of road sat beside it. Coming up alongside the throughway, Mark banked right, exiting the stream of traffic and heading down the road. Red, brown, and yellow hued foliage shadowed much of the street, the line of trees along the quaint street broken only by the occasional house. Rounding a bend, Mark came upon a rotting wooden sign which pointed towards an access road to the right. "WELCOME TO WOMPATUCK STATE PARK" the sign greeted in yellow letters.

Turning down the access road, Mark passed by an empty, wooden guardhouse, its windows fogged with dust and the shelter appearing in disrepair. As he pulled past the shack, the trees fell back and gave way to a rolling meadow to his right, and that is where Mark first viewed his intended destination.

Upon a small hill there sat a rustic, squat building. Some type of lodge, it was constructed entirely out of wood with only a few window panes decorating the building's façade. The roof was only slightly angled, covered with dry, decaying wooden shingles that looked as though they could fall off at any second. Mark pulled into the parking lot, which sat astride the Wompatuck Welcome Center, pulling alongside a boulder and cutting the engine.

As he exited the vehicle, his attention was called skyward by a metallic rattling. Two large flags, one American the other emblazoned with the blue and yellow logo of the state of Massachusetts, whipped furiously in the wind. Faded and worn, they threatened to leave the coil of their aluminum flag poles at any moment. Marching past them, Mark alighted onto a small curb and headed towards the front door of the establishment.

Once inside, Mark paused for a moment and took in his surroundings. The building reeked of mildew and old age. There was a noticeable hint of ozone in the air, and much of the wood upon the walls seemed to be rotted. As he walked forward, his feet scuffed upon the concrete flooring and he noticed the bench to his left was adorned with a sign indicating it was out of order. *A bench can be out of order?* Two ancient and industrial looking water fountains clung to the wall besides the bench, staggered for people of differing heights. Each fountain was encrusted with a fine coating of lime and calcium belying their age.

Placing his hands in the pocket of his hooded sweatshirt, Mark exited the lobby and entered another room. Passing through the doorway, he instantly recognized the room from memory; this was why he had come here. Several glass-encased dioramas lined the walls, each depicting a different animal native to Southeastern Massachusetts. The paper landscapes depicting differing environments were yellowed and curling. However, the stuffed animals encased within the glass still appeared in remarkable condition.

Mark passed by one scene which depicted a large seagull landing upon a rock. The ocean beyond it was faded and turning pink, but the bird looked alive, albeit frozen in place. Its wings were spread wide, the beak open and glassy, and its black eyes stared back at Mark. The taxidermist who had stuffed the seagull had done an impeccable job.

Mark paused and inspected the next case. A raccoon reared back, its fangs bared and claws stretched forth in a menacing way. It appeared as if the animal was suspended in time, as if at any moment it would spring to life and leap at Enos. The only thing which indicated the furry menace was dead were the papier-mâché rocks upon which it stood; they were badly faded, and the paper was fraying at spots.

"Can I help you, sir?" a voice sounded.

Mark turned away from the diorama and looked in the direction from which the voice had come. An average looking fellow stood behind an information stand, leaning against the counter. He wore all earth tones, the green and yellow patch upon his shoulder indicating he was a forest ranger.

"Yeah, actually you can," Mark answered. "I have a few questions about local wildlife."

"Okay," the man answered, standing up straight. Turning around, he retrieved a small form from the desk behind him and touched pen to paper. "What school are you from?"

"I'm sorry?" Mark asked, moving towards the desk.

The ranger looked up, seemingly annoyed. "You know, where do you teach?"

"Oh no, I'm not a teacher," Mark replied, withdrawing his hands from his shirt and gesturing wildly. "I just have a few questions."

"Seriously?" The ranger inquired, his face indicating that he did not know how to proceed.

"Um, yeah." Mark nodded.

With an air of trepidation the ranger lowered his pen and placed the form back upon the desk. Turning back around, he leaned against the counter in front of him. "Sorry, we just usually don't get people your age in here unless they're elementary school teachers or something."

"Sorry?" Mark shrugged.

"No, no." The ranger waved. "So what can I do for you?"

"Are you familiar with the local animals?" Mark asked.

"For the most part," the ranger said. "What are you interested in—bird watching, hunting?"

"I'm talking more like local predators," Mark answered curtly.

"Predators?" the man asked, his brow furrowed.

"Yeah, look, I was recently attacked by something, and I was hoping you could help me identify just what it was."

"It attacked you?" the ranger asked, looking even more confused. He inspected Mark up and down, obviously searching for some sort of wound. "What did it look like?"

"I think it was a wolf," Mark responded.

"A wolf?" the man questioned. "Not possible in Massachusetts. You were attacked here in Mass right?"

"Yeah," Mark answered, "why isn't that possible?"

"Because there hasn't been a gray wolf population in this region for nearly a century. You'd have to go to Canada to find the nearest wild wolf," he answered. "More likely you were attacked by a coyote. We've got them all over the place here on the South Shore."

"How big does a coyote get?"

The man thought for a minute, "Oh, I don't know, usually around forty, maybe fifty pounds, and usually about two feet tall. Although, I have heard of some getting up to nearly seventy, even eighty pounds."

Mark shook his head. "This thing was big. I'm talking all muscle. It took me to the ground, and it was black."

The ranger frowned, tapping his fingers upon the counter, "I don't know what to tell you, guy. I mean, some dogs can get pretty big, and even a hundred-pound dog will take you to the ground. They are basically all muscle."

"It didn't look completely like a dog though," Mark protested.

"Well, we do have black bears down here, but I don't think you could confuse one of those with a wolf, and they don't tend to attack people."

"You're telling me my two choices are a dog or a coyote?" Mark inquired.

"Yeah, sorry, man." The ranger shrugged. "The only indigenous big carnivore is the coyote, and the only wolves you'll find reside in local zoos or private collections."

"Private collections?" Mark asked, his eyebrows raised. "You know of any around here? Maybe one of them had an animal escape recently."

The ranger laughed and shook his head. "No, sorry, I don't know of any wolf collections around here, and I'd like to think we'd all be informed of a wolf escaping into the wild."

The ranger stopped laughing when he realized that Mark appeared upset, as if he could not come to grips with the fact that it was not a wolf that had attacked him. Grinding his teeth nervously for a moment, an idea popped in his head. The ranger said, "But hey, just 'cause I don't know any local collections or haven't heard of an escape doesn't mean you can't check it out on the web."

Mark looked up at the ranger. "I don't have a computer."

"Well, jeez, son," the ranger harrumphed, "the library is just up the road."

* * *

Mark ascended the concrete steps of the Hingham Public Library. It had been years since he had visited the spot, but despite an extensive makeover he found that little had changed with the building's exterior. The library was still basically two buildings joined as one by a connecting corridor. The main building was squat and trapezoidal in shape. The gray roof was supported by sturdy, white pillars, which were spaced about every six feet along a concrete walkway. The walls of the building were solid red brick, interspaced with the occasional window. The second, smaller building was similar in material, yet it appeared more like a chapel as a sharp, white spire rose out of its sharply angled ceiling.

Mark entered through the front doors and stood in awe at what he had found. He remembered coming to library when he was a young man with his grandfather and spending countless afternoons perusing the library's catalog. The building had been smaller then and had smelled of mold. Now, however, the library was spacious, and where once the walls had been brown, they were now stark white. The shag carpet had been replaced by a dark blue covering, and where there had once been stacks upon stacks of books, there was now row after of row of computers. *Welcome to the information age*, he snorted.

Mark wondered just what the procedure was now to use the library, but found that the elderly women who manned the building's front desk paid him no heed, refusing to look up from their computer monitors. Nonchalantly Mark walked past the desk and into the library's main antechamber. The familiar rows of books had been relegated to a back room, visible from the library's main room, and in a way Mark found this comforting, though he did not know why. *Guess it's nice knowing they're still there*, he shrugged. The library was a virtual ghost town, and Mark sat at the first computer he came across.

He was familiar with the ins and outs of the internet as most people were; he simply hadn't seen much use in purchasing a computer following his exit from the military, and his mother was largely computer illiterate. Arriving at a search page, he pondered just what to type. Pausing for a moment, he finally entered "native carnivores of Massachusetts." There was a short pause, and then a variety of search pages popped up. Looking over his options, Mark selected one and immediately frowned; the information the website contained was almost what the ranger had said verbatim.

Mark returned to the main page and entered "wolf collections in Massachusetts." There was a flurry of activity, and Mark found himself frustrated whilst looking for a page that fit his needs. Most of the websites pertained to Boston area zoos and history websites. There was even one for a New England area casino.

Mark brought up the search page once again and typed in "unexplained animal attacks." The computer produced a new list, and Mark nearly groaned at what he saw. Several sites invited Mark to view grisly, uncensored photos taken in the aftermath of a tiger or lion attack. Others pertained to supernatural, mythological monsters; one in particular exclaimed, "Bigfoot raped my wife!" Mark chuckled before clicking upon one site out of morbid curiosity.

As the page filtered through, Mark's jaw dropped open. There, in the relief of a woodcarving, was the animal that had attacked him. The black fur, the exaggerated canines and the quadruped's stunning muscularity was all beautifully depicted in what the computer told Mark was an eighteenth century woodcarving. Mark looked up at the title of the website and did a double take. "Werewolves: Myth or Reality?" the website asked.

Mark nearly exited the site, but something stopped him. *Werewolves do not exist,* he told himself, but something gnawed at his consciousness. *Of course they're not real, but why does that picture look so much like the thing that attacked me?* Feeling a little bit crazy for doing so, Mark decided to read on.

The site began to relate a series of "real" cases attributed to werewolves. Mark found himself momentarily captivated by a tale of a werewolf-like beast in France that had killed over a hundred people, and later another case in which man-eating wolves had stolen nearly fifty children in India during the late nineties. His interest piqued he scrolled downwards, coming upon a section listing the "Symptoms of Lycanthropy."

He stopped at the first item: "adverse reactions from pets and other animals." The image of the distressed feline swatting at him and clawing Alicia's face flashed in his mind. He shook his head. *Don't be an idiot.* Moving on to the next symptom, a shiver ran up his spine. "Quick healing and faster metabolism" it read. He instantly recalled Doctor Andrews's surprised reaction just hours earlier, and he reflected on how much healthier he had been feeling lately. There were also his hunger fits and the manner in which he had fed following the attack; he realized that such things could also be attributed to a faster metabolism. *This is all just a coincidence, isn't it?*

Mark settled down when he read the other symptoms the site attributed to those afflicted with lycanthropy. Heightened senses, he didn't feel he had been blessed with those. More attention from the opposite sex, he laughed. There was Carol, but attracting the gross chick at work didn't count, he decided. Feeling better, he continued to investigate the website, stopping at the next warning sign, "dreaming you are a wolf." He recalled his last vivid dream, the one in which he and his animal companion had attacked and slaughtered the inhabitants of the local All-Mart. *Does that count as dreaming you are a wolf?* The website made him dizzy as so much of what it ascribed to lycanthropy seemed to fit him to a tee. It all seemed so crazy, yet sensible at the same time.

Calming himself, he almost broke into laughter. He was acting crazy. After all, you couldn't attribute all your knowledge of a subject to a single website, especially one dealing with such outlandish subject matter such as this. No one tested the veracity of kook websites like the one he was viewing and only the feeble minded and mentally ill took what they said as gospel. If he was so easily swayed by such garbage he may as well begin searching for UFOs whilst wearing a tin-foil hat.

"BEWARE!" the webpage instructed. "If you are bitten by a werewolf, you will change come the next cycle of the moon, and you will do those around you harm! If you think you could possibly be afflicted with this curse, seek help before the next full moon!"

Mark forced himself to smile, a small act of defiance as his conscience screamed for him to heed the site's warning. He supposed the website had taken the place of the old gypsy woman so common in those werewolf movies from long ago. "You vill change Mark Enos," his inner monologue mockingly screamed with a bad accent, "you vill change!" Refusing to be shaken by such rubbish, he exited the site and brought up the local weather. Searching for the phases of the moon, which he rembered were commonly found on such pages, he found the section and brought it up. The cartoon picture of the full moon stared back at him, indicating that there would be one that night.

"Oh, no," Mark mocked, attempting to show himself that he was not affected by the website's ridiculous claims. He stopped, however, when a curious thought entered his head. It had been exactly one month since the attack, and that meant that the animal had set upon him on the night of a full moon. Reflecting on this for a minute, he finally shook his head. "What a crock of shit," he muttered before signing out of the computer and sliding away from the table. Standing up, he took one last look at the computer before heading towards the exit, still shaking his head.

XVI

Waiting, Mark had always hated waiting. Ever since he could remember, he had always harbored some deep hatred of the act, constantly wanting to speed things up, incorrigibly impatient. In every facet, he wanted things instantaneously, be it traveling a long distance or a slow drug deal. He supposed it was just a byproduct of modern American society, a product of a world flooded with fast-food restaurants and on-demand movies. His family had labeled it years ago one of his worst personality traits.

Granted the drugs had helped alleviate his demanding nature, the depressants causing his mind to slow as he lost himself in euphoria. However, when they weren't around, as they were not at this very moment, the tick had returned. It had been especially grating during his rehabilitation stage when he had returned stateside. Being shuffled from doctor to doctor around base, he had found himself in a myriad of waiting rooms, spots which by their very nature forced him into the act he could least bear.

It had been especially hard to occupy himself during those visits to the usually drab, unadorned waiting rooms, populated only with the mentally damaged, such as him, and the occasional receptionist. Busying himself with the usual sports magazines that littered such areas, he would even take a gander at the occasional gun magazine, which inevitably showed up at military bases, though he found it odd that they would want the most battle scarred among the serviceman to be perusing advertisements for the newest submachine gun. Eventually he had worn out the sports periodicals and had one day turned to the psychiatric journals that dotted the waiting room tables.

They were usually boring, fraught with technical jargon that only someone who had dedicated himself to the study of psychology or neurology could find entertaining. However, there were the occasional interesting articles. Mark had taken a particular liking to those which dealt with serial killers or madmen of the past. He found that such pieces could be found in one out of every three of these journals.

It piqued his interest, and he found it fascinating how so many academics in the field concerned themselves with the dregs of society, the men and occasional woman who lurked in the darkest sectors of the civilized world. In between the usually droll text, there were meaty sections which grabbed Mark's attention, lines which detailed the gory and horrifying trail these killers had blazed. Mark found it almost comical how many so-called experts obsessed themselves with trying to discern why these people had gone bad, how these doctors attempted to dissect the inner workings of evil men. To Mark it was almost as if these psychiatrists and neurologists possessed some need to explain why these people were different from the rest of flock, constantly trying to tell the world why such people were the exception to the rule.

There was always some new theory of why serial killers came to be. Tumors found during autopsy in the brains of killers, they all had bad childhoods, this one killed because of his repressed homosexuality—it was all too out there for Mark. The problem he found was that so many doctors attempted to create a theory that could be laid like a blanket covering all serial killers; they never left any room for cases to be judged on an individual basis. It also struck him that not one of these academics could simply accept that some people were just born bad; to them this was an unacceptable theory, there had to be a reason for such deviant behavior.

He had fought the urge to laugh at one particular article that postulated that serving in the armed forces contributed to the creation of serial killers. Simply called "The Military Theory," it claimed that some seven percent of the killers the authors had studied had served in the military at some point, and that this was a major factor in their actions later on in life. Mark failed to see how seven percent equated to all such killers, but he was struck by the irony of reading such a thing while waiting to see an army psychiatrist.

Though he found the theories these articles put forth outlandish and downright bullshit, they had inspired him to read further, to learn as much as he could about these various murderers. By the end of his stay, he had checked out nearly every book the base library possessed on serial-killers, devouring them all and becoming somewhat of an expert on many of their lives. It had made for a few concerned looks in the waiting rooms and barracks when he showed up with a book on Dahmer or Gacy, but it had helped pass the time. It helped with the waiting.

Driving back from the library, Mark had this strange, uncomfortable feeling that he was now waiting for something. His heart rate was slightly elevated, small droplets of sweat coalesced on the skin of his forehead, and he had the slight nauseous feeling caused by a small rush of adrenaline flowing through his veins. What was the word he had read in one of those medical texts sitting in the waiting room, hypochondria? It was where hypochondriac, or health-anxiety, was derived. It usually described someone who feared catching some disease, but did this count? His eyes vacantly watching the road ahead as he thought. Mark now pondered whether something as ridiculous as wondering whether or not you were a werewolf counted as a form of hypochondria.

Blinking for the first time in what seemed like ages he caught a quick glimpse of the late afternoon sky, a mixture of purple and yellow hues as the sun began to dip below the horizon. He could view the full moon, its faint outline peering out from behind the still-bright sky. The very sight of it caused his blood pressure to spike, and he could feel himself losing it. Had he not been so caught up in the craziness of the idea, he might have laughed at the ludicrousness of such an irrational fear.

How would it happen? Would it be like the movies? He imagined his body writhing in fear and pain as he morphed into something hideous and awful, a series of bone-snapping transformations affecting his joints, and his fingernails lengthening into butchering meat cleavers. Would he look like a wolf or just a hairy, hulking man-beast? Picturing himself howling at the moon he almost veered off the road as he came to. Laughing at himself, he cursed out loud, "You're a fucking idiot."

Of course this wasn't real. There was a reason such beasts only existed on the silver screen. It was physically impossible for a man to change into a beast. Shape-shifting existed only in the realm of computer generation and the imaginations of animators. Even as he was explaining this to himself, the fact that he could not shake even the most ridiculous of thoughts unnerved him.

What's going on here?

Mark would have understood such paranoia had he still been abusing certain chemicals. Many played tricks with your mind, caused you to leap to the most ludicrous of assumptions and believe the implausible. The thoughts he was entertaining at this very moment would have been explicable in such a situation, and he would have anticipated such things. The problem was he hadn't touched the things in weeks. Was this some sort after effect, a lingering gift from the overuse of such drugs?

That's possible.

It didn't really make a lot of sense, though. While he wasn't the most mentally stable of human beings, Mark also wasn't prone to flirt with the fantastic, albeit without chemical assistance. Pulling onto his road, he wondered what was wrong with his head, why he possessed such a feeling of dread. He felt like a condemned man awaiting his execution, every tick of the clock bringing him closer to some awful event. Shaking his head he admonished himself, *you're being ridiculous.* Still, he couldn't shake the thought that he was star-crossed, destined for something horrible. Pulling into the driveway, he found himself resigned to just waiting for the inevitable. He hated waiting.

XVII

Enos sat hunched over the kitchen table, gently nudging the food on his plate with a fork. He was sweating profusely, and he felt weakened, downright sickly. Every now and then, there was a crippling wave of nausea accompanied by an intense cramping sensation in his stomach. He didn't know what was happening to him. He had felt fine and virile no more than an hour ago, but as the night had worn on, he simply felt ill.

"Stephen called," his mother droned, placing a fork full of food in her gullet. "He says Alicia's doing just fine," she added, not making eye contact with her son while speaking with a mouth full of food.

Mark knew exactly what she was doing; rather than have them sit in awkward silence, she chose to fill the air with inane, idle chit-chat. Girding himself for the next assault on his stomach, he knew he had to act as if he were interested in what his mother was saying to avoid hurting her feelings. "How's the cat?" he croaked.

"I didn't even ask," his mother said, exasperated. Taking another bite, she swallowed before adding, "I'm assuming they'll look to put it down. At least I hope that's what they'll do."

Mark speared a carrot and forced it towards his mouth. Chewing slowly, he swallowed and waited for his body's reaction. It came suddenly, his abdomen seemed to seize up, and he felt sure he would vomit. Clenching his teeth, he rode the wave of nausea to completion and placed his fork down. Mouth watering, he imagined his mother's reaction to her son retching all over the dinner table.

What is the problem here? He hadn't felt ill or weak for well over a month. He was well rested, and with his daily workouts, he felt healthier than he had in years. No drugs had passed through his system since the attack and— *That's it,* he reflected, *it must've been the shot.*

He had received a dosage of the rabies vaccine at the doctor's office earlier, and he had to be suffering from an adverse reaction. However, he noted that he had received earlier doses of the vaccine with no ill effects. *Maybe it was a bad batch. That has to be it,* he convinced himself. *It must've been spoiled or something.*

"So, how's work?" His mother asked, sensing that the conversation was dying down. She continued to busy herself with her plate of food, only looking up when she received no answer, "Mark?"

Clutching his stomach, Mark looked across the table, sweat dripping from his brow. "What?" he groaned.

Placing her fork down, Virginia looked at her clearly ailing son in concern. "Mark, honey, are you all right?"

"Yeah, I'm fine," Mark gasped, "just a little stomach ache."

"It's not the food, is it?" she questioned.

"No," Mark smiled weakly, amused that his mother worried her cooking had made him ill. "I think I'm just reacting to whatever the doctor gave me."

"Well, do you want to go lay down? Honey, you don't look good," she said, trying her best to sound motherly.

Mark nodded, his jaw clenched. "Yeah, I think that'd be best."

Pushing away from the table, he stood up from his chair, stumbling backwards slightly. Steadying himself upon the nearby kitchen counter, he began to trudge towards the hallway, exiting the kitchen. As he entered the hallway, out of his mother's line of sight, he paused for a moment and doubled over. The pain was more intense now, and his skin felt as if it were on fire. Standing up had seemed to aggravate his body, causing the dull pains to become sharp and the nausea to become a full-blown sickness. Inhaling deeply, he rose up and walked several paces down the hall before being forced to double over once again. *This is ridiculous. I can't even fucking move.*

He had never felt like this before. Usually he simply threw up and felt better when he experienced the flu or something like it. This was different; this was far more concentrated and debilitating. He felt paralyzed almost, as if the next step would be his last. Reaching out, he steadied himself against the wall and began to slowly limp down the hall. Every movement was met with stabbing, crippling pain, and his stomach felt as if it would burst at any moment.

After what seemed like an eternity, he finally reached the doorway to his bedroom, and he stumbled through it. Closing the door, he took a deep breath before taking several quick steps and flopping upon his bed. He stopped breathing as a new round of pain gripped his stomach and tore at his insides.

The pain finally subsided, and Mark lay there gasping, his breath coming in short, shallow pants. The softness of his mattress seemed to alleviate the pain, and Mark rested his head upon his pillow. Curling into a ball, he began to tremble uncontrollably, feeling the sweat trickle down the back of his neck and soaking his shirt. Feeling cold momentarily, he was subjected to wave after wave of hot flashes, as if he were suffering from the mother of all common colds. *Jesus, am I going through menopause here?*

He flailed out as his abdomen clenched again, feeling the muscles painfully contract. Gritting his teeth he slapped at the mattress, fighting the urge to scream out. His head throbbing, he allowed himself to breathe once more as the pain slipped away, seeming to drain what little energy he had had left. Closing his eyes, he began to inhale rhythmically before finally drifting off to sleep, the full moon rising ominously just outside his bedroom window.

XVIII

Bill Lamperti stood in his backyard, ignoring the early autumn chill that hung in the air. It was late on a weeknight, and as such he was the only one outside. Elderly and hunched over, he should have been inside preparing for bed, but he couldn't, not tonight.

Just as he had every night for the last month, he was resuming with the search for his missing dog, his last true friend. "Toby," he called plaintively. The echo of his voice lingered for a moment before fading away into the night. "Toby, come here boy," he called again. Whistling through his teeth, he snapped his fragile, spindly fingers for good measure.

The silence he received in response was deafening. Just like every night for the past thirty nights, there was no reply, no dog barking, no jingling chain. A stiff wind buffeted Lamperti, and he ducked his head into his coat. A light fog rolled through the chain-link fence that surrounded his yard, obscuring his feet. It was unusually cold for mid-October, and Lamperti noted that the flowers in his garden would probably go soon with the first frost of the fall.

Hopefully, Toby will have come home by then. Turning in a different direction, he cupped his frail, weathered hands around his mouth. "Toby!" Looking towards the forest which buttressed his property he called out again, "Toby, please come home!"

There was nothing, Lamperti felt as if he might cry. Throughout the month he had wept fitfully several times, and it recalled the dark period shortly after his wife had passed. He couldn't stand the thought of being along once again; the thought was too much to bear. The motion light on his back porch went dark, and Lamperti produced a flashlight from his pocket. Flicking it on, he played the light around the yard and snapped his fingers a few more times, hoping against hope that it would attract his canine companion.

There was a metallic clang from behind him, and Lamperti gasped in shock. Whipping around, he trained the light in the direction of the disturbance and relaxed for a moment. He had left the fence gate open, and the wind had slammed it shut as it passed through. Lamperti watched as the wind took the gate once more, the rusting hinges groaning as it yawed open and screaming in protest as it was shut once more.

The clanging was caused by the U-shaped latch, which remained down, slamming against the aluminum of the fence support structure.

"Oh, jeez," Lamperti wheezed, shuffling over towards the fence. Placing the flashlight between his thighs he secured the door and pulled it shut, pulling the latch down. Tugging at the gate to ensure that it was closed, he paused as he heard a most peculiar sound.

In the distance an animal could be heard howling mournfully. The wail rose and fell before fading away, only to be replaced by a new round of baying. Lamperti stood upright and listened to the sound of the animal's cries. *The forest*, he surmised, *it's coming from the forest.*

Lamperti turned and trained his light upon the woods, but all he could see was the gray trunks of the evergreens which stood beyond his backyard. The howling continued, seemingly getting louder. He surveyed the houses to his right and to his left, but found their windows still darkened, none of his neighbors awakened by the baying animal. Suddenly, the animal stopped calling.

Lamperti shambled forward, still peering into the woods. *It couldn't be Toby, could it?* In all his years with the mutt, he could not recall hearing the dog howl. He couldn't even imagine what it would have sounded like. *Maybe, just maybe, that was Toby calling for his master, calling for help.*

There was the sound of rustling leaves and snapping twigs, and Lamperti moved closer to the fence. The trees were only a few feet away now, and he squinted hard, trying to make out any odd shapes in the woods. "Toby, that you?" he asked, his mouth dry from anticipation.

He received a grunt in response, and there was a new sound, a snuffling noise. Similar to the sound of a dog sampling the air with its snout, Lamperti felt his heart rate increase as he heard it. *Could this really be it, is Toby finally coming back to me?* "Toby? Oh, Toby, come here boy," he beckoned. His heart was a flutter, after a month of longing he was finally getting his friend back.

Something moved in the darkness of the woods, and Lamperti could make out the faintest of shapes. It stood just beyond the luminescence of his flashlight, choosing to remain hidden in the shadows. Whatever it was, Lamperti was now sure that it was not Toby.

"Hello?" he asked. "Anyone there?"

The figure grunted, a thick mist radiating from it as its hot breath condensed in the cold air. It began to growl menacingly, and it moved forward, allowing the light to define its shape a little bit more. Lamperti could now see that he was dealing with a biped, and the figure seemed to be that of a man.

"What the hell?" Lamperti questioned, perplexed by the figures actions. "Look, this isn't funny. What do you want?"

The figure stumbled forward, and Lamperti's light now fully illuminated the intruder. "You?" He gasped, stepping backwards. "What do you want?"

As he retreated he could see the figure advancing towards him. "What's wrong with you?" He protested, "What's wrong with you?"

There was no response however as the intruder continued to come at him slowly. Feeling threatened, Lamperti turned to run, his knees creaking and aged muscles refusing to boost him forward. His heart thundered in his chest and he struggled to propel himself at any great rate of speed, trying desperately to make it to the sliding glass door of his deck and the safety of his house.

He could hear the clanging of metal behind him and knew it meant the intruder had reached the fence and jumped it. It meant that now the aggressor was in the yard with him, no more than a few feet away. Lamperti dropped the flashlight and trudged forward, pumping his arms for added speed to no avail. He had just reached the steps of his porch when he felt the aggressor grab at him from behind.

"No!" He shouted, losing his balance and hitting his face hard upon the wooden steps. His eyes watered, and his nose ached; he was also aware of the coppery taste of blood in his mouth. Rolling over, he raised his hands defensively. "What's wrong with you?" He shouted, "Why are you doing this?"

The intruder roared and brought a hand down upon the old man's face, causing Lamperti to howl in pain. Unable to fully open his eyes, Lamperti was stunned by the force of the blow. It rattled his brain and caused his head to throb. Lashing out blindly, he sought to defend himself, making contact with the aggressor's solid mass. Forcing his eyes open just a bit, he watched as his attacker struck him once again, causing the world to go black.

XIX

Kaplan pulled the cruiser up alongside the lawn. An assortment of rescue vehicles and fire trucks had amassed just ahead. He frowned as he viewed a new presence, however; a smattering of blue and grey vehicles had joined the pack, sporting the words "Massachusetts State Police" on their sides. Concerned looking, gossiping neighbors had gathered just beyond the vehicles, and Kaplan could see some of them weeping, and the most callous among them aiming cell phone cameras towards the fray.

Wearing a concerned look himself he exited the car slowly and surveyed the chaotic scene around him. The dispatcher had not been completely clear over the radio about the situation at hand, and he walked cautiously towards the center of activity, knowing in his heart that nothing good lay ahead.

The sky was overcast, a leaden gray in color. The forecast called for rain later on in the day, but Kaplan felt that it could come down within minutes as the humidity in the air was oppressive, making it hard to breathe. He recognized the area instantly, as he had been there only a month ago. However, he didn't recognize the house he was walking towards.

It was a ranch style home, indistinguishable from the other houses surrounding it, stately in its simplicity and perfectly representative of its no doubt middle-class owner. Sky blue with a red front door and white garage entrance, it sported a small garden in front, the flowers looking wilted and dehydrated. Kaplan sensed that most of the police and rescue personnel were filtering in through a small gate just to the right of the house and he sensed that he too should gravitate towards the entrance.

With a feeling of trepidation, Kaplan plodded through the chain-link fence. He paused for a moment allowing his hand to rest on the fence gate. It appeared as if there were a hundred people gathered in the small yard, with various policemen snapping photos and collecting evidence. Kaplan made eye contact with a fellow officer who stood forlornly at the other end of the yard.

It was McGuire; he looked pale and sickly. His arms were crossed, and as he locked eyes with Kaplan he shook his head slowly in dismay. Kaplan instantly knew he had walked into something disastrous, something bad. Removing his hand from the gate Kaplan passed by a medical technician and came around the corner of the house, stopping dead in his tracks.

At the base of the house's porch laid the crumpled form of an old man. His clothes were torn, and where the flesh was exposed there were deep, red gashes. Several circular and semi-circular marks were present along the length of the body, looking as if someone had taken a cookie cutter to the elderly man's soft tissue. Kaplan watched as several crime scene technicians from the state police rolled over the body and revealed the man's face.

It was bloodied and disfigured, a thick coating of brown-red dried blood obscuring the man's identity. The eyes were closed shut, the expression pained and sorrowful. As messed up as the body's face was, Kaplan instantly recognized the man as the owner of the mutilated dog he had found weeks ago. It was Bill Lamperti.

Kaplan balked at the sight of the damaged face and instantly doubled over. Bracing his hands upon his knees, he furiously began to suck wind, his breath coming in short, ragged gasps. Hyperventilating, he was stricken by the macabre scene, not even flinching as an unknown presence rested a hand upon his shoulder.

"Knew him?" A voice asked.

Still doubled over, Kaplan crouched down and ran a hand over his face before taking a deep breath. Looking back at the old man's corpse he shook his head. "Not really." He sighed. "Well enough, though."

"Yeah, I know what you mean," the voice replied.

Kaplan looked up at the figure to his left. A burly man clad in the cerulean uniform of the Massachusetts State Police. He was an older gentleman, clearly nearing retirement age, but it was apparent that he was still a powerful, strong man. Kaplan stood up looking the man in the face. "Sorry, just needed a minute," he said before offering his hand. "Sergeant Eric Kaplan, Hingham Police."

The burly man smiled, his bushy, gray eyebrows rising on his forehead. "Trooper Matthew Henry of The Massachusetts State Police, Homicide Division," he said, gripping Kaplan's hand. "They tell me you're the big dog around here."

Kaplan blushed, "Well, I don't know about that."

"Nonsense," Henry boomed, "they say you're in charge."

"Well, all right then," Kaplan nodded, withdrawing his hand.

"So, you know how this works, right?" Henry asked.

Kaplan looked at the destroyed body a few feet away, "Thankfully no, I don't really. We don't have many murders around these parts."

"Okay then," Henry crowed, "ostensibly the Mass State Police conduct the homicide investigations in the towns of the commonwealth, except for the big one; Boston's got their own unit. Now that means technically we're running the show here, but I want you to know that we're going to work on this together. Me and the boys from the crime scene unit are simply here to assist you in catching the son of a bitch who did this." He slapped Kaplan upon the shoulder to emphasize his friendly message.

Kaplan nodded and shrugged, "Okay, yeah, sounds good."

"Good." Henry smiled, apparently happy with Kaplan's response.

"So, what happened to him?" Kaplan asked, still looking at the body.

"It appears this poor bastard was killed sometime during the night," Henry answered.

Kaplan looked at the old trooper, his brow furrowed, "How do you know it was last night?"

Henry placed an arm around Kaplan's shoulder, not even relinquishing his grip when the Hingham Policeman cringed in discomfort. Commanding Kaplan's view with an outstretched finger, Henry pointed towards the center of the lawn. "We found a flashlight there in the middle of the yard. The bulb was dim, but it was still on, indicating he had come out here last night."

Henry then pointed towards the fence. "We found blood on the railing of the fence, and we believe the killer entered the yard and later exited over that fence and into the woods." He then removed his hand from Kaplan's shoulder and stood in front of the officer. "Now, the way I figure it is the old man was awakened by some sort of disturbance last night, he comes out to investigate and is surprised as the perpetrator jumps the fence."

Henry moved closer to the body and continued to speak in dramatic tones, "He is grabbed here by the perp, who dispatches him, does his dirty work, and slips back over the fence."

"Was the house ransacked?" Kaplan asked, "Was his wallet gone, any valuables missing?"

Henry stood up straight, his eyebrows indicating he was unsatisfied with Kaplan's line of questioning. "Well, no, his wallet was accounted for, and the woman who found him said that the sliding door was shut, that the house hadn't been entered."

"Who found him?" Kaplan demanded.

Henry thought for a moment. "Um, God I forget her name, some neighbor. Enos I think was her last name."

"Virginia Enos?" Kaplan questioned.

Henry spread his hands wide. "Yeah, I suppose that was it, why you know her?"

"Not personally, but we've met," Kaplan answered.

Henry's facial expression darkened, "You don't think she had anything to do with this do you? Did she and the victim have some sort of troubled past?"

"No," Kaplan answered shaking his head. "Well, I mean I don't know, not to my knowledge."

"So, then what's your angle?" Henry asked.

"I don't know." Kaplan sighed. "I don't really have one, at least not as far as his neighbor's concerned. If you're looking for one, I suppose that in a case like this, my first hunch would be a robbery gone bad. But, if everything's in order like you say, then I'm totally lost. I mean, if it wasn't a robbery, then why murder this old man? I can't imagine he has many enemies; I doubt he even left the house that often."

Henry thought for a minute before offering, "Hey, man, there are sick psychos everywhere."

"That's your explanation?" Kaplan spat. "Sick psychos? That theory seems a little flimsy." Kaplan was immediately embarrassed by his reaction, and he girded himself for the backlash.

Henry lifted his hands defensively. "Look, let's not get off on the wrong foot. Sometimes motives only become apparent when we catch the bastards who are responsible."

"Sorry," Kaplan said, rubbing a hand over his forehead, still a little flushed by his outburst and the sight of Lamperti's corpse.

"Don't you worry about that," Henry soothed, lightly tapping Kaplan's shoulder, "I understand. People get emotional around these types of things all the time. Not every day you see a dead body."

"Well, thanks for understanding," Kaplan said, crossing his arms.

"Not a problem," Henry said. "Now, let me describe to you what we got going on here, catch you up to speed."

"Okay," Kaplan said, motioning for the trooper to continue.

"I've got a crime scene unit team here collecting evidence from the house and the yard, as well as from the body itself. We've got two canine teams, along with a group of troopers combing through the woods searching for any sign of the killer, and we've got one canine team patrolling the yard, looking for anything we might've missed."

"Again sounds good, what can I offer you?" Kaplan asked.

"I think we got it, buddy," Henry responded, again placing his hand upon Kaplan's shoulder and squeezing rhythmically. "I think we got it."

XX

The housefly buzzed around the room, its translucent wings flapping furiously. Navigating a meandering, twisting flight path, it finally alighted upon Enos' nose. Forearms twitching in front of its red compound eyes, it began to skitter up the length of Mark's proboscis before he angrily slapped it away.

Rudely awakened, he pried his head off his pillow and yawned. Groggily shaking his head, he attempted to jostle himself awake, only to wince at the taste in his mouth. It was a horrible flavor, tasting as if he had been gargling with sour milk and skunked beer. Flicking his tongue a few times in vain, he found he could not wash out the horrible tang; perhaps he had vomited during the night, he thought.

Blinking repeatedly, he waited for the return of the nausea which had plagued him the night before only to find that it was not coming. A pleasant little surprise, he began to stretch out his limbs, hearing the joints pop and crack as he did so. There was a sticky feeling about him, as if he had bathed in syrup. The clothes which he was wearing stuck to his skin in places and pulled upon his body hair as the cloth peeled away from his flesh. *Must've sweat really bad last night,* he acknowledged.

He rolled out of bed and noted the time upon the clock. It was early in the morning; the sun couldn't have been up for more than a few hours. A loud belch reminded him of the rank aftertaste which had pervaded his mouth. Shaking his head as if that would rid his aching body of the taste, he staggered into the hallway, scratching his crotch.

The floorboards creaked as he did so, and he found he had to step quickly, as they were freezing as always. Lurching into the bathroom, he flicked on the light and quickly opened the medicine cabinet searching for the Listerine. Clutching it, he fumbled with the top for a moment before placing the bottle to his lips and taking a prodigious amount into his mouth.

He swished the green liquid around his mouth, relishing the fact that it quickly replaced the horrible, raw taste in his mouth with mint and alcohol. Whipping his head back he gargled loudly, allowing the liquid to foam out of his mouth before spitting the entirety of the mouthwash into the sink. He watched as the emerald liquid swirled around the drain and took note of the red flecks which commingled with the foam. *Were my gums bleeding last night?*

Confused by the presence of dried blood in his saliva, he slowly twisted the cap back upon the Listerine bottle and placed it back where he had found it in the cabinet. Closing the small door, he gasped and jumped back as the mirror upon the flap revealed his reflection.

There was a liberal coating of dried brown-black blood upon his face. He was covered in it. It spread from his nostrils, around his mouth and continued down his neck. Looking downwards, he was horrified to find that the blood had continued to flow to his chest, soaking through his tee shirt and caking to his pectorals. It stained his pants and covered much of his forearms.

Mark wiggled his fingers, finding that the skin clung to that of the adjoining digit, having to be peeled apart. He must've bled out during the night he concluded, and he began to search for the wound. Combing back his hair and lifting up his shirt he frantically searched for the source of the blood. Surely, he had cut himself upon something while flailing about in bed.

There was no wound to be found, nothing that could account for the amount with which he was covered. Thinking for a minute he came to what he believed was a logical conclusion, *nosebleed.* It had to have been a nosebleed, and a particularly bad one at that. Nosebleeds were usually painless, and that would account for why he had not woken up, why he had continued to sleep as he bled.

Turning on the faucet he began to scrub his hands vigorously under the running water with a bar of soap. He watched as the blood slowly flaked off, leaving a pink hue in the bottom of the basin. The once white bar of soap was now tarnished, turning a horrible yellow-brown. The process of removing the dried liquid was laborious, and he slammed down the bar of soap.

The faucet still running, he began to strip, wrestling off his shirt before shimmying out of his pants. He groaned as he noticed that the blood had seeped through to his boxers, turning the once blue fabric a light purple. Removing them he leapt into the shower and began to bathe himself.

Scrubbing his body with his mother's pumice stone, he watched as the water at the bottom of the tub appeared like cranberry juice. Doing away with the stone, he lathered the entirety of his body before stepping underneath the running water again and letting the foam run down the drain.

Turning off the spigot, he stood in shower, hands against the wall, and allowed the excess water to drip off of him. Gasping momentarily he began to laugh, the sound of his mirth reverberating in his ears. *What a ridiculous way to wake up.* Pulling aside the shower curtain, he stepped out of the shower and retrieved a towel to dry himself with.

As he toweled himself, he turned the sink off and retrieved his bloody clothes from the floor before setting out for his bedroom. He tiptoed carefully down the hall, conscious of the fact that his mother may not have been up yet and crept into his bedroom. The window next to his bed was open, the drapes billowing in the cold morning air. He didn't necessarily remember opening the transom, but he regretted it now as the cool air stung his still drying skin. Dropping his clothes, he ambled towards it and began to slam it shut only to pause as he was doing so.

There was a noticeable murmur just outside his window. The low buzzing that was instantly recognizable as distant crowd noise. It was subdued, only occasionally wafting by, but there was something else. He could also hear a lower rumbling, and it took Mark a minute or two before he could identify it. It was the sound of several running truck engines.

Mark closed the window and dressed quickly, grabbing a sweatshirt and pair of khakis from the floor. Donning them, he clutched at a pair of weathered looking tennis shoes and tried to place them on as he walked down the hall, stumbling as he did so. Flying down the hallway, he peered out the living room window and viewed the large crowd which had assembled across the street. There were ambulances, fire trucks, and a myriad of police cruisers.

"Oh shit," he whispered. Drawing away from the window he looked down the hallway and called out, "Hey, Ma!"

There was no answer.

"Hey, Ma, wake up!" he insisted. "I think Lamperti's had a heart attack or a stroke!"

Again there was no answer. Annoyed he marched down the hall, mumbling to himself as he did so, "Jesus Christ, would you wake the fuck up?"

Not bothering to knock, he pushed open the door to his mother's bedroom and stomped into it. Stopping short, he saw that her bed was empty, a mass of pillows and wrinkled sheets where she would normally sleep. She had to be outside, he ascertained. *Must've already joined the crowd.* He took off for the front door seeking to join her.

He flung the door open and ran outside, towards the group of onlookers who had assembled just behind the rescue vehicles. He hardly recognized many of them, but he saw that most of them wore concerned looks and furrowed brows; clearly, something bad had happened. Lingering on the outskirts of the group he searched for a recognizable face before finally selecting one.

An older woman with a grizzled face stood near the front of the group. Periodically, she raised a cigarette to her pursed, ugly lips before allowing a cloud of gray smoke to billow from her mouth. She was Ms. Bolduc, the neighborhood gossip and his mother's best friend. He instantly recognized her from her hideous short, white hair and cragged skin. She wore her trademark tank top, even in the morning chill, allowing the loose skin of her arms to flap repulsively with every hand gesture she made.

He began to navigate the crowd towards her, calling out the woman's name as he approached. "Ms. Bolduc," he shouted, trying to gain her attention. "Ms. Bolduc!"

She looked and nodded at him as came closer.

"Ms. Bolduc, what happened?" He panted.

Taking another drag from her cigarette, she feigned remorse. "Oh, it's just terrible, honey."

"What is?"

"Mr. Lamperti's dead," the old hag rasped.

Mark looked towards the old man's house, attempting to catch a glimpse of something. "That sucks," he sighed "What was it, heart attack, stroke, old age?"

"Murder," she deadpanned.

Mark snapped his head back and looked at Bolduc, "Murder? Somebody murdered the old man?"

"Yeah, isn't it awful?" She croaked, "Your poor mother was bringing him coffee this morning and found the body."

"She did?" Mark asked, exasperated.

"Hmm mmm," The woman nodded, not opening her mouth for fear the butt would tumble from her lips.

"Where's my mother now?" Mark demanded.

Bolduc pinched the dwindling cigarette with her fingers and nodded behind Mark, "Over there."

Mark wheeled around, catching a glimpse of his mother seated in the rear of an ambulance. Her eyes were red and blotchy; she had clearly been crying. Her head bobbed up and down, her mouth occasionally moving though from this distance it was impossible to hear what she was saying. A police officer stood in front her, taking notes and it appeared as if he was questioning Mark's mother.

Pushing through the crowd Mark took off, tearing towards his beleaguered mother.

XXI

Kaplan and Henry were crouched over Lamperti's body, the trooper leading an extensive overview of the old man's wounds. With his hands encased in latex gloves, Henry pointed towards a point on Lamperti's battered face. "You see this area right here?"

Kaplan leaned closer, looking at where Henry had directed him to. On the body's right temple there was a particularly bloody area. The hair was matted down by greasy, brown blood, obscuring much of the area, but Kaplan could clearly see a large gash and he noticed that the spot appeared to be concave. It was dimpled in relation to the rest of the man's head. Kaplan looked up. "There's a dent."

"That's what we call blunt force trauma, and a real bleeder from the looks of it," Henry reported, smiling, although Kaplan found nothing he was saying particularly amusing.

"Any idea what type of weapon the killer used?" Kaplan asked.

"Real good idea," Henry nodded, pointing behind the officer.

Kaplan craned his neck. A rock, roughly the size of a grapefruit, was situated just a few feet away. A plastic marker was parked next to it, a black number one drawn in permanent marker upon its white face. The rock was stained in areas with black liquid. Looking back at Henry, Kaplan questioned, "The killer used that rock?"

"That's what we're thinking," Henry affirmed.

Kaplan looked towards the fence and the woods beyond it. "So, the killer jumps the fence, spooks the old man, they struggle, and the killer knocks him off with a rock?"

"Sounds good to me." Henry nodded.

Kaplan looked back down at the body and shook his head. "It still sounds like a robbery gone bad. Old man hears something outside, comes out to investigate, guy jumps him and kills him in the ensuing struggle. But why isn't anything missing?"

"Maybe the killer was interrupted?" Henry offered.

Kaplan frowned. "No, that can't be it. The guy had all night you said. The body wasn't discovered until this morning. It's got to be something else. Look at the condition of this guy; somebody did a real number on him."

Henry opened his mouth, ready to offer his opinion, but they were cut off by the sound of barking dogs. Henry's eyes went wide with excitement. "Oh boy, they've got something."

Confused, Kaplan watched as the older trooper leapt up and began galloping towards the din. Kaplan attempted to protest leaving the body, but found that Henry was already out of shouting distance and rounding the corner of the house. Standing up, Kaplan began to follow.

Kaplan began to walk slowly, watching the older man jog clumsily out of view. The barking of the canines had intensified, and Kaplan became concerned, breaking out into a slow trot. Coming around the house he could see two large German Shepherds, their jaws continuously flapping as they bayed and growled.

Two muscular police officers struggled to contain the frothing mutts, the muscles of each man's forearms straining as they held fast to the leashes restraining their respective dogs. The black and tan dogs sprang forth periodically and snapped at their target. Kaplan looked to see just what had spooked them so much and was shocked to see Mark Enos, the young man he had met a month earlier, on the other side of the fence holding his hands up in surrender.

Enos had a shocked and frightened look upon his face, standing nervously in front of the threatening dogs, only the chain-link fence protecting him from their wrath. Kaplan watched as Henry arrived in front of the canines and held out his finger towards the scared young man. "Stop right there, mister!"

Kaplan began to rumble forward, seeking to intervene on Enos' behalf.

"What's your name, son?" Henry growled at Enos.

Enos continued to hold his hands up as the dogs refused to cease their barking. "Mark."

"Mark what?" Henry demanded.

"Enos," Mark stammered. "I live across the street."

"If you live across the street what are you doing over here?" Henry grumbled, staring at Enos intently.

"My mother's here, sir. I'm just here to check on her. See if she's all right," Mark answered as he lowered his hands just a bit.

"You know Mr. Lamperti, got any problems with him?" Henry interrogated, his eyes looking suspiciously at Enos.

"What?" Mark asked, unsure of how to answer.

Thankfully for him, Kaplan arrived at the scene and grabbed Henry's outstretched arm. "What the hell are you doing?" Kaplan demanded of Henry. "He lives across the street; he's not a suspect."

Henry glared at Kaplan. "How the hell do you know that?" The trooper motioned towards the still baying dogs. "He's sure got my hounds all riled up."

"His mother found the body; they're probably detecting her scent on him," Kaplan explained.

He then turned towards the K-9 officers. "Would you shut those things up?"

Henry hesitated at first, his brow still lowered in anger, but he eventually lowered his arm and nodded at the K-9 officers, who dutifully tried to silence the dogs. Still suspicious, he inspected the still shaking Enos. "Don't go too far, kid. We might have a few questions for you."

Kaplan placed his arm around Henry's shoulder and began to lead him away from the scene before turning his head towards Enos. "Sorry, Mark. How's the hand?"

Enos placed his hands by his side and smiled meekly at Kaplan. "It's good, real good." He held up his once-injured hand for inspection.

"Well, that's great." Kaplan smiled. "Now, go check on your mom."

Mark nodded in appreciation, watching as the officers retreated towards the backyard.

"Look, I didn't mean to embarrass you back there," Kaplan said to Henry.

"Well, you failed." Henry bristled. "How do you know that kid's not a suspect? What, do you know him well?"

"Well enough," Kaplan lied. The sight of Enos had jogged his memory and caused him formulate a new possible theory. Once they were out of earshot of much of the crowd, Kaplan stopped and stood in front of Henry. "Listen, I just thought of something. Are you sure we're not looking at this the wrong way, I mean, is it possible our attacker wasn't human?"

Henry looked at Kaplan fish eyed. "What do you mean?"

"About a month ago that kid you were just talking to was attacked by an animal just up the road, thing really tore up his hand," Kaplan reported.

"Yeah, and?" Henry asked.

"Well, he was walking Lamperti's dog at the time. About a week later, animal control found the dog torn to shreds a few streets over. Now, is it possible that the same animal came back here and attacked the old man? Maybe it caught the dog's scent and came snooping around Lamperti's house. Maybe that's what he heard and that's what brought him out into the backyard."

"You're asking me if I believe some animal is responsible for attacking the old man?" Henry asked incredulously.

"Why not?" Kaplan rejoined, "It already attacked one person before."

Henry thought about Kaplan's theory for a moment before asking, "Well, how do you explain the rock?"

Kaplan frowned. "I don't know, maybe he fell and hit his head on it when he was being attacked. I mean look at the state of his body, and it looks like those are bite marks on his lower half."

Sensing that Henry was suspicious of Kaplan's theory, the officer continued, "And it would explain why nothing was stolen from his house and why his wallet was still on him."

"What did animal control say happened to the dog?" Henry questioned.

"They said it was probably coyotes or a big dog," Kaplan replied.

Henry stroked his chin before vigorously shaking his head. "No, this wasn't an animal attack. That rock was picked up and used to beat him about the face, there's no animal that can do that other than a human. Sorry, I can't buy that explanation."

"But—" Kaplan protested, only to be cut off.

"And I've found in these types of cases it's usually someone known to the victim, and you'd better hope it wasn't that young man who got my dogs excited, mister," Henry scolded, tapping a finger upon Kaplan's chest.

"He'd have to be pretty fucking stupid to kill this guy and then come stand in the crowd watching the cops," Kaplan defended.

"What are you talking about?" Henry said, exasperated. "I've heard of killers doing that all the time, getting their jollies from watching us work the scene."

Kaplan began to speak, but found that he had no response and quickly closed his mouth, slumping his shoulders as he did so.

Henry seemed to take comfort from his display of resignation. Patting Kaplan's shoulder, he smiled, "We can discuss theory later on. Right now, let's get back to work, buddy."

XXII

Dissociative Identity Disorder, that's what the articles had called it. After his brief encounter with the officers, Mark had attempted to come to his mother's aid only to be rebuffed by the army of paramedics, police officers, and rescue personnel present. "We need a few moments alone with her," they had explained sternly. "You can be with her when we're done." Pushed back into the crowd, he stood silently amongst the neighbors, lost in his own thoughts. That's when the term he had been searching for had come forth in his mind.

Dissociative Identity Disorder, or multiple personality disorder, he recalled the terminology from one of the articles interspersed amongst those on the killers who so interested him. He recalled reading the piece in a fit of boredom, during an interminably long wait to be analyzed by one of the base doctors. Struggling to recall the details, he hardly noticed the awestruck whispers of his neighbors as a news chopper thundered overhead, hovering for a short while before circling around and taking off.

The affliction had formed the basis for many famous stories including the infamous tale of Dr. Jekyll and Mr. Hyde. Mark remembered reading the novella for a class in high school and writing some paper on the duality of human nature, the war between good and evil in every human being, although he had ripped those terms off from the book's forward. In fact, Mark had always regarded the idea that two or more personalities could exist within one mind as total horseshit; just another cheap parlor trick thought up by psychologists and exploited by a million defense lawyers and attention seekers. However, in light of recent events, the idea of two entities in one body now seemed like a plausible idea, a reasonable hypothesis that could explain what had occurred here.

What had the article listed as the symptoms of the disorder? He shuddered as he recalled with stunning clarity the signs most sufferers of the disease exhibited as many of these symptoms, he realized, could pertain to him. There were so many he could apply to himself. Lack of intimacy or personal connections, he certainly had experienced that throughout his life. Depression, he had exhibited signs of that in the past. Unexplainable body pains, though this hadn't happened before, the memory of him writhing in pain the night previous did not escape him. However, the one which concerned him the most was the most important, severe and unexplained memory loss. He couldn't account for last night. Originally assuming he had just passed out, he now searched for alternative answers, as he didn't even remember falling asleep. He had been sick and then . . . what? His mind had gone blank, blacked out as if he had been drunk.

Was it possible that he had developed some form of this disorder? Had he done something last night, albeit under the guise of a separate personality? It seemed outlandish and unlikely, but given the circumstances of how he had awoken and where he now found himself, anything seemed possible, nothing could be discounted. Was it possible he had become a different person last night and had killed his elderly neighbor, and if so, why? Was it the manifestation of some long harbored ill will towards the old man?

Mark shook his head. *No.* As far as he could remember he had never entertained any violent or hateful thoughts about Mr. Lamperti. He was just some gentle old man, living silently across the way. He had been a good friend to Mark's mother and Mark couldn't recall one time ever seeing the man curse or get angry when neighborhood kids would occasionally knock out one of his windows with an errant fly ball. He had always been a gentleman, someone the younger generation in the neighborhood regarded as harmless and kind hearted. Mark even recalled one time when

Stephen and several friends in a fit of drunkenness had vandalized the old man's mailbox, and Lamperti hadn't even said boo about it, silently cleaning it up without complaint and then going about his business as if nothing had occurred. As the memories passed through his head, Mark was aware of a tinge of sadness which tugged at his heart. In a strange way he was going to miss the old man, or at least his gentle presence.

No, he had never thought of harming Lamperti, so the explanation that he had acted out of some subconscious rage or long held resentment of the man didn't hold much water. Besides the whole multiple personalities thing didn't make a hell of a lot of sense to Mark either. He had never exhibited such behavior before, and he sincerely doubted that such a mental disease would manifest itself so late in life. Besides, he recalled that all those symptoms he had rattled off could also be attributed to Post Traumatic Stress Disorder, something he was well aware he suffered from.

Still, something bothered him, caused a leaden feeling to settle in his stomach. The way the dogs had barked at him, the sheer anger in eyes and the vicious nature with which they had gnashed their teeth irked him immensely. They hadn't barked like that at anyone else in the crowd, and admittedly now as he watched them, they seemed slightly agitated, and he was certain the animals were casting unnerving glances his way, their gleaming brown eyes seeming to work him over.

There was also the cadence of their barking and as it played in Mark's head. He was certain he could hear them announcing to the world, "You did it! You did it!" It was harsh, rough, and grating on the ears, but the conviction with which they had set upon him and their determination to get at him was unnerving. Something clearly wasn't right here.

Besides, if it had not been him, who else would hurt the old man? As far as Mark could remember, nothing like this had ever happened in the old neighborhood. Stephen used to lament how boring and mundane the area was as a teenager, constantly whining that, "Nothing ever happens here." It seemed inconceivable to Mark that someone had broken into the man's house and dispatched him. Though maybe Stephen had gotten his wish all these years later. Perhaps Mark was just being crazy. *Why wouldn't someone choose Lamperti's house?*

This entire time Mark had discounted the thought that he was not responsible. The very idea that it was someone else's fault now eased his mind. It comforted him. It wasn't out of the realm of possibility that some transient or low-life had murdered Mark's elderly neighbor. *Lamperti was the perfect victim,* Mark reflected. He was a frail old man who lived alone and, as far as Mark could recall, possessed no weapons or security system. It also occurred to Mark that he didn't even know how Lamperti had met his end. Maybe he had been shot, or scared so badly that his heart had simply given out. Imagining the hundreds of possibilities with which the hypothetical criminal had killed the old man, Mark became giddily lost in his morbid exercise. Of course he hadn't killed Lamperti; it had to have been someone else.

Absolving himself of all guilt, Mark felt the stress recede from his body, and it felt as though a great burden had been lifted from his shoulders. That was until he remembered the pile of bloody clothes which now sat in his room. The stark reality of those crimson-stained garments brought his head out of the clouds and returned the butterflies to his stomach. Preparing for another exercise in self-flagellation, his thoughts were broken by a stern voice.

"All right, son," a stern faced, ebony-skinned policeman commanded from beyond the crowd. "Yo, I'm talking to you," he barked, adding a whistle to draw Mark's attention.

"Me?" Mark asked meekly.

"Yeah, you," the cop responded humorlessly. "Let's go."

Mark swallowed hard. He had been caught, the jig was up. Undoubtedly they had found some key piece of evidence which pointed directly at him. He was going away in handcuffs; they were going to send him to jail for the rest of his life. Accepting this harsh reality, he stepped forward, gingerly approaching the policeman.

The policeman dutifully squeezed his shoulder with thick, sausage-like fingers and pulled Mark close to him. Mark prepared to turn around, waiting for the cold steel to close painfully around his wrists. "All right, man, you can go get your mother now," the policeman said, softening his grip and his tone.

Confused at first, Mark looked at the man before nodding his mouth to dry to speak. "Thank you," he croaked as he walked away. *You're losing your mind, Mark.*

XXIII

The news cameras rolled, and there was a flurry of newspaperman who had arrived to cover the death of Bill Lamperti for their respective organizations. Many in the crowd preened for the cameras and attempted to get in on the action, posing and waving behind several of the news anchors who had arrived to do their pieces for the nightly news, to the point that the proceedings took on the air of a movie opening or a triumphant sports celebration. It was a macabre spectacle, and to many outsiders it made for an unflattering indictment on the men, women, and children of this particular neighborhood.

Many of the neighbors came forth and offered their take on the incident for the benefit of the cameras, including of course Ms. Bolduc. Discarding her cigarette, the old hag prepared herself for her fifteen minutes of fame, working herself up to the point where her lip quivered and her eyes welled up with crocodile tears. "It's terrible, just terrible," she croaked, the harshness of her Boston accent ratcheted up for the interview. "You know you think something like this can never happen where you live and then . . . " Her voice trailed off, and she had to collect herself, her face betraying that she was on the verge of tears. Her acting was impeccable; this would be on the news tonight for sure.

"Were you close to the victim?" The newswoman asked, her own make-up-caked face a mask of forced concern.

"Oh yeah, oh yeah," Bolduc nodded, the camera coming in for a close up as she had to collect herself again. Lightly sobbing now, she looked forlornly into the newswoman's eyes. "We're really going to miss him; he was such a great friend."

This was a lie of course. Though Ms. Bolduc and Lamperti had lived in the neighborhood for years, they had never been particularly close. In fact, besides the occasional exchange of pleasantries, the two never spoke. It didn't matter to Bolduc of course; she couldn't wait to brag to the ladies at the local salon about her appearance on television.

A smattering of neighbors gladly gave statements to the local papers, all giving their opinion and theories on what had taken place, waiting anxiously to see their names in print the next morning. Mark and his mother had long since left the scene, but that hadn't stopped many of the reporters from approaching the front door, asking to speak to the woman who had discovered the body. Mark had promptly shooed them away, refusing to participate in the narcissistic exercise taking place between the residents and the press.

One of the most revolting scenes had been when the medical technicians had finally wheeled the body out from the backyard. An amorphous figure tied down to a stretcher and wrapped in a white blanket, cameramen and neighbors jockeyed for position, each attempting to get the best view of the formless corpse. Cameras snapped, and a few of the teenagers in the crowd shouted over the din, "Let us see it!"

It wasn't until after the ambulance closed its doors and rumbled off that many of the assembled media began to lose interest, confident that they now had their footage or story. Even as many in the news vans began to pack it up, many of the onlookers stayed, waiting to spy something new, and reveling in the carnival-like atmosphere Lamperti's death had created.

With all the commotion, it was understandable that one would think Lamperti's death was quite the event, but it received little play beyond his local community. It made the Boston news channels of course, even reaching as far Manchester and Providence, but it wasn't sensationalized, and it hardly grabbed the attention of those outside Talbot Road and Hingham. A mere blip on the radar of the local consciousness, it hardly registered with those watching their television. The news anchors of course acted quite solemnly and concerned as they announced the occurrence before cutting away to their on-the-spot reporters, who promptly rolled the footage they had collected earlier. Ms. Bolduc was ecstatic when many of the networks used her dreadful performance as the centerpiece of their reporting, the footage portraying her as the worried neighbor in mourning. Of course each network kicked it back to the studio where each one of the anchors shook their heads in mock sorrow and closed with similar lines of, "The police have released no information on suspects, and the investigation is ongoing."

In nearly every case, however, the news of Lamperti's death was followed with a delightful fluff piece on a local fair or a rescued kitten returned to her young owner. The once dour news anchors all perking up and delivering the most cheerful of dribble. Just like that, Lamperti's murder was removed from the collective consciousness. It was a sad reflection not only on the state of network news broadcasts, but also on the audience. Hardly anyone watching had much of a reaction to the murder, giving it nothing more than a collective shrug of their shoulders.

In a country where terrorism, constant warfare, and gang warfare dominated the headlines, the murder of an elderly man, no matter how brutal, failed to raise any eyebrows. Many went back to what they were doing, that is if they had even been paying attention at all. Outside of Ms. Bolduc's performance and Virginia's Enos shock, not many were openly concerned about the death of Bill Lamperti. Most of the neighbors attributed it to a home invasion gone horribly wrong and regarded it as an anomaly, an extraordinary action which surely wouldn't happen in the neighborhood again. At the end of the day, many didn't deem Bill Lamperti's murder to be newsworthy.

XXIV

Kaplan turned right and left, the bloody crime scene in his rearview mirror. Lost in his thoughts, he was grateful for the brief moments of solitude the drive to the station house would afford him. He was shaken, bothered immensely by what he had seen, and he needed to take some time to gather his thoughts and reflect on what had just gone down.

He had always prided himself on his ability to remain calm under pressure, to appear cool and collected even when his mind was in great distress. He believed that he had kept it together admirably at the crime scene. Kaplan seriously doubted that Henry had even detected the slightest amount of squirming and discomfort from his rock-solid façade. It was all an act of course; like any human, he had recoiled from the sight of a mangled body. It was alarming to him that someone could have inflicted such savage wounds upon one of the most helpless members of society, and his emotions had vacillated between disgust and anger as he conducted his investigation. It also troubled him enormously that he had come in contact with this person no more than a month ago. In that moment Lamperti had been a living, breathing human being, and now he was just a heap of hamburger lying in a yard.

He had spent the better part of four hours listening to Henry go over the crime scene and examine the body itself. Kaplan didn't know if that was a normal time frame, and he had noted that Henry had remained at the crime scene as he left. Truth be told, he had sort of zoned out on Henry, choosing to mull events over in his own mind. *Who could do such a thing?* He asked himself. *Why would someone do such a thing?*

This last question is what gnawed at Kaplan the most. There was no discernable motive as far as he could see. At one point he had entered the victim's house, and the immaculate order Lamperti had maintained had impressed him. Not one thing was out of place as far as Kaplan could see, and he had noted along with the rest of the crime scene team that the old man's bed was still made. The only thing that concerned Kaplan about the house was that much of the furniture and décor was from the seventies. It had been like walking through a time warp, and there was even the hint of mildew which had hung in the air. It didn't appear as if anything had been stolen from Lamperti's house, and he couldn't really see what anyone would want to steal from a man of such modest means. The minute Kaplan had entered the domicile, he knew in his gut that his robbery-gone-bad scenario was probably out the window.

So what happened?

Was it a pack of kids playing some cruel, twisted game? Kaplan recalled a recent murder in Mount Vernon, New Hampshire in which four teenagers had hacked a woman to death in her sleep before slitting her young daughter's throat. It seemed farfetched, but he supposed it was possible that such bad apples could be amongst the teenagers of Hingham. Lamperti was a prime target for something so awful; he was old, frail, and lived alone. That meant that the killer or killers had to have been local, that they had to have possessed some working knowledge of the old man and his situation. Of course in this scenario Kaplan would have to concede that Henry's "sick psycho" theory had been correct.

No, that's not what happened.

He shook his head, admonishing himself for even entertaining such a preposterous hypothesis. It wasn't some traveling band of satanic teens, of that he was completely sure. He had to review the facts of the case. Something had lured Lamperti from the safety of his home, and that something or someone had attacked him there in the backyard. It had been dark, hence the flashlight they had recovered near his body, and whoever or whatever had set upon Lamperti had been far stronger than the old man. Kaplan went back to his other theory, the one he had felt a little embarrassed broaching with Henry.

Why is the notion that an animal was responsible so ludicrous?

The wounds had been extraordinarily violent. Nothing had been taken from the house. The killer lacked any rational motive, unless of course you were an animal. Then the killing made perfect sense. Lamperti could have surprised the animal or cornered it in his yard; perhaps the beast had even viewed the old man as food. It wasn't out of the realm of possibility, the old man's neighbor had been attacked just a month earlier, and Kaplan winced as he recalled Toby the victim's dog torn asunder. As he pondered the possibility of a rogue predator prowling the woods of his beloved town Kaplan felt a pit develop in his chest, a surge of guilt wash over him.

If there was something out there, a dangerous animal, he could have prevented all of this. He had been there the night Mark Enos was attacked, and he had seen the remains of Lamperti's dog. Maybe he shouldn't have taken that animal controller's advice that it was just a coyote; maybe there was something bigger and more threatening out there in the forest. He could have sounded the alarm, gotten the ball rolling on a search party for this thing.

He was a good cop. He truly believed that. He always had the best interests of those he served at heart. He hadn't failed to notify those in command of possible coyote attacks out of laziness; rather it had been an action committed in good faith, a utilization of his police discretion. He had taken the animal controller at his word and believed it was their issue; they were the ones who usually handled such issues and would obviously hunt the things down if they believed they posed a danger. Kaplan would have been more than happy to assist them in that endeavor had they asked, only the call had never come, and he hadn't given the matter much thought. No new calls had originated about animal attacks or even unusual animal sightings in the intervening days. He had also ordered the animal controller to cremate the dog, believing that it was better to keep the old man's hope alive rather than tell him the awful truth. The old man seemed to be having a hard enough time as it was from where Kaplan had stood, and he simply assumed the thought of Toby running free would pacify the old man and make him happy. He hadn't needed to know that his dog was mutilated by . . . by what?

Kaplan's brow furrowed at this thought. Lamperti may have been a fragile individual, but he was still a human male. It would have had to have been something of comparable or considerable size to bring him down and not let him get away. What the hell around here could do that? Shaking his head, he tossed his animal theory aside. If something that large had been lurking outside Lamperti's window, surely he would have phoned the police rather than going out to confront it. Lions, tigers, and bears didn't roam the forests of southeastern Massachusetts.

It was at this moment Kaplan recalled the principle of Occam's razor, which is that the simplest explanation is usually the correct one. There wasn't any creature lurking in the woods, and there weren't any murderous teens banding together to butcher an old neighbor. That brought Kaplan back to square one. Something had to have motivated the attack on Bill Lamperti; he just didn't know what. *Maybe someone held a grudge against the old man, a neighborly dispute? Or was it a relative eager to collect the life insurance policy Lamperti held, a financial motive? Did Lamperti even have life insurance?* His mind was cluttered even further by this drive as his imagination concocted a hundred scenarios for why someone would brutally murder Lamperti. Rather than clear his thoughts, these few moments alone had convoluted them.

Cursing himself for not focusing more, he lightly slapped the steering wheel just as he pulled into the station house. At least something like this was an anomaly. Things like this didn't happen in a small town. Of that he was grateful, as it meant he wouldn't have to view such a scene of gore again. Oh sure, there'd be the occasional nasty car wreck, but for some reason that thought sat well with Kaplan, as they were relatively common occurrences at certain times of year. Besides, most of those involved in such accidents tended to be under the influence, and Kaplan viewed it as social Darwinism in action, a cosmic and karmic just desserts for those inclined to climb behind the wheel in such a state. In this type of setting, brutal murders were not run-of-the-mill events. It eased his mind. He assured himself that a homicide like this one was just an isolated incident. *Isn't it?*

XXV

As the day wore on the crowd grew thinner. Many of the onlookers became bored with the macabre display and went home, all eager to return to the comfort of their living rooms and the glow of their television screens. The vehicles also started to disperse. One by one they rumbled off until only a few squad cars and police vans remained. The occasional news chopper hovered overhead throughout the day, gathering footage for the local channels.

A thin ribbon of yellow crime scene tape had been draped across Lamperti's driveway, and Mark watched as it billowed in the wind. Rocking back and forth in his chair, he took in the police activity across the street, even enduring the occasional glares of the trooper who had questioned him hours before. Sitting on the deck of his house, he had waited patiently, sure that he would be interrogated at some point, but they had never come for him.

His mother seemed to be suffering from shock, rattled by the sight of the old man's mutilated corpse, and the medical technicians had dispensed a few pills to calm her nerves before sending her home. Questioned thoroughly by the police, she had said little to Mark after returning, and her quivering lips betrayed the fact that she could burst into tears at any minute. Stephen had rushed over after work to check on her and remained inside the house.

Mark was in a state of shock himself. The bloody clothes, the lack of wounds, and now the murdered neighbor—he couldn't be responsible for the murder, could he? He continually reviewed the facts in his head and was unsure of what to make of them. His window had been open this morning he recalled. Was it possible that he had slipped out in the night and killed the old man?

He recalled an old news story in which an Englishman had claimed he strangled his wife to death whilst having a nightmare. Mark had thought the man was full of shit, a guilty murderer concocting a preposterous excuse, but was it now reasonable? He had been racked by some frightful dreams himself as of late, was it feasible that he had lashed out and hurt someone while in the midst of a nightmare?

The events of the previous day continued to replay in Mark's head, and he kept focusing on the website he had viewed at the library. "You will change and do harm those around you," it had warned. It had all seemed so comical the day before, but now as he watched the police mill about the old man's house, not so much. *Could this really be true?* Mark questioned, *Did I change last night?*

He had been covered in blood, and then there was the horrible flavor in his mouth that morning. It had been foul, raw and coppery; was it the rotten aftertaste of the old man's flesh? *Jesus Christ, did I take a bite out of him?* The very thought made him ill, and it suddenly struck Mark that it had been the night of a full moon. *This isn't possible, is it?* Could it be, Mark waffled, could he really be cursed? He dismissed such crazy thoughts. *Come on, man, werewolves don't exist.* Still, he wrestled with the fact that he may be culpable, that he may in fact be a murderer.

No, his inner monologue shouted, *you're not a killer.* It was a nosebleed, plain and simple. *Besides you were too sick to hurt anyone last night, dumbass,* he scolded. He had been ill the night before, feverish even. *That's it, you must've gotten up in the middle of the night and opened the window to cool yourself.* The illness could also explain the awful flavor which had filled his mouth, he must've vomited during the night, the bile coating his cheeks before he had swallowed it.

Still wrestling with his own thoughts, Mark heard the screen door behind him open and clang shut. The ancient floorboards of the porch groaned as Stephen sidled up besides Mark. "How's she doing?" he asked.

"She's fine." Stephen sighed. "Just a little shaken up."

"Did she take those pills the medics gave her?"

"No," Stephen shook his head, "flushed 'em down the toilet. Said she just needs to rest."

"Probably true, she's had a hell of a day."

"I hear that," Stephen said, looking across the street. "It's so messed up. I never figured that'd be how the old man went."

"I know, poor bastard," Mark agreed.

"How you holding up? Mom mentioned something about the police talking to you."

"Um, I'm fine I guess," Mark stuttered.

"You guess?" Stephen prodded.

Mark bit his lip, rocking in his chair and thinking hard. Swallowing, he asked, "Do you believe it's possible for a sleepwalker to kill someone?"

Stephen looked dismayed, "What the hell type of question is that?"

"I don't know." Mark shrugged. "Do you think it's possible?"

"No, I don't think it's fucking possible," Stephen spat. "Why do you ask?"

Mark stopped rocking and looked down at the porch floor. "I don't know, man, I guess I just feel responsible in a way for his death."

"Whose, Lamperti's?" Stephen questioned.

"Yes," Mark said.

"In what way?" Mark's older brother demanded.

"I don't know what to say, man, I'm just wondering if maybe I had a bad nightmare and . . . " he trailed off.

"Oh Jesus, Mark," Stephen harrumphed, "you're wondering if you killed the fucking guy?"

"I don't know," Mark stammered. "I don't know what I'm saying."

Stephen appeared annoyed by his brother's line of questioning. "I think you'd know if you had killed him Mark, and no, asshole, I don't think you had a nightmare, sleep walked over to our neighbor's house, and murdered him. Jesus, man, what's wrong with you? Why would you even think something like that?"

Mark went back to rocking and shrugged his shoulders, "I . . . I guess I'm just talking out of my ass." He thought about telling his brother of the blood-stained clothes and the open window, but thought better of it. "Just forget about it," he added.

Stephen looked as if he were about to scream at his petulant little sibling, but his facial features lightened. "Fine," he sighed, "maybe it's you who needs to get more rest."

"Maybe," Mark agreed.

Stephen stepped forward and leaned against the porch railing. The cool, crisp autumn air smelled of wet leaves and fresh cut grass. The sun had begun to dip below the horizon, and the police across the street had switched on klieg lights to combat the fading daylight. In the gray haze of dusk, Mark and Stephen strained to see much of what was going in the yard across the street, and the elder brother dipped his head in resignation. "Strange stuff going on here, man, strange stuff. First, you get attacked by some dog, and then old man Lamperti gets it."

"Yeah," Mark replied, thinking about the confluence of bizarre circumstances which had surrounded him in the past twenty-four hours. "Strange stuff."

Stephen stood back from the railing. "Well, I've got to get home, get back to the kids. Are you and Mom going to be okay alone here tonight?"

Mark thought about the question, staring at the retreating sun. Soon, darkness would descend and the full moon would rise high in the sky. Hesitating at first, Mark finally shook off the strange thoughts which plagued him. *This is bullshit.* "Yeah," he answered confidently, "we'll be just fine."

XXVI

Hingham Chief of Police Richard Patterson sifted through the grisly photos, letting loose with a whistle. Moving onto the next picture he winced. "Oh Christ, look at that." He was dressed in a crisp, dark blue uniform, and the skin on his bald forehead wrinkled as he displayed his displeasure with the images in front of him. Setting the photos down on his desk he looked up at Kaplan and Henry, who were seated across from him. "So, who was he?"

"Name was Bill Lamperti, lived up on Talbot Road," Kaplan answered. "Heard of him?"

"Nah." Patterson shook his head.

Kaplan slouched back in his chair. "Apparently he worked at the shipyard over in Quincy for most of his life, retired when they shut it down. Wife died a few years back, been living alone ever since."

"So, what happened? What was it, a robbery gone bad?"

"That's what I thought, but the woman that found the body, a next door neighbor, assured us that nothing was out of place," Kaplan responded.

"Didn't look like there was much worth taking anyways," Henry snorted.

Casting a glare in the trooper's direction, Kaplan continued, "Mr. Lamperti was obviously a man of modest means, and yes, it didn't look like he had much in the way of valuables."

"Teenagers might have seen an easy target," Patterson said, "frail old man living alone."

"That's one pissed off teenager," Henry offered. "I mean, hell, they did a number on him. Somebody who does something like that, they must have a lot of anger directed at the victim."

"What are you saying? That this was personal?" Patterson questioned.

"That's exactly what I'm saying, Chief. Shit like this, most times the perpetrator knew the victim, and the intensity of the wounds usually indicates a lot of bad feelings directed at the dead person. I'm saying I like the kid," Henry answered, looking at Kaplan derisively.

"I told you, he's not our guy," Kaplan replied, waving his hand dismissively.

"How do you know that really?" Henry retorted, shifting in his chair.

"Somebody care to fill me in?" Patterson interjected, "Who's the kid?"

Frowning, Kaplan looked across the desk. "Trooper Henry is speaking of Lamperti's neighbor, Mark Enos. He's nothing, not really of any concern."

"The dogs at the crime scene seemed to think differently; fuckers were chomping at the bit when they laid eyes on that kid. It was like he was a nice porterhouse sitting on a plate," Henry intoned.

"And as I told Trooper Henry that was probably because Mr. Enos's mother is the one that found the body. They probably smelled her scent on him," Kaplan hissed, the annoyance in his voice barely concealed.

"And I'll counter by saying that's a little convenient, isn't it? Maybe the two of them were in on it together. I mean, do we really know just how chummy the victim and Ms. Enos really were? Maybe something was missing from the house, something they wanted. They form their plan. Son offs the old man, steals whatever they're after, and mother, after just happening to find the body, assures us that nothing's missing from the house," Henry claimed.

"Oh, I think that's making a huge leap from nothing," Kaplan spat. "There's no evidence of such a scheme here. Lamperti was a neighborhood favorite from what I gather, and it wasn't that uncommon for members of the neighborhood to check in on him. Besides, the dogs weren't going nuts when they saw her."

"So why they'd go ape shit when they saw the son?" Henry beamed.

"Oh goddamn it," Kaplan groaned, realizing he had hung himself with that last statement. "I'm telling you they didn't conspire to kill Lamperti."

"Well, then who killed the old man?" Patterson asked.

Kaplan threw up his hands. "I don't know, Chief, but I know it wasn't this kid. He's just not a nefarious character."

"Do you know him well?" Patterson asked.

"Yeah, I'd say," Kaplan answered. "The kid was attacked by some dog, or something, like a month ago while he was walking Lamperti's dog. I responded to the call, and I pulled the kid's record out of boredom. He's got nothing on his record besides a few speeding tickets and a citation for underage drinking when he was twenty, for Christ's sake. He's a military man to boot, real disciplined no doubt. It'd be a huge leap for him to go mutilate the old man across the street. He's harmless, just a normal twenty-something. Looks like a good kid."

"Looks can be deceiving," Henry chimed in. "What about the old man's dog? You said it was all messed up, maybe that was the kid's work, and now he's graduating to bigger prey. They say these psycho killers usually start with animals. Hell, maybe he got his jollies over in the war and can't stop himself now that he's stateside."

"I don't remember hearing about a mutilated dog." Patterson frowned at Kaplan.

Sighing, Kaplan replied, "Animal control found it about a week after the kid was attacked. They told me it was probably whatever attacked Enos finishing off its intended prey. A coyote or something, and I think it's a preposterous hypothesis to think that Enos murdered the dog, bit himself, and passed out in the street before murdering the dog's owner a month later."

"What happened to the dog's remains?" Patterson demanded.

Kaplan sighed. "I had them cremated."

"So there's no way to know what the hell attacked this kid?" Patterson interrogated.

Kaplan shrugged, "I took animal control's word for it that it was a coyote or another dog. I didn't think it was that big of a deal. Besides, I figured it was best if the old man never knew his dog was torn to shreds."

"Jesus Christ, Eric," Patterson scolded.

"Maybe the dog bit Enos while he was doing his dirty work," Henry chimed in nonchalantly.

"Oh, come on," Kaplan rejoined, "Chief, I'm telling you Enos is a good kid; he's not our guy. The real killer's still out there."

"Maybe you knew the kid's a bad seed and burned the dog's remains to protect him," Henry threw out.

"Holy shit," Kaplan exasperated, "is there anyone you've met so far who isn't involved in the conspiracy to kill Bill Lamperti?"

Henry threw his head back, letting loose with a full-throated belly laugh.

"All right, all right," Patterson interjected. Running a hand over his bald head and sinking into his chair, he paused for a minute before leaning back over his desk, "Are you two going to be able to work together? Can you actually stand to be in the same room as each other?"

"Oh, I think we're right as rain, go together like peas and carrots." Henry smiled. "I've found this kind of discussion is normal in these type of investigations; just part of fostering a good team atmosphere. I've liked working with your officer here so far, Chief, real top notch."

Kaplan looked at Henry. *Right as rain, peas and carrots; who talks like that? And real top notch? You just implied I was a crooked cop, covering up evidence, you asshole.* Composing himself he nodded back at the Hingham Police Chief. "Yeah, I've got no problem working with the trooper here." He felt ill at ease as the lie passed his lips.

"All right then, Trooper Henry, Sergeant Kaplan here will act as our liaison and he will assist you with your investigation if that's acceptable."

"Oh, that'd be more than acceptable, Chief Patterson, we're all are after the same goals here." Henry beamed.

"In the meantime, consider yourself to have the run of the department. Anything you need in terms of manpower, space, or just in general, do not hesitate to ask," Patterson said.

"That's mighty fine of you, Chief, mighty fine," Henry stated before looking over at Kaplan and baring his teeth in a grotesque looking grin. "This is gonna be fun."

This is going to be awful, Kaplan thought, managing to force a grin and nodding at the trooper.

XXVII

Mark watched as the moon ascended into the sky. A cerulean orb, it hung ominously there. He had not retreated indoors, even as the forecasted rain had come and gone in the early evening, leaving only a few wispy, dark clouds to sail across the lunar face. A picture of tranquility, it stood in stark contrast to the turmoil brewing inside Mark's body. He could feel it coming, bracing himself for the creeping onslaught.

As his core seized up and his stomach brewed, Mark doubled over in his rocking chair. He felt hot and feverish, recalling the sensations which had buffeted him one night previous. His muscles felt as though they were tearing and his bones, breaking. Mark groaned in pain as another spasm rocked his abdomen. The police had left the area hours before, apparently content in their take of evidence and eager to beat the rain, and as such, no one was around to hear Mark's anguished cries. The only things that stirred around him were the fluttering crime scene tape across the street and Lamperti's creaking gate.

Stumbling from his chair, he fell to the porch floor, still clutching at his stomach. "Help me," he pleaded through clenched teeth. The sweat poured from his scalp, trickling down his forehead and dripping upon the wooden deck. As yet another wave of cramping rippled through him, he slapped out his hands, his fingernails tearing into the rotted wood.

On trembling legs he stood and tore off his sweatshirt. It was as if his skin was on fire, threatening to spontaneously combust. His mouth was awash in viscous, glycerin like saliva and he had to repeatedly spit out the excess fluid. He was confused and frightened, eager for the pain to subside; yet it refused to do so. *You need to get inside.* Turning around he clumsily entered the house.

The lights were off inside, as his mother had never emerged from her room after Stephen had left. Mark was sure his moaning would awake her, but it didn't seem to be disturbing her rest. Taking a few steps into the hallway, he stumbled and crumpled to the ground. On all fours, he spat once again, his teeth feeling as though they were about to fall out of his head. "Oh my God," he gasped, "Oh my God."

Pounding his fists upon the ground as he was ratcheted by yet another painful spasm he waited for the lights to turn on in his mother's room, sure that loud noises would alert her to his suffering. There was nothing. *No one is coming to save you.*

Crawling desperately towards his room, he inched forward and felt his stomach heave. No vomit was forthcoming, but he gagged loudly. Looking pathetic and weak, he clawed his way down the hall only to collapse a few feet from his door.

With his cheek pressed against the cold floor, he debated calling out for his mother. *No,* he decided, *get to your room.* Something was clearly wrong with him. This was the second night in a row he had found himself to be in the throes of some unidentified illness. He had felt fine all day and could not for the life of him think of a single thing he had done to bring on such pain. *This is no bad reaction to what they gave you,* his inner monologue screamed, *this is something else.* Taking a deep breath, he began to panic as a peculiar thought crossed his mind. *Oh my God, it's happening. We're changing.* "No," he yelped. He didn't want to change, didn't want to hurt people. Shaking his head, he dismissed the thought. *Shut the fuck up,* he scolded, *there is no such thing as a werewolf. You're just sick; now get off the floor, you fucking pussy!*

Rising to all fours he took a deep breath and willed himself towards the doorway. Ignoring the twisting, writhing pain in his gut, he pushed open his door and crawled across the ransom. Counting to three, he forced himself to stand up and leapt for the bed, gratefully feeling the soft give of his mattress as he collapsed upon it. Believing it would relax him and cure his ills, he clutched at the sheets as the pain overtook him. It washed over his body like some awful wave, and he assumed the fetal position in response.

Sweating profusely, he began to sob quietly. The pain was too intense; he simply couldn't handle it. The cramps and muscle spasms forced him to flail about. He arched his back, kicked out with his legs, and slapped his arms around the bed. His sobbing became throaty, roaring groans, and his face became angry looking. Clawing at his chest, he began to tear at his ruddy, sweaty skin.

In the throes of powerful spasms, he rolled right off the bed, landing underneath the window. Pounding on the floor with clenched fists, his moaning became more forceful. Guttural and throaty sounding, he believed he sounded inhuman, like something out of a bad horror movie. Unsure of whether or not it was in his head, he began to feel totally overwhelmed by the pain. Unable to endure the agony any longer, he blacked out.

Outside, the wind whistled through the trees, plucking several leaves from their branches. The leaves tumbled and floated earthward, whipped into a series of mini cyclones by the currents. The bare, spindly branches appeared like the fingers of an ogre, and they reached skyward, obscuring the moon's face. As the wind howled and twisted, it was joined by a new sound, one far more threatening. A mournful wail, sounding like an air siren, rose in the distance. Changing in pitch as it reached its crescendo, the unseen animal bayed again and again, a seeming dirge of death. The hunt had begun anew.

XXVIII

The four-door, mid-sized sedan pulled off the road and into the parking lot. As it did so, it emitted a horrible squealing pulse, revealing that its fan belt was going. As the tires righted themselves, the screeching came to a halt while the vehicle hummed along. The parking lot was a long, twisting labyrinth connecting a number of apartment buildings into a singular complex.

The car slowed as it came across the first in a series of yellow speed bumps. The suspension groaned as the car bucked over the bump, and the driver accelerated over the next two in a jarring fashion. Continuing to the last apartment building, it pulled into an open parking space.

Margot Roday cut the engine and flicked off the headlights. Sitting in darkness for a moment, she let out a long sigh. It had been a long day, nearly thirteen hours spent cooking on the line.

She needed a shower and was looking forward to a relaxing night in front of the television set.

She looked in the rearview mirror and stared at her reflection. She was middle aged, large boned, and slightly masculine looking. *No wonder you live alone*, she chided herself while inspecting her face. Disgusted, she hit the rearview mirror and began to gather her belongings. Clutching her purse and a garment bag, she opened the door and exited the vehicle.

As she slammed the door shut, the car's alarm began to sound, a series of rising, annoying chirping and beeping. "Oh, shit," she hissed, fumbling through the pockets of her purple trench coat for her car keys. The car continued to whoop and holler, the headlights flashing rhythmically along with the interior lights. "Shut up," she commanded, depressing a button on her key ring. The car darkened once again, giving two final chirps before falling silent.

Crash!

Margot gasped at the noise as it erupted behind a dumpster just a few feet away. There was the rustling of plastic and the rattle of aluminum cans as they hit the ground. A motion light situated on a nearby street pole flicked on and illuminated the dumpster area. Clutching her chest, Margot began to breathe again as she realized there was nothing there.

It must've been a raccoon. She chuckled nervously. The apartment complex had a real problem with raccoons and skunks digging through the resident's trash and feasting upon the refuse. By the sound of the crash, Margot reasoned, it must have been a particularly large raccoon. Eager to leave the area before the pest returned, she began to waddle towards her building.

A two-storied apartment building with a white façade, it was not particularly remarkable looking. It was roughly two hundred feet long, and most of the windows flickered with a blue light, denoting that most of the residents were glued to their television sets. The thick smell of stale cigarette smoke hung in the air, and Margot dug her face into her jacket in an effort to escape the odor. However, she recoiled from her own stink. She reeked of fry oil and cheap whitefish. *Shower for sure.*

The rattling of a kicked can sounded behind her, followed by a strange wheezing sound. She froze. It was an odd noise, a raspy, phlegm-clogged gasping similar to that of an asthmatic in the midst of an attack or someone with a bad chest cold. She could not explain why, but it made the hairs on the back of her neck stand on end, and she slowly turned and faced the dumpster.

The motion light silhouetted the front of the dumpster and the debris strewn around it. While it was impossible to make out much of anything with distinction, she was certain that no one was there, yet the panting continued. "Hello?" She called, "Is someone there?"

There was a flurry of movement and something scurried out from behind the trash container and quickly crouched behind a nearby car. Margot began to back away, whatever it was had been large and clearly not your average raccoon. Fiddling with her keys, she turned and staggered towards the door, hearing the unidentified beast growling behind her.

Whimpering, she dropped her bags and began to jockey for the right key upon her key ring. She could hear the gravel crunch under the animal's feet, and she was sure it was approaching her. Sobbing, she finally located the correct key, slid it into the lock, and to her relief heard the click as the door unlocked. Flinging the door open, she moved to enter the apartment building only to be hit from behind.

Wham!

Instantly, she was flung to the ground from the force of the strike. The air exploded from her lungs, and a hollow feeling filled her chest. Her head bounced off the floor as she hit, and her temples throbbed from the impact. In tremendous pain she struggled to get up and flee the attacking animal.

She could feel its hot breath playing upon the skin of her exposed calf, and she moved to scream, but nothing came out. She could not breathe. There was a trickle of hot saliva upon her flesh, and then she felt the beast's teeth clamp down upon her leg. Flailing about, she felt herself pulled back towards the door as the animal began to claw at her back. Still trying to cry out, she was horrified as she heard the sound of her own ripping flesh.

* * *

Ken Greco sat on his couch munching loudly upon potato chips. The television set flickered in front of him, a procession of moving images, although he could not hear anything that was being said as his stereo blared loudly. A rhythmic pulsing of bass drums and screaming electric guitars, it was impossible to hear anything in the apartment over the sounds of heavy metal.

His brother Pete exited the bathroom, the horrid smell of last night's dinner wafting by Ken's nose. "Oh dude, what the fuck?" Ken protested, "Light a fucking match."

"What?" Pete screamed, unable to hear his brother.

"I said light a fucking match!" Ken cried out.

Still not able to make out what his brother was demanding, Pete stomped towards the stereo and flicked it off. "What did you say?"

"I said—," Ken began, stopping suddenly when a muffled scream came through the walls. His brother's confused look told Ken that he was not hearing things. "What the hell was that?"

"I don't know," Pete said.

Dropping the bag of chips, Ken knelt upon the couch and pressed his hear up to the wall. Unable to make out anything with a great deal of clarity he heard only series of bumps and thuds.

"Hear anything?" Pete whispered, edging closer to the couch.

"Shhhh," Ken hissed, telling his brother to be silent. The thuds seemed to be slowing, and Ken removed his head from the wall. Turning towards his brother he shrugged his shoulders. "I don't know what I just heard."

There was new sound, a scratching noise, and Ken turned towards his front door. His brother's fluffy, brown Himalayan cat sat pawing at the front door. Looking up at its owners plaintively, the bundle of hair begged to be released from the confines of the apartment.

"JP get away from there," Ken demanded, leaping from the couch and shooing the cat away from the door with his shoe. As he did so, he found that the scratching did not cease. Loud and noticeable, Ken realized that something was scratching at the wood on the other side of the door. His eyes went wide, and he looked back at his brother.

Pete held his arms wide and mouthed, "What is that?"

Ken mirrored his brother's posture, signaling that he had no clue. Slowly, he peered through the peephole in their apartment door. The hallway outside appeared empty and devoid of life, yet Ken knew that wasn't possible because the scratching persisted. In the wake of the scream, it was eerie and nerve-racking, just completely out of place to Ken. It refused to stop, filling the apartment with the grating noise.

Ken decided he had to know just what was pawing at his door. Most likely it was just someone else's cat, he assured himself. *Nothing to worry about, you're just being paranoid.* Still, he slid the chain latch into place for some added protection before undoing the deadbolt and, without consulting his brother, opened the door a crack. Peering down, he immediately slammed the door shut.

"Holy fucking shit!" He exclaimed to his brother while he fumbled with the deadbolt.

"What is it?" Pete demanded, but before Ken could answer there was a roar from the other side of the entryway, a throaty, blood-curdling bellow. Pete froze as whatever was on the other side of the door began to shoulder its way in. Ken placed his weight against the door, attempting to hold its shut and deny entry to the monster on the other side.

"What the fuck?" He shouted at his brother, "get over here and help me before it gets in!"

Pete shook himself out of his frozen state and lurched towards the door to assist his sibling. The thing on the other side continued to roar and claw at the door, continually bumping it open just a few feet before the chain latch and Ken's weight forced it shut. As Pete laid his hands upon the portal, there was the sickening sound of splintering wood, and he found himself flung backwards, the door landing on him as he hit the floor.

Disorientated and in pain, he was jarred back into focus by the screams of his brother. Turning to his right he could see his younger sibling struggling to fight off an unseen opponent. His view obscured by the door, Pete watched in horror as Ken's head snapped back and the younger sibling squealed through clenched teeth. There was a wet, sloshing sound and blood spurted through the gap in Ken's front teeth, the hot liquid smacking Pete between the eyes.

Frightened beyond belief, Pete struggled to free himself from the weight of the door that pinned him to the ground. Wriggling free, he forgot his brother and ran for his bedroom, choosing not to catch a glimpse of the unidentified assailant. His heart racing he jumped into his room and slammed the door shut, throwing a nearby dresser in front of the entryway for good measure. Backing away, he tripped backwards over the edge of his bed and clambered towards the other side of the mattress before hunkering down. Still huffing and puffing he searched frantically for his cell phone, but stopped suddenly when he realized Ken had stopped screaming.

Trying to control his breathing, he peered over his bed and stared in terror at the doorway. There was a raspy wheezing coming from the other room, and Pete felt a lump in his throat as a shadow fell over the cracks in the doorway. There was a thump, and the dresser shifted slightly as whatever it was on the other side attempted to enter the room.

Hopeful at the possibility his makeshift barrier would hold, Pete continued to stare just as the unknown intruder threw its full weight against the door in a far more violent attempt to gain access to the room. Pete yelped as the hinges gave way and the attacker burst forth into the room, the door splintering over his impromptu barricade.

Outside of the building, Pete's muffled screams could be heard, dark shadows flickering across the yellow light filtering out his window. There was also something else, the snarls and roars of an enraged beast filled the air. As Pete unleashed a high pitched wail, a torrent of blood smacked against the window, crimson light now shining outwards. Soon, everything became still; an uneasy silence hung in the air only to be pierced by the screech of one clearly unhappy cat.

XXIX

Rob Lambert sat contently in the driver's seat of his truck, marveling at the moon's reflection off the glassy surface of the water ahead. His leg propped upon the dashboard, he tapped his foot lightly upon the windshield keeping rhythm with the country tune that spilled forth from the car speakers. "...*Work, work, all week long...,*" the singer warbled and Lambert attempted to sing along before resorting to lightly humming along as he realized his singing voice was horrible, *like nails across a chalkboard.* Breathing in deeply, he reached over to the passenger side and pulled a greasy little clam from the white bag at his side, popping the tender little morsel in his mouth. Closing his eyes as he chewed, he was tempted to moan in ecstasy as he savored the salty sweetness of the clam; the juices cascading down his tongue. Swallowing, he leaned his head back, still keeping time with his foot.

His wife would kill him if she knew he was eating fried clams and a large side of fries. He had been struggling with heart problems and high cholesterol for years, but who could resist that which came out of a grease stained bag? *Besides,* Lambert smiled, *eating yourself to death would be a good way to go.* What was the point of living longer if you had to deny yourself the finer things in life in order to do so? It wasn't like he could get clams for much longer anyways, in just a few weeks it'd be winter. Who the hell wanted fried clams in the dead of winter? This was good beach food, the stuff of summer. Opening his eyes, Lambert's gaze returned to the water. Nobody came to the beach in the fall; it was why he liked it, just a nice peaceful place where he could be alone and divulge in his favorite vice. Licking his lips, he popped another clam in his mouth chewing slowly, enjoying every bite.

To his rear the muffled sounds of dogs barking came forth, becoming more insistent with every moment. Lambert couldn't blame them, stuck in a cramped, dark cage in the back of some strange vehicle. No doubt they were frightened, probably smelled his clams too. Turning up the volume on the radio he drowned them out, continuing to devour the remnants of his greasy meal. He knew he should take the dogs back to the pound and offload them, but he wasn't ready to call it a day just yet. He got few "quiet" moments like these, at home his wife would just be on his ass; wouldn't even let him chill in front of the TV. The overtime pay he was receiving right now didn't hurt either.

"*Rob?*" The dashboard handset crackled, "*Hey, Lambert, you still on?*"

Lambert sighed, wiping his greasy hand on his shirt before reaching over his gut and grabbing the receiver, "Yeah, I'm here, go ahead."

"*Where are you, a bar?*"

Grumbling, Lambert switched off the car radio; the crooning Southern accent emanating from his dashboard ceasing to exist. "No," Lambert harrumphed, "just the radio what's up? Did my Goddamn wife call again?"

"*No,*" the radio hissed, "*I've got a woman over on Triphammer, says something's trying to get her dogs.*"

"Some *thing's* trying to get her dogs?" Lambert croaked, "What is it a coyote?"

"*Probably, you want me to try someone else? I think Sam's on over in Rockland.*"

"No, no," Lambert responded, "I got it." Shifting in his seat, Lambert pulled his leg down and flung the receiver at the dashboard, the small handset bobbing up and down, suspended by its curled chord. He turned the key in the ignition and the vehicle rumbled to life. In response the dogs in the back began to howl and whine, their barking reaching a fever pitch. "Shut up!" Lambert insisted, pounding upon his seat for good measure before shifting the car into gear and exiting the parking lot. As he eased the truck into traffic he looking longingly towards the passenger seat, lamenting with grease stained lips that his beloved clams would have to wait.

Lambert drove the truck slowly towards the curb, the brakes squealing as he brought the vehicle to a halt in front of a frond of bushes just a few yards away from a well lit house. *A veritable Mcmansion*, he grumbled. A stately house, it would have suited most people's taste, but it was available only to those residing in the upper middle class, a strata Lambert was far from belonging to. Deriding the fact that it was indistinguishable from the neighboring houses was Lambert's way of convincing himself he wouldn't want such a house were he able to afford it anyways. Turning off the car, Lambert exited the vehicle; the door hinges groaning as he did so. Slamming it shut he retrieved his animal snare from the truck's side panel as the dogs continuing to yip and whimper from with-in. "Shut up, shut up," he barked before taking a deep breath and waddling towards the homestead.

He had barely set foot upon the driveway when the porch light went on, a middle aged woman stepping out onto the front step, clad in a pink bathrobe and a cocker spaniel tucked beneath her arm. Lambert watched as another spaniel, with a pink ribbon in its hair, crawled in between her feet.

"Did you call animal control ma'am?" Lambert asked as he approached the house.

"There's something in the back," she nodded, not even bothering to engage the animal control officer with a polite word of welcome. "I took my girls out back to do their business and it came at us. It was trying to get my spaniels."

Lambert inspected the woman as he got closer. Her skin shimmered in the dull light of the porch and in most cases she would be considered attractive as her short, blonde hair accentuated her Nordic features perfectly. However, she now looked worried, positively agitated, and her pained expression drew attention to the wrinkles surrounding her mouth and eyes in an absolutely unflattering light.

"It?" Lambert questioned, removing his focus from the woman's physical appearance.

"It was big, and black," she responded, raising the spaniel in her arm to her face like a child with a teddy bear. "Please hurry Lilly's still out there."

"Lilly?" Lambert asked, "Your child?"

"No," she shook her head, "Lilly my spaniel."

Christ, Lambert thought, *she has another one?* "Well, sit tight," Lambert instructed, "I'll get it."

Shooing her dog into the house, she closed the door behind her and Lambert could hear the click as she locked the door. *What the hell does she think is out here?* Shaking his head, Lambert raised his snare, the noose dangling from the long line. Whatever was out here the woman was acting as if it was something big and dangerous and he wondered for a moment whether or not the snare would keep it at bay. It was probably just a large dog or a coyote, anxious to gnaw down on this woman's pets, yet Lambert could never be certain. For a moment the image of the dead dog he had found weeks earlier, its mutilated remains scattered amongst the brush, flashed in his head. Could this be the unknown creature that had done that? What had that cop said had attacked the kid and the dog? A wolf? Lambert wasn't sure of any wolves prowling nearby, he was sure it wasn't possible, but then again he certainly didn't want to find out.

Moving into the shadows towards the rear of the house he could feel his skin flush hot as a mixture of fear and adrenaline crept upon him. His mind began to run wild, beginning to think about the news report he had heard earlier, the elderly man mutilated in his own backyard on Talbot Road. Might it have been an animal that did it? A torrent of fearful images flooded his thoughts, fraying his nerves and causing his heart to race. *Calm yourself man*, he soothed, *probably just someone's escaped pit-bull.* Shaking his head, so as to free himself from his own clouded thoughts, he continued onto the backyard. His mouth dry from fear, he struggled to whistle. "Here Lilly, Lilly," he cooed, "come on girl, I'm not gonna hurt you."

Instantly, the bushes at the perimeter of the yard began to tremble, twigs snapping as something large moved quickly through the undergrowth. Lambert's heart sank and he let loose with an embarrassing whimper, clearly that had been no

cocker spaniel. Backing up slowly his blood ran
cold as he heard a low, threatening growl emanate
from the shadows of the forest. Whatever it was,
it sounded large and intimidating. He needed
more than just a snare. The unseen animal moved
again, the crashing in the darkness announcing
its travels. Still backing up, Lambert had moved
into the front yard, the light of the front porch
offering cold comfort in the face of a threatening
beast. Still searching the darkness for the animal
now menacing him Lambert's heart stopped as the
air filled with noise.

The headlights of his truck began flashing
intermittently, the car alarm blaring with a series
of siren noises and whoops. Dropping his snare,
Lambert rushed towards the vehicle, clutching
his ears as he came closer. The alarm reverted
to sounding the horn every few seconds, a truly
deafening noise for anyone who came close. To his
chagrin and horror, both doors were already pulled
wide open and his keys inexplicably dangled from
the ignition. The radio was turned to maximum
volume, an unidentifiable pop song booming
forth. Still clutching his ears, Lambert reached in
and disabled the alarm, removing the keys so as
to cut off the music. Breathing heavily, Lambert
sought to collect his thoughts in the overwhelming
silence which now followed the noise.

Slowly, his hearing returned, the barking of
the dogs becoming louder and louder. He was still
in the process of collecting himself as the screech

of several whining hinges filled the air and he knew instantly a number of dog cages had been flung open. Removing himself from the front seat he watched in shock as several of the dogs he had spent the day catching ran headlong into the forest. "Get back here!" Lambert screamed, knowing full well that it was futile effort. Waddling after them in a half-hearted effort, he listened in defeat as the barking of the dogs became muffled and distant, knowing full well they were all long gone. Bewildered and struggling to calm his beating heart, Lambert looked at the yawning cages, the doors waving at him in a provocative manner. Turning, he inspected the open doors of his truck and the radio. *This is no animal,* Lambert reflected, *it's a bunch of kids, fucking with the fat guy.* Looking at the passenger side he bristled as he realized whoever it was had spilled his precious fried food upon the vehicle floor. His long desired meal was now wasted, nothing more than crushed breading and shellfish upon the rubber flooring.

Lambert's fear morphed into an intense anger, his vision turned white. Leaning over the driver's seat he ripped open the glove compartment and withdrew the small revolver he kept for emergency situations. Checking that it was loaded, he slammed the vehicle's doors shut and began stomping back towards the backyard. If these kids thought they were going to have fun at his expense, he was going to make them piss their pants and cry for their mommies. Marching into the shadows cocksure and full of anger Lambert shouted into the darkness, "Get your little asses out here you assholes!"

There was no answer in response, but Lambert was sure that just beyond the tree line a bunch of teenagers giggled at him from the safety of the shadows. This made him angrier; no one made a fool out of him. "I am not fucking around you pieces of shit. I am a law enforcement officer and I do have a gun and I sure as hell will use it unless you get the hell out here by the count of three!"

Cocking his gun, Lambert began to count, "One!" There was nothing.

"Two!" Now the bushes began to rustle, something rushed him from the shadows and without thinking Lambert turned and fired.

Blam!

The gunshot thundered in his ears and Lambert began to gasp as he came to his senses, realizing he may have just shot a kid. Fumbling with his belt, he produced his flashlight and shined it in the direction of where he had fired. He swallowed hard as the light fell over his target. He saw the mop of blonde and black fur first before following the beam of light to where the top of the head should have been, now just a red, soupy mass with only the bottom jaw intact and identifiable. He looked back at the house realizing what he had done. Clearly, he had just dispatched Lilly, the woman's missing cocker spaniel.

As he struggled with what to do with the carcass there was another rustling in the bushes to his rear. Lambert heard the sound of heavy footfalls before whatever it was thundered into the open. Swiveling, he trained his light upon the noise and yelped in fear as he illuminated the velvet, black pelt of a large canine. Catching only a quick glimpse of its fangs and yellow eyes, he depressed the trigger instinctively.

Blam!

The gun shuddered and Lambert watched as the animal momentarily staggered before continuing to the front of the house and out of his field of vision. He shivered in fear; the thing had been huge and menacing looking. And he had hit it. This thought brought an intense feeling of dread over Lambert. Not only was something large and threatening out there, but he had wounded it and probably pissed it off. Forgetting about Lilly's destroyed body Lambert began to run awkwardly back to his truck, seeking to flee the area. Arriving at the driver's side door he dropped his flashlight and began to fumble around with the door handle before realizing it was locked. Whimpering, he moved to the other door and tried to open it, crying out as he realized it too was locked. Feeling for his keys he caught sight of them upon the passenger seat, realizing in horror that he must have thrown them there before locking the doors and stomping into the backyard.

His heart thundered in his ears and he began to perspire, his breathing coming at a rapid clip. This stopped when he heard a rustling behind him. Wheeling around, he trained his gun on the forest, straining to see or hear anything. There was a metallic screech behind him as something raked across the rear bumper of the truck and Lambert pivoted in that direction, unable to see anything despite the light of the full moon. Still focused upon the rear end of the vehicle, Lambert had no time to react as the beast sprung forth from the trees behind him. Instantly, the fangs clamped around his throat stifling his attempted scream. Lambert struggled to free himself but was pulled to the ground with stunning speed. Kicking and flailing, he was dragged into the forest, leaving nothing but his truck and few fried clams in his wake.

XXX

The clock upon the wall continued to tick, each jittery movement of its spindly hand audibly counting down the seconds. It was an annoying sound, and Mark found it to be unnecessary in this age of digital clocks. However, that was under usual circumstances. Right now he was so grateful for the reassuring click the clock emitted every second, piercing the uncomfortable silence which hung over the room like a pall of smoke.

Slouching in the uncomfortably rigid chair, he could feel the thick polyester of his fatigues grating upon his skin as his weight pulled the material against the flesh of his rear end. He sat motionlessly, staring blankly across the desk at the man across from him. A younger man with sharp, angular features, his dark skin betrayed his ancestral roots to be of the Indian subcontinent, and it stood in stark contrast to the chalky gray color of his army fatigues. Dr. Christman, or Adam as he liked to be called by his patients, was Mark's main liaison with the psychiatry department on base. His hands folded upon his desk, he ran his tongue over his lips and leaned forward. "So, you were afraid over there?" His tone was calm, and he spoke in almost a whisper.

Mark fought back the urge to frown, or show his displeasure with the question. Christman was always asking repetitive, obvious questions, and Mark wondered just what the man was searching for. "I wasn't not afraid," Mark deadpanned, the sarcasm and annoyance barely hidden in his answer.

Christman frowned, his distaste for the response painfully evident. "Now Mark," he scolded lightly, "we're not going to get anywhere if you don't respond properly."

Mark sat up a little bit in his chair, lightly lifting up his hands in surrender. "Sorry, sorry, my bad." Breathing deeply he sighed. "Yes, I was afraid over there."

"Okay," Christman nodded, seemingly pleased by his patient's new reply. "Do you want to talk about it? Anything in particular that caused you anxiety, some incident which really stands out in your mind? Anything at all really, go ahead." Anticipating Mark's reply, Christman leaned back in his chair, placing his hands beneath his chin.

Mark sat there blankly, unsure of how to respond. *Anything in particular, you fucking asshole?*

I was in a warzone, dick. Maintaining his calm though annoyed demeanor, Mark shrugged his shoulders and shook his head, "No, nothing stands out."

Christman leaned forward again, "Oh, come on Mark. You have to open up to me, or else nothing's ever going to get better." Pausing for a moment something dawned on him, a new tool with which he could prod his young patient with, "And the sooner you get better, the quicker you get to go home."

Home, the word struck Mark. It was an abstract idea, since his home life had been in shambles long before he found himself in this austere room, with its sickly white walls and uncomfortable office furniture, but it was a comforting one. Home was certainly better than here, and it was infinitely better than Iraq. He wanted to go back home. Straightening out, he nodded his head slowly. "Okay." His eyebrows rose, and looking at the floor, he began to speak, "Um, yeah, okay, the whole IED thing freaked me out, really rattled my nerves."

"And what about them?" Christman interrogated.

Was this guy serious? "Um, you know," Mark shrugged, "just the very unpredictability of them I suppose, that they could be anywhere. You step upon a sidewalk or turn around the wrong bend and all of a sudden you're gone, blown to pieces."

"And the concept of death unnerves you?"

Mark looked up at Christman and sighed. "I mean yeah, I know as a soldier it's one of the hazards that comes with the job, but that doesn't really mean you're ready for it. I mean, I'm young; it's not something you want to be thinking about, especially constantly, at such an age. Dying is something you do when you're old. You realize it's an inevitably of life, but you don't want it to be so quickly."

Christman sat back, and Mark couldn't help but notice the faint beginnings of a smile at the corners of the psychiatrist's lips. *He's enjoying this,* Mark noted. *He loves the fact that I'm pouring my guts out.*

"So these thoughts overwhelmed you?" Christman asked.

Mark frowned, "I suppose they did. Over there it is a constant thought. Death is a constant companion. Not just your death per se, but also the death of civilians, and even the enemy. After awhile you just get too caught up in your thoughts, too engrossed with the stench of dead and dying things. I suppose I just kind of lost all rational perspective. I guess I couldn't handle it."

"Did you yourself inflict death upon people, Mark?" Christman demanded.

"That's a little awkward of a question to put to someone, isn't it?" Mark answered, surprised that his own inner monologue had voiced itself.

Christman shrugged. "Sorry, I mean did you yourself have to kill the enemy? I mean all these constant thoughts of death—did it strike you when you had to cause the death of someone else?"

"Yes," Mark whispered.

"Even if they were trying to kill you in turn, to cause your death?"

Mark simply nodded his response.

"How did it make you feel, Mark? How did it feel to kill someone?"

Mark shrugged.

"Do you consider yourself a violent man, Mark?" Christman pressed.

Mark's head snapped up, his mouth open, searching for the right answer. Unable to speak, he suddenly became aware once again of the sound of the clicking clock. The noise was more violent now, far more pronounced. As the hand continued to move around the clock, the noise began to morph into something not all together recognizable, and Mark became confused, his brow furrowing. Looking from the clock to the stone-faced visage of Dr. Christman, the psychiatrist still patiently awaiting an answer, he noticed the periphery of his vision begin to become blurry and the room begin to fade away . . .

The murmur of the crowd caused him to rustle, but it was the sound of barking dogs that forced him to finally open his eyes. Shivering from the cold, he was disoriented and confused. The left side of his face ached as it was pressed against the freezing asphalt. With a cough, his body ejected a stream of yellow spittle. The now too-familiar, awful taste was in his mouth. Enos gagged as the flavor rolled over his tongue; it was raw and fishy in nature, threatening to induce a fit of vomiting at any moment.

Suffering from the cold, he lifted his head off the ground, only to be horrified with what he saw. He was naked, covered only with a fine film of blood and hair; it enveloped him, seeping into nearly every crevice of his naked body. Rather than being in his bed, he found himself camped next to a trash dumpster, the refuse of countless homesteads surrounding him. Examining himself, he was bewildered, not completely grasping the totality of his circumstances. *How did I get here? Whose blood is this?*

He gazed up at the sky and found it to be a purple-gray. Coupled with the freezing temperatures, Enos surmised that the sun was just now dawning, and it was early morning. A forest of dead, ash-colored trees flanked his position, and from his vantage point behind the dumpster he could view the front ends of a few cars off to his left. He was obviously in the parking lot of a residential or business complex of some sort, just where exactly, he did not know.

The barking of the dogs was muffled, as if the animals were off in the distance. Yet, there was a frightening closeness to their calls. Enos found the baying of the dogs to be alarmingly similar to those of the canine units which had confronted him just twenty-four hours before. Clearly, the racket they were causing along with the sound of chattering masses warranted investigation.

Moving his aching body, he grasped the lid of the green dumpster and lifted himself up in order to peer over the trash container. Staring in the direction he perceived the dogs to be, he gasped and immediately ducked down, crouching close to the dumpster. Did he really just see that? Was this really happening?

His heart began to race, and he forgot how cold he was. Hyperventilating, he clutched at his chest and began to sweat. Withdrawing his hand, he stared in disgust as his blood-stained fingers. "Oh my God," he gasped, "Jesus Christ." *Calm down Mark, you're going to give yourself a heart attack.* Doubling over, he began to consciously control his breathing, taking deep, rhythmic inhalations. Closing his eyes, he waited until his respiration assumed a normal pace and his heart slowed to its basal rate.

Sitting back against the cold metal of the trash dumpster, he steeled his nerves for another look over the container. Crouching down he raised himself up so that only the top of his head was visible. He could not believe what he saw.

Just a hundred yards away a swarm of police and rescue personnel milled about the entrance of what Mark could only assume was an apartment building. The scene was reminiscent of what had taken place earlier outside of Mr. Lamperti's house. A myriad of police cruisers, some white, others blue and grey, were arrayed around the structure's entrance, their blue siren lights playing upon the building's façade.

A group of onlookers stood outside, braving the cold in their pajamas and robes, confirming Mark's belief that it was early morning. Some of them appeared horrified; others looked groggy as though just waking up. Still others looked downright angry that their sleep had been disturbed and they voiced their displeasure loudly to anyone within shouting distance.

The dogs that had rustled Mark awake with their incessant squawking were arranged in teams of two, prowling the grounds of the apartment building. Mark watched in fear as the animals patrolled the area, their noses pressed to the ground. Each animal unleashed a throaty bark periodically as if conversing with the other canines, only to be scolded by the officers leashing them. Mark knew it was only a matter of time before they caught his scent and set upon him.

There was a tremendous thundering sound as a news chopper raced overhead, causing Mark to reflexively duck back behind the trash container. The whipping blades thumping through the air, coupled with the unceasing murmur of the crowd brought back horrible flashbacks of the warzone. Closing his eyes he could see the Blackhawk helicopters circling over the devastated cityscape, and he began to rock back and forth.

There was no calming himself now. Sobbing lightly, he began to wrestle with the thoughts racing through his head. He had no recollection of the previous night. Like the evening before that, he only remembered a feeling of tremendous pain before his mind went blank. *There is no doubt now,* he reasoned. He had awoken covered in blood once again, and this time no more than a few hundred feet from the scene of some unspeakable crime rather than in his bed. *I'm a murderer.* It was unfathomable to him the harm he had no doubt caused the night previous. *How many people did I hurt last night?*

He had changed last night, he surmised. *Oh my god, this is really happening.* He began to believe, began to recognize that something was remiss here. "What the fuck bit me?" He sobbed, still rocking back and forth, "what the fuck bit me?"

It had been a full moon last night, just like the night before; two nights with the same result leading to one conclusion. "I'm a werewolf," Mark whispered, vocalizing his troubling thoughts.

"I'm a fucking werewolf," he said again, louder this time.

How many people did I kill last night? He fretted, *more than one?* Grappling with this question, he suddenly realized something horrible, morbid in nature, and thoroughly grotesque. He knew now what the horrible taste was, recognizing his conclusion as fact. It was the sickening aftertaste of raw meat, human flesh he had swallowed the night before while dismembering his unfortunate victims. Breathing heavily, Mark doubled over and retched everywhere.

Sputtering and coughing, he looked down and viewed the former contents of his stomach.

It was a red, chunky liquid, flecks of what looked like meat and hair littering the viscous material. Overwhelmed by this sight, Mark's stomach heaved once again, the vomit smacking upon the asphalt. Mark struggled to recover his breath, spitting repeatedly. Long spindles of drool hung from his gaping jaws.

Feeling sorry for himself momentarily, he was snapped back into focus once again by the barking of the dogs. It was louder now and rang in his ears with surprising clarity. Unable to actually gauge their distance, the noise assured him they were in close proximity. He had to get out of there. Fighting the urge to vomit once again, he stumbled forward, staying low so as not to draw any attention. Scared out of his mind, he crawled forward, slipping into the dead forest and fighting his way through the dense brush towards home.

XXXI

Kaplan approached the apartment building's entrance with a great sense of trepidation. He felt as if he were in slow motion, as though he were in a dream-like state. Propelled on legs of stone, he crouched under a string of yellow crime scene tape and walked through the crowd of rescue personnel.

He was dismayed by their demure and sorrowful expressions. Many of the officers possessed the thousand-yard stare of a combat veteran; as if they had lost their faith in morality and all that is holy, Kaplan reflected. He felt thoroughly unprepared for what he was about to see, and as he came near the columned entrance way of the structure, he felt even more lost.

The base of the white columns were stained a light crimson, and a now dried black puddle had coalesced at the bottom of the concrete stairs. As the crowd parted, Kaplan placed a hand to his mouth as he now viewed the mutilated body of a heavy set woman. She lay face down, her arms stretched forward as though she had been struggling to get away until her very last breath. Her back was a bloody mess, the purple coat she had been wearing torn away along with her flesh, revealing her brown and green innards. In a macabre thought, Kaplan reflected that the woman's back looked like that of a turkey after Thanksgiving dinner.

Moving closer, Kaplan viewed a series of marks upon her pasty legs where the meat had been removed in a semi-circular pattern similar to that of Lamperti's body. Cameramen moved from one point of the body to another while a small gathering of crime scene technicians pored over the surrounding area. Kaplan stood silent, not looking any of them in the eye, until a familiar voice greeted him, "Howdy partner."

Kaplan looked up slowly and nodded at the approaching Henry.

"I'd be lying if I said it was good to see you under the circumstances," the trooper continued.

Kaplan looked back at the woman's body, struggling to speak as his mouth had gone dry. "Wha—" he croaked, before clearing his throat. "Who was she?"

Henry descended from the concrete stairs and stood by Kaplan's side. "Meet Margot Roday. Worked at some greasy spoon over in Weymouth. Her boss said she worked late last night and we found her work gear in the bag she was carrying."

"What happened to her?" Kaplan questioned.

"Far as we can tell she was ambushed from behind, and as you can see, the bastard really tore into her," Henry said, motioning towards the body. His angry tone enhanced his harsh Massachusetts accent to the point where the word bastard was now pronounced 'bastahd,' the *r* mysteriously disappearing. "Can't tell for sure until we get an autopsy, but I'm assuming cause of death is she just bled out from her wounds. I mean look at her." He gestured. "It's like he just stripped the meat off her bones."

"Was it our guy?"

"If I had to hazard a guess, I'd bet on it. That's why I had them call you in," Henry answered. "You think this is bad, you should see what he did to the others."

Kaplan snapped out of his haze and cast a forlorn look Henry's way. "There are others?"

"Oh yeah, buddy, I've got two more stiffs upstairs," he replied callously. "You're gonna need booties for this." He dangled a pair of cloth slipper coverings and winked at Kaplan. "It's a real wet one up there."

Kaplan grabbed the coverings and dutifully slipped them over his shoes. When he was done, he found Henry was now offering a pair of latex gloves. Donning the gloves, Kaplan stopped. "There're no dead kids up there, right?" He didn't know if he could handle the sight of a mutilated child.

"No," Henry assured him. "I've got two brothers in their twenties up there, Peter and Kenneth Greco."

Kaplan breathed a sigh of relief. "Okay." Finishing with his gloves, he nodded at Henry. "All right let's go."

Henry led them up the small staircase, helping his temporary colleague navigate around the woman's body. Kaplan took one more painful look down at the corpse, wincing as he got an overhead look at Ms. Roday's inner workings.

As they entered the building, Kaplan found it to be even more overcrowded than outside. A crowd of uniformed personnel were gathered upon the narrow stairwell ahead, and a considerable number milled about in the narrow hallway above. Kaplan watched as members of the crime scene unit filtered in, and out of a doorway just beyond the stairway landing, those exiting emerged with a pained look upon their faces.

"I'm assuming you gleaned these people's identities from their wallets?" Kaplan asked as they climbed the small flight of stairs.

"You'd be correct, buddy," Henry answered.

"So, just like Lamperti, robbery wasn't the motive."

"Just like the Lamperti case," Henry replied, "I don't think our boy's in it for money. I guess we can throw your animal attack theory out the window, and I suppose you were right about the Enos kid."

Waiting for Kaplan to finish ascending the stairs, Henry beamed. "My sick psycho theory isn't looking so bad now is it?"

Kaplan didn't respond, choosing to slip past Henry and approach the open doorway. Even from a few feet away Kaplan could see that the entranceway was damaged, the wood of the doorframe cracked and splintered in spots. Taking a few last steps, Kaplan stopped short at the apartment entrance, unsure of how to proceed.

The white door of the apartment lay on the floor just beyond where it should be. It was scratched and heavily damaged, the hinges bent with the wood around them having cracked. Blood was spattered upon the door's face in a fan shaped pattern. Kaplan did not have to look far for the source of the splatter.

A young man was next to the door, his face clenched in the throes of agony. His body was in worse shape than the woman's outside. The chest cavity had been torn open, his yellow, stringy intestines strewn about. Kaplan was thankful for the fact that the black fleece shirt he was wearing obscured much of the damage as bits of torn fabric intermingled with shredded flesh. Stepping back in horror, Kaplan became aware of Henry's presence just behind him.

"That's Kenneth Greco, younger of the two," Henry informed. "Believe it or not, he's in better shape than his brother."

"Where's he?" Kaplan asked his voice barely above a whisper.

"Bedroom just ahead." Henry nodded.

Kaplan moved into the apartment slowly, making sure as to not come to close to the mutilated corpse. Walking on wobbly knees, he headed towards an open bedroom door just a few feet away. Like the apartment door, it too was in shambles, now nothing more than a few planks of wood laid over a damaged dresser. Kaplan found himself not able to move after arriving at the precipice of the bedroom. "Oh my God," he moaned.

Blood was splattered upon the bedroom's walls, as if someone had taken red paint and cast it in every direction. The blood had pooled upon the floor, seeping into the carpet, turning it from tan in color to a deep crimson. The body of the room's occupant lay splayed upon the bed. His white tank top ripped away and his entrails on full display. That would have been disgusting enough without the fact that the body had been decapitated, nothing more than a red stump where is head should have been.

Henry arrived next to Kaplan as if on cue. "See what I meant?"

"Where the hell is his head?" Kaplan demanded.

"Other side of the bed," Henry replied nonchalantly.

Kaplan moved in slowly and peered around the bed, finding the man's missing cranium. The head was slack-jawed, the tongue sticking out as if it had been ripped off mid-scream, and the bulging eyes stared directly at Kaplan. "Oh, Jesus Christ," he yelped. "What the fuck did he do that with?"

"I have no clue, honestly, but we've scoured this entire place and it doesn't appear he used one of the kitchen knives as far as I can tell. I mean, hell, it looks like he just ripped it off," Henry answered.

"This is way worse than yesterday, way worse," Kaplan exclaimed, waving his arms around animatedly.

"Our guy's really taking it up a notch," Henry nodded, "He's got to be strong as hell too. I hate to speak ill of the dead, but it's not as if that woman outside was exactly dainty; she couldn't have been a pushover. Then he came in here, overpowers two young men in their prime, and guts them on top of that. Fuck, he even tears this poor bastard's head off. I'm telling you we're looking for a roid head or something, big son of a bitch."

Kaplan looked around the room. "This had to have been loud as hell. Nobody heard anything?"

"Nobody's come forward. It seems our two dead young guys here, Ken and Pete, were quite the partiers. Neighbors said loud noises coming from their apartment wasn't anything new."

"Oh, bullshit," Kaplan spat, "you're telling me these people couldn't tell the difference between people partying and people screaming bloody blue murder?"

"Apparently not, my friend." Henry shrugged. "In fact, the guy who discovered the mess was just some poor schmuck going out for his morning coffee."

"Jesus Christ, this is the suburbs not the city, damn it," Kaplan remarked. "People are desensitized to shit like this. They call the cops for Christ's sake out here."

"I hear you buddy, but the neighbor's lack of action doesn't change the fact that we're dealing with one sick puppy, compadre."

"I know, I know, it's still just infuriating," Kaplan said, retreating from the bedroom.

"No, I don't think you do know," Henry said calmly.

"What do you mean?" Kaplan asked, struggling to contain his emotions and his breakfast.

"Medical Examiner found what he believed to be teeth marks on the first victim's body during yesterday's autopsy."

"The bastard bit him?"

"Didn't just bite him buddy, he tore out some nice chunks for himself, real fine cuts of meat."

Fighting the urge to gag, Kaplan bristled at Henry's frequently uncouth manner at these crime scenes. He realized that it reflected the older man's years of experience around dead bodies, but Kaplan found it disrespectful and patently offensive. Still, he managed to compose himself and ignore the trooper's attitude, all while keeping down his food. "What are you saying? He ate parts of him?"

"Bingo," Henry winked, "and judging by the mark's on Big Bertha outside and the condition of these two poor souls, I'd say he had himself quite a feast last night too."

"You're not saying that's his motive are you?"

"Not saying anything just yet." Henry waved. "Just saying we're dealing with a guy who's clearly in it for the thrill of kill, and the usual stuff like money and revenge isn't coming into play."

Kaplan rubbed his chin before snapping his fingers. "Wait, what if the victims are connected? What if it's like a gang hit or something?"

"A gang hit?" Henry snorted. "Look buddy, I don't know about you, but I'm going to say it's safe to assume that an eighty-year-old man, a middle-aged line cook, and two young guys have no connection with each other, let alone a fucking gang."

Kaplan looked down, feeling a little embarrassed.

Recognizing this, Henry softened his tone and placed his hand upon Kaplan's shoulder. "Look, I understand what you're trying to do. You're trying to make sense of all this, but sometimes things happen at random. Sometimes, there is no sense to be made at all."

Kaplan looked up at Henry, still feeling a bit dejected. "Yeah, I guess." He then nodded his head, gathering his thoughts. "We usually don't deal with shit like this here."

Henry removed his hand and held it up. "Hey, believe you me, this is all new on this end as well. This is some Dahmer shit if I've ever seen it, and then some." He fell silent for a moment before asking, "You want to see something fucked up?"

Kaplan spread his hands in disbelief. "This isn't fucked up enough?"

Henry caught himself and waved his hand dismissively. "No, no it is, but I'm saying there is something really just messed up over here." He grabbed Kaplan by the shoulder and led him toward the bathroom, which was situated next to the bedroom they had just exited. Pushing the door open, Henry pointed downwards. "The son of a bitch even took out the cat."

Kaplan stared downwards at the bloody fur ball that had once been the Greco's cat. The body had been gnawed away in the center right down to the spine. Kaplan noted that the feline now looked like the discarded remnants of a fish dinner with only the head, forearms, and rear section remaining. Blood and bits of fur were strewn about the bathroom. Staring down at the sad, mangled animal, its insides torn asunder just as those of its owners, Kaplan began to have flashbacks of the mutilated body of Toby the dog.

He found these confusing at first and believed them to be just his mind associating the two acts as they were both animals. However, he began to sweat profusely and something gave way inside of him. His stomach churned as he began to realize what was happening. Overwhelmed by images of death and gruesome scenery, his body entered into a state of revolt, and as the bubbling in his gut became worse, he removed himself from the bathroom and pushed past Henry.

"Hey where you going?" Henry called after the distressed officer. Picking up speed, Kaplan fled to the hallway and rushed down the stairs, chucking people out of his way as he ran outside and nimbly leapt over the body of Margot Roday.

Getting just a few steps from the apartment building he doubled over, spewing forth the contents of his stomach in spectacular fashion while receiving a smattering of "eewwws" and "ahhhs" from the assembled crowd of onlookers.

XXXII

Mark stumbled through the open window, crashing to the floor. Rubbing his aching head, he assumed the fetal position and began rocking back and forth on the bedroom carpet. Getting home had been a hellish experience involving traversing through miles of forest as branches and twigs scraped at his naked body. Occasionally, when coming upon a road, Mark had been forced to dash across in the buff with only his hands to cover his nether regions from prying eyes.

"Mark, honey, are you all right?" His mother called through the walls. Enos panicked as he heard the door open and he leapt from the floor, rushing towards the entryway.

As his mother entered the room he placed both hands upon her shoulders and began leading her out. "Mom, I think I've done something horrible."

Virginia looked aghast as she viewed her son's nude body. Her mouth moved as she attempted to speak, but it was instantly clear that she did not know exactly what to say. Mark was covered in dried blood, his blonde hair matted to his face, and he stood stark naked, staring at her with a crazed look. "Oh My god, Mark, what happened to you?" she asked finally.

Still pushing her into the hallway, Mark answered her, "Ma, are you listening to me? I've done something awful."

Seeming to ignore his comments, she continued to look him up and down. "Are you hurt? Where did all this blood come from?"

She grasped back at his shoulders, gently resisting his pushing, "You smell terrible, honey; what is going on?"

Enraged by her refusal to listen, Mark tightened his grip on her blouse and jostled her forcefully, "Jesus Christ, Mom, would you fucking listen to me!"

Virginia fell silent, raising her hands in a defensive posture. Her son appeared delirious, seething with anger. His blood-soaked chest heaved up and down rhythmically. His red-yellow teeth were clenched, and he glared at her with dismay.

Mark softened his facial features as his mother ceased to speak. He had not meant to frighten her, but he was scared himself. Lessening his grip upon her lapels, he began to speak, "Mom, I think I really hurt someone last night."

"What are you talking about?" Virginia stammered.

"And . . . " he breathed deeply before continuing, "I think I'm the one who did that to Mr. Lamperti yesterday."

His mother's face darkened. "That's not funny, Mark. That is not funny."

"Listen to me!" He screamed, grabbing her tightly once again, "I am not joking here!"

His mother fell silent again, her lips trembling.

"Look, something's not right with me, Ma. I think I'm really the one who's doing these things, I'm blacking out at night, and I truly think I'm the one hurting these people."

"Mark, what is wrong with you?" She whimpered.

Mark hesitated with his answer. *She wouldn't understand, would she?* Sighing he began to speak, "Mom, I think after that thing attacked me last month, I began to change."

"Yes, I know." His mother bobbed her head animatedly. "You've been really good all month, no more bad dre—."

"No, not like that," he hissed, forcefully cutting her off. "No, I mean physically; I really feel that thing infected me with something, something not natural."

Virginia searched her son's crazed eyes. "Mark, I don't understand. Do you mean like rabies? Is that it, do you think it was rabid?"

"No," Mark growled, "I mean I don't think it was a natural animal. I'm saying that thing cursed me."

Virginia remained silent, not sure how to respond to her son's statement.

"I'm a werewolf, Mom," Mark explained. "That thing attacked me on the night of the full moon, and now I change during the full moon. I changed two nights ago, and I attacked poor Mr. Lamperti."

Appearing at a loss at first, Virginia began to sob loudly. She believed her son had finally cracked, succumbing to delirium, and she continued to cry over his continued rambling.

"And then last night I changed, and I'm sure I did something terrible at an apartment complex across town, Mom." His mother continued to cry and began to struggle against his grip. Clutching her wrists now, Mark went on speaking, "Look, Mom, you've got to believe me. I'm telling you for your own sake. It's a full moon tonight, and there's no telling what I'll do when I transform. I could even hurt you."

Virginia stifled her sobs and looked at her son through watery eyes. "What is wrong with you, Mark? Werewolves don't exist, honey; you've just been watching too much TV."

"I thought the same thing, Mom, but I know differently now. I woke up behind a fucking dumpster for Christ's sake, and there were cops everywhere." Still gripping her wrists, he nodded at his naked body, "And look at me. I'm just covered in blood. The same thing happened to me yesterday morning after you found Lamperti."

Sniffling, she stopped fighting his grasp. Swallowing hard she croaked, "Mark, I'm only saying this as your mother, but I think something's really wrong with you and—"

"Of course there's something wrong with me, woman!" He snarled, "I'm a fucking werewolf!"

Maintaining a calm tone in the face of her son's repeated yelling, Virginia continued, "And I was going to say we need to get you help, you need to see someone."

Mark released her wrists, throwing them towards the floor in disgust. "I don't need someone's help, Ma, I need yours. I mean, we've got to do something. You need to buy some rope to tie me down, or some silver chains, maybe even a silver bullet, just in case."

Virginia stood in the hallway, rubbing her wrists and glaring at her son. "You're not a werewolf, Mark."

"Look, I'm going to get in the shower and then we'll take a ride over to the hardware store for stuff to contain me with," Mark insisted, ignoring his mother's matter-of-fact statement. Brushing by her he entered the bathroom and closed the door.

Virginia stood in the hallway waiting for the squeal of the metal faucets to sound allowing the water to run before lowering her head into her hands and sobbing gently.

XXXIII

Mark exited the bathroom, still toweling himself off. Ignoring conventions, he remained in the buff, using the towel to dry his hair and squeezing it into his ears. Bare bottomed, he continued down the hall and into his room. Washing off the blood today had been worse than the previous occurrence. The scrubbing had left his skin raw and this had irritated the myriad of scratches which had been inflicted on his body during his run through the woods.

Throwing the towel upon his bed, he opened his closet and began to search for something to wear. He wanted something loose and comfortable, an article of clothing which would not press upon his already agitated skin. Looking through the racks, he growled in frustration before turning towards the floor and retrieving the sweats he had doffed one day earlier.

Grabbing the sweat stained clothes, he had a moment of reflection, he must've rid himself of the garments during his transformation. It was a painful reminder of the circumstances in which he found himself. *This is really happening,* he thought. He had always believed lycanthropes resided in the realm of fiction, only existing in the world of entertainment. Now he knew otherwise. Now he knew what went bump in the middle of the night.

Recalling the litany of werewolf films he had viewed as a child, he had always thought that the cursed beings transformed in their clothes, remaining covered, albeit in shredded fabric. *Apparently not,* he mused. *This isn't funny, Mark,* the tiny voice inside him scolded, *you've hurt people.* Shaking his head at this, he slipped on his sweatpants and headed for the hall.

Donning his shirt as he walked towards the kitchen, Mark became aware of hushed voices emanating from the room. Was his mother talking to herself? "Ma, I'm ready to go whenever you are," he called.

No sooner had he spoken when the whispering parties fell silent. This caused Mark to slacken his pace as he approached the kitchen, "Ma?"

There was the sound of his mother clearing her throat and she responded, "I'm in here."

Cautiously, Mark rounded the corner and entered the kitchen. His mother sat at the kitchen table, a steaming mug of coffee clutched between her hands. Her eyes were swollen and red.

Virginia's face betrayed the woman's worriment and sadness. To her side, with a hand upon her shoulder, stood Mark's brother, Stephen, wearing an equally pained expression.

For a moment, the three stared at each other in a bit of awkward silence before Stephen spoke, "So, what's up man?"

His brother's tone sounded forced and condescending and immediately got Mark's back up. "What are you doing here?" He demanded, "Shouldn't you be at work?"

Stephen remained calm and he brushed back a lock of black hair which had fallen in his face, "Well yeah, but Mom called me down here."

"What for?" Mark asked, glaring at his mother.

Stephen appeared uncomfortable, fidgeting with his posture and crossing his arms. "Well, she told me about your conversation, said you might be having some problems."

"I'm fine, man," Mark hissed through clenched teeth. He was annoyed by his mother's transgression, infuriated by the fact that she had called his brother down here. Remembering his mother's final sentences to him before entering the shower, he believed he knew where the conversation was going. *You need help.*

Entering the kitchen, he stomped past his family and towards the counter where the coffee maker was located. Filling a mug with the black brew, he stood seething by the kitchen sink, slowly sipping from his cup.

An uncomfortable silence descended upon the kitchen and hung like a pall over the Enos family. Mark continued to drink, his rigid body posture betraying his anger. Virginia rose her own cup to her mouth, her hands trembling.

Deciding to break the silence once again, Stephen turned towards his brother. "So do you run around on all fours or walk upright like the Wolfman?" he cracked.

Mark slammed his cup down upon the counter. "Fuck you, man, this really isn't funny."

"Oh, come on, dude, do you hear yourself?" Stephen barked. "You really think you're a fucking werewolf?"

"I think I really hurt people last night," Mark retorted, "and I tried to tell you yesterday about Lamperti." There was tinge of sadness which tugged at his heart, coupled with blind rage. Stephen was supposed to be his one true companion, the only person he could fully rely upon, and now he was turning on him. The tone of his brother's voice told Mark that he was now alone, that his brother was now an enemy, no longer on his side. The stunning isolation which descended upon him following this realization was soul crushing, exacerbating everything he was already going through.

"You're full of shit," Stephen shot back. "You didn't kill Lamperti, and you're just having a reaction to those happy pills the army sent you home with."

"Fuck you, asshole, I haven't touched those in a month. In fact, I threw most of them down the drain," Mark replied, edging towards his brother. If Stephen was truly an enemy he would be treated like one. Mark balled his fists and prepared for combat.

"My ass you did," Stephen barked, pointing a finger towards his younger brother, "you don't think me and Mom know about your little stash? Think we don't know about the top drawer in your dresser? We just didn't intervene because we knew you'd probably fucking snap. Army fucked you up man, and you need to get some serious fucking help."

"You piece of shit," Mark growled. A blind rage came upon him and he could see only red.

"Call me whatever you want," Stephen retorted, "but you're not a killer Mark, you're just a fuck up."

Virginia stood up from the table and quickly intervened; she had seen plenty of sibling fights over the years. "Boys, boys, please," she pleaded. Turning towards Stephen she placed a hand on his chest. "This is not what I called you over here for," she scolded.

She then turned towards Mark her face becoming sickly sweet and her tone raising an octave, "Sweetie, we're just worried about you. We just want you to get help."

Stephen softened his tone as well, "Yeah man, I'm sorry. That was uncalled for. We are just worried about you."

Mark backed away, his brow furrowing. "Help? Who the hell can help me? What are you saying, you want me to go see a shrink?"

"Yes," Stephen sighed.

"Your brother's already called South Shore, they say they can put us in touch with some nice mental health representatives," Virginia cooed.

"Mental health?" Mark spat, continuing to retreat until he felt the countertop against his back. He felt surrounded; it was like the walls were closing in on him. He felt like a cornered animal.

"Yes, honey, now why don't you go pack some of your things," his mother recommended.

"No, absolutely not," Mark answered, swatting at his mother's hands. "No shrink can cure me. I'm a god damn werewolf. I'm fucking cursed!"

At this Stephen moved forward and spoke in soothing tones while trying to restrain his brother, "Look man, we're just going to get you some help."

As Stephen placed his hands upon his body, Mark reacted badly, lashing out and pushing his older brother. "Get the fuck off me!"

Stephen continued to try and arrest his younger sibling, "it's for your own good dude, trust me."

The two began to struggle with one another and Virginia protested, "Guys, guys! Stop right now!"

Ignoring the pleas of their mother, the Enos brothers continued to tangle. "Calm down man," Stephen grunted.

"Get the fuck away," Mark hissed.

Stephen, grabbing Mark by the shoulders shook his brother violently, "you need help dude. You didn't kill anyone man and there are no such thing as a werewolf."

Freeing himself, Mark flung Stephen backwards. "Fuck you!" Mark screamed as he landed a right cross to his older brother's jaw. There was the wet smack of knuckles meeting flesh, and Stephen crumpled to the floor, clutching his aching cheek. Not waiting to review the aftermath, Mark took off running, pushing out the front door and disappearing down the street.

XXXIV

Kaplan trudged gingerly to the water cooler, leaning down and filling a Dixie cup with the cool, refreshing liquid. Taking a swig, he let it sit in his mouth before swallowing it down. It had taken him hours to rinse the horrid taste of vomit from his mouth and even longer to regain a feeling of normalcy.

In that time, however, Henry had made sure to inform everyone in the department of Kaplan's gastrointestinal mishap at the crime scene, even making sure an amateur cell phone video of the display had made its way around the staff. Kaplan had faced an onslaught of ribbing from his colleagues, been the butt of a thousand jokes, and had been subject to more than one round of mock applause since returning to the station. While he had smiled and taken it good naturedly, internally he was a seething, roiling pit of anger.

He resented Henry's attitude, his callous comments, and found him to be a coarse, unpleasant old man. Kaplan found himself clenching his fists every time the trooper referred to him as "buddy." *I'm not your friend, asshole,* he had wanted to scream on more than one occasion. *Hell, just twenty-four hours ago you were impugning my good name to the Chief of Police.* "Build's a good team, my ass," he muttered before taking another sip from the paper cup.

"Sergeant Kaplan?" A feminine voice called from down the hallway.

"What?" Kaplan asked rather curtly, expecting yet another insult to be hurled his way. Glaring down the hall, he softened his expression as viewed a frightened looking older woman standing with her fingers interlocked just a few feet away. She appeared nervous, the big doe-like eyes behind her thick glasses looking as if they could tear up at any moment. *Oh Shit,* he cursed himself, *it's the dispatcher.* Ruth, he believed her name was. Clearing his throat, he stood up straight. "Uh, sorry Ruth what is it?"

Ruth seemed to relax as Kaplan changed his tone. "There's a call out for you, says Trooper Henry wants you over at seven Talbot Road."

"Okay thanks," Kaplan nodded. *Now what?* He asked as he crushed the tiny paper cup and tossed it in the garbage.

* * *

Kaplan trekked up the driveway, the static filled sound of police radios permeating the air. The area was now all too familiar to him as this would be his third trip in over a month. *This isn't going to be good*, he thought. Nothing originating from this neighborhood had turned out well for him. *At least there'll be no body to examine, no shredded corpse.*

There were two squad cars parked in the driveway besides his own. One of them, he noted ominously, belonged to a member of the state police; it had to be Henry since he had called Kaplan to the residence. Coming up on the decrepit little house, he called out to a Hingham Policeman standing on the porch, "How's it going, Dan?"

Officer Dan Leduc was a veteran member of the force. The years had not been kind to him, and the skin on his face sagged in places, and a prodigious beer gut hung over his utility belt, causing his blue uniform top to become unflatteringly tight. "I'm good, Eric, you?" Leduc wheezed, mopping his brow with a handkerchief despite the fact that it was no more than forty-five degrees out.

"I've been better," Kaplan winked, acknowledging the morbid events he had been part of the last two days, along with his little episode this morning.

"I heard," Leduc snorted.

"What's going on inside?"

Leduc crossed his arms and sighed, "Well it sounded pretty straight forward to me at first, just a simple case of domestic violence."

"Domestic violence?" Kaplan questioned, "What, did the kid hit his mom?"

"His mom?" Leduc asked, confused at first. "No, one brother took a swing at the other."

"Oh," Kaplan nodded, moderately relieved at this information. Motioning towards the state police squad car, he asked, "So what's with the, you know?"

"Well the guy and his mother started explaining what happened, I called it in, and next thing I know that asshole trooper shows up, kicks me out, and tells me to call you in," Leduc harrumphed.

Kaplan looked the portly officer over, noting that the man had the look of a jilted prom date. "He wanted me called in?"

"Yeah, he's waiting for you inside," Leduc affirmed.

Ascending the white porch steps, Kaplan slapped Leduc on the shoulder as he headed inside. "All right, man, wish me luck."

Leduc huffed in response before leaning against the wooden railing. Kaplan opened the screen door, wincing as it unleashed its telltale screech. The common room he entered into was darkened, not a light on and the drapes drawn. The hallway to his left was in a similar state, possessing the look of some moribund inner-city alleyway. Only the kitchen straight ahead bore any trace of life. Light filtered in through a dingy skylight overhead allowing several faded shadows to play upon the floor, there was the muffled sound of voices, and the smell of stale coffee hung in the air.

Entering the cramped kitchen, Kaplan found three individuals huddled around a table. While the trooper had his back to him, Kaplan instantly recognized Henry, and he also could identify the woman of the table as Virginia Enos, her hideous perm nestled upon her head along with the red, puffy eyes which the officer was beginning to think the norm for this particular individual. The only one Kaplan could not place was a man in his mid to late twenties clutching a white plastic bag of ice to his swollen, purple cheek. His black hair obscured his face, and it was clear to Kaplan that it was not Mark Enos. Realizing that conversation had stopped and all eyes were now on him, Kaplan cleared his throat and offered, "Um, Hello."

"Hello, Sergeant," Henry greeted, "you remember Mrs. Enos of course."

The trooper motioned towards Virginia, prompting the woman to nod politely. "Hello, Officer."

"Hi," Kaplan replied hesitantly.

"And this is her oldest boy, Stephen," Henry continued.

Kaplan responded with a brief head bob before asking, "Where's Mark?"

"Well, that is the million dollar question my friend," Henry thundered.

"I don't understand," Kaplan stammered, a little lost by the proceedings.

"I won't belabor these good people the task of recounting their story once again, so I'll let you in,"

Henry sounded boisterously. Crossing his arms, he paused suddenly and looked at Virginia, "If that's okay with you Mrs. Enos of course."

"Of course," Virginia permitted, waving her hand.

Henry then assumed his previous gruff tone and looked at Kaplan, "It seems that this morning Mrs. Enos here heard quite the commotion coming from her son's bedroom and went to investigate, you know, see if everything was okay. Before she could even get in the door her son, Mark, came at her like a crazy man covered head to toe in blood."

"Blood?" Kaplan questioned.

"That's right; he was rambling about having hurt some people the night before, and as he accosted his poor mother—"

"Wait, he hurt you too?" Kaplan interjected, directing his question at Mrs. Enos.

She placed her hands nervously upon her crotch. "Well, no, he didn't hit me. He more or less grabbed at me and shook me a little."

"Anyways, as I was saying," Henry cut back in, "the young man stated that he believed he was also responsible for Mr. Lamperti's untimely end two nights before that."

"What?" Kaplan probed, "What do you men he *believed* he was responsible?"

"Oh, well that's where this story only gets better, buddy, it seems our friend Mark believes he's a werewolf," Henry harrumphed.

"A werewolf?" Kaplan asked in disbelief, suddenly feeling the urge to sit down.

"Yeah, you know changes with the full moon, sprouts fur and fangs before terrorizing the countryside, the whole nine yards," Henry chuckled before frowning and looking at the Enoses. "Sorry, I meant no disrespect," he coughed.

"I don't get it," Kaplan gestured, lost completely.

"The Enoses here were just informing me of their relative's tenuous mental state. They say Mark's not entirely well en la cabesa," Henry said, knocking himself lightly about the head for effect. "Mark, they tell me, was discharged from the military recently due to the fact that he suffered from post traumatic stress disorder, and since then he's been heavily dosing himself with a steady diet of drugs he has hidden in his room, attempting to deal with the night terrors he suffers from. In fact, the kid cracked his older brother Stephen here in the jaw when the family attempted to intervene and get him some help."

Kaplan, though still processing the information, was put off by Henry's tone; it was cavalier and condescending, as if he had no respect for the people in front of him despite the fact he was speaking of their embattled relative. Kaplan also sensed an angry tone simmering underneath the trooper's recounting of events and surmised that it was directed towards him. Ignoring this, Kaplan looked at the Enoses. "So what happened after Mark hit his brother?"

"He ran out of the house," Stephen mumbled, unable to fully move his jaw just yet.

"Still covered in blood?"

"No," Virginia offered, "he had taken a shower in the meantime, just after he grabbed me and before hitting Stephen."

"And now he's just out there?" Kaplan questioned, "Does he have a car?"

"No," Stephen grumbled, "he just took off running."

"Does he have any friends in the area, a girlfriend maybe? Maybe there's somewhere he could lay low for a while," Kaplan interrogated.

"I've already covered this, buddy," Henry interrupted. "The family tells me Mark's kind of a loner, a real lone wolf, no pun intended, and he doesn't have a girlfriend."

"Where does that leave us?" Kaplan asked of Henry.

"Us?" Henry asked, standing up from the table. "Well *I* now have to find our friend Mark."

Henry placed a hand on Kaplan's shoulder and squeezed tight, indicating he wanted the officer silent. Leading Kaplan towards the front door, he paused and looked back at the Enoses, smiling as he did so. "Sit tight for a moment, folks, I'll send in an officer with instructions, and don't you worry now, we'll find Mark and get him back to you safe and sound." With a nod he proceeded to lead Kaplan out the front door and onto the porch.

As they emerged outside, Henry directed the portly Leduc, "Officer, I'm gonna need you to get inside and take those people into protective custody, there's no telling what their batshit crazy relative is capable of. And I'm gonna need you to call down another unit here in case the son of a bitch shows back up."

Leduc hesitated, unsure of whether or not to follow the state trooper's orders, looking plaintively at Kaplan. Pausing momentarily, Kaplan nodded slowly, instructing Leduc to do as Henry said. With an angry disposition, Leduc waddled into the house leaving the two men on the porch.

"Okay, so what's the plan?" Kaplan asked.

"The plan?" Henry growled, his steely gaze piercing through Kaplan. "There wouldn't have to be a plan if it weren't for you."

"What are you talking about?" Kaplan demanded.

"We had the son of a bitch yesterday right there," Henry hissed, pointing towards Lamperti's front yard. "And you called me off, told me you knew the guy. I knew it was him, the dogs don't go crazy for nothing."

"Now look, that's not fair," Kaplan defended.

"Not fair?" Henry bristled, "Look, I don't know what your reasons were for interfering, and I don't much care. Maybe you thought you did know the kid, or maybe you just don't like dealing with the Staties; hell, I'll even take into account that it's probably your first murder investigation, and you just plain fucked it up. The bottom line though is that you cut him loose, and then he went and killed those three poor people last night, and that really pisses me off."

"You're blaming me?" Kaplan asked incredulously.

"Damn right, I'm blaming you. As far as I'm concerned, those people's blood is on your hands, and God forbid he hurts anyone else, Kaplan. God forbid."

"How the hell was I supposed to know he was crazy?" Kaplan protested.

"It doesn't matter," Henry shot back. "The fact is you let him go when we had him, and I'll be taking up the matter with your superior officers. Now if you'll excuse me I've got to go find the sick bastard." Henry glared at Kaplan for a moment before storming off the porch and towards his car, leaving the Hingham policeman to wallow in his thoughts.

XXXV

Now *this* was newsworthy. There were now four mutilated bodies all murdered with in the span of forty-eight hours, and the press ate this sort of thing up. Organizations from all over flocked to the tiny seaside community of Hingham to chronicle the carnage left by this new killer, yet to be bestowed with a clever nickname which the press had seemed to pin on these individuals since Jack the Ripper. Though this was technically a spree-killer by definition, most of these news outlets abandoned such conventions. "Serial Killer in Suburbia" had a much more threatening and ominous ring to it.

Though not even sure if the murder of Bill Lamperti and these three new bodies were even connected the press lumped them all together anyways, gleaming what little information they could from loose-lipped patrolmen who stood guard behind reams of yellow crime scene tape. Not possessing anywhere near a complete story, the reporters blabbed away in front of the cameras anyway. Sensationalized news made for much higher ratings than straight facts did. Besides, in a world dominated by the internet, it was either report immediately or forever hold your peace. You could always make a correction or a retraction later, and few would hold you accountable if your gaffe was small enough.

Cameramen and reporters milled about the town doing "Man on the Street" interviews, all the while drumming up a sense of fear and dread amongst the townsfolk. Assembled media members had almost leapt for joy as they captured footage of the muscular policeman scrambling from the entrance of the police station and blowing chunks, every second of his agonized vomiting captured. Dozens of close-ups captured his sweaty countenance and boom mikes, his belabored breathing. It made for wonderful footage and added to the aura surrounding these killings. Sex sells, but members of the American public also have an unceasing desire for gore and mayhem; scenes of a policeman losing it over what he saw served to pique the viewing audience's interest. *If he can't take it,* they would think, *it must be really bad.*

Though the cameras would never reveal what was actually inside the building, supposedly out of respect for the dead, but primarily because the police would not allow it, they would titillate the audience with certain scenes. More than one of the cameramen assembled took long shots of the fallen Margot Roday, not enough to explicitly show her mutilated body, but enough to imply terrible things had befallen her. It would stimulate the public's imagination, cause them to picture horrible scenes of violence. Some would see a faceless butcher, hacking away at his hapless victim while others would envisage familiar monsters of the past, Dahmer, Bundy, Gacy, and the like.

By mid-afternoon, with nary a peep from the police, the media had whipped the town of Hingham into near frenzy, convincing them that a killer lurked in the shadows, already selecting his next victim. A remarkable state of hysteria, it stood in stark contrast to the reaction of many just a day before. The murder of one elderly man had been regarded as a tragedy, but a negligible one. Now, however, there was a palpable sense of panic in the streets. Hingham was a town under siege, and all largely due to media-induced paranoia.

* * *

Chief Patterson marched down the narrow corridor, carefully adjusting his uniform and wondering if those around him noticed the slight pep in his step. Clutching his prepared speech in his sweaty left palm, he struggled to maintain his composure as he knew there was an array of news camera and microphones waiting for him at the department entrance. This was big, his first time on real network news, nothing like the low-budget community television he had appeared on in previous years with its non-existent audience.

He would become synonymous with catching this killer; people would identify him as the man who had headed the investigation that ultimately led to Mark Enos's arrest. It didn't matter that his involvement had been limited, that the real credit belonged to the man walking to his left, Matt Henry. He spied Henry out of the corner of his eye, inspecting the trooper, who had donned his customary straight-brimmed blue hat, complete with its gold braids, and blue uniform jacket before shining his black jack boots for the cameras. Patterson envied the man, his aging yet chiseled jaw jutting forward and his barrel chest puffed out, he looked like the consummate police officer, quite the contrast to Patterson with his double chin, bald head, and doughy mid-section. There was no doubt in Patterson's mind that Henry would come across better on camera, and he sought to minimize the man's involvement in the press conference.

"Just so we're clear, I'll be making the initial statement before we open this up to questions, right?" Patterson asked, wondering if his voice betrayed his nervousness.

"Absolutely," Henry answered with his gruff tone, not a trace of disappointment on his face. "I have no interest in talking to these bastards."

Looking ever more confident, he smiled. "I'm just eager to catch this son of a bitch."

Patterson felt relieved, convinced that the limelight would be his and his alone. However, the butterflies again rose in his stomach when a peculiar thought crossed his mind. "You know you can't swear on camera right?"

Henry winked, "I'll try to hold my tongue. Besides, the wife would give me a good ass kicking if she saw me on the news cussing up a storm."

Patterson found himself smiling at the thought of the grizzled trooper cowering before his wife. Then he returned to a more serious expression. Raising the papers in his hand, he turned towards Henry, "And we're sure this Enos kid is definitely our guy?"

"As sure as the sun will rise tomorrow," Henry nodded.

"Good enough for me," Patterson nodded, not breaking stride. Asking these types of questions made his confidence swell, something he needed right before facing the battery of reporters assembled outside. Truthfully, he had felt a sense of inferiority in much of his relations with the state trooper. It was why he had named Kaplan as liaison, feeling that the younger, muscular officer would have an easier time interacting with the brash Henry, and it was also why he had removed Kaplan from the case on Henry's insistence. Hell, he had even chewed Kaplan out, though he hadn't known why, choosing instead to defer to Henry's judgment. Now, however, he felt good about himself, priding himself on the way Henry answered his questions dutifully, as if Patterson were his commanding officer.

He recognized an opportunity when he saw one, and this case was as big as it got. He could profit off of this in a big way. Cable news outlets, news magazines, and papers from around the world would seek him out, eager for an interview; he would become the face of this investigation. If he played it right, he could parlay it into real money. Surely there'd be book and movie deals in the offing. He'd be like that Charles Moose character from the Beltway Sniper attacks. Moose had made himself a pretty penny with his performance during that period, although he had been forced to resign in order to receive any monetary reward from his resulting book deal. *Does Hingham have similar rules regarding a public official receiving money in such a way? Does it matter?* If the money was good enough, he could easily retire. Hell, he remembered reading that Moose was now serving on the force in Honolulu. *That'd be an easy beat.*

Truth was he had taken the job as Hingham police chief because of its undemanding nature. It was life on easy street compared to the beats he had patrolled in Boston and later the gang unit in Brockton of all places. He was lazy by nature, and the job in Hingham had offered more money with a lower crime rate, and he had happily accepted it. Serving for nearly twelve years now in this role, he now salivated at the opportunity to make a quick buck and leave the working world in general.

Moose had gotten the opportunity to communicate with his quarry, who had left tarot cards with messages directed towards him and had later even called to taunt him. Patterson had had no such chance to engage this killer as this spree had only now gone on for less than forty-eight hours. Time, it was something he had been sorely deprived of. The D.C. Sniper attacks had lasted three weeks, giving the news outlets more than ample time to lionize Moose as he had held near daily press conferences; Patterson would receive only a few days worth of media attention. Was it wrong to wish that Enos remained at large for a little while, all the longer for Patterson to get his name out there?

Of course such a sentiment underlined the double-edged sword Patterson was facing. If they captured Enos so quickly, stopping his rampage over a matter of days, Patterson and his force would be commended for their exemplary police work, congratulated for removing a dangerous psychopath from the streets. He would be hailed as a man who could get things done and done quickly. However, if Enos remained at large, Patterson would be subject to the later criticisms that had been hurled at Moose, claims that his incompetence had allowed the madmen to continue their work on the streets of Montgomery County. *I wonder who will play me in the movie version? Moose got Charles Dutton.*

This case was a veritable goldmine for any book or movie, containing outlandish plot elements and a perfect antagonist for Patterson. He couldn't write worth a damn, but they had ghost writers for that sort of thing. *How much does that cost?* There would have to be some embellishment of his involvement, but who would really call him on that? Moose could go fuck himself as far as Patterson was concerned. The Beltway snipers were a couple of losers in a Chevy caprice dropping tarot cards; he had a killer who believed he was a werewolf. *A fucking werewolf!* You couldn't make this stuff up.

Visions of fame and riches still dancing in his head, he briskly exited the building and descended the station steps towards a podium, which had been erected earlier in the day. The lights were blinding, even in the midday sun, and there was the constant click of cameras. Patterson waited for Henry and his assortment of uniformed officers to fall into line behind him before speaking into the podium's lone microphone. "Good afternoon," he began. "We'll begin by releasing a brief statement, and then we'll open it up to your questions. We'd appreciate it if you refrain from any questioning during the reading of the statement."

Pausing for a moment, he took a deep breath and glanced down at his prepared speech before continuing, "As you know, our usually quiet seaside community has been subject to a series of incidents in the last few days. While we will not release certain details of this case, I can confirm that three people were found murdered early this morning and we believe the murder of one William Lamperti the previous day is also connected to this case. For the moment we will withhold the identities of the three victims found this morning.

"The Hingham police Department, in conjunction with the Massachusetts State Police, would like to announce that we now have a suspect in these heinous crimes. Earlier today we have identified one Mark Enos, a Hingham resident and former member of the United States Army, as the primary suspect in all four murders. Mister Enos remains at large, his whereabouts unknown and as such we ask for anyone with knowledge of his location to come forward and contact the Hingham Police. Mister Enos is also believed to be a highly unstable, dangerous individual, and as such we ask that Hingham residents remain indoors between sundown and sunup. This is not a curfew; I repeat this is not a curfew . . . "

* * *

No sooner had Patterson wrapped up his press conference that the residents of Hingham erupted. Hundreds of them who had viewed or listened to the police chief on their television sets or car radios voiced their questions and concerns to one another. "If they want us to stay indoors, why wouldn't they have just issued a curfew?"

"How the hell did they let this guy get away, and why haven't they captured him yet?"

"Why aren't they canceling school and bussing children back to their homes?"

"Why won't they tell us the names of the victims?"

Rather than coming across as confident and in total control, the image most people now had of the police chief was that of a bumbling, ineffectual fool. Henry had pushed for a curfew, believing that by removing residents from the streets, it would make hunting Enos down easier. Henry had also pointed out that all of the murders had been committed at night, and as Enos believed himself a werewolf, he would be active as there was to be a full moon that night. However, Patterson had rejected the idea, choosing instead to merely recommend that people stay indoors, a move he had intended to show that he respected the freedom of his fellow residents and would not trample upon it in order to pursue a fugitive. He believed that by not disrupting the daily routine of Hingham's residents, it would portray him as a policeman who was sympathetic to those he served and would convey a sense of overwhelming confidence in the police's ability to capture one renegade veteran without interfering in the lives of the general public.

Instead, it further served to stoke the fear and paranoia of many in the town as they perceived the move as one of weakness. "The police know they can't keep us off the streets, so they're just throwing their hands up in defeat. If they can't control us, the law abiding citizens, how do they expect to catch this madman?" the community seemed to say. People reacted badly as parents left work to scoop up their children from the schoolyards, businesses shuttered their doors early, and many Hingham residents simply packed up and left town. It was pandemonium as many in the community rushed to get home and buttress themselves indoors, the streets in downtown were clogged with traffic within minutes of the press conference, and the shelves of the few local grocers still open were picked bare. It was the type of things usually reserved for a massive storm or a national emergency.

It didn't take long for mass hysteria to spread to surrounding communities such as Hull and Cohasset. Their borders were close to the Enos's Hingham residence, and many in those towns found it not unreasonable to wonder if he had slinked his way into their placid communities. Their fears stemmed from the belief that if Hingham's people locked themselves indoors, Enos would move on to more fertile hunting grounds in the surrounding municipalities, ones whose residents were unhindered from milling about at night.

Tips poured in from all over to the Hingham Police Department, most, if not all of them originating from unreliable sources. More than quite a few asked if there was a reward being offered for Enos's capture, despite the fact that Patterson had never mentioned any such thing in his meeting with the press. Some claimed they had seen a wolf-like beast prowling about their yards the previous two nights, and others claimed they knew Mark Enos's whereabouts, though half of them managed to get his physical description wrong despite the fact that his photo had been displayed during the news conference. Ms. Bolduc, ever so fearful of losing the spotlight, also called in a tip, claiming that she had seen Mark Enos sneak back into his house, though the police officers guarding the premises quickly dispelled such a notion. A few callers even offered to join in the manhunt, claiming that they possessed the silver bullets needed for such a hunt; they were promptly hung up on. By late afternoon, early evening the volume of calls was so overwhelming and the information so unreliable that Patterson pulled his officers off of the phones, letting the calls go to the department's answering machine instead.

The local newscasts had lost their monopoly on the story as well. Many of the cable news networks had jumped upon the story, intrigued by the murderer's unique motive and the gory details. It was a tale tailor made for the headlines, a quiet town racked by a spate of grisly murders. Add to the fact that the killer remained at large, the promise that more gore was to come as he eluded the grasp of the local constabulary, and you had something many even outside of Hingham couldn't keep their eyes off of.

Within an hour of Patterson's press conference, millions knew what Enos looked like and were aware of his back story. The various news outlets had regaled the public with tales of macabre dealings, illustrating in many of their viewer's minds the savagery with which the murders had taken place. Pilfering video and commentators from local affiliates the main cable news stations came stunningly close to disclosing the more disgusting images and details of the Enos case. One news outlet even managed to find Mark's squad mates Glen Kelly and Steve Frey, demanding that they detail what life had been like with this monster now terrorizing his hometown. When pressed Kelly, not the most photogenic person and incredibly camera shy, shrugged his shoulders before mumbling, "He was a little weird, I guess."

Media pundits on these stations also seized upon the case, Mark Enos becoming nothing more than a tool with which to make their own political statements. The talking heads on the left slammed the military for not doing more to help this disturbed young man. They also claimed Mark Enos was the natural byproduct of a brutal military structure which had been thrust into an unnecessary and costly war; some even went so far as to claim Mark Enos was George Bush's fault. Those on the right claimed that Mark Enos was the result of a culture immersed in violent movies and videogames. The fact that he claimed to be a werewolf, a tidbit leaked by Patterson in his conference, served to illustrate the fact that Mark Enos was the result of a disturbed mind overstimulated by the desensitizing violence of television. He was the poster child for why Hollywood needed to pull back and why the government needed to step in and enforce a tougher entertainment rating system.

Despite the fact that he became the lead on many of these news outlets, many of whom scrapped their normal programming to focus on him; Mark Enos eventually became a non-story. Few focused on why this seemingly good-natured man had gone bad. They simply knew what his motives were, and none of them focused on the factors which had turned him into a monster. These facts were left for scholars and academics to pick over later on, each one of them no doubt eventually appearing in their own documentaries on Mark Enos. No, the real Mark Enos was replaced by a media-created image of Mark Enos. He wasn't a troubled young individual anymore, he was a bloodthirsty monster lurking in the shadows, and he had become a political pawn for many on these news shows. In the end the true story of Mark Enos was lost, drowned out in the chorus of sensationalized news and media driven hysteria.

XXXVI

Mark continued to run, the massive intake of air burning his lungs. His legs were growing weary, his body signaling its refusal to press any further at this pace. Unsure of where he was exactly, he finally slowed, doubling over and sucking in wind. He had nowhere to go, no intended destination.

Alone now, at the end of a residential cul-de-sac, he had reached a dead end literally and figuratively. There was no going back now; he knew that, at least just not yet. His family simply couldn't understand what he was going through, believing him to be a crazy person. Though he felt terrible about cold cocking his older brother, he knew it was for the best, and one day he would be able to explain it to Stephen. He felt isolated, completely alone, like he was on some far off deserted isle. *If I can't turn to my family, then whom can I turn to?*

The thought of being abandoned by his family angered him and he remembered in that instant just why he had hit his brother. Stephen had been the only one he was sure he could reach out to and now that bridge had been burned. It wasn't his fault, Mark assured himself. He hadn't meant to push Stephen away, clearly it was his brother's fault. If Stephen had just listened to him, rather than speaking to him in the same patronizing tone his mother so often adopted, he wouldn't be running through strange neighborhoods right now. *So be it*, Mark huffed. *Stephen was dead to him now, nothing more than an enemy.*

Maybe going to the police would be the right thing for him. They'd lock him away in a cell, and maybe that's what he needed; that way he wouldn't be able to hurt anyone. *No.* He shook his head. *They wouldn't get it and they'd probably kick my ass for hurting those people.*

As he returned to his normal pace of breathing and his heartbeat slowed, Mark stood up, trying to get a bearing on where he was. Quaint little houses surrounded him, their windows staring blankly towards the street. Not willing to turn back the way he had come, he began to jog forward again, running up the driveway of the house facing him and disappearing into the woods beyond the backyard.

The forest slowed him down, the dense tangle of trees and roots forcing him to move at a more deliberate pace. The leaves crunched beneath his feet, the occasional branch slapping at his shirt. Ahead he could see that the tree line ended briefly before picking up again on the other side of a road. Determined to get to the pathway he picked up his feet and broke through the trees, emerging onto the strip of asphalt.

It was confusing at first; the road was full of potholes and the once black roadbed was now a light shade of gray. Granules of sand filled in the cracks which lined the path, and rusted railroad tracks cut across the pathway before disappearing back into the woods a little further up the trail. The road looked abandoned, like something out of a post-apocalyptic wasteland, but there was something familiar about the scene to him. This notion nagged at Mark, and it bewildered him so. *Why the hell do I feel like I've been here before?*

There was the high pitched *cling-cling* of a small bell, and Mark looked up just a mountain biker whizzed by him. "Comin' through," the biker wheezed as he passed. As he watched the man, clad in his spandex outfit and absurd looking helmet pedal away, Mark suddenly realized where he was. He had indeed been here before; he had spent countless hours riding his own bike down such paths as a child. He was in Wompatuck.

There was something comforting about this realization, something insulating. Comfortable in these surroundings, Mark began to follow the abandoned railroad tracks down the well-worn bike path. He remembered his grandfather had informed him once that the park had once been part of a Naval Ammunition Depot during the Second World War, and these tracks had belonged to the trains which supplied the United States Atlantic Fleet. They were not tracks in the traditional sense, as their wooden slats had long since been removed or rotted away as the park paved them over. Rather, they were just two parallel, iron rails rusted black and running along the road.

He remembered that the park was dotted with what seemed like a hundred abandoned bunkers and other structures, places where he could lie low; surely these tracks would inevitably lead him to one. The tracks ran off the road diagonally and disappeared into the forest. Without hesitation Mark followed them into the woods, pausing periodically to clear away a clump of leaves or other debris to see the tracks.

The forest floor was littered with the evidence of a million illicit gatherings that had occurred within the park's boundaries, ranging from used condoms and empty beer cans to empty syringes. Pushing away the refuse with his feet, Mark trudged through the woods, finally stepping out into a clearing. He allowed himself a sigh of relief as he spied a hulking, decrepit structure across from him.

The trail here was overgrown green and brown grass sprouting from the asphalt and obscuring the tracks, but that was okay as he no longer required them. The one-story building ahead of him may not have been tall, but it made up for that in length; it was roughly as long as a football field. While the majority of the structure was constructed of thick concrete, the roof and other supports were metal, and these had corroded badly, leaving the site littered with flakes of rust. It was dilapidated, a derelict frame of what once was a solid building, now covered in a liberal coating of vulgar and nonsensical graffiti.

Mark approached the building and passed through the weeds, which formed a makeshift moat around it, some reaching as high as his waist. Placing his hands upon the concrete, he used what remained of a rubber truck stop to lift himself up and into the building. He remembered such sites, and there was no doubt in his mind that he had been here at least once before. He and Stephen had spent countless summer days during their youth exploring the abandoned buildings of Wompatuck and playing soldier in the park's ruined bunkers.

Rapping his knuckles against a rusted support beam, he marveled at the holes in the steel framework of what once had been the structure's ceiling above; some sections had simply collapsed all together. His grandfather had told him that when the navy had left, they had removed the windows and doorways of the buildings, exposing them all to the elements. Mark had always wondered why they had done that. *Why not simply demolish them all?* Now the buildings served as an idle curiosity for the hikers and bikers who toured the park by day while doubling as convenient hideouts for bored teenagers looking to party at night.

Chunks of concrete littered the floor along with corroded pieces of steel, and as he kicked around a particularly jagged piece, a terrible, sickening thought crossed Mark's mind. *What about suicide?* It wasn't as if there was a treatment for lycanthropy, no cure for what ailed him. He had seen enough movies to realize that the werewolf's bloodlust only ended when it was killed. It would be all too easy to pick up that piece of metal and slice his wrists down to the bones. It would be painful for sure, but at least he would spare someone an unspeakable death by his hands.

Shaking his head, he quickly dismissed the thought. *That's not the answer.* He just needed a place to lay low, to collect himself and contemplate his course of action. Surely his family would forgive him if given time to cool down, and then they would discuss how to proceed. *I can figure out a way to live with this disease, can't I?* There had to be a way. Clearing away a piece of concrete, he sat on the floor, resting his head upon the wall. The sunlight struck his eyes, and it occurred to him that he had been running aimlessly for hours. As he realized this, the exhaustion overtook his body, and his eyelids began to flutter. He just needed to rest for a bit, a short nap before planning out what he wanted to do. Content with his decision, he closed his eyes and drifted off to sleep.

XXXVII

Stephen sat on the hard bench, still clutching his throbbing jaw. The physical pain had subsided hours ago, yet that wasn't why he continued to rub the wounded area. It was a deep psychological torment which kept him holding the section of cheek which Mark had made contact with. He had simply believed his brother to be going through a tough moment in life, a terrible bump in the road. It wasn't until he found himself at the local constabulary that he realized his brother was going through something more serious, that his young life had taken some miserable detour that could never be rectified.

Thus he sat holding his wounded jawbone. He couldn't tell at first what truly hurt; surely it had been his pride at first, but now it had evolved into something more. Millions of thoughts raced through his mind, each one nibbling at his conscious, and the totality of the mass gnawing away at his psyche. Silently he watched as the policemen filed into the room across the way. Many of them chatted amongst themselves, a few even laughed talking of lighter subjects than the task at hand. The enormity of the danger his brother was in hit him as a group of stern faced state troopers entered the room, their gleaming jackboots clacking upon the dull linoleum.

How had he gotten here? He asked, cursing himself for not taking note of his brother's obvious cries of anguish. Had he acted sooner, perhaps none of this would have come to pass, he would not be sitting here, and he may have saved lives. The very thought caused him to shake his head. *Mark's not a killer.* He cursed himself. *Is he?*

Where did this all start? He pondered. *It was the goddamn military,* he decided. *They transformed Mark into a monster, a mindless killing machine.* It was all so clear now; his brother had been forged into a tool of war and molded for the stresses of combat, removed from the daily grind of civilian life. They had created a machine, a serial killer that no one now knew how to shut off. It was like throwing an active grenade into a crowd and being shocked at the results. Clearly Mark was not safe to be amongst the general public; clearly it was the government's fault.

This line of thought comforted Stephen as it absolved him and his family of any malfeasance, declared them not guilty of any negligence.

It was refreshing, a load off his back and ultimately, Stephen noted, a bold-faced lie. Hundreds of thousands of soldiers had returned home from the terror wars, and they had all adjusted to life stateside. Even among those who had experienced problems assimilating to civilian life none, as far as he knew, had become mass murderers, let alone declared themselves werewolves. The government didn't create monsters, and the military served to protect the people, not unleash killers amongst it; that had only been some deep seeded New England liberalism talking, some long held distrust of the army ingrained in many residents of the Northeast, a relic of Vietnam. No, Stephen realized, the underpinnings of his brother's behavior had started earlier in life, well before he had ever joined up.

It had started with their father's untimely death no doubt. Mark had never recovered from it, and Stephen imagined a host of ugly feelings stirring within young Mark's brain. Maybe if he had started paying more attention at such a young age he could have stopped all of this, prevented everything from going into motion.

Stephen had never declared himself to be the man of the house following his father's passing; it simply wasn't his personality. Though he was the oldest, he had never been a real domineering person, not once feeling the need to take the reins. *And why should I have?* He yelled internally. He too had been young at the time of his father's funeral, and he had always felt it was the place of the adults to lead, not for some young child. Later he had felt like he had his own life to lead, completely self-absorbed like most adolescents. It wasn't his responsibility to ensure that his younger brother recovered from some deep, emotional wound, to make sure that young Mark adjusted to the normal pace of life.

Sure losing the presence of his father had hurt, but as the old saying goes "time heals all wounds." *Why didn't Mark simply get over it?* Even in his halcyon days of high school Stephen had realized Mark was a little off, his personality slightly askew, but he had paid it no heed. His mind was of course on other things, like getting laid and making sure to keep up on the latest schoolyard gossip.

After high school Stephen had focused primarily on getting some type of employment, doing anything he could to get out of his broken household. He had somehow scrounged up enough money and financial aid to attend college, nothing prestigious of course, but a major milestone for anyone of his background. He had married his high school sweetheart and produced a few rug rats, all of this coming after he had been awarded with a job by the state, a little gift coming via his college roommate's uncle, a Massachusetts state senator. It was only now, huddled upon an uncomfortable bench, that Stephen realized that in his rush to leave his mother's house, he had left Mark behind.

He cursed himself, lamenting that he should have been there more for his mentally ailing younger sibling. Looking back, he noted that he had really been the only one Mark would open up too, Mark's only friend. Clearly their father's death had stunted his brother's mental development, and Stephen groaned as he remembered all those documentaries on television describing how most serial killers suffered some type of deep psychological trauma in their younger years.

Then there were Mark's open pleas for help which had come in the preceding days. He had stated openly that he felt he had done something awful, even going as far as to say he had killed old Lamperti, yet Stephen had just waved him off. Why shouldn't he have, though? Who would believe that his own flesh and blood was capable of such a terrible act, of murder? *Still,* Stephen reflected, *maybe if you had listened to him you would've saved a few people.* Didn't even the Unabomber's own brother turn him in? *Why couldn't you have done the same?* Slumping over in his chair, he wallowed in his own grief, blaming himself for all that had occurred up to now. *This isn't your fault,* he assured himself. So why did it still feel like it was?

Watching as a few stragglers marched into the meeting room, Stephen became more aware of their hushed conversations. The low murmur of the crowd buzzed in the room, and he only caught intermittent flashes of sentences, the gossip and rumors of the lowly patrolman.

" . . . Heard whoever catches this guy gets busted up two ranks automatically and a week's paid vacation."

" . . . News says killer took out an entire apartment building 'cross town."

" . . . Saw all the guy's guts and everything, fucking gross."

" . . . Can't wait to pop a cap in this guy's ass."

The last statement caught Stephen's attention. *Pop a cap in whose ass, my brother's?* His heart began to race as he realized Mark was in even greater danger than he had reckoned. It would only take one renegade or overeager officer, and Mark would face fatal consequences. Maybe there was still time to help his brother; Stephen just wasn't sure how. If he could find Mark before anyone else did, he could ensure his brother was brought to justice humanely; he could assure his physical safety. In this one act he could atone for the sins of the past, soothe his battered psyche, and restart his relationship with his younger brother. He would never get the chance though if someone "popped a cap" in Mark's ass. How to go about it, though?

Struggling for an answer, Stephen recalled the policeman who had arrived at his mother's house earlier. Not the older, gruff motherfucker, but the younger one. He had seemed congenial and approachable; maybe, just maybe he had Mark's best interests in mind. Stephen had watched as the policeman, Kaplan he believed, had entered the room with a disapproving scowl upon his face. Resolving to approach the policeman, Stephen relinquished his hold upon his jaw and started towards the meeting room, only to have the door rudely shut upon his face.

Dejected, he walked back to the bench waiting patiently as a loud, muffled voice sounded from beyond.

XXXVIII

Henry's black boots clacked upon the linoleum surface as he marched between the rows of desks. In the cramped room where Hingham police officers routinely held their pre-shift roll call he was now king, preparing to bark orders to the room of assembled law enforcement personnel. Arriving at the front of the room, he situated himself behind a dais and rapped his fingers impatiently upon the wooden podium. There was the sound of shuffling paper, and the majority of the men seated or standing ahead of Henry were busily passing sheets of paper to one another, ensuring that each of them possessed a copy of the flyer.

Clearing his throat, Henry lowered his face towards the microphone, "Everyone got one?"

There was a chorus of "yes, sirs" along with a few head bobs, and the activity came to a halt as all focus was placed on the stern-faced trooper at the head of the room.

"Good," Henry smiled, "as some of you may not know, I am Trooper Matthew Henry of the state police, and for all intents and purposes, I'll be heading this little shindig. That understood?"

A similar grunting of approval and nodding of heads followed. Kaplan stood at the very back of the room, by the doorway, with his arms crossed listening intently. True to his word, Henry had taken up the matter of Mark Enos and the incident at the Lamperti crime scene with Kaplan's superiors. After facing a thorough chewing out by Chief of Police Patterson, who had informed him that he had "brought great shame upon the department," he was lucky to even be allowed in the room. Coupled with the earlier vomiting episode, it was shaping up to be one hell of a day for Kaplan.

Still, the yelling and cussing with which he had been assailed with by the various powers that be had not truly bothered Kaplan all that much. Rather, it was Henry's parting statements which really stuck in his craw and caused him great internal strife. *"Their blood is on your hands,"* is what Henry had told him and though he was offended and even incredulous of the statements before, some doubt had begun to creep in. He had allowed Mark Enos to simply walk away and indirectly had become the proximate cause for the deaths of three people later that evening. The simple act of removing Enos from Henry's hook had led to such horrible consequences. *I'm not responsible for this*, Kaplan assured himself, *am I?*

His thoughts were broken up as Henry continued to speak into the microphone. "All right, everybody, get a good look at our suspect," the trooper commanded holding up a white flyer, "the gentleman pictured on here is one Mark Enos. He is twenty-three years old, approximately six-foot-one, and weighing in at one hundred eighty-five pounds. He's a string bean of a fella, but don't you be fooled, he's one mean son of a bitch."

Placing the flyer back upon the podium Henry continued, "Enos is a combat veteran, saw action with the army in Iraq. He was recently discharged from the military due to complications from post traumatic stress disorder, and the good men at the Department of Defense saw fit to send him on his way with a whole slew of medication. A preliminary search by our crime scene unit turned up a variety of controlled substances hidden in the suspect's sock drawer."

Moving to continue, Henry was interrupted when a boyish looking officer in the second row raised his hand. "Yes?" Henry called.

"What specific substances, sir?" the officer asked.

"Uppers, downer, hell, son, you name it, he had it," Henry answered while giving a look that instructed the policeman to never interrupt the trooper again. Moving on, Henry moved to the side of the dais, "Mr. Enos suffers from intense delusions according to his family, and it's probably due to his heavy drug use. The bastard even believes he is a werewolf."

There was a smattering of laughter that rippled through the crowd of policemen. Henry smiled and raised his hand, signaling the crowd to be silent, "I know, I know, he's a crazy son of a bitch. But I'll tell you what isn't funny." His expression became darker. "We believe this guy is responsible for the deaths of four people over the last two days. Now, for those of you who haven't witnessed this guy's handiwork, I'll spare you the slideshow, but let me inform you that it's some grisly shit. He's a mean bastard, and he even whacked his poor brother upside the head this morning when his family attempted to get him professional help."

"Is he a spree killer, sir?" Another officer called out from the crowd.

"In every sense of the word," Henry nodded, "and I don't believe he's done yet." As he said this, he locked eyes with Kaplan at the back of the room and glared at him icily.

Kaplan broke off and stared at the floor. Sadly he had to agree with the trooper's assessment. A spree killer, by general definition Kaplan remembered from his studies, was a murderer who embarked on a murderous rampage in multiple locations with little to no "cooling off" in between. By contrast a serial killer was more deliberate, with the murders occurring over a greater length of time and the victims chosen carefully. Mark Enos appeared to be murdering with abandon, having no connection to any of his victims except for his neighbor, the ill-fated Lamperti.

"As I mentioned before, the kid claims he's a werewolf, and after perusing the internet I have been told by the local weather station that tonight is indeed a full moon, meaning our big bad wolf will probably kill again. The suspect is on foot, with no car, and it seems he's a bit of a loser with no known girlfriend or close friends in the area. He's got about a four hour head start on us, gentleman, so let's get our asses in gear. You, men of the Hingham police, will scour the area from the Enos household on Talbot road to the town borders with Weymouth, Cohasset, Hull, Rockland and Norwell."

"Will we be conducting roadblocks, sir?" The boyish officer interrupted again.

"No," Henry growled, "since our suspect is most likely not in a car, there's no point, and it'll simply piss off the townsfolk, causing traffic and such. Searches are to be done mainly with canine teams and by foot. We will be assisted by the good men of Massachusetts State Police Troop D-One," Henry beamed nodding towards a group of standing, muscular state troopers to his right.

The troopers, clad in their jackboots and doughboy-like hats along with their matching square jaws, nodded back at Henry. "They'll be primarily scouring the border areas as they can cross with no jurisdictional problems, understood?"

Henry inspected the crowd for any signs of dissent, happily finding none. "Just one more thing before we go people; I cannot stress enough how violent this fellow is. He is most likely armed, and should he come at you do not, I say again, do not hesitate to take him down. You put a bullet in him if you have to."

In the back of the room Kaplan shook his head in dismay at this order. *Enos may be a murderer, but he's still just a scared kid.*

"We clear?" Henry demanded, receiving a number of affirmative reactions. "Okay, let's clear out, people, individual orders will be handed out by dispatch or by me personally. Good hunting."

Kaplan hung back, watching the dozens of men filter out of the room. Many chatted with their fellow officers, others simply walked out silently. Through the crowd, Kaplan caught intermittent glimpses of Henry, laughing and no doubt trading old war stories with the other state troopers. Shaking his head, Kaplan joined the line of officers and exited the room.

As he entered the hallway, a young man leapt off one of the benches lining the corridor and made a beeline for the officer. "Officer Kaplan?" The young man asked.

Kaplan recognized the individual as Stephen Enos, the man clutching his swollen jaw in the Enos's kitchen earlier that day. His jaw, though still bruised, appeared healthier and this was made evident by the ease with which he addressed the officer. "Um, yeah. Stephen, right?" Kaplan answered.

"Yeah, that's right," Stephen nodded, extending his hand in greeting. As they shook hands, Stephen continued, "Can I speak to you for a minute?"

"Yeah, definitely," Kaplan replied, leading Stephen away from the group of officers retreating from the conference room. Stopping just a few feet from the doorway Kaplan crossed his arms. "So what's up; what can I do for you, Stephen?"

"Call me Steve," Stephen responded.

"All right, what can I do for you, Steve?"

"It's about my brother," Stephen began, "about what you think is going to happen to him."

"I don't understand," Kaplan replied.

Appearing a little flustered, Stephen began to rephrase his statement, "Look, I don't know what was going on earlier between you and uh, uh—"

"Trooper Henry?" Kaplan offered.

"Right, Trooper Henry," Stephen nodded, "but my mother and I seemed to get a much better vibe from you than from him."

"A better vibe?"

"Yeah, I don't know how to say it exactly, it just seemed he was an angrier guy, you know?" Stephen stuttered.

Kaplan nodded his understanding.

"And it seems like you're a more reasonable person, like you'd actually care what happens to my brother."

Kaplan sighed, "Steve, I hate to be rude, but I'm having a little trouble following you here."

"I just want to know if they're going to hurt my brother," Stephen blurted out. "I know they think he's done terrible things, but I know Mark's not well mentally right now, and anything he did, he did when he wasn't in control of himself. I understand it sounds ridiculous to say, but my brother didn't mean to harm anyone, he's a really good kid going through some tough times, and I'm just afraid when they find him they're really going to mess him up." Stephen sighed before continuing, "And it just seems that out of that entire room of cops you're the only one who gives a shit what happens to my brother."

Kaplan moved to put his hand on Stephen's shoulder, "Steve, calm down."

Stephen shied away, visibly upset, "No, I will not calm down. Now, are they going to hurt my brother or not? Because that trooper sure seemed pissed this morning, and they tore apart my mother's house looking for God knows what, and it doesn't seem like they give a damn about Mark's well being. I understand he hit me, I understand he might have hurt some people, but he's my brother, and I still love him no matter what. So, I'll ask you again, what are they going to do to my brother?"

Kaplan hesitated, struggling to produce an acceptable answer. Henry's previous words rang in his ears, "*Put a bullet in him if you have to.*" Kaplan had never heard another law enforcement member speak in such a way, and he knew it amounted to tacit approval for shooting Mark Enos, but there was no way he could tell the scared, frustrated young man in front of him such a thing. Biting his lip, he decided to lie, "Look, Steve, no one's going to hurt your brother."

"You can promise that?" Stephen pressed.

Kaplan struggled to answer, opening his mouth, but emitting no sound. The hesitation made Stephen's eyes go wide, "What's going to happen?" Receiving no answer, he pressed again, "What's going to happen?"

Kaplan looked down at the floor in resignation, "I don't know, I really don't know."

"Jesus Christ, how do you not know?" Stephen demanded, "Aren't you in charge here; don't you have some authority?"

"I'm not in charge here," Kaplan retorted, "in fact, I'm not even officially involved in the search for your brother. I don't even know if I'm on duty right now."

"Well holy shit, help me here," Stephen pleaded, "There's got to be something you can do."

"I really don't know what you want me to do here, Steve," Kaplan answered.

"I want you to help me," Stephen said animatedly, "help me find my brother before they do."

"And then what?" Kaplan asked, looking Stephen in the eyes.

"And then whatever, arrest him if you have to, stick him in a mental ward, I just want to make sure that he's physically okay, that he's not hurt." Stephen searched for an answer in Kaplan's gaze. "Help me," he begged.

Kaplan was conflicted, unsure of how to answer. Debating internally a figure beyond Stephen's head caught his eye. It was Henry emerging with the group of state troopers into the hallway. Still laughing with the group and appearing quite jovial for a man about to search for a murderer, Henry locked eyes with Kaplan. Smiling maliciously, he winked at Kaplan before continuing the other way down the hall. Kaplan's decision was now made for him. "Okay," he answered, "okay, I'll help you."

"Thank you," Stephen said, waving his clasped hands at Kaplan, "thank you so much."

"Don't thank me yet, kid," Kaplan instructed. "We have to find your brother before they do."

Stephen nodded his understanding.

"Now come on," Kaplan directed, "my car's out back."

XXXIX

Virginia Enos sat solemnly in the Hingham police station's break room. Alone at one of the cheap round tables which dotted the room, she kept her swollen, puffy eyes fixed upon a candy vending machine ahead. With a trembling hand, she raised her paper coffee cup and ingested even more of the liquid. Truth was she drank far too much coffee, she reckoned she was up to five cups a day at least. It made her jittery, contributed to her chronically high blood pressure and, with the liberal amounts of cream and sugar she loaded it with, she had a sneaking suspicion it was the primary culprit for the considerable weight gain she had experienced over the years. Still, of all vices to entertain, she believed that caffeine was healthier and less destructive than smoking or gambling.

Hell of a time to be thinking about your coffee intake Virginia, she scolded herself. Yet that was how her mind worked. Focusing on the trivial and the mundane matters of the day was far more comforting than confronting truly important issues. She never liked to face the ugly facets of her life head on, choosing instead to avoid them or have others do her dirty work for her. It was something she had picked up early in life, compartmentalizing her brain to hide from the smarmy remarks regarding her weight that her classmates leveled at her and that even her own father would make consistently. If you really thought about it, it was the only way she could have motored on, the only conceivable manner Virginia could have survived. It was also, she reflected, most likely the reason she had called Stephen over to confront Mark.

Upon further review, there was really no discernable reason she had called Stephen home from work. She could have handled Mark alone, even though he was acting erratically. It was simply easier to let Stephen take the lead with Mark; she hated confrontation of any kind. Besides, that was always her way with Mark, when something had to be handled, she had usually passed it off to Stephen. It had been that way since her husband had died. She had handled that event badly of course, as was her nature, and the result was that she was inaccessible, unable to be there for her youngest son in his time of need.

This is all my fault, she bewailed. If she had been more assertive with Mark, if only she had been able to act like all good mothers should, none of this would have occurred. She would have calmed Mark down and guided him towards South Shore hospital and their mental health facilities. It would have been handled quietly, Stephen and Mark would never have fought and then . . . and then what? *You'd just be crying in your coffee in the hospital break room rather than the police station's.* That would have been the only difference, she assured herself, same result, different location.

Maybe the present circumstances of where she sat were not her fault, but the overall order of events certainly was. She had been selfish in her mourning years ago, and that had caused the defects in Mark's mind. She should have been more nurturing, a shoulder for her young son to cry upon. Toying with her cup, she cursed herself for not possessing a stiff upper lip. She was too emotionally fragile, and her husband had been the rock upon which she had built her life. When Ron had passed, she had collapsed emotionally and mentally, unable to fulfill the duties of motherhood. Tending to her own broken heart and attempting to put the pieces back together, she had ignored Mark's own ailing spirit. She had created a monster.

She had believed the job she had done raising her two young sons had been admirable, the only crowning achievement of her life, but it was clear now that had all been a lie. Mark's sanity had been a charade hidden beneath a frighteningly thin veneer. *What had been the tipping point?* She wondered. *Had it been the war?* Was that all it took for the walls to come tumbling down; was the heat of combat the catalyst for Mark's descent into madness? Or was it the drugs? Had the chemicals which saturated her young son's brain caused all this chaos? Why had she simply chosen to ignore her son's drug use? Was it her aversion to confrontation again? Did any of this really matter anymore; did it really matter how they had all arrived at this point?

Of course none of it mattered, she resolved. All that mattered was that she would now be known henceforth as the mother of a serial killer. At this moment, she suddenly felt sorry for the mothers of all those famous murderers she had heard about on the nightly news over the years. She felt a tremendous sense of pity for Mrs. Bundy, Mrs. Gacy. What had run through Lee Harvey Oswald's mother's mind or Mark David Chapman's when they had learned their sons were cold-blooded killers? She supposed it was a similar thought process to the one she was going through just now. She would be ostracized, cast out of normal society; surely, the world would consider her responsible.

How would she look into the eyes of the victim's mothers? She couldn't comprehend their pain; here she was feeling sorry for herself, not even considering what they would be going through. They would despise her, curse her for creating the wretched human being that had torn their babies from the world. The very thought of their angry glares was enough to make her lip quiver. She thought for sure she was going to burst into tears once again.

Goddamn you Virginia, she cursed herself in a sudden fit of anger, *you're always crying.* It had been her reaction to anything difficult, the default action of her body whenever confronted with anything close to distressing. *Pull yourself together!* Still, she couldn't shake feeling sorry for herself. Her already non-existent social life was over; she would be shunned by her neighbors. Surely that gossipy bitch, Ms. Bolduc, would see to that, spreading unsubstantiated rumor and innuendo amongst the residents of Talbot Road. Soon people she had interacted with and known for years would treat her like a total stranger, refusing to call upon her or even offer their hand in greeting. She would probably have to move out of the neighborhood.

The only people who would probably be interested in speaking to her would be college professors and psychologists, eager to pick her brain for evidence of why her son had transformed from maladjusted Hingham resident to vicious murderer. In the end, though, she deserved it, she assured herself. The road traveled to the police break room had been a long and winding one, but there was no doubt she had paved the way for her son's descent into madness. As far as she was concerned, she belonged here.

XL

Henry stomped down the corridor, a triumphant, militant air about him. So confident was he that he didn't even try to wipe the smile from his face. He was in his element, flanked by a small grouping of troopers from the Violent Fugitive Apprehension Section of the state police, who had been placed under his command. He was being recognized for what he was, a great leader of men. It was with enormous pride that he realized he was in fact the last man standing in this investigation. Patterson had flopped egregiously at the press conference, and Henry was almost embarrassed to be standing next to the man on camera. It had been clear to him that Patterson had sought the spotlight, a real shithead who wanted to claim credit where none was due, and Henry had been more than willing to let the sniveling little wimp humiliate himself.

There was a reason men like Patterson accepted command positions in Podunk towns like this one. There was little real work to be done; they spent most of their days kissing ass at town council meetings and making appearances at town parades and festivities. They were lazy, soft individuals who recoiled at the thought of any real action. They eschewed anything resembling real police work. Not like him. He was a man of action; he lived for such work.

He reveled in the blood, relished the smell of the crime scene. He saw himself as something akin to a general when it came to these investigations, directing his minions towards victory. It worried him every now and then that he felt nothing but perverse fascination when he came upon a dead body, but he usually shook such concerns away. That was something for limp dick shrinks and analysts to ponder, he had work to do. Besides, everyone dies, some people just met their maker in a more violent fashion than others.

He had risen through the ranks of the state police and he was proud of the hard work he had done to get here. He had spent countless days and nights tagging drunks and writing tickets along the Massachusetts Turnpike. There were all those years in Troop F patrolling Boston's Logan Airport, and then there was that proud, proud day when they had placed him in the Plymouth State Detective Unit with the rank of Lieutenant Detective. He had been a little disappointed he hadn't been placed closer to Boston, as he felt that was where the real action happened, but he had found the gang-infested city of Brockton more than enough to his liking. He liked the give and take of detective work always finding it more than satisfactory when he bagged some drug-dealing punk and threw them in the clink.

He also took great pride in his appearance. Though approaching sixty, he hit the gym hard, maintaining an imposing physique. He was disgusted with how men like Patterson let themselves go, looking sloppy and out of shape. They wouldn't scare an old lady, let alone some gang banger hanging out in Brockton. He also was allowed to wear a suit and tie rather than his trooper uniform, as he was a detective, but he repudiated such ideas, believing that suit and ties were for lawyers and that his trooper uniform was more demanding of respect.

That was why he had had such high hopes for working with Kaplan. *Now there was a policeman.* He looked good in uniform and he had seemed more than willing to go toe to toe with Henry, not backing down like that pencil dick police chief. Kaplan had seemed competent, a good cop, and had things turned out differently, Henry had thought of even offering the man a job. However, such was life. If it sounded too good to be true, then it usually was. Kaplan had turned out to be no different from most small town cops. Rather than investigating a crime, the bastard had been running interference for Enos. Henry didn't really know why Kaplan had been doing such a thing; he just knew that he was. In these small towns, everyone seemed to know everyone and their brother. Maybe Enos had banged Kaplan's sister, who knows, or maybe Kaplan just didn't like the Staties stepping in on his territory.

It hadn't mattered, Henry had gotten the man removed and maybe even cost him his job. It had been easy; all he had had to do was lean on that pussy Patterson. The man was like a little lapdog, doing whatever Henry demanded. This thought made Henry's smile broaden. He took a small measure of sadistic pleasure in imposing his will upon weaker men. He didn't take shit from anybody, besides his wife that is; she was the only one he'd let give him an earful. He certainly wasn't going to take shit from some meddling small town cop like Kaplan either. Regardless of his motives, Kaplan was out of the way and was now permanently on Henry's shit list. Seeing the anger and defeat in Kaplan's face had caused Henry to smile and wink at the young Sergeant, knowing the policeman was helpless to do anything about it, all the better to get under the prick's skin.

Of course Henry had bigger fish to fry. He was focused now on Mark Enos, determined to bring the little bastard to justice. Henry didn't care if Enos was a veteran; no one hurt innocent people in his jurisdiction. He would make Enos pay. He had known Enos was their man the minute the dogs had laid eyes upon him. He would've nailed him that day too, had Kaplan not interfered. Three people would still be alive had he just nabbed the son of a bitch then and there.

There was a part of him that relished the fact that Enos had eluded his grasp. Ever the fan of a good detective novel, Henry felt he had found his perfect foil; his very own super villain. He was a dutiful cop doing his job, determined to keep a serial murderer off the streets. When it was all said and done, when he had captured Mark Enos dead or alive, Henry would seek no recognition. No, unlike that piece of shit Patterson, he would shy away of the cameras, simply taking solace in the fact that he had protected the good people in his charge. There was a quiet pride in such actions, Henry assured himself, something that would have made his father, an ex-policeman, and his grandfather, also an ex-policeman, proud.

Brimming with confidence and anticipating a great victory, Henry had to stop himself from letting loose with a "Yee-haw!" Instead he turned towards the men behind him, still beaming and not breaking stride, "Let's catch this son of a bitch."

"Yes, sir!" They responded in unison, their voices echoing down the halls.

XLI

The sun set slowly upon the tiny hamlet of Hingham, allowing the silvery surface of the full moon to peer over the horizon. As the sky turned black, becoming populated with millions of phosphorescent blue stars, the great white orb hurtled headlong into the sky, rising to its rightful place on top of the world. A cragged, glowing circle the moon loomed large over the surface of the Earth.

The trees swayed softly in the early autumn breeze, and the sea rolled upon the shore giving the town a quiet, natural tranquility refusing to belie the turmoil its law enforcement personnel and the community in general was undergoing. Life had become chaotic and unnerving for the majority of the townsfolk who had nestled into their living rooms, the warm glow of their television lights shining from their windows. Hardly any civilian stirred on the nightscape, choosing the comfort of their homes rather than the cool air of the outdoors and the perceived danger lurking outside. A near silent, peaceful night the surreal environment was punctuated only by the distant howling of some unseen beast.

He flew through the woods, his heavy limbs crashing with considerable force into the undergrowth. Moving through the shadows, he marveled at the occasional plumes of dry leaves kicked up by his clumsy footing and the snapping of dry twigs as he staggered past. To the outsider, it probably looked sloppy, an uncomfortable, choppy series of movements, yet he couldn't have felt more free. It was indescribable, the sense of complete liberty and athleticism he felt as he navigated the forest.

His raspy breathing made it sound as though his airway was impeded, yet his lungs swelled with unimaginable capacity. Reaching out, he could sense what he was sure was a clawed hand parting a heavy growth of branches allowing him to proceed with reckless abandon between the trees. He could feel the slobber dripping from his mouth, believed that his fangs were lightly pinching the soft flesh of his lips as they protruded from his distorted gums.

Looking skyward, he saw the full moon, in all its glory, shimmering through the trees, its countenance flickering in the forest canopy like some defective light bulb. Focusing again on his footing, he sampled the air, sure that his newfound sense of smell would aid him in his quest. Seemingly aware of his movements, he felt out of control, as though he were watching himself move from outside his body, his brain relegated to the role of reluctant passenger. In this moment of freewheeling movement, the more primitive centers of his mind were piloting his shadowy form, only those most animal of instincts allowed to shine through.

There was no recollection of past events, nor any real concern for the future; he was only living in the now, his mind completely uncluttered and concentrating only on the most basic of tasks. There was a pang in his stomach, and a bell went off signaling that he hungered. There was plenty of prey to be found around him, the scent of deer, rabbits and other game animals hanging in the air. If he truly wanted to put his mind to it, he surely could have hunted down some small, furry inhabitant of the forest, but he shook this off. He wanted more of what he had sampled in the previous days. This wasn't simple hunger, it was a fully fledged craving, the very thought of his coming meal causing the saliva to gush forth from his mouth.

Was it Dahmer who callously commented that human flesh tasted like beef? Or was it that newspaperman in the thirties, William Seabrook, who famously commented that the meat of his fellow man tasted like a good cut of veal? Either way he didn't agree with either of them, to him it tasted like some form of salted pork, only with a fishy aftertaste. He had been repulsed by it at first, but he now desired it like nothing else. He supposed it was an acquired taste, something which had a most disagreeable flavor in the beginning only to slowly grow on one, like beer or boiled peanuts.

Did the fact that his brain now recognized human flesh as a food source make him a cannibal? He deduced quickly that it did, that his new found respect for anthropophagi made him that most unusual of serial killers, but it hardly made him unique. Besides the aforementioned Dahmer, he reflected there had been plenty of homicidal cannibals throughout the centuries. In fact many of the periodicals he had read had noted the ubiquity of cannibals in the history of mankind. He had been fascinated by the Leopard Society of the Ivory Coast and its band of cannibalistic members, which flourished well into the mid twentieth century. With morbid interest, he had read the grisly details of how its members dressed in leopard skins, ambushing travelers and dismembering them with leopard claws and teeth before feasting on the remains.

Of course his "favorite" cannibal had been Albert Fish, the so called "Werewolf of Wysteria." He could recall a series of articles dedicated to the early twentieth century killer that he had devoured in his spare time. He remembered cringing at Fish's graphic recollections of dispatching three young children for their meat. *How had Fish described their taste?* Better than any roasted turkey Fish had ever consumed. He supposed he could see that, of course he hadn't been able to delight in the flavors of cooked meat from his victims, not yet at least. In his present state, something deep inside him, embedded in the nether regions of his mind dictated that he begin feasting on their remains raw, gorging himself on their entrails right then and there.

Of course Fish had been completely crazy, making such claims that God had commanded him to torture and castrate little boys. The man was a well-known pedophile, a rapist who delighted in torturing and molesting small children throughout the United States well before he had committed his first murder. *What was it the articles had attributed Fish's mental defects to, a traumatic childhood, right?* Fish's father had died when he was young, and his mother had placed him in some abusive orphanage where the teachers stripped children naked before beating them in front of one another. That orphanage had turned Fish into a sexual deviant and launched him on the path to murder, to cannibalism.

He was no sexual deviant, but maybe there were still similarities between him and Fish. Both of their fathers had died young and their mothers had abandoned them, subjected them to painful and joyless childhoods. Now a new commonality had arisen, their appreciation for the flesh of their fellow man. *No,* he shook it off, *Fish was stark raving mad.* Fish had been crazy, a lunatic, surely he, Mark, was different. Although maybe not, perhaps he was crazy, traipsing through the woods believing himself a cursed being, a veritable lycanthrope. *Of course thinking this way, rationalizing what is happening to you, can you really be crazy?* Weren't such actions the very definition of sanity?

No, he wasn't crazy; this was really happening. Of course he was a werewolf. Or maybe he was something else. Had he really transformed fully? He couldn't really tell at this time, something unseen and unrecognized kept him from clearly identifying what form he was in. Maybe he had merely been possessed like that old Native American legend, the Wendigo, a malevolent cannibalistic spirit that could infect unlucky individuals. Viewing the full moon again, he resolved himself to his original train of thought. No, he was indeed a werewolf, a werewolf on the prowl.

If he was sane, however, he should have control of his actions, and that was clearly not the case, he noted. Even his thoughts were convoluted. What had he been talking about? He did not relish the taste of human flesh. That couldn't have been him thinking like that. *Could it have been?* Commanding his limbs to cease moving, he lamented as they failed to do his bidding. In his present reality, there was no controlling himself. The rational, omnipresent voice inside his head inhabited only a small corner of his brain right now, captive to the seething, angry animal which had wrested control from him. The beast did not rationalize, it did not ponder its existence, and it was wholly subservient to the terrible, primal urges which drove it forward. What little humanity it possessed was tucked away in the furthest recesses of its primitive mind. It hungered, needed to feed immediately. It longed for the kill.

Suddenly, a cacophony of smells wafted past its nostrils. Coming to a complete stop it nestled itself against the trunk of a tree, firmly concealed in the shadows. Inhaling deeply, it took stock of the variety of smells coming across its olfactory centers, attempting desperately to decipher the scent trail. There was the smell of smoke, spiced meats, and the aggravating smell of bug spray. Shaking its head, its ears pricked up as the soft sound of singing filtered through its eardrums. Creeping closer to the tree line, carefully placing its feet so as not to make a sound, it peered forward and viewed the orange flicker of a campfire.

The flame silhouetted the figures seated around it, a crowd of disparate shapes and sizes. Getting low to the ground, it pawed its way ever closer, stopping just behind the tree line, hidden only by a grouping of ferns and ivy. Its eyes glinted in the firelight, and it tensed in anticipation of the strike as it heard one of its victims speak, "Mommy, can we make 'smores now?"

It could hardly contain its excitement as it heard the unmistakable squeal of a young child. It had yet to taste the sweet, supple flesh of young boy or girl; now would be its chance. Licking its lips, it prepared to unleash the full fury of its weapons.

"You have to wait for your father," it heard a woman seated beside the child respond. Though her back was to it, the man-beast in the woods noted her defined muscle tone, her slender neck. She would be an easy kill and provide a bevy of tender, stringy meat. Preparing for the attack, it froze as another figure approached from the other side of the campfire. The amber glow of the fire illuminated the man's huge frame; he was a hulking, muscular brute. Obviously the young child's father, he could be dispatched, but could also do some damage before he was subdued. Determining that the costs outweighed any perceived benefits, it retreated into the woods, resigning itself to locating easier quarry.

Slinking through the trees, it had only gone a few hundred yards when it detected a new presence up ahead. The air emanating here seemed humid, a moist warmth mingling with the cool night air. There was also the heavy smell of menthol along with a bizarre soapy smell. A thunderous, constant sound reverberated in its ears and it moved forward, thoroughly intrigued. The faint yellow glow of artificial light filtered through the trees up ahead and just above the roar of running water there was something else, something indecipherable before. Committing itself to investigate even further it moved forward, recognizing the noise as someone singing, a poor, unassuming soul singing in the shower.

XLII

The manhunt began slowly, with most officers spreading out to predetermined spots Henry had identified as prime locations for Enos to be hiding; that is if he was even still in Hingham proper. This included the Old Burying Ground a hulking mound of earth dotted with an undeterminable number of headstones and tomb markers. Many officers found the atmosphere downright eerie as they swept through the premises, sweeping the area with their flashlights, the beams flickering through the bare limbs of the cemetery's trees. Other areas identified by Henry included the park surrounding Hingham harbor and even the few small islands which dotted the inlet, although just how Henry believed Enos had gotten to these was not explained. The main boulevards of South and Main Streets in the downtown region of Hingham were also heavily patrolled with a small contingent of officers milling about the steps of St. Paul's Catholic Church, its white spire reaching skyward towards the full moon above.

A few unlucky stragglers, however, had been ordered to stay behind at the station house, fielding the few calls which now came over the 911 line as Patterson's phone blackout of the tip line continued. One particular call of note came from a Michael Williams of Marion Street, just a short distance from the Enos house on Talbot Road, who reported hearing strange rustling noises in his backyard. Two officers were immediately dispatched from the main search to investigate Mister Williams's claim.

* * *

Patrolman Paulo Molina brought his squad car to a rolling stop just at the edge of the Williams' house, a stately and quaint split-ranch style home. The houselights were not on, and in the dark of night, the place appeared abandoned. As if reading Molina's mind, his partner Pat Canty switched on the patrol car's searchlight and aimed it at the front of the house. Occasionally the radio would crackle with static, but for the most part they sat in silence, only the rumbling of the vehicle's engine keeping them company. Canty, an older, burly gentleman turned to his younger counterpart. "So, what do you think?"

Molina sighed and shrugged his shoulders. "I guess we go knock on the door."

"Think this one's legit?" Canty asked.

Frustrated and tired Molina rubbed a hand over his close-cropped black hair before shaking his head, "Fucker probably just heard a bunch of raccoons rummaging through his trash cans, and now he thinks the big, bad wolf is at his backdoor."

Cutting the engine, Molina flung open his door and started to exit the car, "Let's get this shit over with."

Molina began marching towards the house, hearing Canty slam his own door and fall in line behind him. *More fucking wild goose chases,* Molina bristled. *I just want to go home!* He was tired, forced to work a double shift due to the search for Enos. Cranky and irritable, he desired nothing more than just a cold beer, some television, and his warm bed. His jaw clenched and muscles flexed he stomped towards the front door, only softening his expression as the door opened.

A man who Molina estimated was in his mid-fifties opened the door. He was frumpy and wrinkled, wearing thick glasses and a robe which hardly covered his beer gut. Opening the screen door in front of the main entrance he leaned out, blinking in the harshness of the still-shining spotlight.

"Are you Mister Williams?" Molina asked, attempting to act as friendly as possible.

"Yeah, that's me," Williams nodded.

"All right what seems to be the issue tonight Mister Williams?" Molina questioned, stopping just outside the transom.

"Me and the wife were about to go to bed when we heard some noises out in the backyard. We figured it was nothing at first until we could hear something moving around the roof, so we thought we'd give you guys a call."

"The roof?" Molina asked incredulously, casting a glance at Canty to his rear.

"Oh Yeah," Williams nodded, "we could hear something scrambling around up there, and after watching the news, we thought we should get you guys over here."

"And is something still on your roof sir?"

"Hell yeah it is," Williams whispered nodding skyward. "We kept the lights off so as to not let him know we heard him. Better for you guys to catch him, you know?"

"Him?" Molina interrogated, finding himself whispering, though he had no idea why.

"Yeah, you know, that Enos fellow," Williams answered.

Molina smiled, holding up his hand. "Look, Mister Williams, I'm sure it's just a few squirrels and not—." Molina found himself cut off by a loud thud originating from above. There was a series of scratching noises, and it was clear that something heavy was ambling across the rooftop of the Williams' house. Molina took a step back, involuntarily clutching at his sidearm and he looked towards Canty for a reaction. Canty had also been taken aback, staring at the rooftop and searching for the source of the disturbance.

"See, I told you!" Williams hissed.

"Get back in the house," Molina commanded. "Is it only you and your wife inside?"

"No," Williams shook his head, "my daughter's in her room."

"Okay, get back inside."

Molina turned and motioned towards Canty, urging him to follow him to the rear of the house from which the sounds seemed to be coming from. As he jogged, Molina retrieved a collapsible baton from his utility belt, unfurling it in one quick and brutal motion. His heart raced with excitement and his breath now came in shallow, ragged gasps. As they rounded the house, Molina felt Canty squeeze at his shoulder and pull him back.

"Yo, what the hell are we doing?" Canty whispered.

"What do you mean? We're going to see what the hell's back there."

"Shouldn't we call for back up?" Canty wheezed, "I mean what if it is that kid?"

"Then it's that kid, come on man we either bag him now or we let him get away. Think about it man, we'll be commended," Molina whispered back. Motioning towards the sounds of someone ambling down the rooftop he watched as the realization of what was possible watched over Canty. He felt alive now; his previously overwhelming fatigue all but vanished. The adrenaline coursing through his veins was infinitely more powerful than any caffeine drink or energy pill he could have taken. This was huge, a chance for something big.

If it was Enos waiting for them in that backyard and they managed to apprehend them, they'd be hailed as heroes, two hardworking cops who rescued a town under siege. There'd be medals, a meteoric rise through the ranks, and maybe they'd even make a few bucks off it. Molina also dreamed of the women he could bag with such a story. *You can get so much pussy with something like this.* Chicks would eat it up; they loved heroes in uniform.

There was a metallic groan, and it became clear that someone or something was climbing down the aluminum gutter that ran along one side of the house. Molina's eyes went wide, and he looked towards Canty, "Come on, he's getting away!"

They came around the back of the house just in time to watch a silhouetted figure drop from the gutter and hit the ground running. Molina broke into a full sprint, clutching his baton in a ready position. "Freeze," he yelled, "Hingham Police Department!"

The figure refused to heed the demand, its heavy footfalls thundering on the grass as whomever it was made for a clump of bushes that led towards an adjoining yard. Molina hastened his pace, determined to bring down his quarry. Coming within a few feet of the figure, he lunged forward, tackling the fleeing suspect to the ground. As he had dropped his baton in the process, he began hurling clenched fists towards the center mass of the downed suspect screaming the entire time through gritted teeth, "I told you to stop!"

Canty arrived behind him, letting loose with a few vicious kicks at the still silhouetted figure. The suspect yelped in return. From behind they heard the creaking of a screen door flung open and they looked up to watch Mister Williams come waddling off of his back deck, a flashlight clutched in his hand and the beam waving wildly. "We've got you, you son of a bitch," he cursed, "you try to hurt my family!"

Still pinning down the flailing suspect Molina became aware of another noise, a shrill shrieking in the distance. Looking up he could see a crying teenage girl, in a state of undress, calling out from her bedroom window. "Stop," She shouted, the tears streaking down her face visible in the dim light of her room, "you're hurting him!" Confused, Molina looked down just in time to watch Williams' flashlight illuminate the bloodied and swollen face of a teenage boy.

Instinctively, Molina pulled back. "Who the fuck is that?"

Williams stepped forward, inspecting the groaning, writhing young man before him. Slapping his knee, he cast an angry look towards the crying teenage girl, still screaming from her window. "It's my daughter's boyfriend," he growled.

XLIII

Unaware of the fear and hysteria which had gripped the town of Hingham, Bob Tranfaglia turned off the hot water and stepped out of the communal shower at the Wompatuck campground. Though the warm steam still rose from the shower room's yellow tiling, he shivered as the cold night air filtered in and slapped at his wet skin. An aging man of sixty-five, he retrieved his white towel and wrapped it around his saggy, hairy body.

He enjoyed camping, truly loved roughing it out in the woods. However, the grit and grime which tended to cake to his skin bothered him immensely, and he was grateful for the showers which populated several of the campground's bathrooms. The tiles were mildewed and the steel faucets a light green, betraying the age of the facility. The pipes which snaked away from the room's sinks were rusted through, now a copper color rather than the proper shiny, gray. Still, everything was in proper working order, and Tranfaglia was just happy to be clean once again.

With a sigh of contentment, he slicked back the few fronds of hair on his head and walked towards a bank of mirrors, whistling as he did so. The mirrors were fogged with condensation as the cold air, wafting in through an open doorway, met the hot steam of the shower room. Waddling in front of one mirror, Tranfaglia placed a liver-spotted hand upon it and began to clear off a section, only to freeze in his tracks.

Something strange had caught his eye as he cleared off the area, something he couldn't quite wrap his mind around. It was a figure, anthropomorphic in appearance, and it appeared to be squatting just outside the shower room. Without his glasses, Tranfaglia was unable to focus and get a clear look at the figure, and his vision problems were exacerbated by the mirrors layer of condensation. As the section fogged up again, he hurriedly wiped it away, squinting at the mirror. "What the—"

Crash!

Tranfaglia was unable to finish his sentence as he was set upon from behind. He was launched headlong towards the wall, and his scalp made contact with the mirror as a result. The shattering glass lacerated his skin, and as he fell, his chin hit the porcelain sink in front of the mirror violently, almost causing the old man to black out.

Lying face down upon the floor and slipping in and out of consciousness Tranfaglia groaned and struggled to get up. Unable to see as the warm blood from his scalp trickled into his eyes, he winced as rested his palms upon broken shards of mirror slicing the skin deeply. Collapsing again, he struggled to breathe as his system went into shock. His vision narrowing, the world going black, he suddenly became aware of a new sensation.

There was a heavy weight upon his back and the tickle of hot breath on the back of his neck. Snapping into focus, he could hear the raspy, congested breathing of his attacker, and he screamed as he felt what seemed like hot knives digging into the meat of shoulder. Struggling to fight off the assailant, Tranfaglia found himself being dragged, naked and flailing, out of the bathroom and into the wilderness beyond.

* * *

Kaplan yawned as he steered the cruiser through the Hingham town center. The lights of the storefront signs and streetlamps shined bright, but there was nary a soul in sight besides a few policemen. Stopping at a red light, he looked over at his passenger, "You really have no idea where he could be?"

Stephen lifted his head off his hand and shrugged his shoulders before shaking his head,

"No, I'm not lying to you. I really have no clue where he'd be."

Kaplan was frustrated; they had been at this for hours, navigating the same roads over and again. As the light turned green Kaplan interrogated, "Come on, you're telling me he has no close friends, no one he would turn to?"

Stephen shrugged, "Mark kind of withdrew, became more of a loner after our dad died. After that he just stopped hanging out with people, went his own way."

"So, what he was a nerd or something in high school?" Kaplan asked.

"No, I didn't say that," Stephen answered, "People liked Mark well enough. He just never really got close to anybody after our Dad's death; I guess it kind of messed him up. They were pretty close and all."

"I see," Kaplan said. "What about girls? Does he have a girlfriend, or even someone he might be seeing?"

"No." Stephen shook his head. "Mark's never dated any girl seriously as far as I know."

Kaplan swallowed hard before asking, "What about a boyfriend?"

"My brother's not gay," Stephen spat. "Like I said, he just doesn't let people get to close to him after my dad, and I'm sure going to war didn't really help him on that front either."

Kaplan nodded, "Sorry, just had to ask." Drumming his fingers upon the steering wheel he questioned, "Well, what about family? Are there any extended family members living around here that he could turn to?"

Stephen shook his head, "My mom's parents kind of looked after us after my dad went, but they both passed away a few years ago. My other grandparents just kind of drifted away after my dad died, and we've just gradually lost contact with them. I really doubt Mark would turn up on their doorstep looking for help. It's really just me, Mark, and my mom."

"Well what about your family? Would Mark go see your wife for help?"

Stephen laughed, "No way, they've never liked each other since high school. Besides, Mark wouldn't want my kids getting involved in this."

"What makes you even think he's still in Hingham then?"

"Because he's got nowhere else to go, man, no money, and like I said, his only family is me and my mom," Stephen replied.

"Well shit, kid," Kaplan sighed as he watched the houses whiz by outside his window. "Where the hell *is* your brother?"

* * *

Patricia Tranfaglia sauntered towards the bathroom entrance, her flip flops slapping at her heels as she did so. Shivering in the cold she adjusted her white sweatshirt jacket and edged towards the men's room. Clearing her throat she listened for the sound of running water and frowned when she heard nothing but the steady plinking of water droplets hitting a puddle. "Bob?" She called out, receiving no response.

Oh lord, she thought, *did he fall asleep on the john again?* "Bob?" She yelled louder this time, hoping to rattle her husband awake. Hearing nothing, she shuffled closer to the door, not daring to enter for fear she would walk in on another man in the most intimate of moments. Again, she heard no reply. It didn't even seem as if anyone was in there. Adjusting her glasses she peeked her head into the open doorway and called again, "Bob, are you in here?"

Her voice echoed throughout the enclosed space, and she gasped as she looked down at the floor. A mirror was shattered upon the wall, the reflective shards littering the floor and glimmering in the artificial light. There was the greasy stain of fresh blood, which had been trampled through and smeared on the tiled surface. A white towel lay strewn besides the sink, stained red with blood. Entering the room further, she spied her husband's belongings nested upon a bench besides the shower room. His clothes were folded neatly on the seat and his glasses perched upon them.

"Oh no," she panted, "Oh God."

Withdrawing from the bathroom, she began to jog away from the facility back towards her campsite.

XLIV

"*All units please be advised,*" the feminine voice crackled over Kaplan's radio, "*possible assault at Wompatuck State Park campground.*"

"Sounds like good times," Kaplan mused, keeping his eyes glued to the road ahead.

Stephen however sprung to life, "Wait, did she just say Wompatuck?"

"Yeah," Kaplan affirmed, "what's so interesting about that?"

"That's got to be Mark," Stephen replied, his voice pitched with excitement.

Kaplan frowned, "What are you talking about? It's probably two drunks fighting over a case of beer."

"No, you don't understand. Wompatuck's like the only place I could imagine Mark going. I can't believe I didn't think about it before."

"I don't follow you," Kaplan said. "Why would your brother go to the park?"

"We used to go there as kids. Mark actually mentioned it a while back. He knows the area around there, and he'd be comfortable there," Stephen answered. Looking at Kaplan he could tell he had not made a convincing case. "Look," he insisted, "I know my brother's there, you have to trust me. We have to go to Wompatuck. Think about it, man, there're plenty of places to hide out in there."

Though not entirely swayed, Kaplan relented, after all they had searched fruitlessly for Mark for hours. "All right kid, we'll check it out."

"Thank you," Stephen said, expressing his gramercy, "Now, please step on it."

Kaplan depressed the gas pedal, the engine of his cruiser roaring in response. With a flick of his finger, the vehicle's siren came to life, the blue lights flashing as they sped down the street.

* * *

Geoff Simmons laid his head upon the pillow, watching as his girlfriend, Alicia Reilly, playfully stripped off her clothing. Alone in their tent, sheltered by a thin piece of blue Nylon from the cold autumn air, he was having the time of his life. Clad in nothing more than her bra and panties, Alicia sat on her knees and looked at her boyfriend. "That's it for now."

"What?" Geoff asked. "Come on, take it all off."

"Nuh-uh," Alicia teased, waving her finger, "not until you take something off."

Smiling, Geoff sat up and hurriedly took off his fleece shirt, flinging it against the wall of the tent. "Okay," he prodded while lying back down upon the sleeping bag, "now keep going."

"You spoiled little shit," Alicia smiled coyly, her long blonde hair tapering just above her heaving breasts. Arching her back she moved her hands and slowly unclasped her bra, holding it in place for a moment.

Geoff was driven crazy by lust, not able to stand his girlfriend's efforts to tantalize him any longer. "Oh, come on baby, just get naked!" He exclaimed with mock anger.

Still holding her brassiere closed Alicia shook her head. "I don't know," she cooed.

"Come on!" Geoff demanded.

"Jesus, all right here it comes," Alicia groaned.

Geoff placed his hands behind his head, ready to take in the spectacle of his beautiful, soon to be topless girlfriend. As she slowly lowered her piece of lingerie Geoff's focus was suddenly drawn to the tent wall. The campfire outside cast a yellow glow upon the light blue fabric just to Alicia's rear, and it now illuminated the clear silhouette of a lurking human being. The dark shadow passed over the tent wall and increased in size. Geoff's eyes went wide as he realized the intruder was moving swiftly towards the tent itself.

"Hey, what the fu—," Geoff began only to be cut off as Alicia was thrown on top of him. The world went topsy-turvy, the two of them screaming and while he was unable to view the outside world through the sea of blue fabric Geoff was sure they were moving. For a brief moment he felt intense heat as the tent was dragged over the fire; the smoldering coals stinging his bare skin.

Alicia continued to wail and the two of them were flung in a series of somersaults as the aluminum tent supports snapped causing yet another part of the tent wall to collapse upon them. The heat inside the shelter was suffocating as they were enveloped in the mess of fabric and pulled to an unknown destination. Geoff cringed as he felt a series of stones and tree roots rake over his back and bruise his flesh. While dealing with the pain, he somehow found the presence of mind to keep his girlfriend situated on top of him, attempting to protect her from the ground onslaught.

This proved to be of no avail as he consistently lost his grip as they were thrown this way and that. There was a hissing sound as a number of tree branches scraped the Nylon surface of the tent and Geoff now knew they were outside of the campsite having entered the forest. There was something else as well; barely audible over their screaming, Geoff believed he could hear a noise similar to the snuffling of a dog.

Suddenly, there was the sound of ripping fabric, and Geoff sensed that a great weight was discharged, causing the tent to pick up more speed. Unable to feel Alicia's warm skin against his own, he instantly realized she had been pulled from the tent. The tent came to a halt, and Geoff struggled to free himself from the collapsed structure. Outside he heard Alicia unleash a blood-curdling scream, and this was accompanied by the sound of a snarling beast which sent a shiver down Geoff's spine.

Fighting to unleash himself and come to the aid of his beloved, Simmons punched at the thin textile only to have a new mess of it fly in his face. Exerting a great deal of energy, he inhaled deeply, choking as he sucked in a liberal section of Nylon. Suffocating in the sea of fabric he began to panic, flailing wildly. Outside Alicia had ceased to scream, but Simmons was unable to take note of this has he was too caught up in his own struggle.

There was more ripping and Geoff was instantly freed from his nylon prison. Gasping for much needed breath, he felt the cold night air touch upon his warm, sweaty skin and viewed the beautiful night sky above. Still acclimating himself to his new surroundings, he became aware of a threatening, guttural growl and felt some type of bladed instrument pierce his skin. Gritting his teeth, he groaned in pain.

Not able to view his attacker in full he began to punch with abandon, swinging his limbs freely. "Get off me!" He screamed, "Get off me!" Still fighting, he found he no longer possessed control over his right hand as the aggressor had grabbed hold of it. Geoff continued to punch away with his left fist and kicked with his legs, stopping only when an intense rush of pain overtook him. There was an audible pop, and Simmons squealed as he felt something give way on his hand.

The agony overwhelmed him, fighting through the fog of adrenaline. Screaming loudly he felt the warm rush of blood wash over his right hand and he moved to clutch it with his left as his attacker released it. "Oh, God damn it!" Simmons cried, "God damn it!"

His assailant grunted, and Geoff felt a hand grasp his ankle, dragging him into the woods kicking and screaming.

XLV

The squad car zoomed up the darkened, wooded pass. Stephen watched with baited breath as the car hugged the curb, threatening to careen into one of many grass-filled ditches. "Slow down, man," he demanded, "I said get us there fast, not kill us."

Grumbling to himself, Kaplan released his hold on the gas pedal as they ramped up a steep slope which carried them past a scenic meadow. The hill crested before rising sharply one final time and allowing the cruiser to continue down the narrow road. At this slower speed, Stephen caught a better glimpse of his surroundings, the vehicles flashing lights serving to illuminate the countryside. To their right he viewed a break in the trees and a darkened warehouse-like building. He smiled weakly, remembering better days with his brother exploring such ruins.

Kaplan however, frowned as they passed the shell of a building, catching sight of the graffiti which defaced nearly every inch of the building's surface. The structures which littered the park had become a haven for bored teenagers and the occasional gang, and as such, Kaplan did not have exactly fond memories of the park. Besides the litany of arrests he had made in the vicinity, more than one of his past girlfriends had forced him to hike the miles of trails which wormed their way through the forested grounds, and these unfortunate travails had brought on not one, but three bouts with poison ivy.

The headlights illuminated a wooden sign to the right, announcing that they had arrived at the park's campgrounds. Turning into the camp entrance, they crept past a small guardhouse with its gate up. The lights were darkened, and it appeared no one was inside. Kaplan reached a fork in the road and turned right, leading them down an intensely narrow roadway. After a passage of several hundred yards, they merged left onto a main road which offered them a choice of four darkened side roads.

"All right, keep your eyes peeled," Kaplan instructed as they slowly passed the first side road. The two of them peered down the throughway, seeing nothing but a strip of asphalt surrounded on both sides by thick forest. The full moon provided the only illumination, casting everything in a subtle, blue hue.

Pulling up to the second road, Kaplan immediately stopped the car. "Shit," he whispered.

Stephen saw it too. The road stood in stark contrast to the adjacent passage. A sea of twinkling lights, a number of police cruisers populated the street all surrounding a white brick structure. Staring intently in the direction of the grouping of vehicles, Stephen attempted to decipher just what they were doing. *Jesus,* he thought, *there has to be a dozen of them.* "Do you think they found him?"

"No," Kaplan answered, still staring at the police vehicles. It was way too many cruisers for a simple case of assault he reflected, and he noted the conspicuous presence of a number of state police vehicles. He had no doubt that the ubiquitous presence of Henry resided down that road. He also realized it probably meant one thing and one thing only, Mark Enos had killed again. A pang of guilt stung at his gut, and he found himself gritting his teeth in response.

"How can you be so sure?" Stephen asked, not taking his eyes off of the policemen.

"We would've heard about it on the radio," Kaplan replied.

"He's here though, right?" Stephen questioned, "I mean they don't call that many cars for just two drunks fighting over a case of beer do they?"

"Yeah, he's here," Kaplan nodded, "and if he messed someone up again, you better hope we find him before they do."

"Why?" Stephen asked, turning to face Kaplan.

"Because they'll shoot him," Kaplan answered stone-faced. Not bothering to acknowledge Stephen's pained expression, Kaplan breathed heavily through his nose. "Come on kid, let's go."

Letting go of the brake, he allowed the cruiser to roll silently past the second road, bypassing the third passage and turning onto the fourth. Turning on his car's searchlight, Kaplan maneuvered the car at a snail's pace. The road was dotted on both sides by a number of grass lots, each denoted with a yellow number on the roadbed in front of it. The majority of campsites sat vacant, and those that were inhabited usually had a large RV parked upon it. *This late in the season only the hardiest of campers would want to sleep in a tent,* Kaplan said to himself.

The two of them inspected each site carefully, attempting to detect anything out of the ordinary. About to give up on this leg of their search, Kaplan nosed the cruiser around a bend before depressing the brake violently and staring breathlessly ahead. "Oh Jesus," he muttered.

Stephen, still inspecting the lots to the side turned and asked, "What?" After following the officer's gaze, he remarked, "Oh shit."

A campsite lay ahead, looking ravaged and disorderly. The fire pit was in disarray, flames spreading beyond the now-broken rock border and licking at the base of a smoldering lawn chair. Other objects had also been caught up in the mini inferno; Kaplan identified several plastic bags of camping goods spewing smoke and flames. The bushes beyond the site appeared matted and trampled down, indicating that something large had been drug through there. Kaplan edged the cruiser forward, coming to a rolling stop in front of the campsite.

Kaplan stared downwards, noticing a faded, yellow marker on the pavement. *Campsite R51,* he noted. Reaching for the radio he stopped himself just as his fingertips made contact with the black receiver. There was no way he could call this in, not just yet. He had to find Enos before Henry and the rest did. Withdrawing his hand he put the cruiser in park and retrieved his sidearm, turning off the safety and chambering a round.

"Whoa, whoa, what the hell are you doing dude?" Stephen asked, "I'm not going to let you go out there and shoot my brother."

"I'm not planning on it, *dude,*" Kaplan answered rudely. "I just want to be prepared for anything." Taking another look at the campsite he looked at Stephen. "Stay in the car, anything happens, use the radio." With a deep breath, Kaplan opened the door and exited the cruiser.

He crept slowly into the campsite, his head on a swivel, scanning the tree line for an impending attack. His pistol at the ready, he moved towards the campfire and inspected the ground. The grass was beaten down, and the rough outline of something square was imprinted into the soil. *Has to be from a tent.* Kaplan also noted something else by the campfire, something which made his heart beat faster. A small pool of viscous looking, red liquid, it reflected the firelight brilliantly and Kaplan knew for sure just what it was: the blood of an unknown victim.

Crouching down to get a better look, he heard a car door slam behind him. Stephen now walked briskly towards the police officer. "I thought I told you to stay in the car," Kaplan hissed.

"Yeah, that wasn't going to happen." Stephen shook him off. Coming to Kaplan's side, Stephen asked, "What is that? Is that blood?"

"'Fraid so," Kaplan answered, "What the hell is wrong with your brother?"

Ignoring the question, Stephen looked ahead, towards the trampled underbrush. "He had to have gone through there right?"

Kaplan stared down the freshly made trail and nodded.

"Well let's go," Stephen prodded, slapping Kaplan on the shoulder. "Maybe we can catch up to him." Not waiting for Kaplan's answer Stephen ran headlong into the woods, following his brother's perceived route.

"Steve!" Kaplan called, "Steve wait!" Hearing nothing but the snapping of twigs as Stephen thundered through the woods, Kaplan stood up and shook his head in annoyance. "God damn it," he muttered before heading into the forest himself.

Henry stood over the shredded corpse of Bob Tranfaglia and shook his head in dismay. "Ah, Son of a bitch," he said to no one in particular.

The nude body of the old man was nestled in the undergrowth just a few yards away from the bathroom entrance, surrounded by a liberal coating of tall crab grass and ferns. The throat had been torn out, pieces of flesh missing from the back of his body, and the face scratched up. Henry detected the shimmering mirror glass still embedded in the dead man's scalp.

"Who called it in?" Henry asked.

"Guy's wife," a burly trooper to Henry's right answered. *Bradley I think*, Henry said to himself, struggling to remember the man's name.

"She found the body?"

"No," Bradley answered, "she thought the guy had been jumped, never even spied the body. We haven't told her the news just yet."

"Poor thing," Henry said through pursed lips. "Well, somebody get a van down here to pick him up and a crime scene team."

"Yes, sir," another trooper answered before retreating from the group gathered around the body.

Perking up, Henry wheeled around and began to walk back towards the collection of police vehicles outside the bathroom taking Bradley in tow. "Listen, Bradley, isn't it?"

"Yes, sir," Bradley affirmed.

"That stiff's fresh; that means our boy is around here. Find me someone who can get me a map of this goddamn place and let's start fanning out so we can catch this son of a bitch."

"Yes sir, already done, we've got a member of the park staff already on his way in," Bradley stated.

"Out-fucking-standing," Henry beamed.

"'Scuse me sir!" A voice called out from the group of cars.

Henry searched for the source, finding a young Hispanic Hingham policeman staring at him. The patrolman leaned against his driver's side door, clutching the receiver of his microphone. *Oh Christ what the hell's this one's name again*, Henry struggled, *Mariscal or Marescal*. "Yes, what is it?" Henry grumbled.

"I've got a call saying we've got an abandoned cruiser two rows up from us outside a messed up campsite. Officers on site say there's evidence of a struggle and blood."

"Hot damn," Henry crowed, looking at Bradley, "they must've found our guy."

"All right, listen up!" Henry boomed, gathering the attention of the assembled officers, "We've possibly located our suspect just two rows up. I want all hands on deck. Let's go get the bastard!"

There was a flurry of activity as the officers began to disperse, some on foot, others jumping back into their vehicles. A team of dogs was unleashed from one car, the air filling with sound of their barking.

"Let's lock and load," Henry instructed Bradley before looking up at the night sky and taking note of the full moon. "Anyone got any silver bullets?" He grinned.

* * *

Kaplan slogged through the underbrush, finally emerging onto a dirt path and nearly running into a stationary Stephen. A pond lay ahead, populated by what seemed like a million lily pads, and the entire scene was rather picturesque as the bright full moon reflected upon the water's silvery surface. "Why'd you stop?" Kaplan asked.

Stephen did not speak, merely directing Kaplan's attention to their feet. "Oh God," Kaplan groaned as the moonlight illuminated a grisly sight.

A young woman, nude but for a black thong, lay prone upon the ground. Her eyes were open wide, her face locked in a mask of horror and pain. The woman's throat had been torn out, and there were deep gouges above her left breast. The sandy soil about her head was now a thick, black mud where she had bled out onto the forest floor.

"My brother did this?" Stephen questioned breathlessly.

Not knowing how to answer exactly, as he sensed the question was almost rhetorical in nature, Kaplan merely patted Stephen's shoulder, attempting to comfort the shocked young man. Looking away from the scene, Kaplan surveyed the surrounding area, his attention eventually drawn by a crumbled bit of fabric resting in some bushes. Leaving Stephen's side he moved closer to investigate.

The shadows shrouded most of the area below the bushes in darkness and Kaplan fumbled about on his keychain before finally producing a small penlight. Flicking it on, he clutched his gun in one hand and the small flashlight in the other. The light was weak, but provided enough illumination for Kaplan to see clearly. What he surmised used to be the young woman's tent was strewn about the branches of the bushes, a tangled mess of shredded blue fabric. Wet bloodstains littered the fabrics surface, and as Kaplan clutched the destroyed tent in his hands something fell, landing with a soft thud at his feet.

Looking down, Kaplan swallowed hard before looking up. "Hey Steve," he called.

"Yeah?" Stephen replied.

"She's got all ten fingers, right?"

Stephen's brow furrowed and he inspected the dead woman's hands thoroughly. Counting to himself he looked back over at Kaplan, "Yeah, why?"

"Then we've got another one somewhere," Kaplan answered calmly.

Intrigued, Stephen walked over to Kaplan's side and looked towards the area the officer's penlight had illuminated. A human thumb, ripped from its socket and trailing a few tendons, sat just beyond Kaplan's toes. "Oh God," Stephen winced, "What the hell are you doing, Mark?"

Kaplan continued to search the ground with his penlight, looking for any sign of a second body.

As he passed over an area of trail, he detected a faint blood trail just a few yards away. "Come on," he prodded, nudging Stephen with his elbow. The two of them followed the trail, walking at a brisk yet deliberate pace.

"Look there!" Stephen pointed. A small, tattered piece of blue fabric, from the tent no doubt, clung to the solitary branch of an evergreen. Kaplan moved towards it, noting that this took the duo past the pond and they were now surrounded by thick forest. Placing the penlight between his teeth he plucked the piece of cloth from the tree and inspected it in his hands before turning his attention back to the trail ahead.

He froze immediately, dropping his penlight from his mouth inadvertently. Standing just a few yards up the pathway, silhouetted in the moonlight, was a lone, hulking figure. The blue glow of the moon danced upon the figure's back allowing Kaplan to glimpse the hunched shoulders and tousled hair of the person standing in front of him. The hair's on the back of his neck stood on end as the newcomer's raspy breathing reached his ears, and he felt his heart rate increase as the intruder growled at him.

Dry mouthed, he lifted his gun slowly and aimed it at the shadowy figure. "Mark," he said sternly, "Mark, you freeze right there."

Stephen came running to his side. "Mark!" He shouted, "Mark, we're here to help you!"

Kaplan watched as the figure turned and took off in response, bounding awkwardly into the woods. Listening to the sound of snapping branches and rustling leaves, he stood shaking, still frozen in place. "Come on," Stephen instructed, grabbing Kaplan and pulling him along, "we've got to follow him."

Kaplan shook his head and regained his focus. *Don't fall to pieces here, Eric.* Grabbing at Stephen he forcibly pulled him back. "Wait man, we can't just rush into this all willy-nilly. We proceed with caution, you hear me?"

Stephen took one plaintive look up the trail before looking back at Kaplan and nodding his understanding. Retrieving his tiny flashlight from the ground, Kaplan motioned for Stephen to follow him.

The dusty trail now morphed into an uneven bed of asphalt, dotted with potholes and frost heaves. Tree roots had forced their way through the tar in places and Kaplan wondered how anyone ever utilized these bike paths. Looking back at Stephen, Kaplan whispered, "Watch your feet."

They moved slower now as Kaplan was fearful of an ambush. *He could be anywhere in these woods,* Kaplan shuddered. Surrounded by trees and denied the aide of moonlight they were sitting ducks for any attack on the trail. Stephen seemed to sense Kaplan's apprehension and kept close to the officer's rear. Unable to see much beyond the scope of his yellow light Kaplan's blood ran cold as a distant sound reached his ears.

Stephen froze as well, the two of them straining to listen as the wind carried the noise by them. There was the snapping of twigs and then the sound of a man screaming in the distance, his cries were muffled, making it difficult for Kaplan to get an accurate gauge on the man's distance, let alone ascertain his location.

"Where is he?" Stephen whispered.

"I don't know," Kaplan answered.

"Mark's got to be with him right?"

"I have no clue, for all we know that is Mark," Kaplan replied. "Right now, just stay quiet."

Stephen ignored Kaplan, rising up from his hunched position and yelling, "Mark!"

"What the fuck are you doing?" Kaplan hissed, "I said stay quiet."

"Mark!" Stephen called, moving past the still frozen Kaplan, "Mark, it's me, Steve, where are you?!"

"Steve!" Kaplan whispered, "Steve, get back here!"

* * *

There was the squeaking of wheels, and other men had run towards the campsite. A number of vehicles had transferred from the bathroom crime scene and now boxed in Kaplan's darkened squad car. Had Henry been a more reflective fellow, he no doubt would have marveled at the artistic beauty of the blue hues of the siren lights mingling with the amber glow of the campfire. As it was however, he had no time to take note of such things hardly even paying heed to crime scene protocol, as exigent circumstances did not allow it.

"Somebody take a few goddamn photos," he barked, stomping into the chaos of the campsite. Already he counted some five individuals milling about the crime scene, no doubt contaminating it and ruining it for further evidentiary searches. Oddly though, this didn't raise his ire, as he was certain they were about to catch Enos in the act. With his steely eyes, he surveyed the damage to the campsite, the fire spread about, and the small pool of what he was sure was blood glistening next to it.

Turning towards the darkened cruiser, he instantly felt concern for the men who had been driving the vehicle. It stood silently, its passenger door slightly ajar. *Probably had to run after the bastard; they could need help.* Searching for the nearest Hingham officer, he spied a portly, young gentleman to his left. "You there," he growled.

The stubby officer pointed towards his chest.

"Yes you," Henry nodded, "whose car is this?"

"Um, um," the chubby policeman stammered, snapping his fingers as he searched for the answer, "I think it's Sergeant Kaplan's."

"Kaplan?" Henry bristled, "what are they, fucking butt buddies?"

The officer didn't know how to respond, thoroughly confused and standing there with his mouth agape. Henry waved him off, kicking up a plume of dirt. It was clear to him now; Kaplan had found Enos's whereabouts and was once again running interference for him. He now viewed the fiery crime scene in a different light now. *Was Kaplan in on this?*

He had covered up for Enos before, even vouching for the bastard to Patterson. Henry had spied him speaking with Enos's brother at the station shortly before they had taken off, and now this. No doubt they had been conspiring, Kaplan and the brother that is, discussing where to rendezvous with Enos. Henry wasn't really sure why Kaplan was aiding and abetting such a disreputable human being, but he was damn sure going to find out. It seemed a tad fishy that Kaplan would find Enos before they did. He was obviously trying to get in the way, spirit Enos away before he could face justice. *Well, that's not going to happen, not on my watch.*

Ahead he spied a trampled grouping of brush and what he was certain was Kaplan's boot print in the sandy ground. Sneering, Henry croaked, "Bring in the dogs, the son of a bitch is here!"

As if on cue three men appeared with a team of dogs, the German Shepherds barking and snarling as they came forth. Henry noted that the animals were chomping at the bit, clearly picking up the scent of something they wanted. *Good boys, tear him to pieces.* "Somebody give me a flashlight," Henry ordered, and an officer stepped forward, dutifully depositing one in Henry's hand.

Flicking it on Henry trained the beam towards the trampled underbrush, "Let's go!"

The men rushed forward, trudging through the camp and surging headlong into the underbrush. Henry went first, finding the footing to be difficult at first. He could hear the dogs still barking away at his back, and he slapped the leaves and bushes in his way out of his sight, determined to get through to the other side.

Stumbling out of the bush he was nearly trampled by the men following in his footsteps. They all spread out and Henry continued forward, carried by his own inertia. Hitting a soft, uneven patch of land he fell forward, hitting the dirt face first. "Goddamn it!" He hissed, his nostrils full of sand. Opening up his eyes, he could hardly focus as they watered from the intense pain he had experienced as he made contact with the hard ground. Bracing himself with his hands he shook his head, attempting to clear his vision. Opening his eyes he searched for the object which had caused his fall. Rising to all fours he looked to his side and scuttled backwards, "Oh good Christ!"

His flashlight had skittered away in the fall and had rolled next to the object which had tripped him up, illuminating it in all its grisly detail. The wide open, glassy eyes of a young woman stared back at Henry; the light illuminating the horrible wounds upon her neck. Henry grit his teeth as he took in the red, glistening mess which marked where her throat had been. Snatching his flashlight he rose to his feet, dusting himself off before inspecting the corpse further.

"Oh sweet Jesus," Henry gasped, shaking his head. Henry had clearly disturbed her original position as her legs laid straight, but her upper torso was now contorted in an unnatural fashion. It was clear that her head had been facing skyward, but had been knocked to the left by the stumbling trooper.

"Are you all right, sir?" Bradley asked, dusting off Henry's shoulder.

"No, I'm not fucking all right," Henry bristled, righting his hat which had surprisingly not fallen off as Henry hit the ground, "I want this bastard caught before anyone else is killed."

"I've got something over here!" An officer called out.

Henry wheeled around, wincing at a small pain in his ankle. *Must've twisted the fucking thing.* The officer who had demanded attention had his back to Henry, his focus clearly on restraining the barking dog he had leashed to his forearm. Henry hobbled over, pushing past the officer and his dog. A small, tattered piece of tarp laid on the ground and Henry moved towards it. Still inspecting the piece of evidence his ears picked up as he detected something above the din of the dogs barking. It was distant and muffled, but he was sure he could hear something or someone.

It was unintelligible, but he was sure it was there. "Voices," he screamed towards the men behind him, "I hear voices! They're over there, let's go!" Ignoring the pain in his ankle he began jogging awkwardly down the path, hearing those in his charge fall into line behind him.

* * *

Stephen continued to run up the pass, ignoring Kaplan's orders. Grunting in frustration, Kaplan jogged after the young man. They continued up the trail, following the sounds of the screaming man, and Kaplan noticed that the painful wailing intensified the further up they ran. Unable to see clearly in the moonlight, Kaplan nearly lost his footing, stubbing his toe against a tree root and hurtling forward. Regaining his balance he looked up just in time to see Stephen veer left off the trail and into the forest.

Kaplan jogged up to the spot and spied Stephen just a few feet away moving towards the entrance of a large ammunition bunker hidden in the overgrowth. Hulking and half-buried in the earth, it was the shape of an aircraft hangar and nearly just as large. A solid structure, it possessed a yawning entranceway in its center; however, no light escaped from within. The calls were loudest here, clearly emanating from the darkened entrance of the concrete structure. They were intensified by the echo chamber that was the bunker and they intermingled with the sounds of a snarling animal. Trudging after Stephen, Kaplan broke into a full sprint catching the young man just ahead of the bunker opening.

"Stay here," Kaplan growled, dropping the penlight and aiming his weapon towards the black void that was the bunker door. There was a final scream and then all was silent, save for a wet sloshing sound, and Kaplan winced, having no desire to imagine just what the source of the noise was. Pointing the gun towards the doorway, Kaplan took a wide stance, "Mark Enos! This is Sergeant Kaplan of the Hingham Police. Come out now with your hands up!"

Stephen lurched forward slapping Kaplan's gun downwards, "What are you doing, man? I said no shooting!"

Kaplan looked at Stephen, his face barely hiding his rage. Sensing this, Stephen withdrew his hand and softened his tone, "Let me talk to him; I know I can get him to come out."

Kaplan inhaled deeply, unclenching his jaw and calming himself. "Fine," he acquiesced and he took a step back, still clutching his gun with both hands.

Stephen moved cautiously towards the bunker entrance. "Mark?" He called, his voice rattling about the bunker interior, "Mark, man, it's me, Steve."

There was a grunt, but it was almost inhuman sounding, more guttural and throaty than the normal man's voice range. It rattled Kaplan's nerves as it thundered forth from the bunker entrance, and he found himself taking another step backwards.

Stephen, however, took another step towards the bunker door. "Dude, if you can hear me in there, I'm sorry about this morning. I didn't mean to talk to you like that."

Another snarl came from the void.

"Mark, man, are you hurt?" Stephen asked moving yet closer to the bunker's mouth, "We can help you. You just have to come out."

There was now a low, threatening growl that came from the inside of the bunker, and Kaplan found that it sent a chill down his spine. He peered inside the bunker, but could make out nothing in the black space beyond the transom. Unable to see beyond the doorway and hearing the noises coming from within, he found his mind begin to race, and for a moment he started to wonder as he spied the sight of the full moon through the forest canopy, *could it be true?* He could feel himself shaking, his forehead begin to perspire. The clumsy stride of the figure on the road just moments earlier and now the animal noises, it was enough to make even a rational man like Kaplan ponder the unthinkable.

"Mark, man, you've got to come out of there and let us help you," Stephen pleaded. "There's all these cops after you, dude. We're you're only hope, trust me."

Kaplan heard a commotion to his right, and he stared through the woods. There was the twinkling of flashlight bulbs obscured through the dense underbrush, and he could hear the barking of dogs along with the muffled calls of their masters. They were out of time; the cavalry was here.

Kaplan turned back towards Stephen, "Whatever you're going to do, kid, to get him out, better do it quick."

* * *

Henry continued to waddle up the path, jogging with a noticeable limp. The dogs continued to bay and howl, eager to be let loose by their masters. Several of the men behind him began to yell as well, "They're up ahead!" Others intoned, "We can hear them!"

Getting a few feet further up the trail Henry could clearly hear the voices now, realizing that they were no more than few hundred yards up ahead. "Come on boys, step on it," he hollered, "Let's catch this sorry son of a bitch!" There was no way Kaplan could save Enos' ass this time in his mind. *Not today, not on my watch.*

* * *

Kaplan could hear the heavy footfalls of the men approaching, the yelling of individuals. He knew there was not much time; soon they would be on top of him and Stephen. Following the same trail of evidence he and the older Enos had followed, the group was headed right for their position.

Stephen's mouth went dry as he sensed their precarious position and their lack of time. His heart began to race as he confronted the prospect of several angry troopers assaulting his brother before he could coax him out of the bunker. Now no more than a foot away from the bunker entrance Stephen made his choice, "Look, Mark I'm coming in there." Placing his hands upon the concrete transom he prepared to hoist himself up and into the dark void ahead.

There was a rustling sound, and the growling emanating from inside the bunker evolved into a full-fledged roar. Kaplan, his attention directed back towards the bunker entrance, detected movement in the darkness, a glimmering silhouette of black on black. Without thinking he raised his gun and squeezed the trigger, firing over Stephen's head.

Blam!

Stephen cupped his hands to his ears and ducked from the line of fire. "No!" he shouted, moving away from the bunker's threshold. Looking up he was just in time to see inside as Kaplan fired off another round.

Blam!

In the brief millisecond that the muzzle flash illuminated the interior of the concrete warehouse,

Stephen was confused by what he saw. Unable to process it fully, he lowered his hands as he sought to wrap his mind around it. *It was an illusion,* he assured himself, no doubt the shadows inside the bunker playing a trick on him. *There's no way you just saw that.*

Kaplan stood shaking, gun still pointed forward just as Henry and a large contingent of police moved past him. Almost in a daze he barely registered the calls of the men and the snarling dogs as they rushed headlong for the bunker vestibule.

"Get me a light in there!" Henry ordered as the officers pushed Stephen aside. The group filtered inside, and shaking free from his frozen state, Kaplan moved to follow. The group stood in stunned silence, and Kaplan pushed his way through, seeking to see what they were looking at. Fighting his way to the front, Kaplan looked down at the concrete floor, now illuminated by the heavy duty flashlights of several officers.

A young man Kaplan could not identify lay on the floor, his body torn to shreds, a pool of blood around him. Inspecting his hands Kaplan, realized he possessed only nine digits, making him the missing owner of the thumb they had found on the trail. There was another presence however, lying next to the mutilated corpse. Mark Enos lay upon the concrete floor, two neat bullet holes smoldering in his right pectoral muscle, inches apart. Though his eyes were closed, his chest moved gently, and as Kaplan looked away from his handiwork he met the surprised gaze of Henry off to right. For a moment they stared at each other, not a word between them. Henry stared in disbelief, not sure of what to make of the scene around him, finding only the stern, angry glare of Kaplan. Remaining silent, Kaplan turned and exited the bunker, the group parting for him as he made his way through the crowd towards Stephen. Only the barking of dogs filled the air as no one uttered a sound, the drama of the moment seeming to grip everyone involved. It was over; they had caught Mark Enos.

XLVI

"We need your gun," McGuire said, gesturing towards Kaplan's sidearm.

"What?" Kaplan asked, the annoyance coming through in his tone as he looked away from the flurry of activity behind him and back at McGuire.

"You know, for forensics testing or some bullshit," McGuire answered. A state trooper stepped forward, a plastic evidence bag held open in his hands.

Frowning, Kaplan removed his weapon from its holster, ensuring that the safety was on before sliding out the gun's magazine. Reaching forward he deposited the pistol and the clip into the bag which the state trooper, who immediately sealed it before walking off.

"So you said you fired two shots?" McGuire questioned, waiting to jot down Kaplan's answer on his open notepad.

"Yeah," Kaplan nodded, still looking around distractedly, searching for one particular person. Surrounded by squad cars the scene was far more chaotic than when Kaplan had left it. His cruiser sat several feet behind him, roped off by crime scene tape along with the rest of the campsite. Helplessly he watched as a number of crime scene technicians rifled through his vehicle, combing it for evidence. Klieg lights illuminated the scene, as the fire had long been put out, and the continuous rumble of a generator sounded throughout the scene. Kaplan noted the number of investigators milling about the campsite snapping photos and marking evidence.

"You sure about that?" McGuire interrogated.

"What?" Kaplan spat, "Yes, I'm sure about that. Why the hell are you talking to me like that, Ian?"

"Whoa, calm down, Eric," McGuire soothed, his hands raised, "Patterson just told me to collect the weapon and take your statement."

"Why the hell are you even taking my statement anyways, don't they have like some state unit that handles this shit?"

"Well yeah," McGuire stammered, his hands held wide, "there'll be a formal inquiry I guess, but Patterson said we need a initial statement from you, and I guess he just figured it'd be easier if I did it."

"Whatever," Kaplan said dismissively, waving his hand, "where's the kid?"

"Which one, the one you shot or the one you came here with?"

"The brother, Stephen, the brother," Kaplan answered. McGuire's question cut at the heart of Kaplan as he replayed it in his head, "*the one you shot.*" It pained him to realize that he had perhaps mortally wounded Mark Enos. He had set out to apprehend Enos peacefully, protect him from Henry's goon squad, and yet it was he who had delivered two bullets to the killer's chest. The delicious irony of the situation did not escape him, and it weighed heavily upon his psyche.

"Oh, the brother," McGuire nodded, "he's been taken back to the station house, they're going to question him there."

Kaplan sighed, lowering his head. Stephen had walked ahead of him on the trail back, rebuffing his attempts to apologize for shooting Mark. Kaplan had tried in vain to explain that he was trying to protect Stephen, but the younger man was distraught, waving the sergeant off as he fought back tears. Henry and the other officers had refused to allow Stephen into the bunker, not allowing him to come to the aid of his wounded brother. It was then that they had set back towards where they came, only to be enveloped by another group of officers who immediately separated the two from one another.

"The other one going to make it?" Kaplan asked.

"What the loonytoon you shot?" McGuire asked, not waiting for an answer, "I don't know. They took him out a few minutes ago. Haven't heard anything."

"Have they identified the two victims?"

"Actually, I heard we've got three here," McGuire answered casually, "but then again, what would I know? They don't tell me things."

"Three?" Kaplan asked.

"I've heard," McGuire answered, with a shrug of his shoulders. Returning to his notepad he asked, "So, it was dark you said?"

"What?" Kaplan asked, momentarily confused, "Um, yeah, yeah it was dark."

"How come you didn't use your flashlight?" McGuire questioned.

"I left the big one in the car," Kaplan admitted embarrassedly, "only had a penlight in there with me."

"So that's how you saw the suspect coming at you?"

"Um, no, I had dropped it at that point," Kaplan answered.

"You dropped it?" McGuire asked exasperatedly, "then how'd you see the guy coming at you?"

"I don't know, I just did," Kaplan responded acidly, "I saw the guy coming, and I fired." He immediately wished he hadn't spoken those last words with such conviction. Truthfully, he had panicked, believing he had seen movement and firing anyways. He could admit to himself now that he had felt some relief when he realized his shots had hit Mark Enos and not some victim attempting to escape to safety.

"Hey man, calm down," McGuire urged, his tone rather conciliatory. Leaning close he whispered,

"Look Eric, between me and you, Patterson says this is all just a formality; they're not going to nail your ass. We're all proud of you for popping this guy, buddy. Worst that's going to happen to you is a few weeks of desk duty."

McGuire straightened up, leaning away from Kaplan, and spoke up in a more authoritative tone, "Now, did you see a weapon as the suspect came towards you?"

Kaplan's brow furrowed, not truly understanding McGuire's body language until he cocked his head as he sense a passing presence behind him. Henry limped through the crime scene, his normally cocksure attitude noticeably absent. His face was a mask of shock and worriment, something Kaplan had believed were two emotions the grizzled trooper was incapable of expressing. As Henry passed he locked his wide open eyes with Kaplan, walking by silently. Kaplan watched the trooper walk off, his attention only drawn away by McGuire.

"Guy's an asshole, huh?" McGuire remarked.

Kaplan merely shrugged his shoulders.

"Danny Leduc was telling me how the asshole chewed you out over at the Enos place," McGuire snorted.

"Just a misunderstanding," Kaplan mumbled, "What were you asking again?"

"Oh yeah, so did you see a weapon as this guy came at you?"

"Um, no," Kaplan shook his head, "I don't recall seeing one specifically."

"What, are you telling me this guy did all this with his bare hands?" McGuire asked in disbelief.

"I, I don't know," Kaplan stammered. Images of mutilated bodies played in Kaplan's head, and he could see into the pained eyes of Peter Greco's decapitated head vividly. *Kid had to have a weapon to do that*, Kaplan assured himself, *right?* The moon hung low in the sky above, and Kaplan once again allowed his mind to drift towards thoughts too ridiculous to be considered serious. For all he knew, they had already found some blood stained blade in the bunker interior.

"I'll just say you believed the kid had a weapon," McGuire said, jotting down a few words, "I can't imagine saying you didn't see a weapon would help you."

"I thought you just said I was fine?" Kaplan asked, spreading his hands.

"You are Er—" McGuire started, only to be cut off by a commotion behind them.

Kaplan was blinded by a white light as a camera shone on his face. "Sergeant Kaplan, Sergeant Kaplan!" A voice behind the camera shouted, "Can you offer a comment? Is it true you shot Mark Enos?"

Shielding his eyes from the light, Kaplan remained silent as a team of officers moved in and scuffled with the cameraman, knocking his camera to the ground. Subduing the journalist they moved him off, disappearing behind a bank of vehicles; their voices muffled.

"Fucking vultures," McGuire chuckled, "they're supposed to be held back at the park entrance. Fucker probably snuck in through the woods." Looking back at the furiously blinking Kaplan he commented, "Better get used to it, buddy, you're famous."

Taken aback by the assessment, Kaplan stared blankly at McGuire.

* * *

It didn't take long for McGuire's prediction to bear out; within an hour most news viewers were fully aware of the name Eric Kaplan. Some, much to Kaplan's chagrin, managed to associate him with the now famous image of a puking cop and the footage ran whenever news outlets touched upon his name. His name was to be forever linked with Mark Enos, and in many ways he became the Frederick Abberline to Enos' Jack the Ripper in the media's eyes, although admittedly, the analogy was a bad one as Abberline had never captured his murderer.

Nearly every channel broke into their regularly scheduled programming to report of Enos' capture or at the very least ran a news ticker at the bottom of the screen. Many news programmers cursed at the fact that Enos had eluded being caught sooner as primetime had passed on the East Coast, although newspaper editors leapt for joy as there was still time to get the information into the next day's edition.

Information was spotty at best, though this didn't hamper the efforts of many reporters who just rushed on camera with nothing more than the word of "anonymous sources." This resulted in a number of conflicting reports as some channels confirmed that Mark Enos had been killed, while others stated that he was in critical condition at a nearby hospital. There was also little consensus on what had happened inside Wompatuck, as some outlets reported that three bodies had been removed, while others detailed a massacre involving dozens of victims had taken place inside the park's campground. Compounding this problem was the fact that the police were not talking. Patterson was now shying away from the cameras, eager to avoid a repeat of that afternoon. About the only thing the news channels could agree on was that Mark Enos had been caught, Eric Kaplan was his captor, and some people had died within the park.

Information trickled in throughout the night, but it was spotty and lacked the sizzle many networks were seeking. The resulting loop of footage played continuously by the mainstream media outlets became a mind-numbing amalgamation of previously aired recordings and the repetitive commentary of newscasters. For many viewers it was like watching the sports highlights on many of the sporting networks. A few newscasts, not content on airing stale footage and seeking something new in the wee hours of the morning, treated audiences to a detailed history of Wompatuck Park. Naturally, the riveted viewers of these channels gave up and did what many of their fellow man had done. They tuned out and went to sleep.

XLVII

Richard Greene meandered through the hospital corridor, patiently moving aside as staff members attempted to pass him. Whistling to himself, he gave off the air of a man who was in no hurry to get to where he was going; there was no trace of urgency in his step. A briefcase by his side, his trench coat was draped over his forearm, revealing his finely tailored black suit and red tie.

Though only in his mid-fifties, Greene's face gave the appearance that he was a full decade older; a world-weary look hung about him. His ebony skin was wrinkled and worn, crow's feet springing from his eyes, and he wore a scruffy mane of white hair atop his head. Rounding a corner, he came face to face with a much younger woman clad in a grey pantsuit.

"Ah, Ms. Sowers," Greene smiled, acknowledging the woman with a head bob.

"Good morning, Judge Greene," Marissa Sowers greeted, straightening her auburn hair.

"Going somewhere?" Greene questioned.

"Actually, I was going to get a cup of coffee," Sowers retorted.

"Nonsense," Greene said, placing a hand on her shoulder and guiding her in the other direction, "how about we just get on with the proceedings? There'll be plenty of time for coffee afterwards."

While a tad perturbed by Greene's actions, Sowers found it hard to get upset as the judge maintained his jovial tone and broad smile. Besides, it never truly paid to get on the judge's bad side. "Absolutely," Sowers agreed, even forcing a grin in response.

As they walked upon the white and black checkered tile Greene noticed two rather large state troopers positioned just outside a hospital room door at the end of the corridor next to an emergency exit, a rather unpleasant reminder of the case before them. A man, roughly in his early thirties, Greene estimated, sat in small wooden chair just off from the room's entryway. Relatively average looking, he had thinning brown hair and wore thick, horn-rimmed glasses along with an ill-fitting blue suit. Looking over a manila folder full of copied pages, he did not motion to leave his seated position until Greene and Sowers approached.

Placing the folder upon the chair he moved toward Greene extending his hand, "Your honor,

I'm Attorney Nick Mears, defense council for Mark Enos."

"Pleased to meet you, Mr. Mears," Greene greeted, shaking the attorney's hand heartily.

"Same to you, sir," Mears replied, shaking the judge's hand rather clumsily. Clasping his free hand over Greene's, his brow furrowed, "Uh, but just a few things, Your Honor."

"Okay, shoot," Greene nodded, forcefully withdrawing his hand from Mears.

"For starters, I was just appointed to this case this morning. I've had little time to review my client's case and minimal contact with my client," Mears said, adjusting his glasses before placing his hands in his coat pockets.

Greene smiled, "Relax Mr. Mears. It's merely an arraignment. You'll have plenty of time to prepare for trial."

"Well, that's just it, Your Honor, I'm not even sure my client's fit to go through with this at this time. He's heavily sedated and not able to speak clearly; I'm not even sure he's coherent," Mears countered.

Greene frowned and turned towards Sowers, "Is this true?"

"The doctors tell me they couldn't remove one of the bullets from his body, as it was too risky, and as such he's been heavily sedated for much of his time here. However, they've agreed to abstain from medicating him until after the arraignment so, he's in pain, but he's definitely coherent," Sowers answered.

"Can he speak?" Greene asked.

"Barely," Mears interjected, intercepting the conversation from his female counterpart, "he has a collapsed right lung as a result of the shooting, and he can just barely squeak out a few words."

"I'm not asking for a soliloquy, Mr. Mears, only how he intends to plead," Greene said rather curtly, annoyed by the defense counsel's enthusiasm. "Now can he do that or not?"

Mears sat opened mouthed, unable to respond.

"I'll take that as a yes," Mears smiled before looking back at Sowers and querying, "Is there a clerk here?"

"Waiting with the family members in the room," Sowers nodded.

"Okay, good, let's get on with it," Greene said, moving past the two attorneys and entering the hospital room. Sowers smiled deviously at Mears before moving towards the room herself. Dejectedly, Mears collected his folder from his chair and his beaten leather briefcase and followed the contingent into the cramped confines of the hospital room.

The room was small, no more than ten feet by ten feet, and was way over capacity as nearly seven people were crowded into it. The majority of space was taken up by the large hospital bed in the center of the room, the prone figure of Mark Enos lying on it. A battery of machines and gauges sat to his rear, the rhythmic beeping of his heart monitor chirping in the background. A little sunlight filtered in from the small window by Enos's bedside, the majority of the room's illumination coming from the harsh ceiling lights overhead.

Stephen and Virginia Enos stood on the left hand side of Mark's bed, in front of the window, and Mears took a position adjacent to them. Nodding in greeting to both he shook hands with the members of the Enos family. Sowers stood at the foot of the bed, whilst Greene and the court clerk were arrayed across from the Enoses.

After a brief whispered conversation, Greene took a sheet of paper from the clerk and motioned for the clerk to begin. She was an elderly woman, squat and frumpy with curly, white hair and thick glasses suspended by a metal chain around her neck. Placing her glasses on her nose, she stepped forward and read aloud from a sheet of paper, "Commonwealth of Massachusetts versus Mark Enos, docket number oh, seven, six, three, five; the honorable Richard Greene presiding. Court is now in session." Stepping back she allowed Greene to move forward.

Greene perused the sheet of paper before turning his attention towards the bed-ridden man in front of him. "Mark Enos," Greene began, "You are hereby charged with seven counts of murder in the first degree by the Commonwealth of Massachusetts. They contend you did willfully and maliciously contribute to the deaths of William Lamperti, Margot Roday, Kenneth Greco, Peter Greco, Robert Tranfaglia, Alicia Reilly, and Geoffrey Simmons, and that you did so with extreme atrocity and cruelty. Do you understand the charges against you?"

Mark, unable to speak above a whisper, merely nodded his acknowledgment. This action prompted Greene to turn towards the clerk. "Let the record show, defendant signaled his comprehension."

"How do you plead?" Greene demanded of Enos.

Mark beckoned for Mears to come close, rising off the bed ever so slightly and wincing as he did so. Wheezing into his attorney's ear it took a moment before Mears nodded his understanding and stood back up. "My client pleads not guilty, Your Honor," Mears stated.

"Very well," Greene nodded as he turned to Sowers and motioning towards the hospital bed. "Do we need to talk about bail here?"

"While we acknowledge Mr. Enos's, present physical state we ask that it be denied if and when the defendant makes a full recovery," Sowers nodded.

"Objections?" Greene interrogated Mears.

"Not at this time, Your Honor," Mears answered.

"Okay then," Greene sighed handing the piece of paper back to the clerk who dutifully accepted it. "The clerk will set a date for trial pending improvement in Mr. Enos's physical state."

Looking down at the forlorn and sickly Enos, Greene shook his head before smiling, "Now, if you'll excuse me, I have other appointments." He then picked up his briefcase and nodded at the clerk, "Court adjourned." With a bob of his head, he acknowledged the two attorneys and exited the room.

Stephen stood in stunned silence by his brother's bedside. The entire proceedings had been so swift, so informal to him. The process had been so cruel and cold, lacking of any drama. While he hadn't known just how it was going to go down, he had expected more, much more. Looking at his mother he found her to be of use, gently patting away tears from beneath her eyes. It seemed like she had done nothing but cry for over a month.

While Sowers and the clerk chatted quietly amongst themselves, the Enoses and their attorney stood in awkward silence. Stephen watched as the dumpy looking Mears collected his things and moved towards his ailing brother patting him on the shoulder. "Well, I guess I'll be in touch." Mears sighed. "Try to get better."

Nodding at the Enoses, Mears moved to exit the room.

Stephen stood disappointed for a moment, contemplating his next course of action. Looking from his bed-ridden brother to his weeping mother and back again, he made up his mind and marched out of the room, chasing after the defense attorney. Catching the lawyer just outside the door Stephen clutched Mears' arm. "Excuse me," he said.

"Yes?" Mears asked, startled by Stephen's sudden appearance.

"I need to speak to you," Stephen said, leading the attorney away from the door and down the hall.

XLVIII

The plump, ruddy faced woman stuck her head in the doorway, rapping her knuckles upon the doorframe. "Lieutenant?" She chimed in her sing-song voice, "there's a newspaper reporter on line three for you."

"I already issued a statement," Henry grumbled, not looking up from the paperwork upon his desk. His office was cramped and orderly, only his desk and a filing cabinet along with an American flag adorned it.

"This one's from New Hampshire, though," his secretary intoned.

Annoyed, Henry set down his pen and stared icily at the woman, "Damn it, Helen, tell that hick he can run with the statement I've already given. I ain't talking to him, tell him to go get something from Patterson, or better yet, tell him to go fuck himself altogether."

"I'll just tell him you're busy," Helen nodded, ignoring the trooper's coarse language and nasty demeanor. She was rather used to it, having been his secretary for several years now. Though, she realized he had been gruffer than usual in the last few weeks.

"Whatever," Henry grumbled, picking up his pen and returning towards the forms upon his desk. The lack of a computer upon his desk in this day and age was noticeable, but Henry considered himself old school, choosing to work off hardcopy rather than some glowing screen. This had led to a fair share of grumbling from his underlings and even from his superiors, who had routinely pushed him to enter the digital age. *Fuck 'em,* Henry had remarked, *when the power goes out, these queers are lost in the dark, but I just keep on tickin'.* Of course he conceded this philosophy was probably why they kept Helen around, as he had long suspected she secretly converted his filings into digital copy.

"Oh and, sir?" Helen called, not having removed herself from the doorway.

Henry sighed, "Yes, Helen?"

"There's an officer from the crime lab here for you."

"What the hell does he want?" Henry demanded.

"You said you wanted to be notified when the preliminary lab results came out," Helen responded.

"Oh shit," Henry remarked, his tone noticeably brighter. Dropping his pen he leaned back in his chair, "By all means, please send him in."

Helen nodded and vanished from the doorway and Henry heard the muffled tones of her high-pitched voice along with a deeper, more masculine intonation. There was the sound of heavy footfalls from the hallway outside, and Henry smiled. *Sounds like the gait of a real man's man.* Henry braced himself for the pride of the force to enter his office, picturing a muscular gentleman who embodied everything it was to be a Massachusetts State trooper. His face fell, however, when a diminutive Asian man with thick eyeglasses entered the room. The man's shoulders were slumped, and he walked awkwardly, hence his heavy strides.

"Lieutenant Henry?" the gentleman asked.

"Yes," Henry nodded, not bothering to hide his disappointment.

"John Wilson from the crime lab," the man said, extending his hand in greeting.

"Nice to meet you, John," Henry said, accepting the man's hand, but not rising from his seat. "What have you got for me?" Henry asked, gesturing towards a manila folder in Wilson's hand.

"Oh, yeah," Wilson smiled uneasily, realizing that Henry had dropped his hand and wasn't going to offer a seat. "Here it is," Wilson said, jutting the folder towards Henry, "the lab results you requested."

"Well all right," Henry smiled, grabbing the folder from Wilson's hand. Wilson looked at the chair across from Henry and wondered if it would be acceptable to sit in it. Uncomfortable just standing there he made a half gesture to seat himself, but found himself intimidated by Henry, fearing an angry response, even though the older man had his nose buried in the folder, perusing the contents. Resigning himself to standing, Wilson placed his hands in the pockets of his oversized leather jacket.

"So, did we nail him?" Henry asked, licking his fingertips and turning a page.

"Um, I'd say so, sir," Wilson responded, straightening his glasses. "His fingerprints were at every scene."

"Every scene?" Henry asked, peering over the folder. "Even the Lamperti place, with all that grass and such?"

"Yes sir, even the Lamperti scene," Wilson replied.

"Hot damn," Henry marveled, "you boys could gleam a print from a nun's tit."

Wilson blushed and smiled in response. He was eager to leave the office, finding Henry's demeanor most unsavory. The older man put him on edge. There was an air about him which indicated that he could go off at any moment, exploding for no reason at all with bombast and fury.

Henry stopped, his bushy eyebrows raised, and he looked up at the nervous Wilson, "Says here you guys can't nail down a murder weapon."

"Nothing definitive," Wilson said sheepishly, "No weapon was ever recovered from the scenes."

Henry seemed unconvinced, glaring at Wilson, "Fucker tore someone's head off; he had to have used something."

Wilson squirmed under Henry's grilling, sweat starting to speckle his forehead. Rocking on his heels he spoke, "Perhaps he did, and we just never found it, including at his mother's house. And as it is, no one can speak with him to ask him how he did it. We did, however, find DNA from the last three victims beneath his fingernails."

"DNA," Henry questioned, "Like skin and shit?"

"Amongst other things," Wilson nodded.

"Jesus H. Christ," Henry marveled, returning to the folder. Reading the pages, he spoke softly to himself, merely repeating the words which appeared on the page. Turning one sheet of paper he stopped abruptly, squinting as if he could not read what was in front of him. Dropping the folder open faced upon his desk he glared at Wilson, his index finger affixed towards a certain spot in the report, "Wait, this can't be accurate, can it?"

XLIX

"So you talked to him?" Mears asked, studying the man seated across from him. Doctor Charles Landis had come highly recommended by Mears' associates, a shrink willing to provide favorable analysis to any defense attorney, provided the price was right. Given his reputation, Mears had expected someone resembling a used car salesman, a real seedy individual. Instead, it was as if Landis had emerged from a time machine, his dress and demeanor more fitting of an Ivy League professor from the mid twentieth century. He was rail thin and shaved bald, the dimples in his skull reflecting the light by his side and drawing attention away from his Romanesque nose and ridiculous gray goatee. Mears noted the tweed jacket and the bowtie wrapped around Landis's neck, as if the good doctor wanted to perpetuate the ivory tower stereotype he seemed to exude.

Landis nodded in response to Mears' question, a trickle of cigarette smoke pouring from his pursed lips. "I did indeed," Landis said, daintily dangling the cigarette in his hand.

"For how long?"

Landis took another drag from his cigarette. "Almost three hours," he answered, the smoke chugging from his mouth as he spoke.

"And he was lucid the entire time?"

"So the nurses told me," Landis replied, waving his hand in a small arc so as to say 'I think so' and allowing the smoke to stream through his spindly little fingers. "He assured me he was in a great deal of pain as they had taken him off of pain killers, albeit temporarily, for the interview."

Mears stifled the urge to cough, he hated the smell of cigarette smoke and normally he forbade it in his cramped little office as there wasn't sufficient ventilation. However, he had decided, against his better judgment it now seemed, to indulge the good doctor's desires and allow him a cigarette in exchange for the information he was now relaying. It was cold outside and as such the lone window in Mears' office was open only a crack, the entire darkened room now filling with the ghostly wisps of Landis' cigarette smoke.

"So what did he say? What did you get from him?" Mears asked, eager to hear what the doctor had to say so has to hasten Landis' departure.

Landis however, did not appear in any hurry to leave, appearing relaxed and speaking slowly and deliberately, seeming to measure his sentences. "A great deal," Landis puffed, "he was surprisingly forthright, nothing like what I expected him to be like."

"He told you everything?"

"Enough," Landis replied. "We touched upon his past experiences, family life, everything leading up to the recent events he was involved in." His cigarette continued to burn, quickly dwindling away in his hand. "It's all there in the report I gave you, Mr. Mears," Landis added, a trace of annoyance in his voice.

"Yes, yes," Mears waved dismissively, picking up a manila folder on his desk. He peered over the top of the folder, "did he admit to the attacks?"

Landis shook his head. "No, he claims he blacked out during them. Claims that was where the…" Landis searched for a correct term before resigning himself to, "where the 'what have you' took over."

"I take it you don't believe him?"

"It's not my job to believe him, Mr. Mears."

"So what's your opinion?" Mears prodded, "what do you think is wrong with him?"

"I barely know him, Mr. Mears. I can't fully diagnose him based on one interview."

"Yeah, but, come on," Mears shrugged, "between you and me. What's wrong with him?"

Landis sat there for a moment, an indiscernible expression upon his face, a mixture of disgust and exasperation as he stared down Mears. Not taking his eyes off of Mears he took one long drag off his cigarette, the glowing ember almost touching the filter. Expelling the smoke cloud from his lungs he sighed, "I'll tell you exactly what I told him."

"He asked for your opinion?"

"He did."

"What did you say?"

"After he pushed me to divulge my opinion I told him that if I had to hazard a guess I would have to say that he has always been a man with a propensity for brutality, who harbored violent tendencies deep in the recesses of his mind. No doubt they first manifested themselves when his father, the dominant male figure in his life, died when he was a child. It sounds like he was neglected at home and he was never allowed to grieve his father's passing properly. If I had to imagine him as a youth, I would fancy him a quiet young man with a disagreeable attitude and a most unpleasant disposition. He believes he wasn't picked on by his peers once he reached grade school because he wasn't a small child, but I believe it was because the other children chose to give him a wide berth. I would imagine they feared him and sought the company of others. Really, who wants to befriend the surly, quiet little brute in the corner who threatens to snap at any moment at any age, let alone as a child?"

"You asked him that?"

Landis continued, ignoring Mears. "He's not an ugly man and I can't imagine he repelled a lot of young girls with his looks as he reached adolescence and beyond. If I was pressed, I would say he's had at least a few sexual experiences in his life and this would preclude sexual repression as the root cause of his recent problems. I doubt though, that he's ever been truly intimate with a member of the opposite sex. I can't imagine any of his relationships lasted long enough to form a real emotional bond. Once a woman got past his physical appearance I can't believe they'd like what they found. I don't think Mr. Enos has ever been able to connect with any human being, male or female, and I would think that this emotional isolation would cause him to harvest a multitude of ugly, angry feelings over the course of his young life. The war provided him with a natural outlet for these feelings and I doubt anyone really sought to dissuade him from acting upon these urges because, after all, an angry, violent soldier is a good soldier."

"That's where he developed Post Traumatic Stress Disorder"

"That's one theory," Landis harrumphed, annoyed by the attorney's interruption.

"You have a better one?"

"Maybe he did indeed crack under the weight of combat stressors, only a fool would question the horrific things veterans have witnessed. Or, maybe he cracked because of how much he enjoyed the experience, the freedom to inflict pain, to release all that ugliness bottled up inside him."

"You said *that* to him?" Mears protested to no avail as Landis continued with his monologue.

"Either way, it doesn't matter why he cracked, we need only know that he arrived home in a sorry state and the army pumped him full of drugs in response. They took efforts to ensure that he appeared copasetic when he returned stateside. Though in reality he was just a doped up, mentally fried young man. He confirmed himself that he was under the influence when what he claims was a werewolf bit him on the hand. He claims he changed that night and that the bite was the catalyst for all the awfulness that followed."

"You don't believe it was, doctor?"

Landis shook his head, "Werewolves don't exist, Mr. Mears. They exist only in ancient myths, Hollywood films and in the mind's eye of a multitude of paranoid schizophrenics."

"I know that," Mears spat.

"Whatever bit him wasn't the cause of this tragedy, Mr. Mears."

"What was?"

"As I questioned him Mr. Enos revealed that sometime after he was bitten he ceased his drug use. Just like that, cold turkey. There's not a doubt in my mind that those chemicals kept Mr. Enos docile, kept him from acting upon his darkest instincts. Have you ever been to the circus, Mr. Mears?"

Mears furrowed his brow in confusion, beginning to dislike the good doctor more and more. The way he spoke over Mears, his condescending attitude and his cigarette smoke and now this bizarre question. *Probably going to analyze my answer,* Mears thought. "Um, yes, as I recall I have at one point in my life."

"Remember the tigers jumping through hoops? The trainer sticking his head in the lion's mouth?"

"I don't know, maybe."

"Know how they can get such wild beasts to perform such tricks?"

Mears shook his head no, bewildered.

"Because they're drugged, Mr. Mears. The trainer can stick his head in the lion's mouth because it's tranquilized, in a daze. That's how I picture Mr. Enos before he stopped taking his drugs, a dazed lion. Once he removed the drugs he returned to his basal mental state, he became that man I see with a propensity for violence."

"Why werewolves?"

Landis shrugged, "Maybe he saw a film shortly before he was attacked. He claims he gleamed most of his information pertaining to the subject from a website he viewed at the local library. It detailed a variety of 'symptoms' one suffers when cursed by a werewolf. After he viewed that list, Mr. Mears, it became a self-fulfilling prophecy."

"What do you mean?"

"Mr. Enos used that information to explain away all that he was experiencing. In that regard the fact that he slept for a day was the result of the curse coursing through his veins rather than the result of having exhausted his body with his erratic sleep patterns. His renewed appetite after the attack was because he was now a wild animal, not because his body thirsted for the nutrients he had starved it of through the use of a number of chemicals which act as appetite suppressants. His increasing physical health and vitality was because he was now a werewolf, not because he had ceased the use of drugs and so on and so on. The werewolf also became a useful excuse for acting upon his most terrible of impulses."

"How so?"

"Because the werewolf is the perfect archetype for Mr. Enos' ascribed behavior. It illustrates the duality of man as clearly as the equally fictitious Dr. Jekyll and Mr. Hyde. It reflects that dark side within all of us we'd prefer to keep hidden from the rest of the world. Mr. Enos probably perceives himself as a good man, an innocent individual, and claiming he is a werewolf allows him to perpetuate that perception. It deflects blame, allows Mr. Enos to shirk his responsibility. He didn't kill those people; it was the monster he became at night. He doesn't have any recollections of the attacks because he believes he lost control to the curse. It allows him to keep a clean conscience. He's not a killer; he's a victim of an ancient curse. But in my opinion it's all a lie Mr. Mears; the moon holds no more sway over Mr. Enos than you or I. He murdered those people and concocted this story to assuage his own feelings of guilt. If it was up to me, and I'm glad it's not, he'd be put down like the rabid dog he is."

"And you said as much to him?" Mears asked, dumbfounded.

"He asked me for my honest opinion," Landis shrugged.

"How'd he respond?"

"He sought leave of me," Landis replied, smiling weakly, "before calling for a nurse to sedate him."

Mears dropped the folder, struggling to find the words he wanted. "So, let me get this straight. You believe my client was already prone to violence, that his war experience only heightened these propensities, causing him to seek the use of drugs to suppress these tendencies. That when he ceased using these drugs after returning home and being attacked by some, I don't know, large dog, he began to act upon these urges in the most horrific manner and then concocted a cover story that he was, in fact, a werewolf so as to shield himself from any feelings of guilt over having committed these horrific acts. Is that right?"

"Couldn't have said it better myself."

Mears' shoulders slumped, "So, then he's not crazy?"

"Oh no, Mr. Mears" Landis responded. "I didn't say he wasn't crazy, I know how my money's made in these situations, Mr. Mears. I believe your client's as crazy as they come, you've got the grounds for a good case in my opinion."

Mears' face brightened, "Okay then, we're in business. What's he got?"

Landis sucked out the remaining life of his cigarette and Mears was certain the embers must have burned the doctor's fingertips. Reaching across the desk, Landis discarded the butt in the soda can Mears had set up for him as a makeshift ashtray. Blowing out a stream of smoke, he tapped the folder upon Mears' desk. "It's all in there, Mr. Mears, all in there."

* * *

Mark watched as the nurse placed the needle into the IV, relishing the coming high. Truth be told, he hadn't needed the pain killers for some time, his wounds were healing just fine. There was a general soreness when he attempted to move and he ached constantly, but the pain was more of a nuisance than a debilitation. Still, the hospital staff insisted on pumping him full of pain killers, heavily sedating him, and he wasn't one to protest as he enjoyed the familiar highs he had denied himself for some time. He watched as the clear liquid meandered down the plastic tube, disappearing below the lip of a gauze bandage and the explosion of pleasure was instantaneous as the chemicals entered his bloodstream and were distributed throughout his body.

With a sigh of pleasure he leaned back upon his pillow, a drool laden smile upon his dazed face. Despite his euphoria as the opiates numbed his nerve endings and tickled his brain he was still aware of a lingering sense of anger and displeasure at Landis' earlier comments to him. The doctor had excoriated him, torn his claims apart. True, Mark had pressed the man for his honest opinion, but he hadn't expected Landis to be so blunt.

All feelings of anger aside, Mark had been shocked at the astonishing accuracy of Landis' assertions regarding his past. Still, Mark had resented Landis' contention that he had always been a man prone to violence. He hadn't remembered ever wanting to harm another individual and he couldn't recall ever having struck another man until he had gone to war. Once there, he couldn't remember enjoying it. Feeling as if he was floating away, Mark sought to dismiss the doctor's claims and simply enjoy the wave of pleasure he was experiencing.

If what he said was so wrong, why are you so pissed off? The little voice in his head called out.

Landis hadn't been right; he had connected with other human beings before.

There was Stephen. *You punched him.*

His mother. *You hardly speak.*

His army buddies, Frey and Kelly. *You've lost touch.*

The policeman, Kaplan? *He shot you.*

Landis wasn't right; the drugs hadn't been muzzling the beast within. He had felt more in control once he rid himself of the chemicals. *You killed seven people when you were "in control".*

Landis wasn't right; the werewolf was not some deflection strategy. Sure, there was the website, but you couldn't explain away everything that had happened. The rapid healing, the sickness that overtook him when the full moon rose, those were real. *Were they?* If it wasn't real then why couldn't he remember what he had done? *Can't you?*

Landis wasn't right, he wasn't a violent man. *You protest too much.*

His thoughts began to drift, his eyes rolling back into his head as the drugs took full effect. Losing all bodily control, his eyes closed and he began to dream.

Dreamed he saw himself leap over Lamperti's fence, chasing down the old man. "What's wrong with you?" The old man screeched over and again as Mark struck him. He remembered the first bite, his teeth struggling to pierce the flesh. He could sense the saltiness of the blood.

He dreamed himself on top of Margot Roday, sensing her overwhelming fear. He remembered the warmth of her calf as he dug in and reveled in the sound of her anguish cries. It had been such sweet music to his ears.

He remembered mimicking the scratching coming from the Greco door, peering angrily at Ken as he opened the door out of curiosity. In his rage he had felt the strength of ten men when he broke through the doorway and began to tear into the soft underbelly of his victim. He dreamed he was in Pete's room, remembered tearing at the flesh of his neck with teeth now well versed in ripping into human hide. He saw himself ripping the head from the body by the sheer force of will. He dreamed he caught his own reflection in the bathroom mirror as he set upon the cat, marveled at his blood stained nude form.

He remembered the feeling of sheer glee as he felt the camper's thumb pop from its socket into his mouth. He remembered feasting upon the body until he had been interrupted. He saw a face at a darkened doorway, Stephen's face. He remembered the rage he had felt when he laid eyes upon it, saw himself rushing in for the kill just as the blast of light blinded him with its intensity and the sound rang in his ears.

He awoke, still in a daze, flailing wildly and screaming. Unsure of where he was, he screamed, a scream borne not of frustration but rather at the horror of what he had done. He saw himself for what he was, not a fur covered beast, but a madman, a murderer. The fangs and claws had been replaced with the blood stained smile he had worn as he butchered those innocent people unlucky enough to cross his path. Still screaming and seeking to free himself from his bed, he was shocked as he felt the grip of what felt like ten nurses grab his wildly flailing limbs.

"Sedate him!" One called.

"He's already under!" Another responded.

"Just do it!" Another voice rang out over his screams.

The pinprick of the needle barely registered as his body went limp and the world went mercifully black.

L

"What's it called again?" Greene asked, placing his coat upon a rack and moving behind his desk.

"Clinical Lycanthropy, Your Honor," Mears answered, shifting in his chair before crossing his legs. "It's a rare psychiatric syndrome where the afflicted believe they can or have transformed into a wolf. I've been on the phone with at least half a dozen doctors who all assure me that while it's not all that common, it is in fact real."

Greene sat behind his desk, a wonderfully ornate oak piece, tapping his fingers upon his chin deep in thought. "And this, uh, affliction, is the center piece of your client's defense?"

Mears squirmed uncomfortably in his chair. "Yes, Your Honor it is. My client's brother and I spoke at length after the arraignment; he informed me that Mister Enos had told his mother that he believed he was a werewolf."

"Yes, I read the police report, Mr. Mears. It is in there," Greene said.

"Well, Your Honor, this explains everything. If my client truly believed that he was a werewolf, then he was in fact suffering from the disease clinical lycanthropy. He was delusional and not entirely in control of his own actions, and therefore could not have acted with malice aforethought. He deserves to be punished, don't get me wrong, but far less harshly than the system demands."

"Oh please," the previously silent Sowers spat derisively. Seated to Mears's left she had been summoned to the meeting in Greene's office as well. "I'm sorry, Your Honor, but I would have a real problem in explaining the actions of the defendant away with nonsensical psycho-babble." Turning towards Mears she tore into him, "The preponderance of evidence against your client is overwhelming. Fingerprints, DNA, character witnesses, it's all there. Not to mention a litany of other facts we can bring to bear. For instance are you aware that while on base your client checked out several books dealing with serial murder? We have the library records to prove it. It's not inconceivable that due to his fascination with such cases he developed some morbid fantasies which he eventually acted out after returning home. I'm sorry, I won't allow such actions to be ascribed to some made-up mental disorder."

"It's a real disease," Mears countered, "and I don't recall showing interest in the histories of serial

killers being a crime. The doctors I have spoken
to explained to me that clinical lycanthropy is
usually brought on by some other form of neurosis
or can be caused by heavy drug use. A nineteen
seventy-seven study published in no less reputable
a source than the American Journal of Psychiatry
detailed the case of a forty-nine-year-old woman
suffering from the disease, which included her
seeing a wolf in the mirror rather than her own
reflection and howling at the moon at night. She
was later diagnosed with chronic schizophrenic
psychosis. That same report also related the case
of a young army private under the influence of
LSD who wandered the woods of Germany for days
believing he had transformed into a wolf. Now, I've
got a stack of reports from the United States Army
diagnosing my client with severe post traumatic
stress disorder and also from the Massachusetts
State Police stating that the evidence they collected
from my client's room hinted at heavy drug use.
I contend that the combination of my client's
psychosis and drug use culminated in his belief
that he was a werewolf."

"So, his war experiences and drug use caused
all this? What about a lot of veterans who return
home traumatized and use recreational drugs?
Are they at risk for this disease?" Sowers asked
incredulously.

"She's right, Mister Mears," Greene chimed in.
"Many people suffering from mental illness also
abuse drugs, but they don't go on killing sprees."

"That's true, Your Honor," Mears acknowledged. "But we'll contend that my client developed this belief after being attacked by what was most likely a large dog the month prior to the murders. He did not get a good look at the animal. The attack occurred on the night of a full moon, and given his tenuous mental state at the time, it is not unreasonable that he developed such irrational thoughts. That event precipitated all of this and was the point where my client came to believe that he had been bitten by a lycanthrope and was therefore now a werewolf."

"Is there any precedent for this defense, anything pertinent in past case law?" Greene questioned.

"Not in this country," Mears answered. Sensing the displeasure his response had caused in Greene's expression, he quickly countered, "But similar cases abound in the historical record. The most pertinent case I could find was that of Manuel Blanco Romasanta from Spain, also known as the wolf-man of Allariz. Apparently, mister Romasanta was a traveling soap salesman in Galicia, Spain who confessed to murdering nine women in Eighteen fifty-one. Each of the victims was found to have been killed by hand, and they all appeared to have been half eaten. Romasanta claimed that he was a werewolf and had murdered the women while in wolf form."

"And the finding?" Greene intoned.

"Well, he was sentenced to death," Mears smiled, adjusting is glasses, "but his sentence was commuted to life in prison when a French psychologist testified that Mr. Romasanta was suffering from clinical lycanthropy."

"I trust you won't be entering a nineteenth century Spanish court finding as evidence at trial Mister Mears?" Greene asked, appearing bemused by Mears's recount.

"No, Your Honor, I won't," Mears answered, feeling more at ease, "I use it only to highlight the fact that this disease exists, and because the circumstances of the Romasanta case are so similar to my client's."

"And these doctors you spoke of, have they interviewed your client?" Greene interrogated.

"Not yet, Your Honor, but we will have a number of experts analyze my client's mental state once he improves physically."

"I'm sorry, are you contending that your client should be found not guilty because of some ascribed mental defect, because he truly believed he was a werewolf?" Sowers demanded, fearful that Mears was swaying the judge.

"No, look," Mears answered, flustered by the prosecutor's query, "I'm not saying that he's not a danger to society right now and should be let loose on the streets. I simply don't believe that he belongs in a prison cell. He should be committed, given the proper help he needs at a mental hospital, or something like that. Send him to Bridgewater State for evaluation and treatment. I mean, he's a veteran, for Christ sake. He went to war to defend Americans. Why would he return home and start slaughtering them if there wasn't something seriously wrong with him mentally?"

"That's not my problem," Sowers hissed. "Your veteran did come home and start murdering people, seven innocent people, and I'm sorry, I could care less what his explanation is. The families of the victims deserve justice, and that means putting your client behind bars for the rest of his life. Besides, your client already received treatment from the best doctors the army could afford, and that clearly did not help."

"Treatment," Mears snorted sarcastically. "Even the secretary of Veterans Affairs has admitted that the military's treatment of traumatized soldiers has fallen woefully short of being effective and needs to be reformed. They gave him a bunch of pills, a few question and answer sessions, and then let him rejoin society a broken, troubled young man."

Sowers turned back to Greene, "I'm sorry, Your Honor, are we really going to be more lenient on this defendant because he claims to suffer from some mental illness? Because let me tell you there's plenty of murderers who claim to have blacked out or been suffering from temporary insanity when committing their crimes. David Berkowitz, the Son of Sam, claimed to be hearing voices during his killing spree, and he didn't get off. Just recently, John Odgren, that autistic child from Sudbury, claimed temporary insanity after slashing a classmate to death, and he was sentenced to life.

I don't see why we should waste the court's time with such a frivolous and dishonest defense. I appreciate Mr. Enos's service to his country, and I'm sorry it affected him mentally, but he still slaughtered seven people."

"And I counter that my client lacked one of the principal foundations for a murder conviction," Mears defied. "If my client does in fact suffer from such delirium, he was not in control of his own actions and therefore his own mind. He lacked the *mens rea*, the criminal mindset. He didn't murder those people with malice aforethought. He truly believed that he was a werewolf and acted as such. I would also like to point out that you just admitted his wartime service affected his mental state."

"And that means he should be treated less harshly?" Sowers crowed.

Greene put up his hand to silence the quarreling attorneys. "I must admit, Mister Mears, I'm not entirely inclined to give credence to such theories or defenses as the one you're proposing."

Sowers sat back in her chair, a broad smile across her face.

"However, I am inclined to allow you to present the most vigorous defense of your client, and I'll be damned if a possible conviction in this case is overturned simply because I refused to hear you out. Therefore, pending an examination of your client, I will allow you to proceed."

"Your honor," Sowers protested in disbelief.

"You'll make your client available for the state's own doctors to analyze of course," Greene motioned towards Mears, ignoring Sowers.

"Of course," Mears affirmed.

Picking up a pen, Greene flipped through an appointment book on his desk before looking up at the prosecutor seated ahead of him. "So, when should I pencil your doctors in Ms. Sowers?"

Sowers looked at the judge exasperated, her mouth open, unable to answer. Dejected, she finally slumped back in her chair before responding to Greene's request.

LI

Kaplan sat at his desk, perusing the morning paper. Periodically sipping from his coffee mug, his focus never wavered from the printed pages of the sports section. As the phone rang, he devoured one last section of the article he was reading before casually lifting the receiver to his ear, "Sergeant Kaplan's desk."

"Hi, Eric, it's Matt Henry," came the voice on the other end.

Kaplan cringed as the raspy, baritone registered in his head. Maintaining his calm demeanor he responded, "Hi, Matt, what's up?"

There was a sigh on the other end of the line before Henry began to speak, "Well, I know we didn't part on the best of terms, friend, and after speaking it over with the wife, I decided to call and apologize to ya."

Is this guy serious? Placing the paper down Kaplan leaned back in his chair, ready to take in the unexpected apology. He'd be lying if he said the thought of Henry groveling for forgiveness didn't amuse him. In the short span they had known one another, Henry had impugned Kaplan's reputation, caused him to be the butt of a million jokes in the workplace due to his vomiting episode, and had momentarily threatened Kaplan's standing in the eyes of his superiors. Now the trooper apparently believed he could soothe over hurt feelings with a few words of apology. Though it struck him that even Patterson had not made such a gesture towards him in the interim, apparently too much of a coward to apologize. He too, however, was guilty of inaction, as he had not spoken to Stephen since that fateful night and thus had never been able to apologize to him. *Oh well*, he shrugged, *at least this is going to be good.* Formulating his response, Kaplan decided to lie, "Not a thing man, I didn't take it too personally."

"Yeah?" Henry asked, his tone sounding noticeably brighter.

"Yeah, it was no problem. I understand you just got a little fired up over catching the guy." Kaplan felt sick as the words, laden with false sentiment, dripped from his mouth.

"Hell yeah, I was," Henry rejoined, "but still what I said to you was a little harsh buddy. It was never your fault the bastard killed those poor people. I mean, shit, you're the guy who ended up catching him in the end." The words pained Henry to speak and he clutched his receiver a little tighter. He envied Kaplan for capturing Enos, yet he was also relieved that the Sergeant wasn't the meddling ass he had believed him to be. Truth be told he had been shocked when he saw Mark Enos lying there with two bullets in his chest; Henry hadn't believed Kaplan was capable of such an act.

Kaplan found himself smiling as Henry spoke, though the thought of shooting Enos still pained him. There was something satisfying in hearing the trooper beg for forgiveness, even offering praise for a favorable response.

"How's that going by the way?" Henry questioned.

"How's what going?"

"You know, the shooting thing," Henry prodded.

"Oh, that's fine I guess," Kaplan answered, "standard procedure stuff; kid's brother even gave me a favorable statement apparently. They say I'll be cleared in using my weapon, but for now just a few weeks of desk duty."

"The kid's brother vouched for you?" Henry asked.

"Yeah," Kaplan breathed into the receiver. He had been equally as surprised when he heard that Stephen's statement was not damning in the least. It had seemed a gesture of acceptance on Stephen's part, that maybe he hadn't taken his brother's shooting too hard. Kaplan was wont to find out the depth of Stephen's acceptance however.

"Well that's good, real good," Henry's voice came. "I trust you've heard the son of a bitch's lawyer's new line of defense."

"No, I haven't," Kaplan answered. "Truthfully I haven't been paying too much attention to the case," he lied again, though this time he didn't know why. The story of Mark Enos's murderous rampage had filled the pages of the local papers and national news outlets. For weeks it had captivated headlines everywhere before being superseded by the next overhyped story of the day. Kaplan himself had of course received a number of interview requests and though he had refused to participate, desiring a return to anonymity, he had kept abreast of any developments in the Enos case, constantly scouring the papers for stories pertaining to "The Werewolf Murders."

"This shithead lawyer's arguing that because the kid believed he was a goddamn wolf-man that he wasn't responsible for his actions," Henry spat, "like its news that Enos was bat-shit crazy."

"Eh, he's just doing his job," Kaplan offered.

"Well it just pisses me off that if you claim to be loopy enough you can wipe your hands of any responsibility in this society. Nobody owns up to nothing in this country anymore," Henry opined. "Of course the motherfucker's a lunatic, and he should rot in jail because of it."

Kaplan snorted in amusement.

"What's so funny?" Henry demanded.

"Lunatic," Kaplan said, "you used the word lunatic."

"Yeah so?" Henry asked, his tone becoming more agitated.

"You know, lunatic," Kaplan smiled. "The word stems from the word lunar, get it?"

"Oh, Oh, I get it," Henry responded, the tenor of his voice softening, "like moon shit, and the kid thought he was a werewolf. Good stuff."

Kaplan began to lose interest in speaking to Henry, desiring to hang up the phone. However, he sensed that the trooper wanted to continue their conversation, and his attention drifted back to the newspaper before him.

"Don't you worry, though, I just had one of the lab boys in my office, and he assured me that it's a slam dunk," Henry said. "We've got the bastard dead to rights."

"Oh?" Kaplan replied, pretending to pay attention.

"Yeah, we've got the fucker's prints at the Lamperti scene and the Greco apartment. Son of a bitch didn't even use gloves."

"That's good," Kaplan grunted, moving onto another article. *Big game coming up this Sunday*, Kaplan thought to himself.

"And we got the bastard's DNA on six of the bodies, lab report tells me they got it from some shit, like the traces of saliva in the victim's wounds; apparently he was taking bites out of 'em just like we thought."

"Mmm hmmm," Kaplan replied. This was old news, already established stuff. He had heard all this before and even most of the newspapers had reported as such. *When is this bastard going to hang up? Besides,* Kaplan reflected, *we definitely knew Enos was responsible when we found him next to that mutilated body.* Kaplan winced as he recalled the shredded corpse and Mark Enos entirely covered in his victim's blood.

Of course he knew Enos was guilty, yet the trooper seemed content to relate already established facts, seeking to educate his younger protégé.

"You know, it's the damndest thing though," Henry rasped.

Oh God, here we go. This guy really isn't going to get off the phone. Kaplan tapped the receiver upon his head, restraining his annoyance as he sensed the older man wanted to wax nostalgic. Taking a breath he asked, "Oh yeah, what's that?"

"Lab techs took dental casts off of Enos while he was in the hospital and obtained his dental records."

"Yeah?" Kaplan asked, returning to his newspaper.

"They couldn't match the casts or the records to the bite marks on the victims, say nothing lines up."

Kaplan slammed down the paper, his focus suddenly fixated on the phone. "Wait, what?"

LII

Stephen sat at his brother's bedside, watching him slumber. Mark's chest rose and fell in a gentle cadence, an air hose running from his nose helping him breathe. Stephen had insisted on being by his brother's side nearly every night since he had landed in the hospital; even to the point of neglecting his own young family.

Something had stirred within him since that fateful day that Mark had been shot. He still felt guilty for not noticing the warning signs of his only brother's slide into dementia; the fact that he had called Mark outright crazy that day still gnawed at his gut. Mark had even reached out for help after the murder of their elderly neighbor, mumbling that he believed himself responsible for the event, and Stephen had simply dismissed his statements, refusing to give them any credence. Of course the guilt which weighed upon Stephen was exacerbated by the fact his brother could not hold a conversation just yet.

It was strange to him still that though his only brother had gone off to war, Stephen had never seriously worried about Mark's safety or well-being. Sure he had given it a passing thought here and there as the images rolled across the nightly newscasts, but he had always just assumed Mark would return home safe and sound. He cursed himself for the fact that it never occurred to him that even though the war had not physically wounded his younger sibling, it had irreparably damaged his mind, that his brother desperately needed his help. For many nights now, Stephen had engaged in deep self-loathing for being so self-indulgent, for being so focused on his own life. In a way, being by Mark's side nightly was a form of atonement, a way for Stephen to unburden his conscience.

Despite the fact that Mark was fast asleep, Stephen continued to speak, believing that his brother could still hear him. "Mom apologizes for not coming down here more often," he said. "She's not dealing with all this too well."

"All these reporters keep calling her for statements, wanting to get her on camera. She hardly leaves the house now, well not that she left the house a lot before," he said, smiling. Returning to his original train of thought he frowned, "But she really feels like she can't go about life as normal anymore, says too many people stare at her and whisper when she's at the grocery store or the gas station. Hell, she's even closing the drapes now so people can't look in on her, fucking lives in the dark now almost."

Stephen's thoughts turned to the events of the night Mark was caught. In the flash of light he had seen something, or thought he had witnessed something peculiar. He knew it was the form of his advancing brother he had spied, but still something had seemed off, simply not all right. His brother had appeared enraged, grotesque looking even, Stephen thought, his face possessing the look of something primal and atavistic and certainly not human. Still, he hadn't pressed the matter in the brief bedside chats he had engaged in with his younger sibling. He had never asked just what Mark was feeling at that moment, not that Mark could answer. *Probably wouldn't get a straight answer anyways, he is, after all, a little crazy.*

He shook his head at such a thought, *Not right to think of your own flesh and blood like that.* It was hard not to allow such notions to creep into his head. The media, after all, portrayed Mark as a killer with no remorse, an oddity who was to be analyzed by a myriad of talking heads each offering their own opinions of his mental state. Perhaps the constant bombardment of voices discussing his brother's psychological health, depicting him as a cartoonish monster and not the man Stephen knew had skewed his attitude towards Mark. *He's not crazy; he just needs help.*

"So, I talked to the lawyer today," Stephen offered, the talk of Mark's mentality jogging his memory. "He said this new defense could possibly work, keep you out of like a real hardcore prison." He frowned again, "Of course he was pretty straightforward on that subject, said even if it does work you're still probably going away for a long time. Nice guy though, really like him. I think you would too if you were well enough to really speak with him."

The door of the hospital room opened slowly, a young nurse sticking her head in. "I'm sorry Mr. Enos, but visiting hours are well over. We're gonna have to kick you out."

"Not a problem," Stephen nodded, collecting his things. Standing from his chair he sighed and looked at Mark. "Well, goodnight, man. I'll see you tomorrow."

Walking by the nurse he smiled. "Goodnight, thank you again."

"Not a problem," she responded. "You have a goodnight now."

Letting him pass, she entered the room and retrieved a chart hanging from the foot of Mark's bed. Checking the bevy of monitors which hung behind the young man's head, she made several marks upon the chart before placing it back in its original position. Taking a visual inventory of her patient's health, she lifted his sheets to just below his chin, assuring that he was most comfortable. Turning to exit the room she switched off the lights before closing the door.

For a few moments the room was dark and silent, save for the hiss of Mark's air tube and the rhythmic beeping of his heart monitor. What little light that filtered into the room came via the full moon as it rose slowly just outside of Mark's bedside window. Sleeping soundly, he began to stir as the blue light spilled onto his bed covers, the lunar illumination slowly creeping along the length of his body.

The heart monitor by his bedside began to chirp more frequently, slowly at first before picking up a greater rapidity. Mark began to stir, his eyes still closed, his brow creasing in concern. Turning his head left and right, he lurched upright, his abdomen cramping up. Shuddering in pain his eyes remained shut tightly, as if he were in the throes of a most violent nightmare. Slamming his head back upon the mattress he started tossing and turning violently.

His heart monitor began to beep faster and faster, acquiring a line of green spikes at a frenetic pace. His breathing became irregular and raspy, his mouth flying open as he gasped for air. As the sweat dripped from his forehead he began to groan, clutching and clawing at his chest and throwing off the sheets.

His moans became deeper, more resonant and inhuman sounding. As a gargling sound developed at the back of his throat, he tore the air hose from his nose and continued shaking his head. As another debilitating ripple of pain shuddered through his body, he arched his back and flung his head backwards. Struggling to catch a breath, his mouth flew open allowing the fangs sprouting forth from his mouth to be silhouetted in the moonlight. . .

* * *

Patrolman Jared Manarini stood lazily by the entrance of the hospital room. Shoulders slumped and thumbs tucked into his belt loops, he leaned back against the wall, sighing not from exhaustion but rather boredom. He needed the extra money that came from these shifts, the department wrote them up as something akin to traffic details or court appearances and that meant overtime pay for officers like him. What he didn't need however, and what he hadn't been prepared for, was the long periods of boredom and dead air which came with keeping watch over the gimp serial killer in the other room.

He felt as if his mind was on autopilot, its only task being to keep track of the passage of time, a painful thankless little task. He wasn't allowed a magazine or a newspaper; the department believed it would appear unprofessional and lackadaisical for its officers to be occupying themselves with periodicals when they were supposed to be keeping watch over a dangerous felon. There wasn't much else with which to entertain himself as the nursing staff in the hospital consisted of middle-aged, stocky, angry little women. *Not one piece of ass among them,* he lamented, *nothing to look at.* Nothing, could break the monotony of this goddamned shift. Checking his watch, he thought he might cry as he realized he had only been at his post for less than an hour. The next officer wouldn't join him for another three. It was going to be a long night; he had to do something to entertain himself. *Christ, I'm going to go stir crazy.*

Recalling a catchy little number he had heard on his way in he began to mentally play it back in his head, keeping rhythm by tapping his fingers upon his belt. Humming to himself, he pursed his lips, preparing to whistle, when he heard it. The muffled sounds of a struggle sounded behind him and his brow furrowed in confusion. The kid was supposed to be bed-ridden, unable to move.

Slam!

It came again, louder this time, a metallic clanging as machines and instruments fell to the floor; like a collection of pots and pans crashing down from the ceiling. Manarini moved away from the wall, unsure of what to do next. Beyond the oak door, through the rectangular darkened window, it was clear something tumultuous was occurring. Mouth dry and hands trembling, he unclipped the holster upon his belt, his fingers tapping upon the stock of his sidearm as he began to shiver from adrenaline.

An alarm sounded overhead, a high pitched series of chirps and Manarini's focus was taken off of the door as a group of nurses came running around the corner. He watched as two squat and concerned looking women, trotting at a pace which for them constituted a sprint, came barreling down the hallway. Pushing their way past the confused policeman they barreled into the room, the halogen light bulbs within springing to life.

Life went into slow motion for Manarini, there was a momentary pause as the lights came up and the two women let loose with matching high pitch screams. His heart thundering in his ears, Manarini drew his gun and sprang into action. Bursting forth across the transom, he was met rudely with a sensation of incredible pain as something forcefully made contact with his face.

Clutching at his now broken nose, he dropped the gun and crumpled to the floor. Momentarily blinded, he sensed rather than saw something of great size and weight move past him, his ears ringing with the women's screams and something new; a series of deep, raspy snorts, like a dog with a cold or a feral hog. Opening his eyes, he could barely view his surroundings as his eyes watered and his vision began to cloud red with what he realized was his own blood filtering across his eyeballs. Lying prostrate upon the floor, he turned his head and watched as a blurred figure, in what he believed was a hospital gown, raced awkwardly down the hallway before pushing past the double-wide exit doors and disappearing into the darkness.

EPILOGUE

Kaplan walked to the window, clutching the mug of piping hot coffee in his hand. Sipping slowly, he marveled at how the newly fallen snow that rested upon the frosted limbs of the evergreens in his backyard reflected the pale, blue light of the full moon. It had been an excruciatingly long day, nearly twelve hours of continuous work. Swallowing, he leaned his head back; eyes closed, and sighed in exhaustion. It had been nearly a month since Enos escaped and the resulting firestorm and widespread panic had fast tracked his return to active duty, which was good. However, it had also meant hours upon hours of overtime, searching fruitlessly for the escaped murderer, which was bad.

Taking another sip from his mug he inspected his living room, frowning at the lack of décor present, a true bachelor pad. With a shrug he reflected that it would be Christmas soon, surely a lush, green tree and a little trimming would brighten up the place. That was if he could find the time, there was more work to be done before he could think of embracing the spirit of the holidays and he wasn't feeling particularly festive at the moment. Frowning, his mind turned once again to Enos, not that he thought about much else these days. Enos was out there, somewhere, and as he turned back to the window Kaplan squinted past his reflection into the forest beyond; allowing himself to wonder whether or not Enos was staring right back at him from the darkness.

The calls to the station house hadn't stopped. Each day hundreds upon hundreds of calls reporting strange, shadowy figures lurking in resident's backyards; prowling their darkened streets. Kaplan believed none of them were real, just panicked housewives catching glimpses of shadows and fog outside their windows. Still, the sightings came day in and day out. Enos had been spotted prowling around schools, alleyways and shopping centers. He had reportedly been sighted in surrounding towns, neighboring states and even Canada, but Kaplan knew he was still in town, he sensed that the killer was close.

The police hadn't been left with much and Virginia Enos was a useless source of information; a veritable hermit now. The hospital witnesses were not of much value either as the nurses couldn't describe just what they had seen and there wasn't much to be gleamed from the security cameras, just grainy black and white footage depicting an obscure figure rampaging down the hallway before fleeing into the night. The patrolman outside of Enos' room hadn't been much help either, remembering only that someone or something had socked him in the face. The poor guy had been left not with coherent images of an escaping maniac, only a gnarly gash stretching from his forehead to his swollen nose. Kaplan himself barely remembered inspecting the hospital room, only the image of Enos' tattered bed sheets sticking with him.

It hadn't fully clicked until Henry had relayed the discrepancy between the bite marks on the victims and Enos' dental records. It was then that the pieces had fallen into place. Although, thinking back about it now, he supposed he had always known. He hadn't been there when the authorities told Stephen about his brother's escape, but he imagined the young man's eyes going wide and the sweat beginning to dot his brow as he listened. It was obvious to Kaplan that Stephen was cognizant of his brother's fate. He knew the young man had long harbored doubts about what they had witnessed in the forest that night and it was clear that his suspicions had not been confirmed until his brother disappeared the night of the next full moon. Kaplan was sure that Stephen didn't buy his brother was merely a sick young man; he knew what his sibling truly was. Kaplan had heard through the grapevine that Stephen had abruptly quit his job upon hearing the news and Kaplan himself had viewed the for sale sign posted outside of Stephen's now empty house. *Kid must be scared out of his mind, running for his life,* Kaplan thought. *Nobody likes to find out what really lurks in the dark.* There were countless times he wished he didn't.

Tattered bed sheets, that's what really did it for him, *there's always tattered bed sheets in the morning.* Kaplan winced as he rotated his shoulder slowly; the soreness from where Lambert's bullet had hit him hadn't quite subsided yet. He didn't like preying upon humans and he hadn't intended to take Lambert that night, at least not until he started firing his gun recklessly. He couldn't have fools like that running around his town, someone could have been hurt. At least he liked to think that was the reason he had killed Lambert, not because of any petty malice or resentment on his part. He did have to admit though that he hadn't appreciated being confronted with his own leftovers when Lambert had discovered Toby the dog's filleted corpse.

He hadn't wanted to know the name of the dog and deep down Kaplan knew it was the real reason he had ordered Lambert to cremate the body; not some altruistic motive to protect the feelings of a lonely old man. He had had the dog disappear to protect himself, the last thing he wanted to do was console someone whose dog he had feasted upon days earlier.

It wasn't hard to cover up the kill, plenty of underbrush to cover up the animal control officer's corpse and that of the small cocker spaniel the dumb bastard had shot. The dog owner didn't think a thing when a Hingham police officer assured her all was well before driving the animal control truck off her property, no one in the suburbs questioned the actions of a cop. While he regretted killing Lambert for the most part, he did remember the macabre sense of satisfaction he felt as the rear end of the truck disappeared beneath the brackish waters of the Quincy Quarry. He had been exhilarated by the feeling of literally getting away with murder, still reveling in the thrill of the kill if only for a moment.

It had scared him; he wondered if it was how Enos felt after bringing down one of his victims. He shuddered as he thought of the monster he had created. If he truly was committed to safeguarding the citizens under his jurisdiction, his justification for dispatching Lambert, he would have killed Enos long before the light of full moon had been allowed to transform the young man. Kaplan knew Enos was one sick puppy, but he felt a tremendous sense of responsibility towards the young man. After all, it had been his bite that had started the entire sad saga. He still remembered how hard it was for him when he first succumbed to the curse after being bitten by a strange "dog" while backpacking through Europe as a teenager. The fear and the confusion had been overwhelming. Perhaps, deep down, Kaplan was happy to now have a kindred spirit; an apprentice of sorts.

Well, maybe that wasn't completely accurate, he did remember praying that he hadn't transferred the curse to the young man that fateful night. He had convinced himself that the curse hadn't been passed along only to recognize, much to his horror and dismay, the hallmarks of this terrible, peculiar affliction at the Lamperti crime scene. The old man's tattered remains brought flashbacks of Kaplan's first kill, an elderly vagrant in Antwerp, nearly two decades previous. He remembered running, clad in blood stained tattered clothes through the streets; scared out of his wits. Somehow, he still had no idea how, he had managed to escape without suspicion. Reflecting upon it now, Kaplan realized it was clearly why he had helped Mark in the beginning. Why he had sought to counter Henry's initial suspicions regarding Enos.

Surely, Enos was just what he had been back then, a scared kid, struggling to comprehend what he had become and deal with what he had done. The similarity however, stopped there in his mind. The increasing savagery of Enos' actions had struck Kaplan, his profound sense of guilt increasing with the body count. These intense feelings of remorse had been the true causation for his episode outside the Greco crime scene, not an aversion to blood and gore as Henry had thought. He realized his own culpability stared back at him from the unflinching gaze of the victim's lifeless eyes.

Enos, or at least the animal inside of him, had to be brought under control before more people died. The beast had to be tamed. Kaplan had learned to restrain himself after all, though he found that the change had become beastlier the more he penned it in. He now fully resembled an animal when he transformed. He had often wondered if this was the tradeoff for greater control, or just a natural progression of the curse, but as he had been preoccupied with Enos he hadn't thought about it in months. The bloodlust could never fully be erased however, something Kaplan feared now as the full moon rose once again. Kaplan had learned to satiate his beastly cravings over the years by munching upon the poor house pets of Massachusetts' South Shore and the occasional Deer or Raccoon. After locating Enos it was his sincere hope that he could teach his creation to turn its fangs and claws upon furry quadrupeds rather than the next innocent human being or ornery State Trooper it encountered. Not that it would do much good as Enos had already been fingered as a murderer; Kaplan had at least been able to cover up his crimes. Still, it was worth a shot.

Placing the now finished cup of coffee down Kaplan stretched his aching shoulder once again before cracking his knuckles and neck. It was time to go. Slipping off his shoes he slid the sliding door before him open and stepped out onto his back porch. The cool night air was soothing upon his rapidly heating skin. His increasing heartbeat began to thunder in his ears and his breathing became a series of short snorts. Stumbling and staggering into the backyard, he headed for the forest, stripping himself of article after article of clothing as he did so. Hunched and disfigured, he disappeared into the darkness, leaving only a trail of increasingly bizarre footprints in his wake.

Overhead, the full moon rose over the canopy of pointed pines, their snow white tips angling towards the heavens. A cold wind whistled through the winter landscape, eddying and whirling pockets of lightly falling snow. As the howl of the wind gusts began to die down a new, more pronounced sound rose above it. Mournful and ominous, the beast's howl rose steadily, increasing in resonance before falling rhythmically and cresting again. In the distance, an identical howl could be heard calling out in response...

Also by Tim Garrity:

Vargulf

Copies available now on Amazon.com

CPSIA information can be obtained at www.ICGtesting.com
Printed in the USA
LVOW132146290812

296613LV00010B/1/P